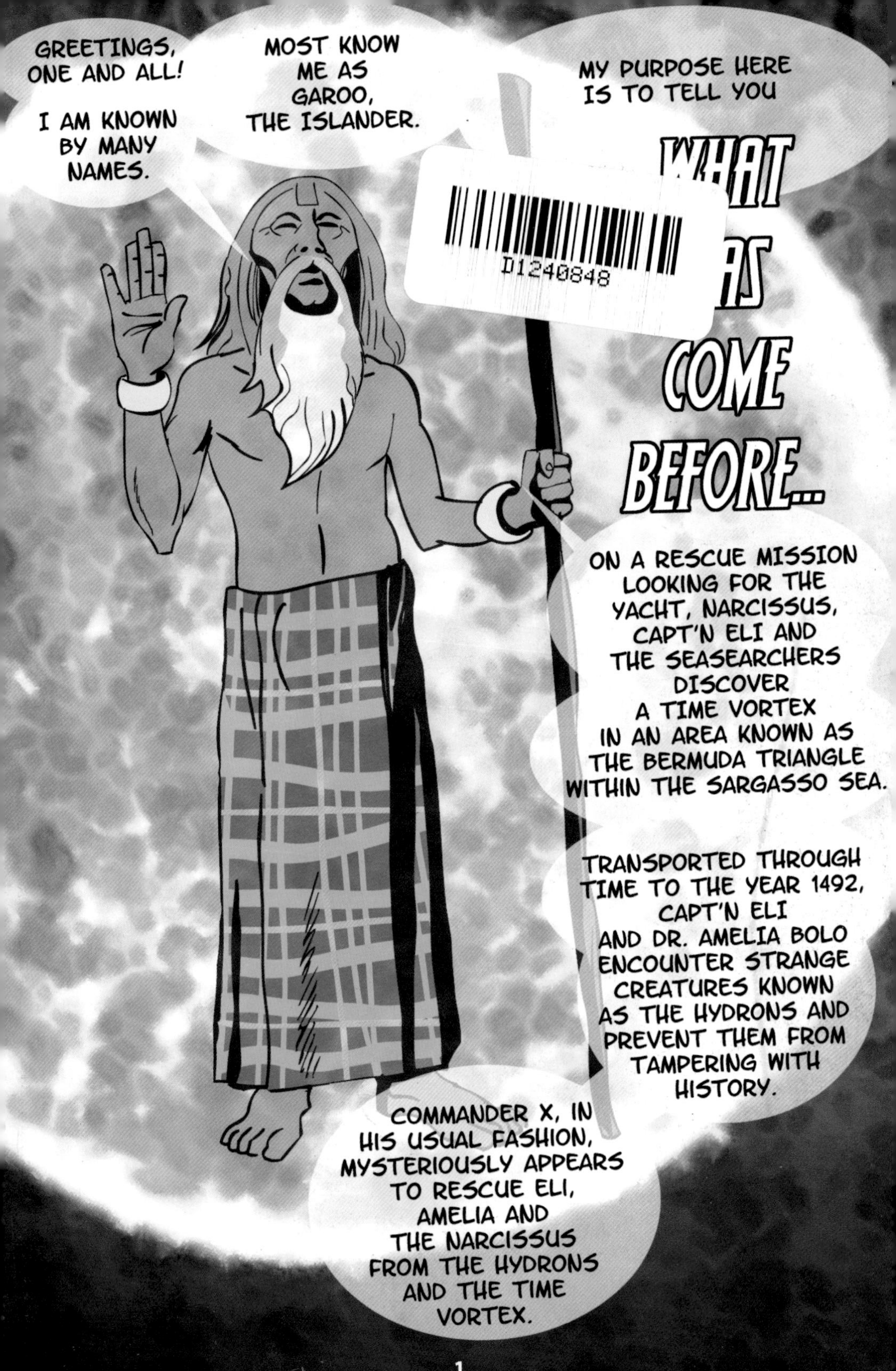
GREETINGS, ONE AND ALL!
I AM KNOWN BY MANY NAMES.
MOST KNOW ME AS GAROO, THE ISLANDER.
MY PURPOSE HERE IS TO TELL YOU
WHAT
COME
BEFORE...
ON A RESCUE MISSION LOOKING FOR THE YACHT, NARCISSUS, CAPT'N ELI AND THE SEASEARCHERS DISCOVER A TIME VORTEX IN AN AREA KNOWN AS THE BERMUDA TRIANGLE WITHIN THE SARGASSO SEA.
TRANSPORTED THROUGH TIME TO THE YEAR 1492, CAPT'N ELI AND DR. AMELIA BOLO ENCOUNTER STRANGE CREATURES KNOWN AS THE HYDRONS AND PREVENT THEM FROM TAMPERING WITH HISTORY.
COMMANDER X, IN HIS USUAL FASHION, MYSTERIOUSLY APPEARS TO RESCUE ELI, AMELIA AND THE NARCISSUS FROM THE HYDRONS AND THE TIME VORTEX.

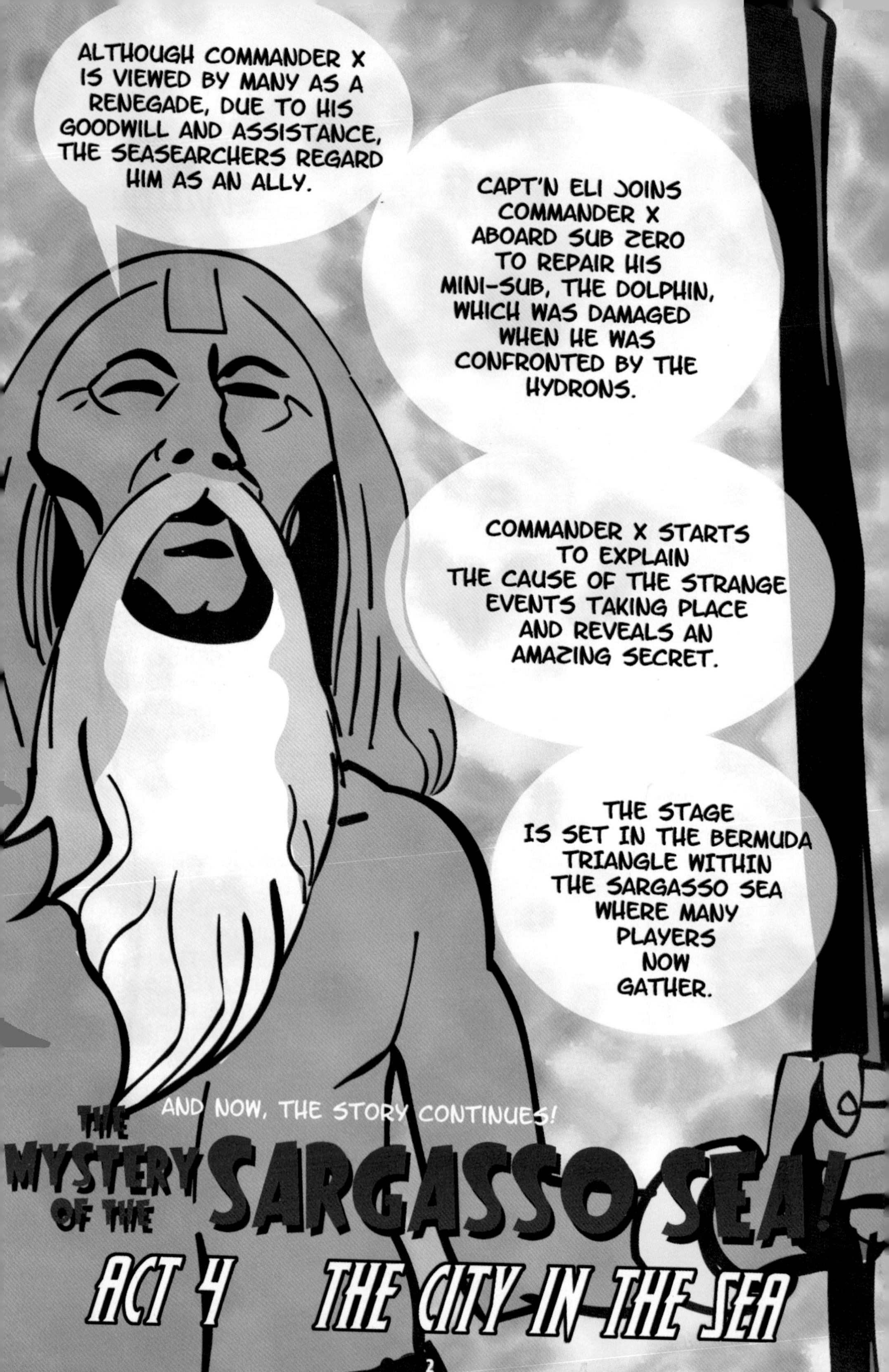
ALTHOUGH COMMANDER X IS VIEWED BY MANY AS A RENEGADE, DUE TO HIS GOODWILL AND ASSISTANCE, THE SEASEARCHERS REGARD HIM AS AN ALLY.
CAPT'N ELI JOINS COMMANDER X ABOARD SUB ZERO TO REPAIR HIS MINI-SUB, THE DOLPHIN, WHICH WAS DAMAGED WHEN HE WAS CONFRONTED BY THE HYDRONS.
COMMANDER X STARTS TO EXPLAIN THE CAUSE OF THE STRANGE EVENTS TAKING PLACE AND REVEALS AN AMAZING SECRET.
THE STAGE IS SET IN THE BERMUDA TRIANGLE WITHIN THE SARGASSO SEA WHERE MANY PLAYERS NOW GATHER.
AND NOW, THE STORY CONTINUES!
THE MYSTERY OF THE SARGASSO SEA!
ACT 4 THE CITY IN THE SEA

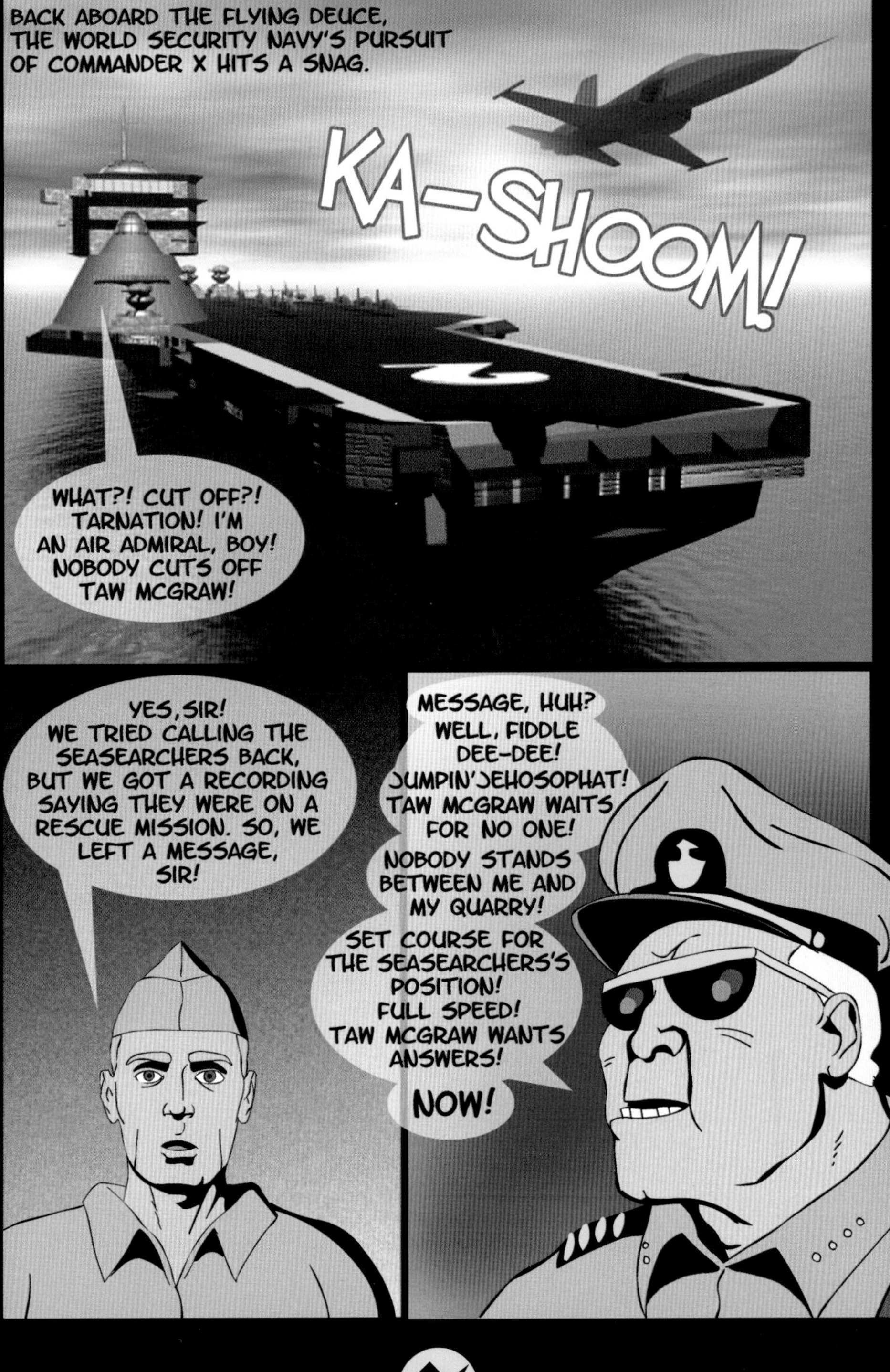
BACK ABOARD THE FLYING DEUCE, THE WORLD SECURITY NAVY'S PURSUIT OF COMMANDER X HITS A SNAG.
KA-SHOOM!
WHAT?! CUT OFF?! TARNATION! I'M AN AIR ADMIRAL, BOY! NOBODY CUTS OFF TAW MCGRAW!
YES, SIR! WE TRIED CALLING THE SEASEARCHERS BACK, BUT WE GOT A RECORDING SAYING THEY WERE ON A RESCUE MISSION. SO, WE LEFT A MESSAGE, SIR!
MESSAGE, HUH? WELL, FIDDLE DEE-DEE! JUMPIN' JEHOSOPHAT! TAW MCGRAW WAITS FOR NO ONE!
NOBODY STANDS BETWEEN ME AND MY QUARRY!
SET COURSE FOR THE SEASEARCHERS'S POSITION! FULL SPEED! TAW MCGRAW WANTS ANSWERS!
NOW!

ABOARD SUB ZERO, COMMANDER X AND ELI DIVE DEEP BENEATH THE ATLANTIC.

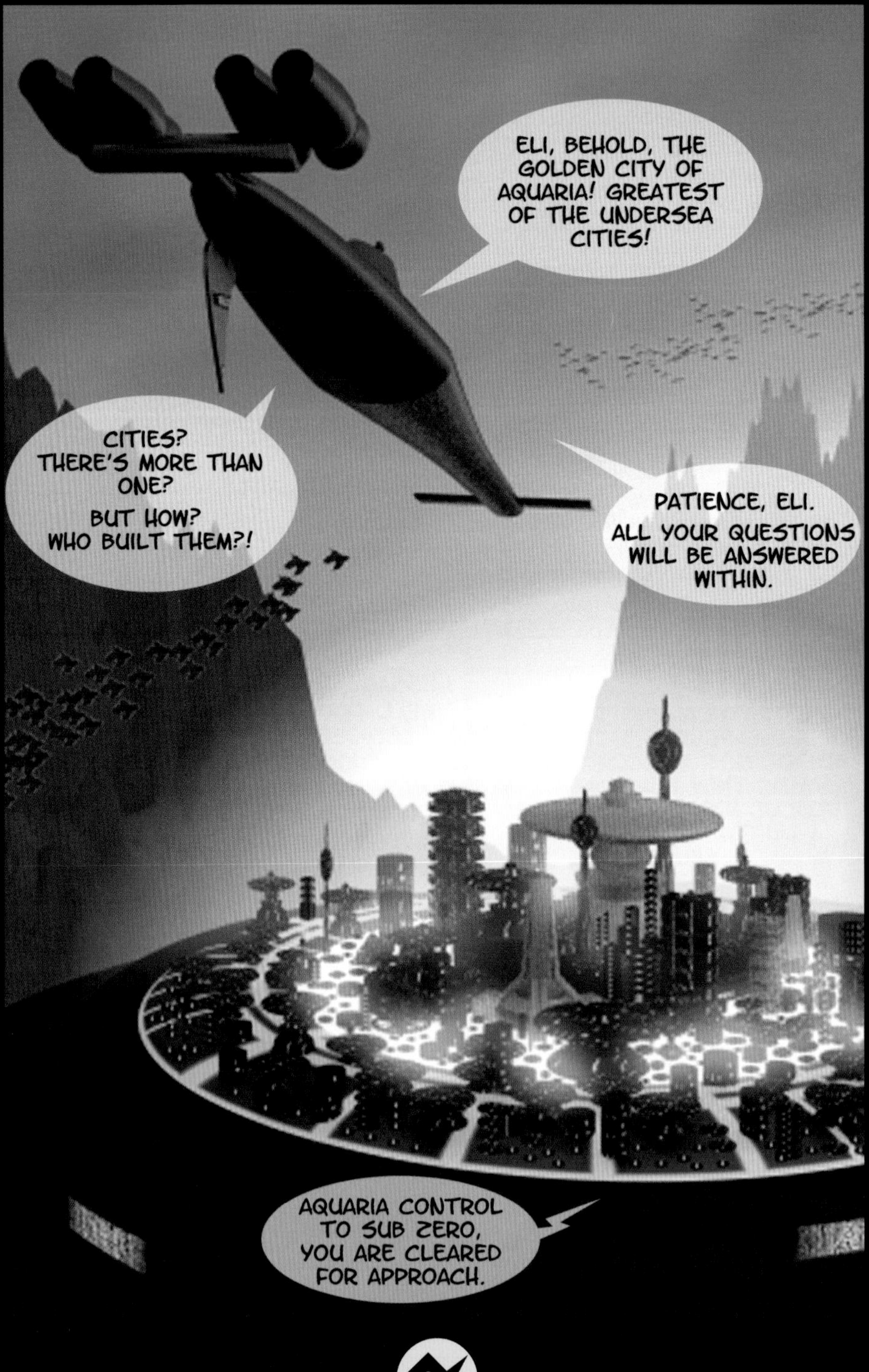
ELI, BEHOLD, THE GOLDEN CITY OF AQUARIA! GREATEST OF THE UNDERSEA CITIES!
CITIES? THERE'S MORE THAN ONE?
BUT HOW? WHO BUILT THEM?!
PATIENCE, ELI.
ALL YOUR QUESTIONS WILL BE ANSWERED WITHIN.
AQUARIA CONTROL TO SUB ZERO, YOU ARE CLEARED FOR APPROACH.

Act 4 - The City in the Sea

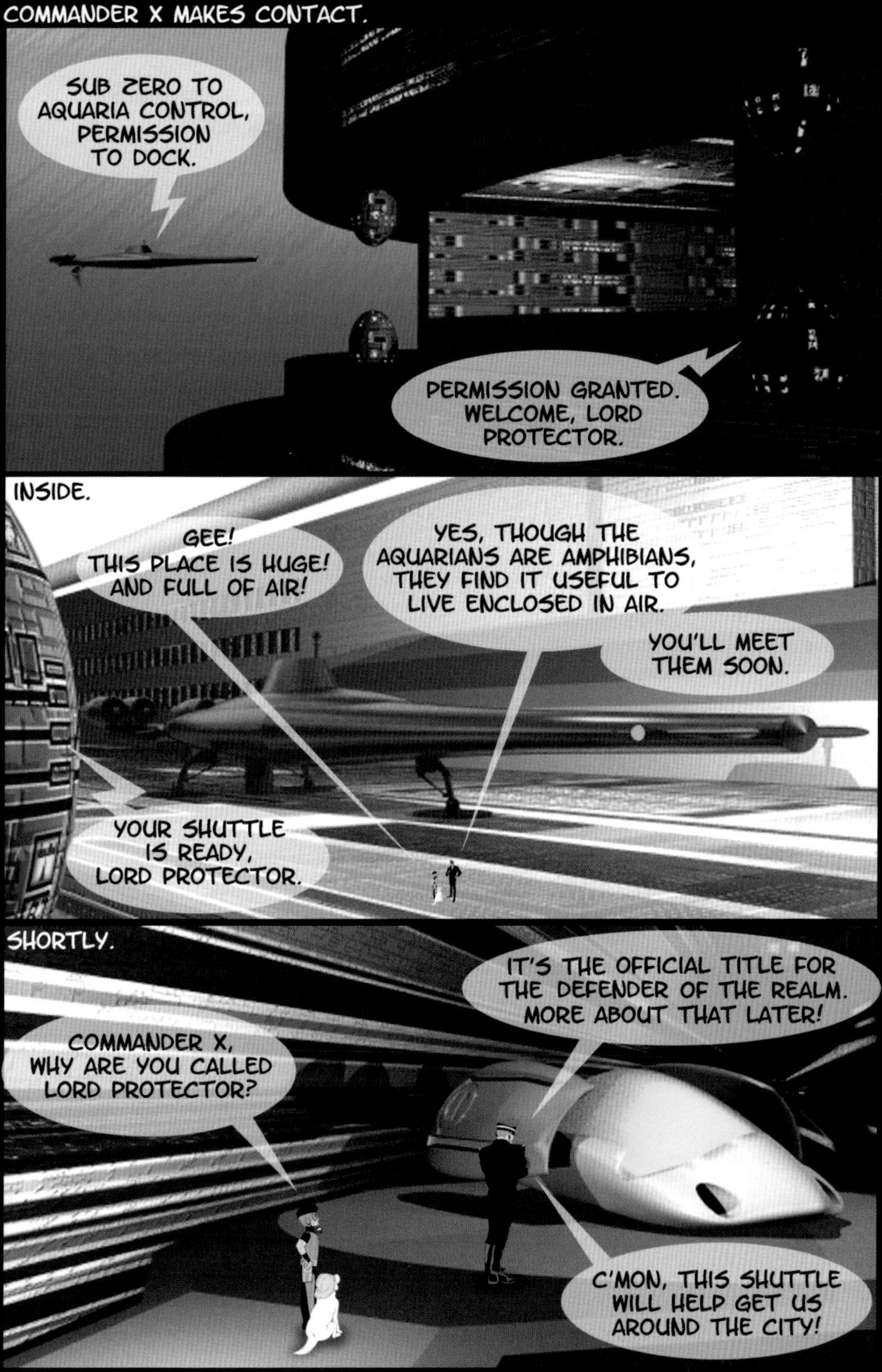
COMMANDER X MAKES CONTACT.
SUB ZERO TO AQUARIA CONTROL, PERMISSION TO DOCK.
PERMISSION GRANTED. WELCOME, LORD PROTECTOR.
INSIDE.
GEE! THIS PLACE IS HUGE! AND FULL OF AIR!
YES, THOUGH THE AQUARIANS ARE AMPHIBIANS, THEY FIND IT USEFUL TO LIVE ENCLOSED IN AIR.
YOU'LL MEET THEM SOON.
YOUR SHUTTLE IS READY, LORD PROTECTOR.
SHORTLY.
COMMANDER X, WHY ARE YOU CALLED LORD PROTECTOR?
IT'S THE OFFICIAL TITLE FOR THE DEFENDER OF THE REALM. MORE ABOUT THAT LATER!
C'MON, THIS SHUTTLE WILL HELP GET US AROUND THE CITY!

THE SHUTTLE GLIDES SILENTLY THROUGH THE CITY.

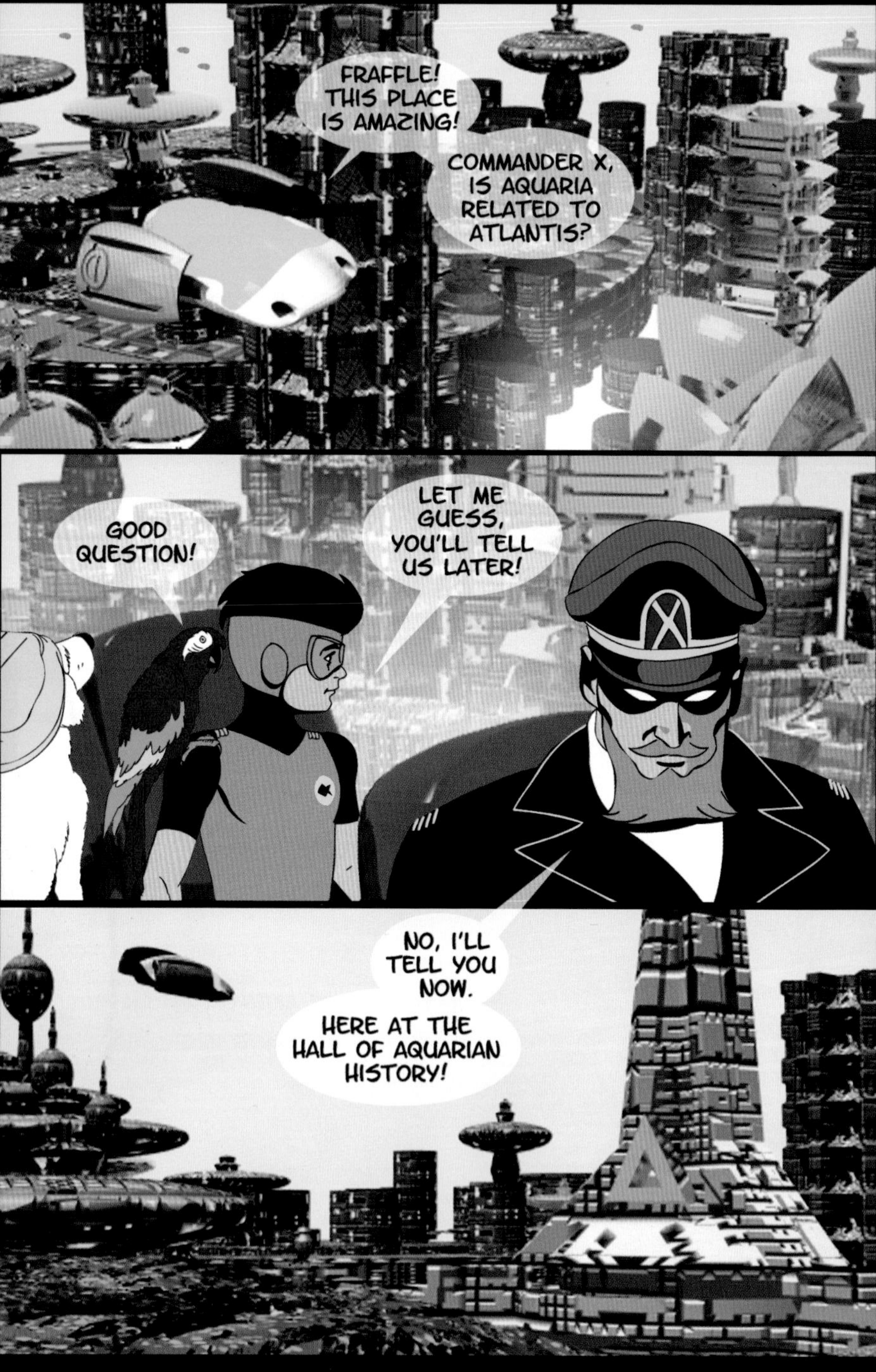
FRAFFLE! THIS PLACE IS AMAZING!
COMMANDER X, IS AQUARIA RELATED TO ATLANTIS?
GOOD QUESTION!
LET ME GUESS, YOU'LL TELL US LATER!
NO, I'LL TELL YOU NOW.
HERE AT THE HALL OF AQUARIAN HISTORY!

Act 4 - The City in the Sea

WITHIN THE VAST MUSEUM.

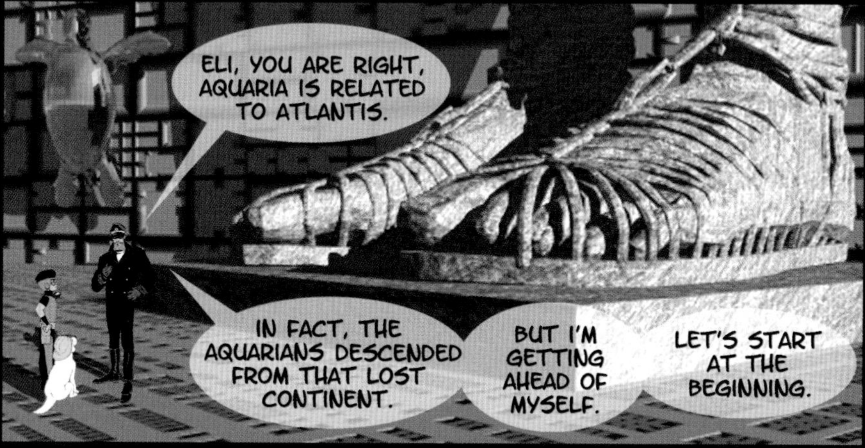
ELI, YOU ARE RIGHT, AQUARIA IS RELATED TO ATLANTIS.
IN FACT, THE AQUARIANS DESCENDED FROM THAT LOST CONTINENT.
BUT I'M GETTING AHEAD OF MYSELF.
LET'S START AT THE BEGINNING.

DOWN THE HALL.

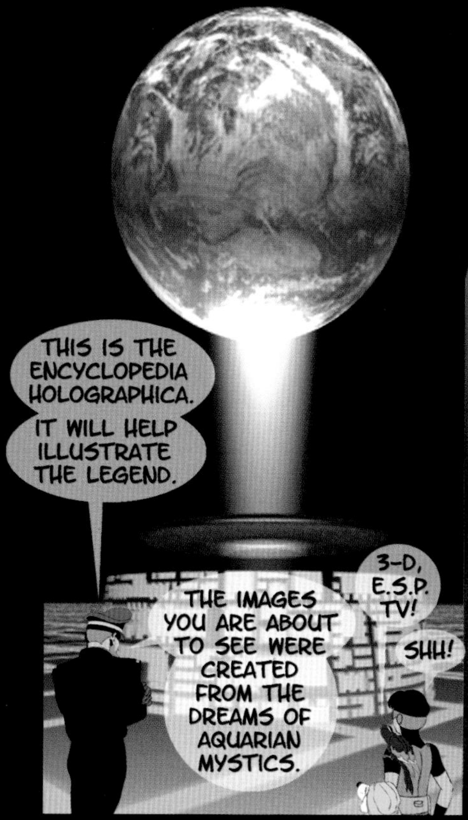
THIS IS THE ENCYCLOPEDIA HOLOGRAPHICA.
IT WILL HELP ILLUSTRATE THE LEGEND.
THE IMAGES YOU ARE ABOUT TO SEE WERE CREATED FROM THE DREAMS OF AQUARIAN MYSTICS.
3-D, E.S.P. TV!
SHH!

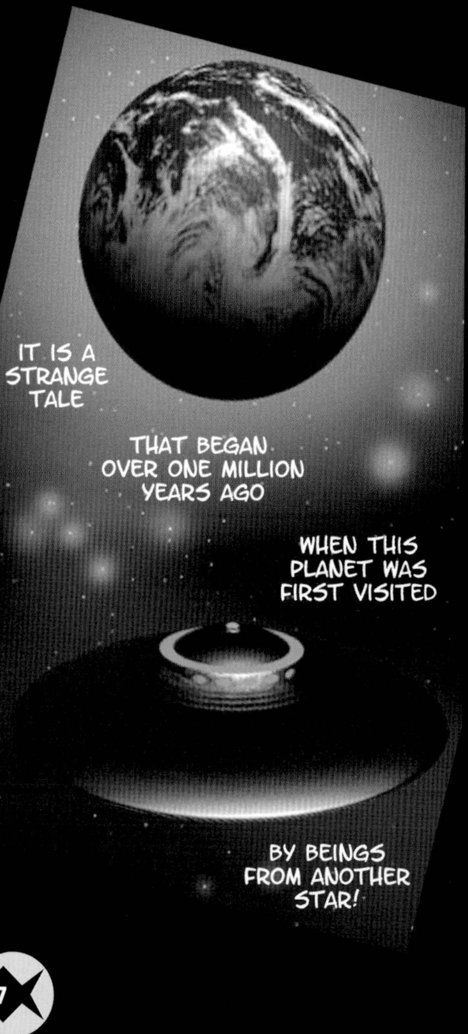
IT IS A STRANGE TALE
THAT BEGAN OVER ONE MILLION YEARS AGO
WHEN THIS PLANET WAS FIRST VISITED
BY BEINGS FROM ANOTHER STAR!

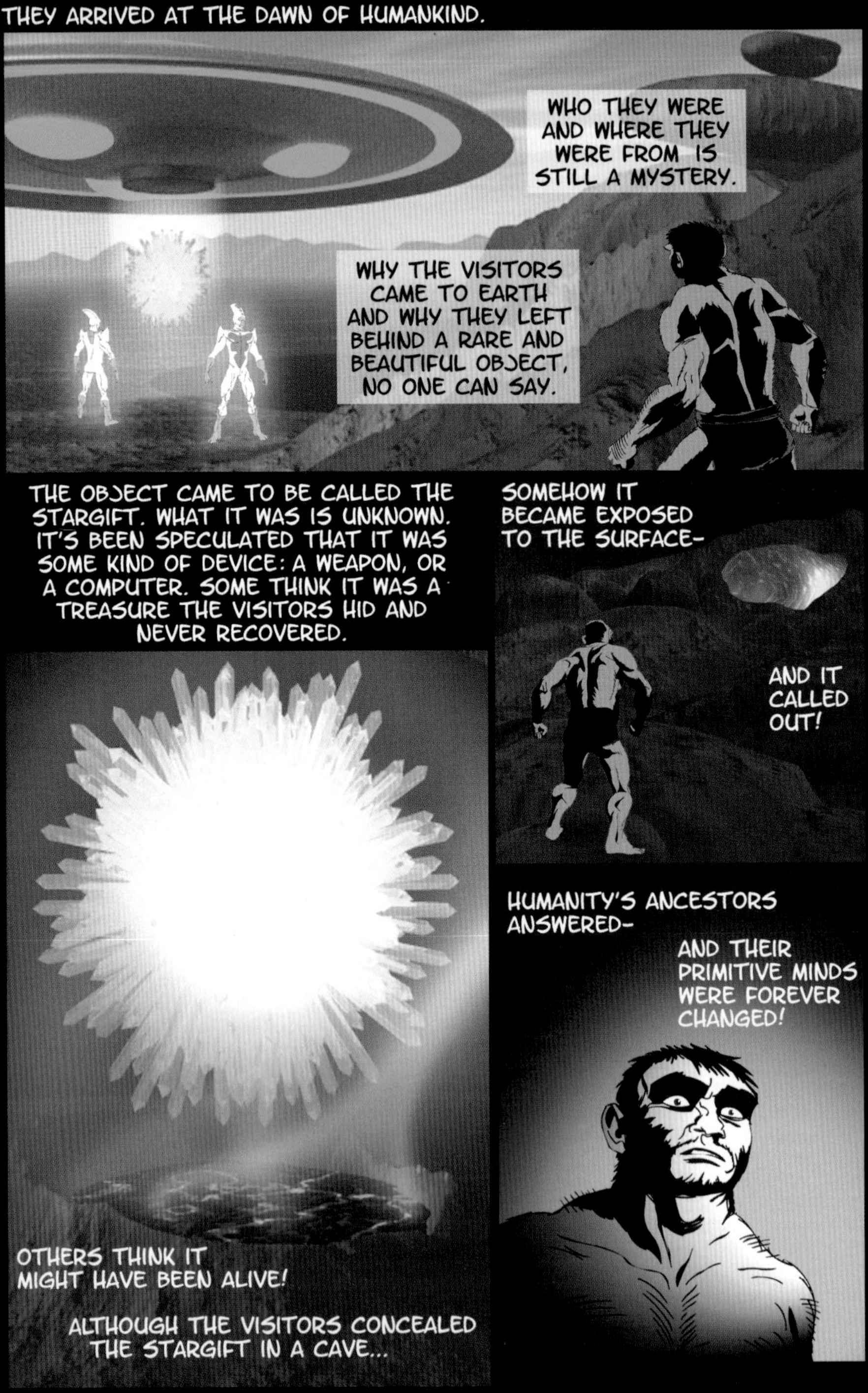
THEY ARRIVED AT THE DAWN OF HUMANKIND.
WHO THEY WERE AND WHERE THEY WERE FROM IS STILL A MYSTERY.
WHY THE VISITORS CAME TO EARTH AND WHY THEY LEFT BEHIND A RARE AND BEAUTIFUL OBJECT, NO ONE CAN SAY.
THE OBJECT CAME TO BE CALLED THE STARGIFT. WHAT IT WAS IS UNKNOWN. IT'S BEEN SPECULATED THAT IT WAS SOME KIND OF DEVICE: A WEAPON, OR A COMPUTER. SOME THINK IT WAS A TREASURE THE VISITORS HID AND NEVER RECOVERED.
OTHERS THINK IT MIGHT HAVE BEEN ALIVE!
ALTHOUGH THE VISITORS CONCEALED THE STARGIFT IN A CAVE...
SOMEHOW IT BECAME EXPOSED TO THE SURFACE-
AND IT CALLED OUT!
HUMANITY'S ANCESTORS ANSWERED-
AND THEIR PRIMITIVE MINDS WERE FOREVER CHANGED!

Act 4 - The City in the Sea

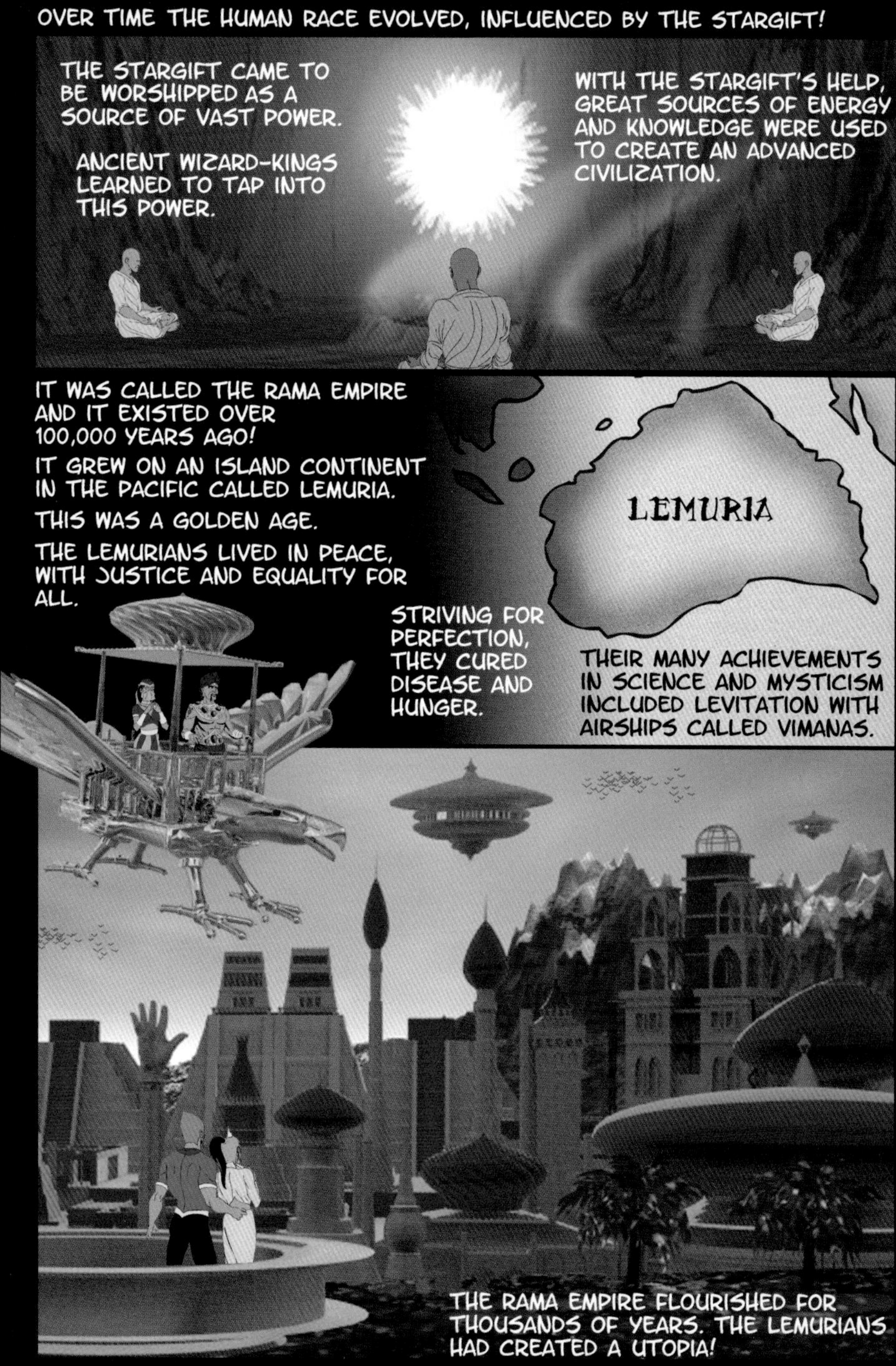
OVER TIME THE HUMAN RACE EVOLVED, INFLUENCED BY THE STARGIFT!
THE STARGIFT CAME TO BE WORSHIPPED AS A SOURCE OF VAST POWER.
ANCIENT WIZARD-KINGS LEARNED TO TAP INTO THIS POWER.
WITH THE STARGIFT'S HELP, GREAT SOURCES OF ENERGY AND KNOWLEDGE WERE USED TO CREATE AN ADVANCED CIVILIZATION.
IT WAS CALLED THE RAMA EMPIRE AND IT EXISTED OVER 100,000 YEARS AGO!
IT GREW ON AN ISLAND CONTINENT IN THE PACIFIC CALLED LEMURIA.
THIS WAS A GOLDEN AGE.
THE LEMURIANS LIVED IN PEACE, WITH JUSTICE AND EQUALITY FOR ALL.
LEMURIA
STRIVING FOR PERFECTION, THEY CURED DISEASE AND HUNGER.
THEIR MANY ACHIEVEMENTS IN SCIENCE AND MYSTICISM INCLUDED LEVITATION WITH AIRSHIPS CALLED VIMANAS.
THE RAMA EMPIRE FLOURISHED FOR THOUSANDS OF YEARS. THE LEMURIANS HAD CREATED A UTOPIA!

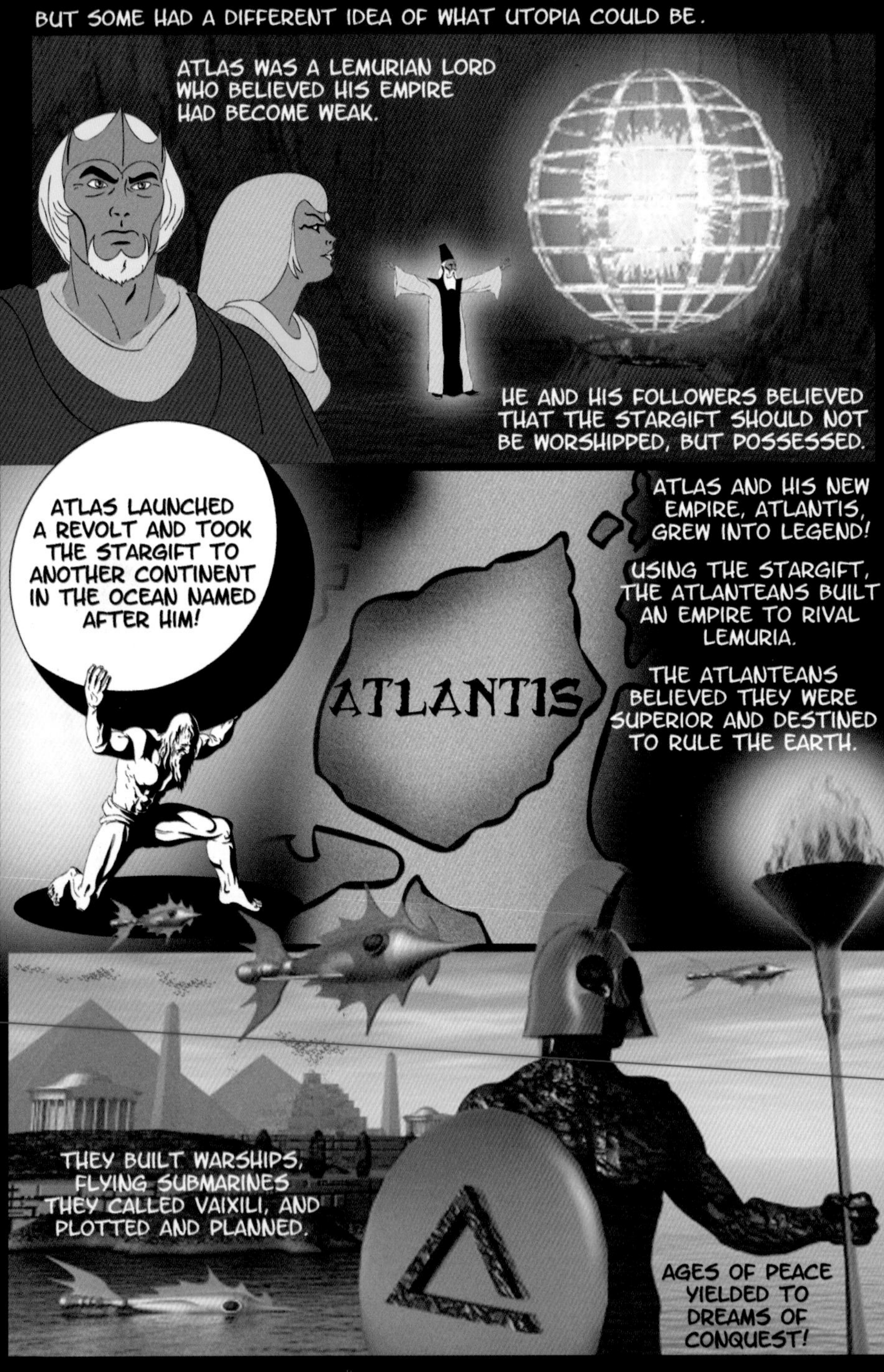
BUT SOME HAD A DIFFERENT IDEA OF WHAT UTOPIA COULD BE.
ATLAS WAS A LEMURIAN LORD WHO BELIEVED HIS EMPIRE HAD BECOME WEAK.
HE AND HIS FOLLOWERS BELIEVED THAT THE STARGIFT SHOULD NOT BE WORSHIPPED, BUT POSSESSED.
ATLAS LAUNCHED A REVOLT AND TOOK THE STARGIFT TO ANOTHER CONTINENT IN THE OCEAN NAMED AFTER HIM!
ATLANTIS
ATLAS AND HIS NEW EMPIRE, ATLANTIS, GREW INTO LEGEND!
USING THE STARGIFT, THE ATLANTEANS BUILT AN EMPIRE TO RIVAL LEMURIA.
THE ATLANTEANS BELIEVED THEY WERE SUPERIOR AND DESTINED TO RULE THE EARTH.
THEY BUILT WARSHIPS, FLYING SUBMARINES THEY CALLED VAIXILI, AND PLOTTED AND PLANNED.
AGES OF PEACE YIELDED TO DREAMS OF CONQUEST!

ACT 4 - THE CITY IN THE SEA

WAR FOR DOMINATION OF THE EARTH WAS INEVITABLE.

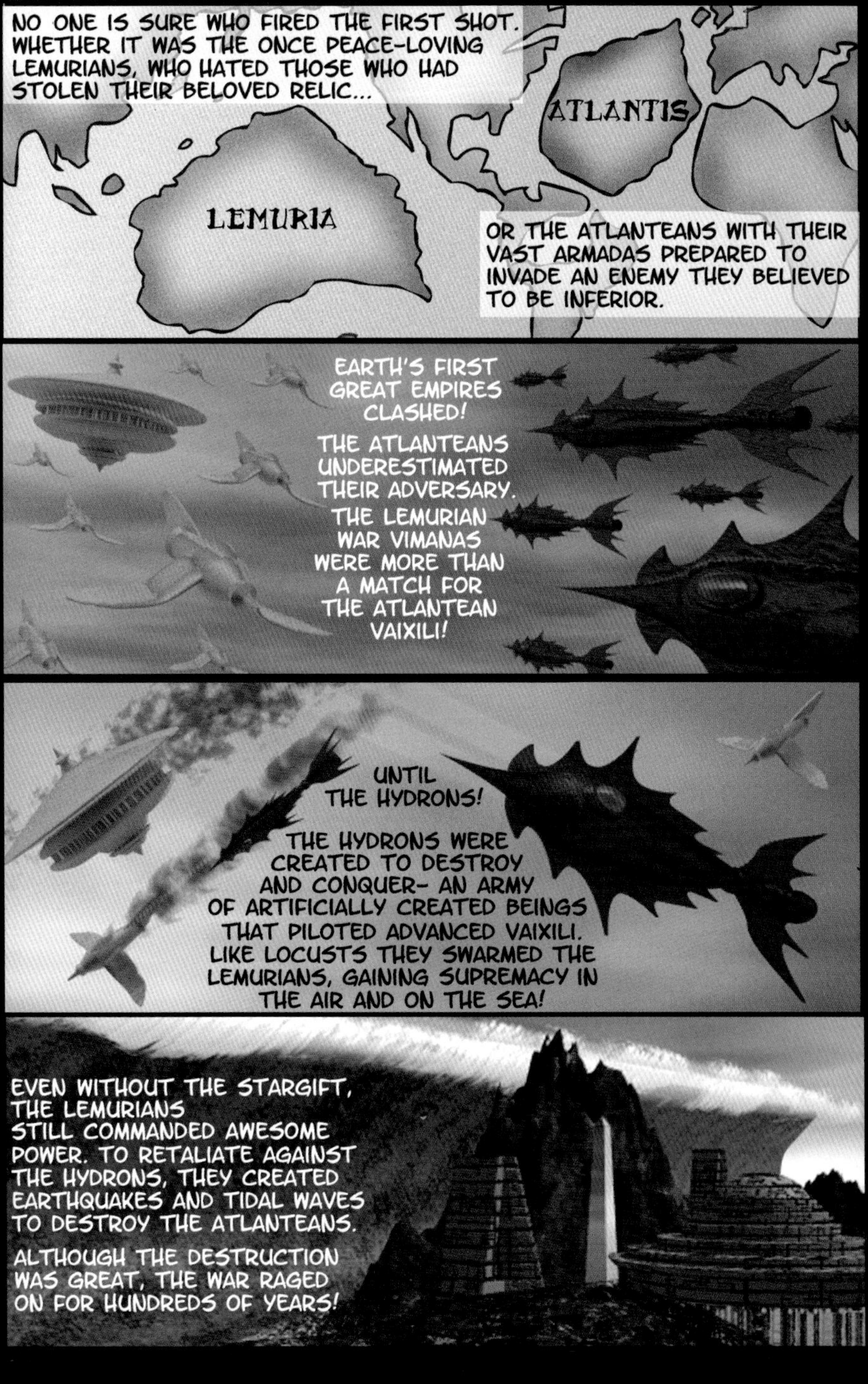
NO ONE IS SURE WHO FIRED THE FIRST SHOT. WHETHER IT WAS THE ONCE PEACE-LOVING LEMURIANS, WHO HATED THOSE WHO HAD STOLEN THEIR BELOVED RELIC...
ATLANTIS
LEMURIA
OR THE ATLANTEANS WITH THEIR VAST ARMADAS PREPARED TO INVADE AN ENEMY THEY BELIEVED TO BE INFERIOR.
EARTH'S FIRST GREAT EMPIRES CLASHED!
THE ATLANTEANS UNDERESTIMATED THEIR ADVERSARY.
THE LEMURIAN WAR VIMANAS WERE MORE THAN A MATCH FOR THE ATLANTEAN VAIXILI!
UNTIL THE HYDRONS!
THE HYDRONS WERE CREATED TO DESTROY AND CONQUER- AN ARMY OF ARTIFICIALLY CREATED BEINGS THAT PILOTED ADVANCED VAIXILI. LIKE LOCUSTS THEY SWARMED THE LEMURIANS, GAINING SUPREMACY IN THE AIR AND ON THE SEA!
EVEN WITHOUT THE STARGIFT, THE LEMURIANS STILL COMMANDED AWESOME POWER. TO RETALIATE AGAINST THE HYDRONS, THEY CREATED EARTHQUAKES AND TIDAL WAVES TO DESTROY THE ATLANTEANS.
ALTHOUGH THE DESTRUCTION WAS GREAT, THE WAR RAGED ON FOR HUNDREDS OF YEARS!

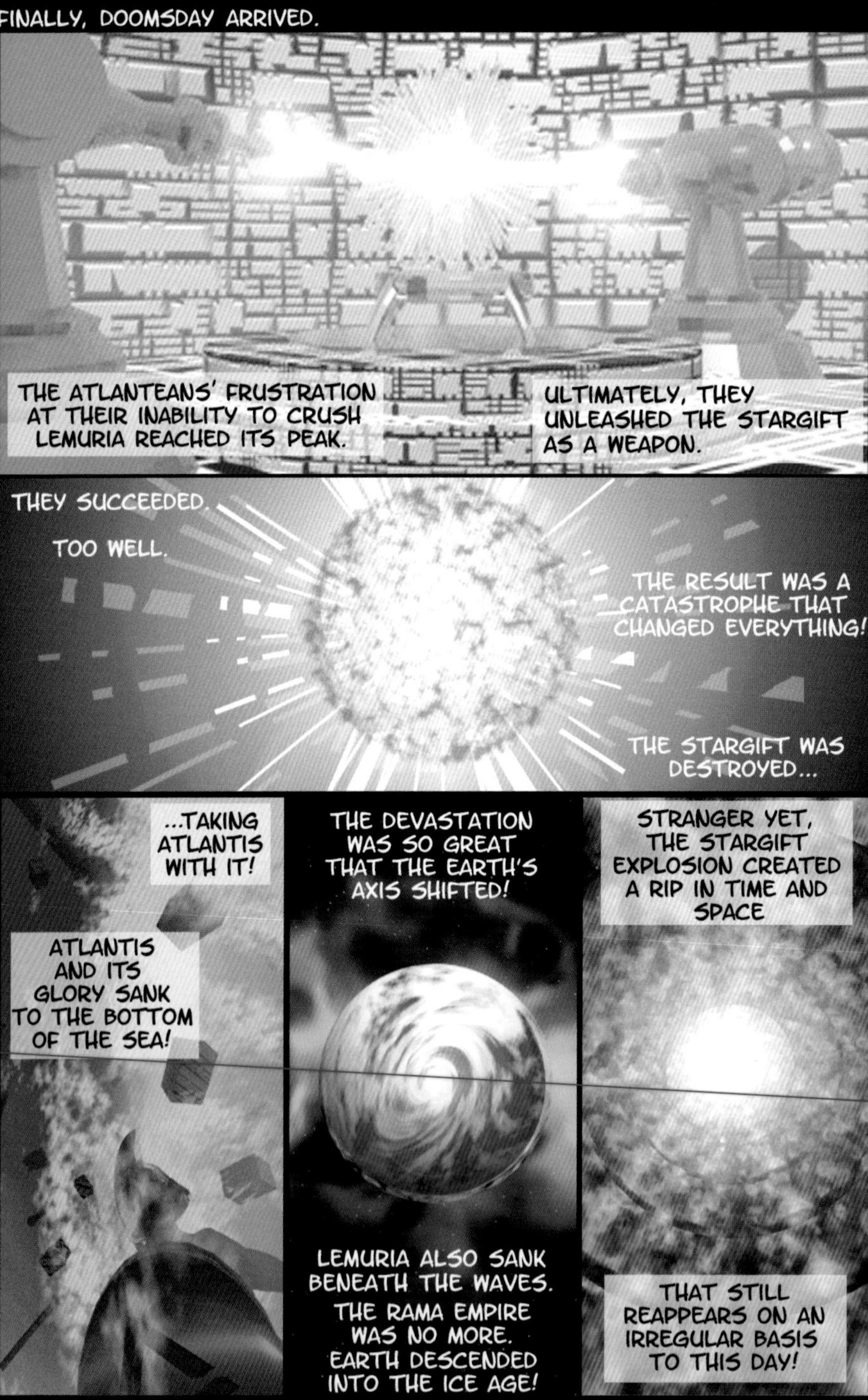
FINALLY, DOOMSDAY ARRIVED.
THE ATLANTEANS' FRUSTRATION AT THEIR INABILITY TO CRUSH LEMURIA REACHED ITS PEAK.
ULTIMATELY, THEY UNLEASHED THE STARGIFT AS A WEAPON.
THEY SUCCEEDED.
TOO WELL.
THE RESULT WAS A CATASTROPHE THAT CHANGED EVERYTHING!
THE STARGIFT WAS DESTROYED...
...TAKING ATLANTIS WITH IT!
ATLANTIS AND ITS GLORY SANK TO THE BOTTOM OF THE SEA!
THE DEVASTATION WAS SO GREAT THAT THE EARTH'S AXIS SHIFTED!
LEMURIA ALSO SANK BENEATH THE WAVES.
THE RAMA EMPIRE WAS NO MORE.
EARTH DESCENDED INTO THE ICE AGE!
STRANGER YET, THE STARGIFT EXPLOSION CREATED A RIP IN TIME AND SPACE
THAT STILL REAPPEARS ON AN IRREGULAR BASIS TO THIS DAY!

Act 4 - The City in the Sea

ELI, ROGER AND BARNEY
CONTINUE TO VIEW IMAGES OF THE PAST WITH COMMANDER X.

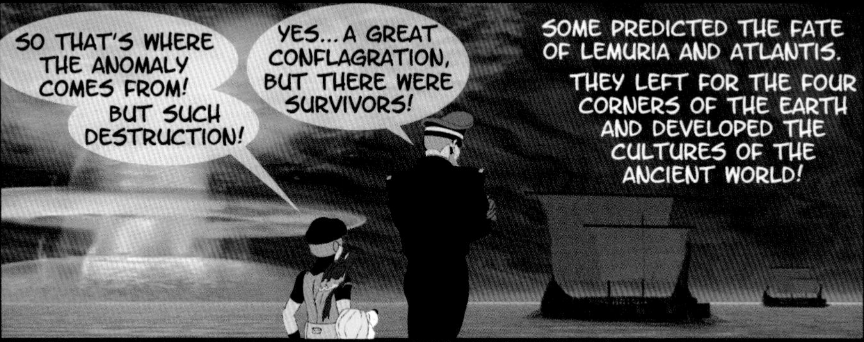
SO THAT'S WHERE THE ANOMALY COMES FROM!
BUT SUCH DESTRUCTION!
YES... A GREAT CONFLAGRATION, BUT THERE WERE SURVIVORS!
SOME PREDICTED THE FATE OF LEMURIA AND ATLANTIS.
THEY LEFT FOR THE FOUR CORNERS OF THE EARTH AND DEVELOPED THE CULTURES OF THE ANCIENT WORLD!

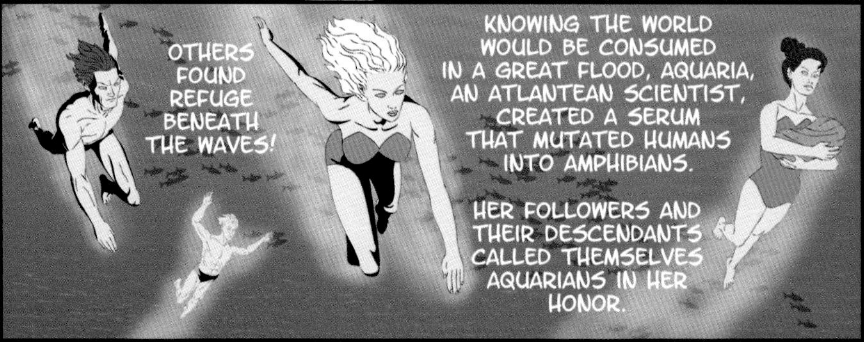
OTHERS FOUND REFUGE BENEATH THE WAVES!
KNOWING THE WORLD WOULD BE CONSUMED IN A GREAT FLOOD, AQUARIA, AN ATLANTEAN SCIENTIST, CREATED A SERUM THAT MUTATED HUMANS INTO AMPHIBIANS.
HER FOLLOWERS AND THEIR DESCENDANTS CALLED THEMSELVES AQUARIANS IN HER HONOR.

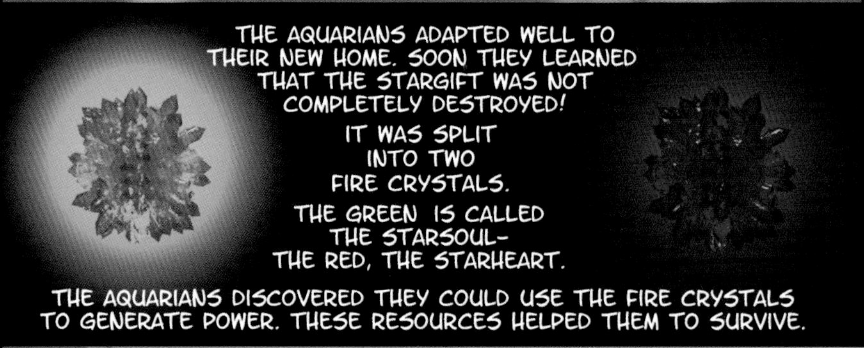
THE AQUARIANS ADAPTED WELL TO THEIR NEW HOME. SOON THEY LEARNED THAT THE STARGIFT WAS NOT COMPLETELY DESTROYED!
IT WAS SPLIT INTO TWO FIRE CRYSTALS.
THE GREEN IS CALLED THE STARSOUL- THE RED, THE STARHEART.
THE AQUARIANS DISCOVERED THEY COULD USE THE FIRE CRYSTALS TO GENERATE POWER. THESE RESOURCES HELPED THEM TO SURVIVE.

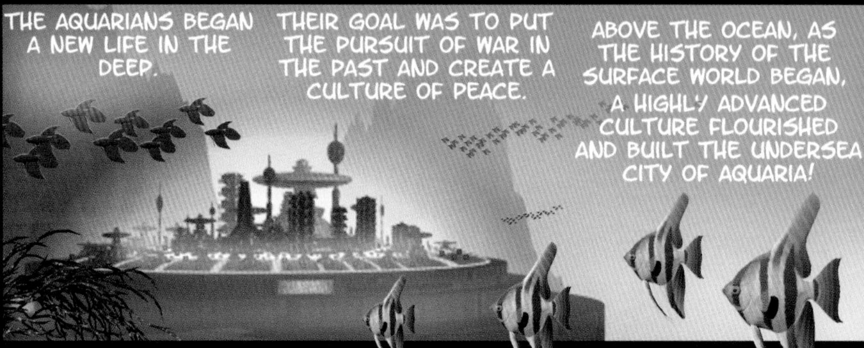
THE AQUARIANS BEGAN A NEW LIFE IN THE DEEP.
THEIR GOAL WAS TO PUT THE PURSUIT OF WAR IN THE PAST AND CREATE A CULTURE OF PEACE.
ABOVE THE OCEAN, AS THE HISTORY OF THE SURFACE WORLD BEGAN, A HIGHLY ADVANCED CULTURE FLOURISHED AND BUILT THE UNDERSEA CITY OF AQUARIA!

ANOTHER UNDERSEA CULTURE FLOURISHED AS WELL! LEMURIAN SCIENCE-MYSTICS CREATED THEIR OWN METHOD TO CONVERT THEMSELVES INTO WATER-BREATHERS. IN THE DEPTHS OF THE PACIFIC, THEIR DESCENDANTS LIVE TO THIS DAY. THEY ARE CALLED SHARK RIDERS.

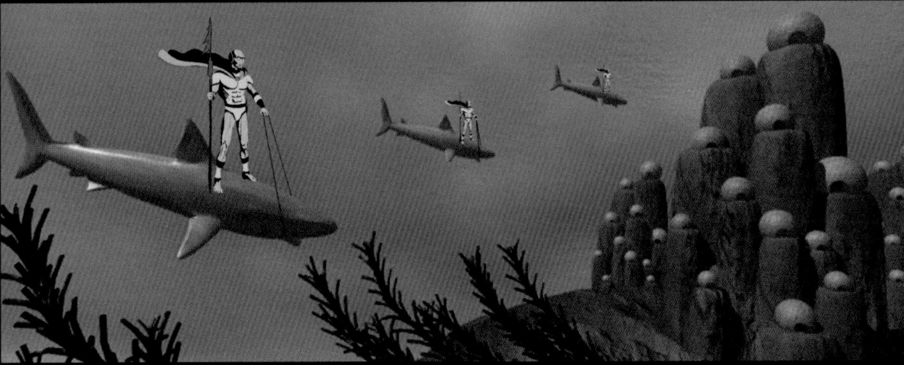

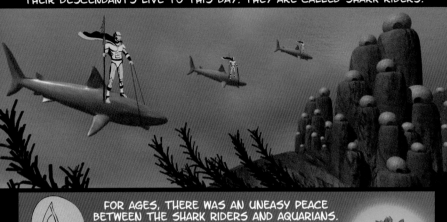

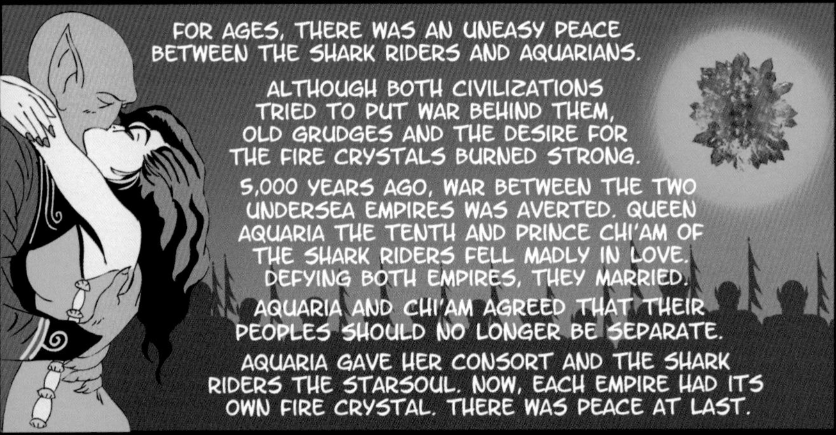
FOR AGES, THERE WAS AN UNEASY PEACE BETWEEN THE SHARK RIDERS AND AQUARIANS.
ALTHOUGH BOTH CIVILIZATIONS TRIED TO PUT WAR BEHIND THEM, OLD GRUDGES AND THE DESIRE FOR THE FIRE CRYSTALS BURNED STRONG.
5,000 YEARS AGO, WAR BETWEEN THE TWO UNDERSEA EMPIRES WAS AVERTED. QUEEN AQUARIA THE TENTH AND PRINCE CHI'AM OF THE SHARK RIDERS FELL MADLY IN LOVE. DEFYING BOTH EMPIRES, THEY MARRIED.
AQUARIA AND CHI'AM AGREED THAT THEIR PEOPLES SHOULD NO LONGER BE SEPARATE.
AQUARIA GAVE HER CONSORT AND THE SHARK RIDERS THE STARSOUL. NOW, EACH EMPIRE HAD ITS OWN FIRE CRYSTAL. THERE WAS PEACE AT LAST.

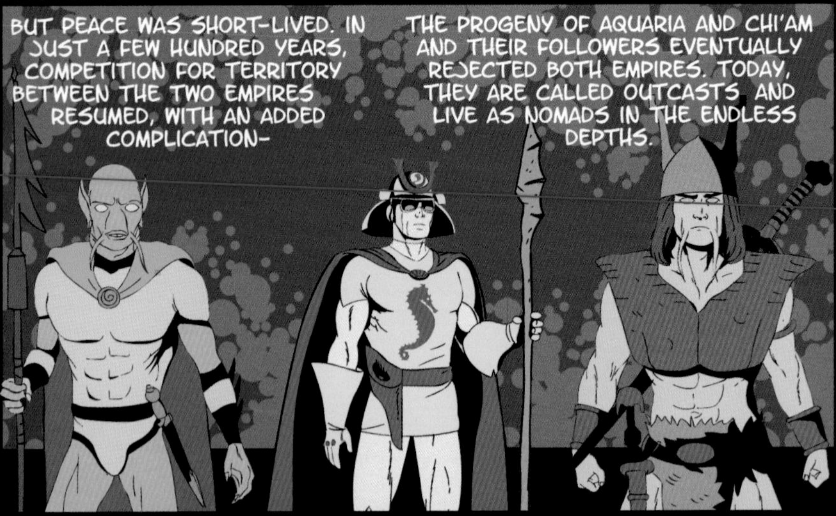
BUT PEACE WAS SHORT-LIVED. IN JUST A FEW HUNDRED YEARS, COMPETITION FOR TERRITORY BETWEEN THE TWO EMPIRES RESUMED, WITH AN ADDED COMPLICATION-
THE PROGENY OF AQUARIA AND CHI'AM AND THEIR FOLLOWERS EVENTUALLY REJECTED BOTH EMPIRES. TODAY, THEY ARE CALLED OUTCASTS AND LIVE AS NOMADS IN THE ENDLESS DEPTHS.

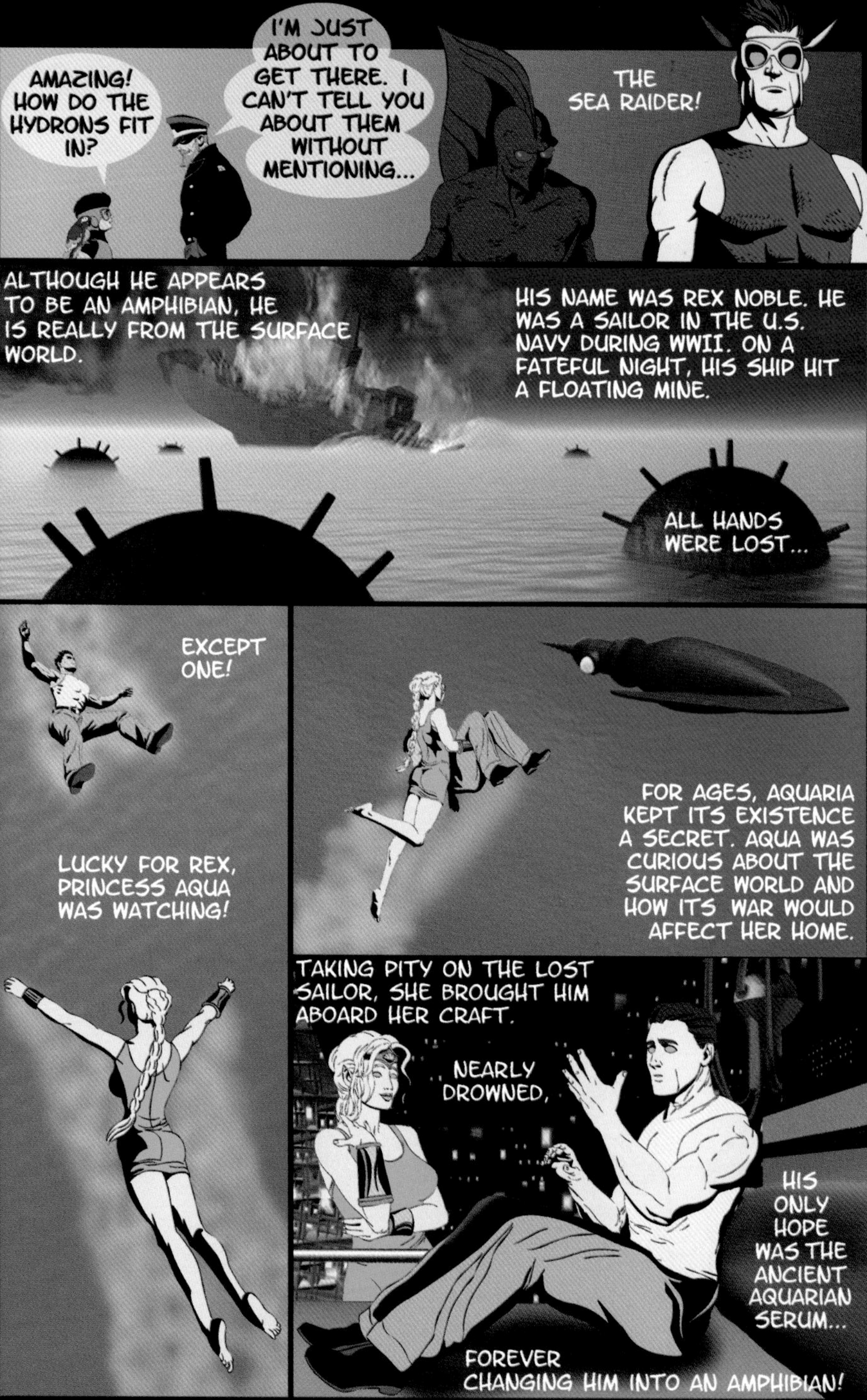
AMAZING! HOW DO THE HYDRONS FIT IN?
I'M JUST ABOUT TO GET THERE. I CAN'T TELL YOU ABOUT THEM WITHOUT MENTIONING...
THE SEA RAIDER!
ALTHOUGH HE APPEARS TO BE AN AMPHIBIAN, HE IS REALLY FROM THE SURFACE WORLD.
HIS NAME WAS REX NOBLE. HE WAS A SAILOR IN THE U.S. NAVY DURING WWII. ON A FATEFUL NIGHT, HIS SHIP HIT A FLOATING MINE.
ALL HANDS WERE LOST...
EXCEPT ONE!
LUCKY FOR REX, PRINCESS AQUA WAS WATCHING!
FOR AGES, AQUARIA KEPT ITS EXISTENCE A SECRET. AQUA WAS CURIOUS ABOUT THE SURFACE WORLD AND HOW ITS WAR WOULD AFFECT HER HOME.
TAKING PITY ON THE LOST SAILOR, SHE BROUGHT HIM ABOARD HER CRAFT.
NEARLY DROWNED,
HIS ONLY HOPE WAS THE ANCIENT AQUARIAN SERUM...
FOREVER CHANGING HIM INTO AN AMPHIBIAN!

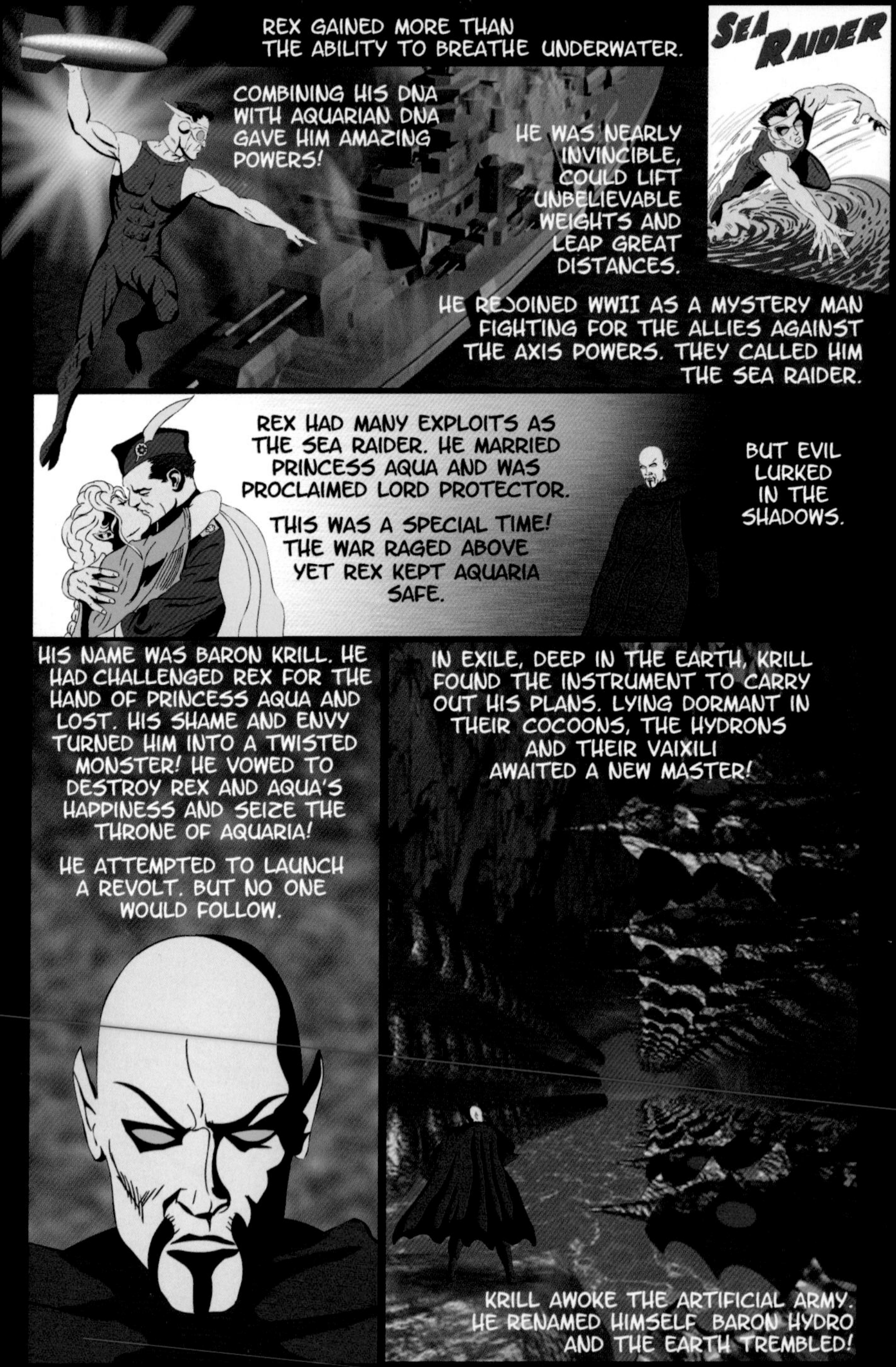
REX GAINED MORE THAN THE ABILITY TO BREATHE UNDERWATER.
SEA RAIDER
COMBINING HIS DNA WITH AQUARIAN DNA GAVE HIM AMAZING POWERS!
HE WAS NEARLY INVINCIBLE, COULD LIFT UNBELIEVABLE WEIGHTS AND LEAP GREAT DISTANCES.
HE REJOINED WWII AS A MYSTERY MAN FIGHTING FOR THE ALLIES AGAINST THE AXIS POWERS. THEY CALLED HIM THE SEA RAIDER.
REX HAD MANY EXPLOITS AS THE SEA RAIDER. HE MARRIED PRINCESS AQUA AND WAS PROCLAIMED LORD PROTECTOR.
THIS WAS A SPECIAL TIME! THE WAR RAGED ABOVE YET REX KEPT AQUARIA SAFE.
BUT EVIL LURKED IN THE SHADOWS.
HIS NAME WAS BARON KRILL. HE HAD CHALLENGED REX FOR THE HAND OF PRINCESS AQUA AND LOST. HIS SHAME AND ENVY TURNED HIM INTO A TWISTED MONSTER! HE VOWED TO DESTROY REX AND AQUA'S HAPPINESS AND SEIZE THE THRONE OF AQUARIA!
HE ATTEMPTED TO LAUNCH A REVOLT. BUT NO ONE WOULD FOLLOW.
IN EXILE, DEEP IN THE EARTH, KRILL FOUND THE INSTRUMENT TO CARRY OUT HIS PLANS. LYING DORMANT IN THEIR COCOONS, THE HYDRONS AND THEIR VAIXILI AWAITED A NEW MASTER!
KRILL AWOKE THE ARTIFICIAL ARMY. HE RENAMED HIMSELF BARON HYDRO AND THE EARTH TREMBLED!

Act 4 - The City in the Sea

BARON HYDRO THOUGHT HE COULD FURTHER HIS PLANS
BY JOINING THE AXIS POWERS.

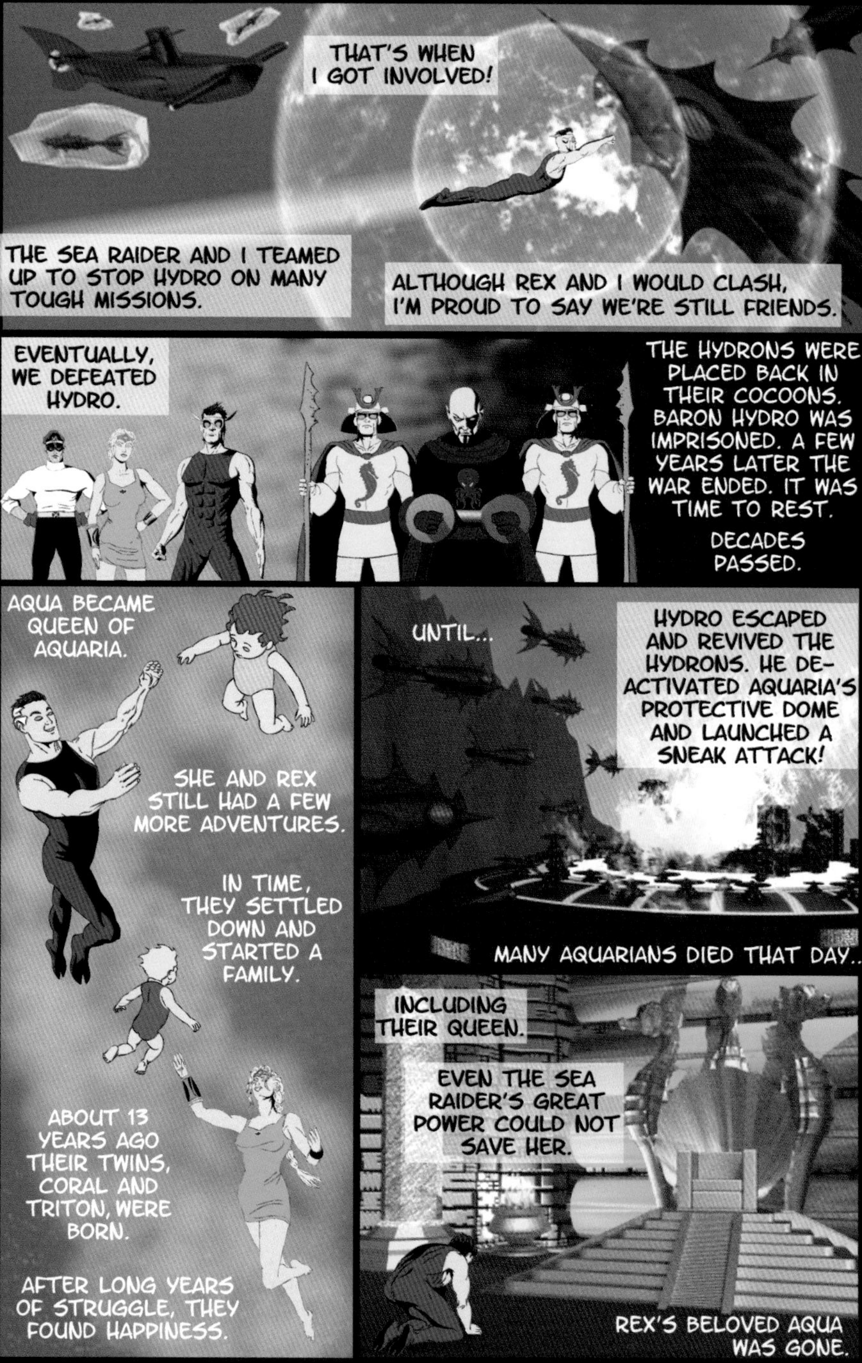

THAT'S WHEN I GOT INVOLVED!
THE SEA RAIDER AND I TEAMED UP TO STOP HYDRO ON MANY TOUGH MISSIONS.
ALTHOUGH REX AND I WOULD CLASH, I'M PROUD TO SAY WE'RE STILL FRIENDS.
EVENTUALLY, WE DEFEATED HYDRO.
THE HYDRONS WERE PLACED BACK IN THEIR COCOONS. BARON HYDRO WAS IMPRISONED. A FEW YEARS LATER THE WAR ENDED. IT WAS TIME TO REST.
DECADES PASSED.
AQUA BECAME QUEEN OF AQUARIA.
SHE AND REX STILL HAD A FEW MORE ADVENTURES.
IN TIME, THEY SETTLED DOWN AND STARTED A FAMILY.
ABOUT 13 YEARS AGO THEIR TWINS, CORAL AND TRITON, WERE BORN.
AFTER LONG YEARS OF STRUGGLE, THEY FOUND HAPPINESS.
UNTIL...
HYDRO ESCAPED AND REVIVED THE HYDRONS. HE DE-ACTIVATED AQUARIA'S PROTECTIVE DOME AND LAUNCHED A SNEAK ATTACK!
MANY AQUARIANS DIED THAT DAY...
INCLUDING THEIR QUEEN.
EVEN THE SEA RAIDER'S GREAT POWER COULD NOT SAVE HER.
REX'S BELOVED AQUA WAS GONE.

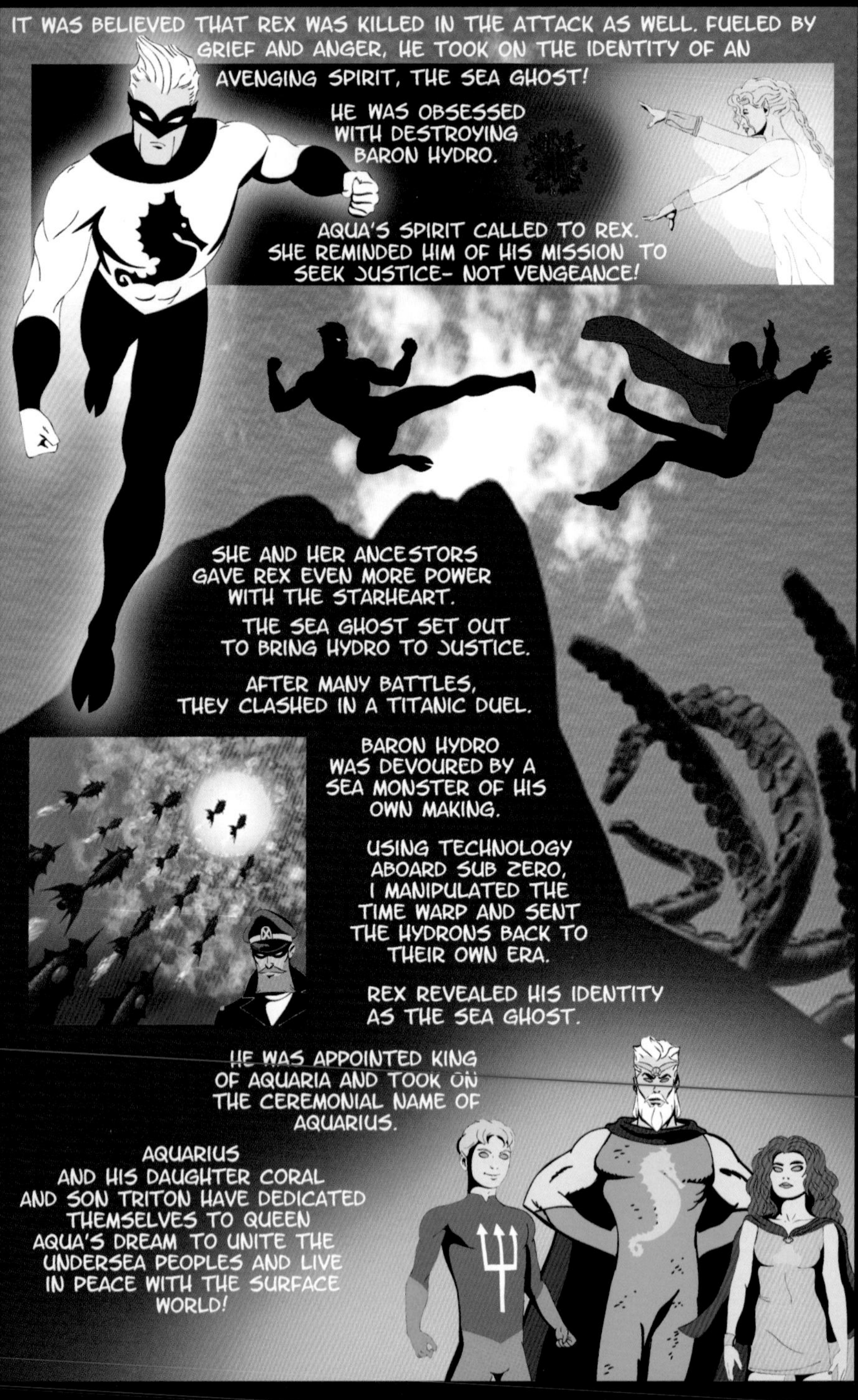
IT WAS BELIEVED THAT REX WAS KILLED IN THE ATTACK AS WELL. FUELED BY GRIEF AND ANGER, HE TOOK ON THE IDENTITY OF AN AVENGING SPIRIT, THE SEA GHOST!
HE WAS OBSESSED WITH DESTROYING BARON HYDRO.
AQUA'S SPIRIT CALLED TO REX. SHE REMINDED HIM OF HIS MISSION TO SEEK JUSTICE- NOT VENGEANCE!
SHE AND HER ANCESTORS GAVE REX EVEN MORE POWER WITH THE STARHEART.
THE SEA GHOST SET OUT TO BRING HYDRO TO JUSTICE.
AFTER MANY BATTLES, THEY CLASHED IN A TITANIC DUEL.
BARON HYDRO WAS DEVOURED BY A SEA MONSTER OF HIS OWN MAKING.
USING TECHNOLOGY ABOARD SUB ZERO, I MANIPULATED THE TIME WARP AND SENT THE HYDRONS BACK TO THEIR OWN ERA.
REX REVEALED HIS IDENTITY AS THE SEA GHOST.
HE WAS APPOINTED KING OF AQUARIA AND TOOK ON THE CEREMONIAL NAME OF AQUARIUS.
AQUARIUS AND HIS DAUGHTER CORAL AND SON TRITON HAVE DEDICATED THEMSELVES TO QUEEN AQUA'S DREAM TO UNITE THE UNDERSEA PEOPLES AND LIVE IN PEACE WITH THE SURFACE WORLD!

Act 4 - The City in the Sea

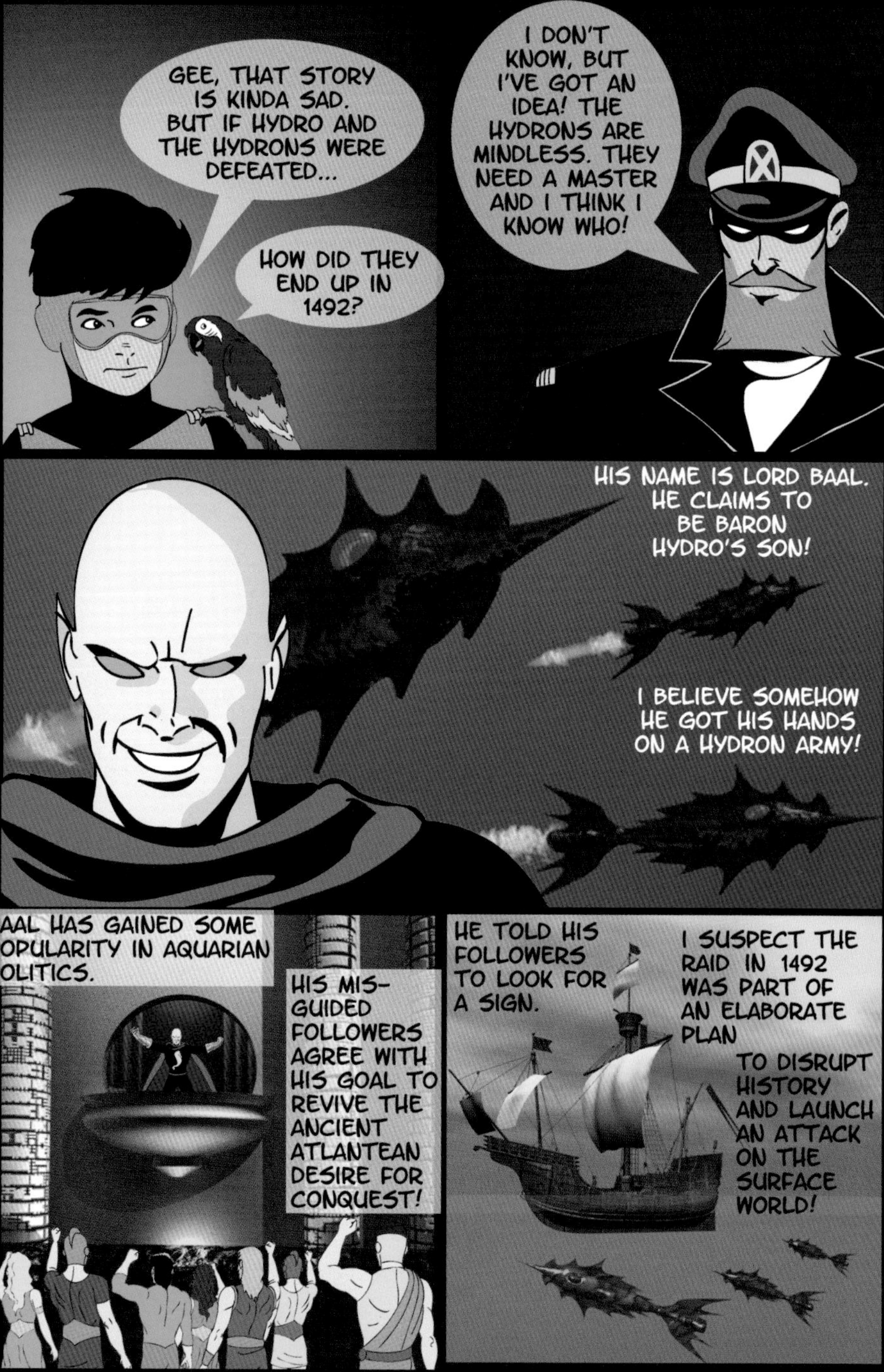
GEE, THAT STORY IS KINDA SAD. BUT IF HYDRO AND THE HYDRONS WERE DEFEATED...
HOW DID THEY END UP IN 1492?
I DON'T KNOW, BUT I'VE GOT AN IDEA! THE HYDRONS ARE MINDLESS. THEY NEED A MASTER AND I THINK I KNOW WHO!
HIS NAME IS LORD BAAL. HE CLAIMS TO BE BARON HYDRO'S SON!
I BELIEVE SOMEHOW HE GOT HIS HANDS ON A HYDRON ARMY!
BAAL HAS GAINED SOME POPULARITY IN AQUARIAN POLITICS.
HIS MIS-GUIDED FOLLOWERS AGREE WITH HIS GOAL TO REVIVE THE ANCIENT ATLANTEAN DESIRE FOR CONQUEST!
HE TOLD HIS FOLLOWERS TO LOOK FOR A SIGN.
I SUSPECT THE RAID IN 1492 WAS PART OF AN ELABORATE PLAN
TO DISRUPT HISTORY AND LAUNCH AN ATTACK ON THE SURFACE WORLD!

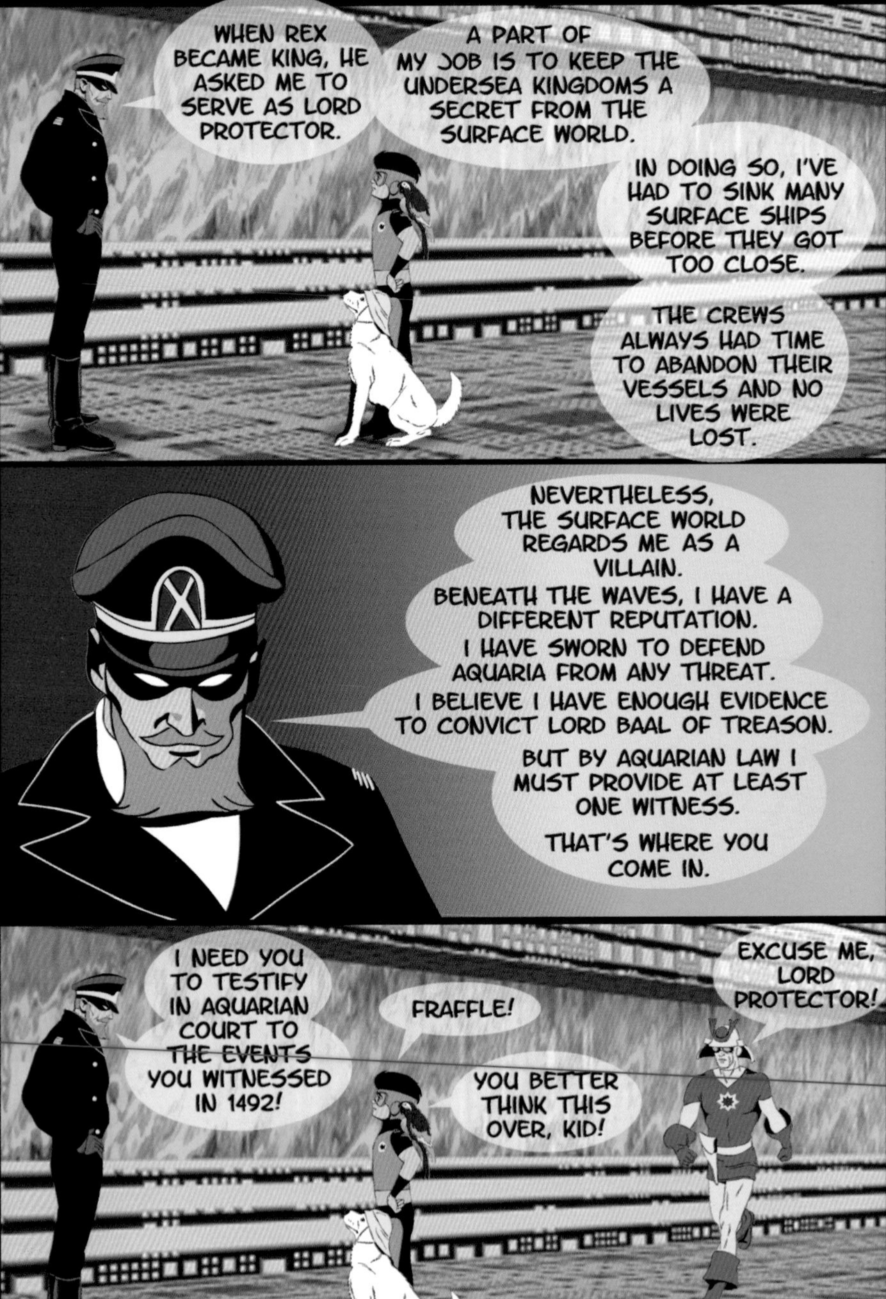
WHEN REX BECAME KING, HE ASKED ME TO SERVE AS LORD PROTECTOR.
A PART OF MY JOB IS TO KEEP THE UNDERSEA KINGDOMS A SECRET FROM THE SURFACE WORLD.
IN DOING SO, I'VE HAD TO SINK MANY SURFACE SHIPS BEFORE THEY GOT TOO CLOSE.
THE CREWS ALWAYS HAD TIME TO ABANDON THEIR VESSELS AND NO LIVES WERE LOST.
NEVERTHELESS, THE SURFACE WORLD REGARDS ME AS A VILLAIN.
BENEATH THE WAVES, I HAVE A DIFFERENT REPUTATION.
I HAVE SWORN TO DEFEND AQUARIA FROM ANY THREAT.
I BELIEVE I HAVE ENOUGH EVIDENCE TO CONVICT LORD BAAL OF TREASON.
BUT BY AQUARIAN LAW I MUST PROVIDE AT LEAST ONE WITNESS.
THAT'S WHERE YOU COME IN.
I NEED YOU TO TESTIFY IN AQUARIAN COURT TO THE EVENTS YOU WITNESSED IN 1492!
FRAFFLE!
YOU BETTER THINK THIS OVER, KID!
EXCUSE ME, LORD PROTECTOR!

Act 4 - The City in the Sea

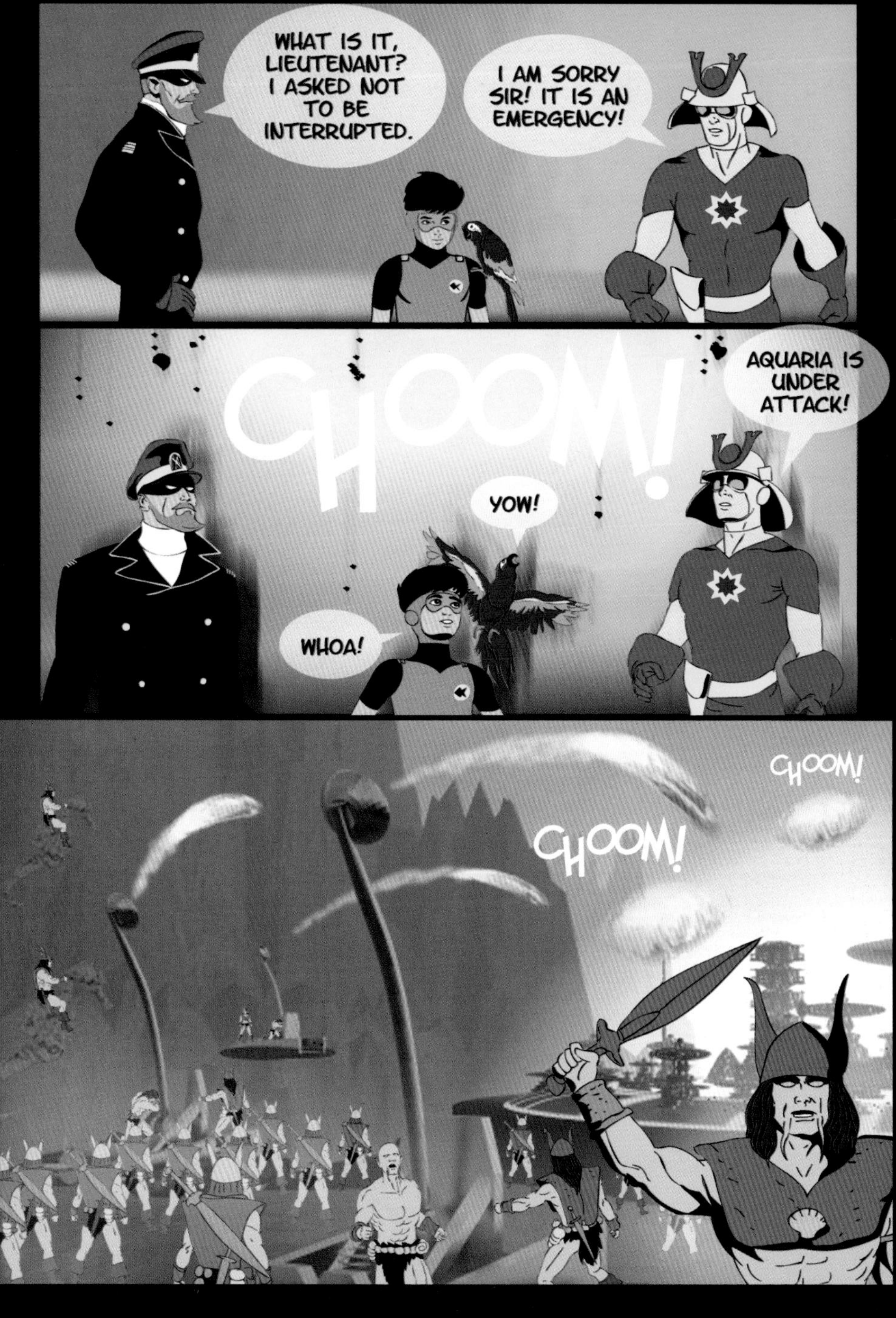
WHAT IS IT, LIEUTENANT? I ASKED NOT TO BE INTERRUPTED.
I AM SORRY SIR! IT IS AN EMERGENCY!
CHOOM!
AQUARIA IS UNDER ATTACK!
YOW!
WHOA!
CHOOM!
CHOOM!

BACK ONBOARD THE SEASCAPE
THE CREW DISCUSSES THE NARCISSUS.

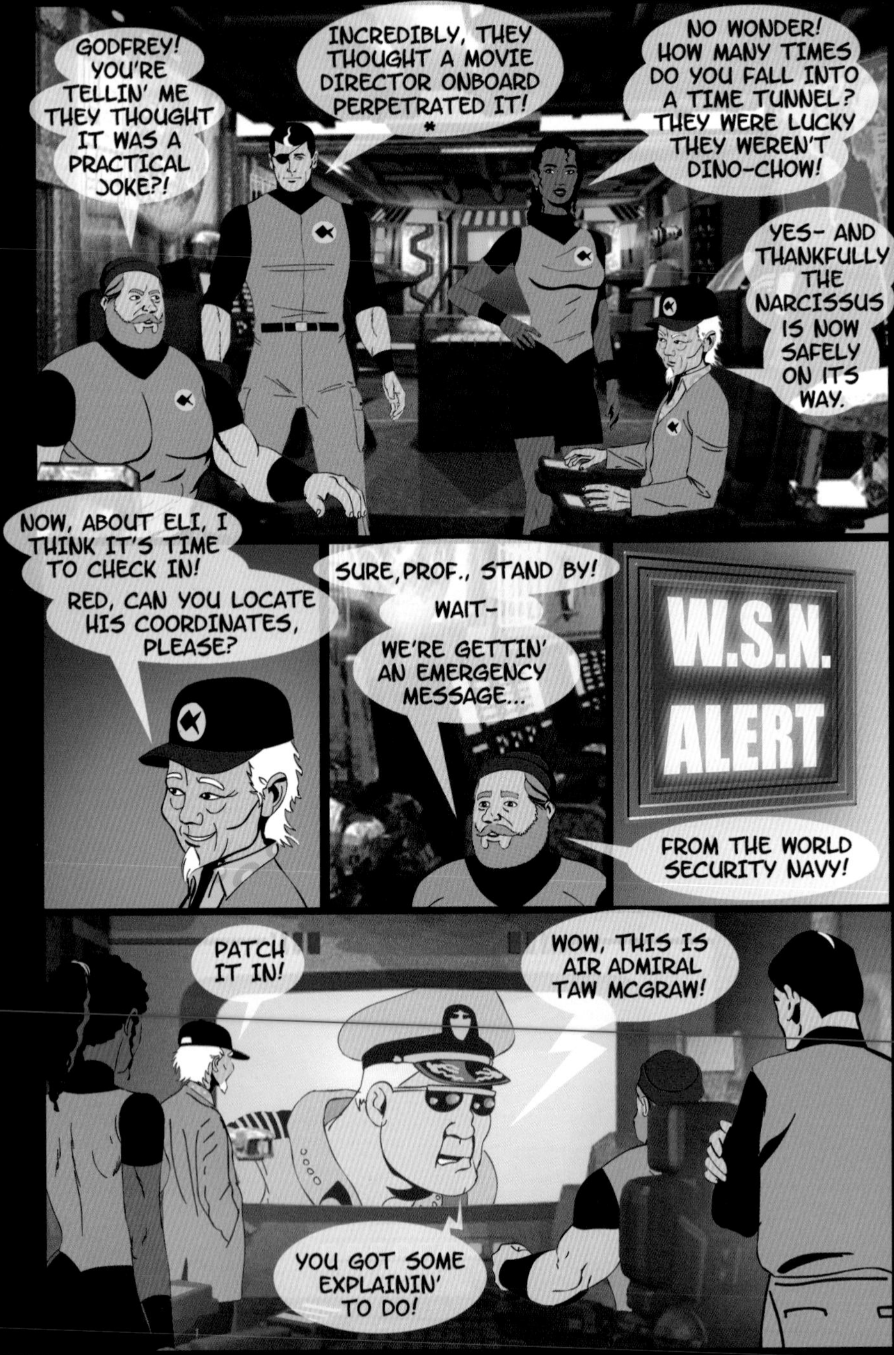
GODFREY! YOU'RE TELLIN' ME THEY THOUGHT IT WAS A PRACTICAL JOKE?!
INCREDIBLY, THEY THOUGHT A MOVIE DIRECTOR ONBOARD PERPETRATED IT! *
NO WONDER! HOW MANY TIMES DO YOU FALL INTO A TIME TUNNEL? THEY WERE LUCKY THEY WEREN'T DINO-CHOW!
YES- AND THANKFULLY THE NARCISSUS IS NOW SAFELY ON ITS WAY.
NOW, ABOUT ELI, I THINK IT'S TIME TO CHECK IN!
RED, CAN YOU LOCATE HIS COORDINATES, PLEASE?
SURE, PROF., STAND BY!
WAIT-
WE'RE GETTIN' AN EMERGENCY MESSAGE...
W.S.N. ALERT
FROM THE WORLD SECURITY NAVY!
PATCH IT IN!
WOW, THIS IS AIR ADMIRAL TAW MCGRAW!
YOU GOT SOME EXPLAININ' TO DO!

* SEE VOLUME 1

END OF ACT 4

Act 5 - The Battle for Aquaria

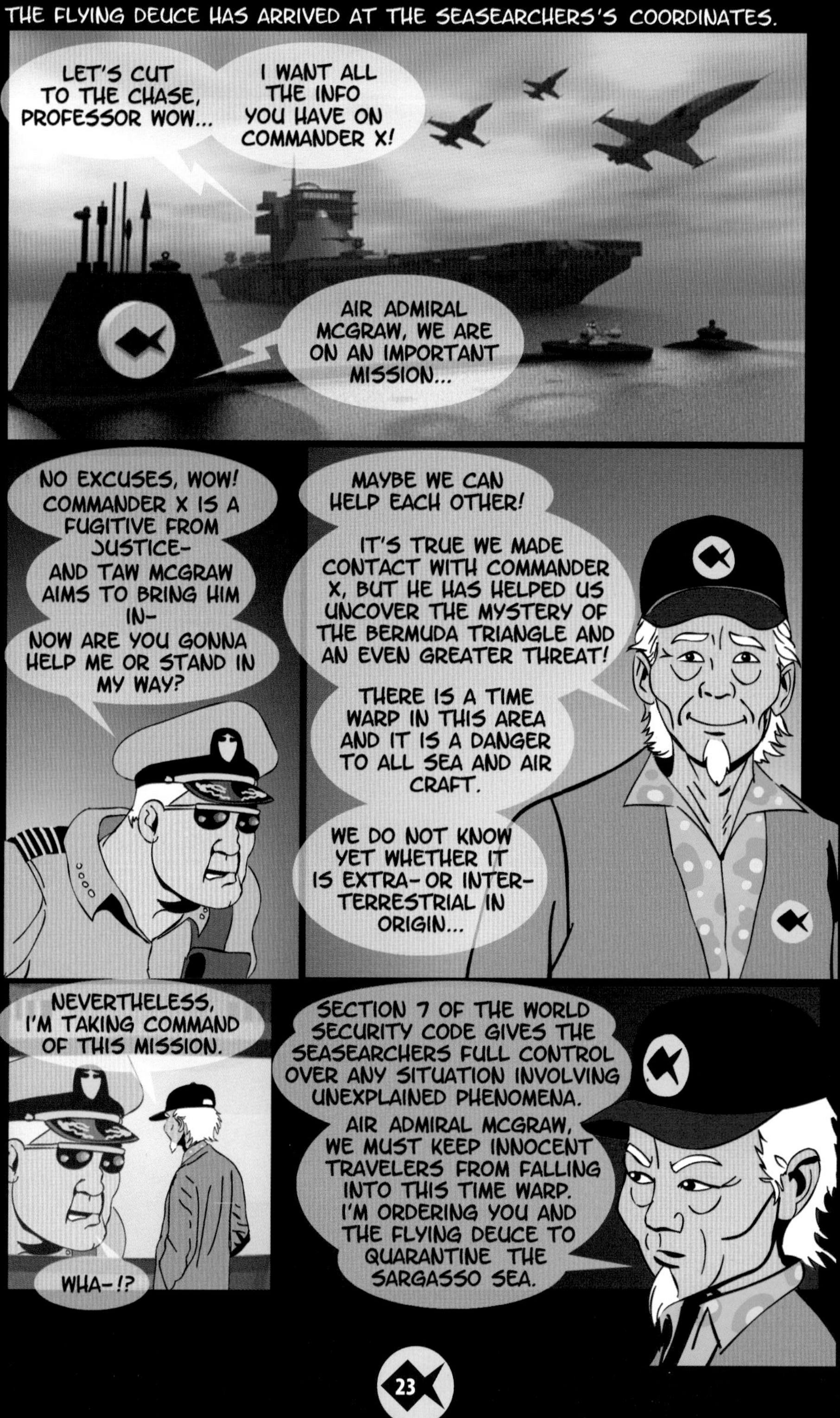
THE FLYING DEUCE HAS ARRIVED AT THE SEASEARCHERS'S COORDINATES.
LET'S CUT TO THE CHASE, PROFESSOR WOW...
I WANT ALL THE INFO YOU HAVE ON COMMANDER X!
AIR ADMIRAL MCGRAW, WE ARE ON AN IMPORTANT MISSION...
NO EXCUSES, WOW! COMMANDER X IS A FUGITIVE FROM JUSTICE-
AND TAW MCGRAW AIMS TO BRING HIM IN-
NOW ARE YOU GONNA HELP ME OR STAND IN MY WAY?
MAYBE WE CAN HELP EACH OTHER!
IT'S TRUE WE MADE CONTACT WITH COMMANDER X, BUT HE HAS HELPED US UNCOVER THE MYSTERY OF THE BERMUDA TRIANGLE AND AN EVEN GREATER THREAT!
THERE IS A TIME WARP IN THIS AREA AND IT IS A DANGER TO ALL SEA AND AIR CRAFT.
WE DO NOT KNOW YET WHETHER IT IS EXTRA- OR INTER-TERRESTRIAL IN ORIGIN...
NEVERTHELESS, I'M TAKING COMMAND OF THIS MISSION.
WHA-!?
SECTION 7 OF THE WORLD SECURITY CODE GIVES THE SEASEARCHERS FULL CONTROL OVER ANY SITUATION INVOLVING UNEXPLAINED PHENOMENA.
AIR ADMIRAL MCGRAW, WE MUST KEEP INNOCENT TRAVELERS FROM FALLING INTO THIS TIME WARP. I'M ORDERING YOU AND THE FLYING DEUCE TO QUARANTINE THE SARGASSO SEA.

MEANWHILE, AT THE BOTTOM OF THE SEA.

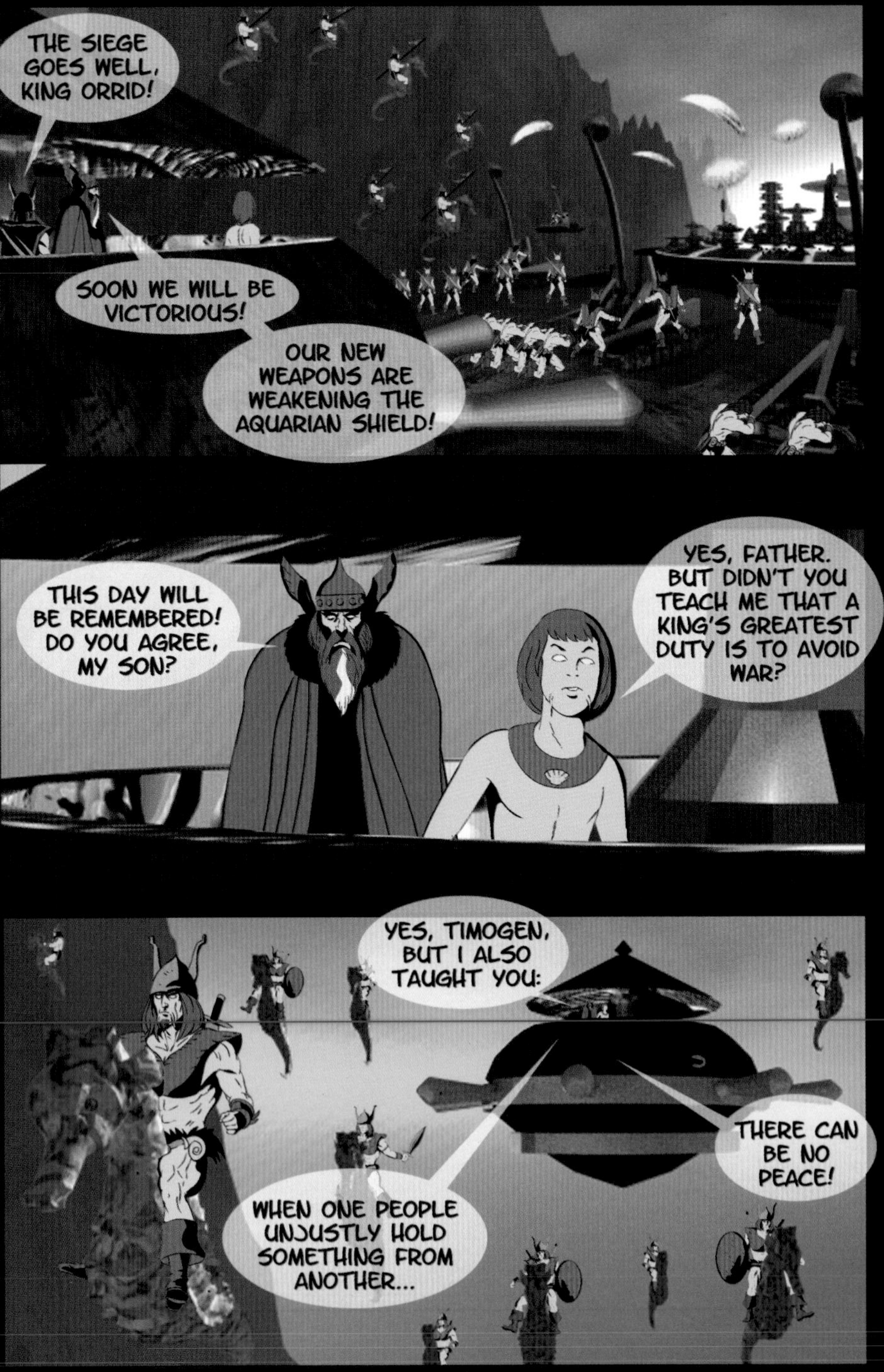
THE SIEGE GOES WELL, KING ORRID!
SOON WE WILL BE VICTORIOUS!
OUR NEW WEAPONS ARE WEAKENING THE AQUARIAN SHIELD!
THIS DAY WILL BE REMEMBERED! DO YOU AGREE, MY SON?
YES, FATHER. BUT DIDN'T YOU TEACH ME THAT A KING'S GREATEST DUTY IS TO AVOID WAR?
YES, TIMOGEN, BUT I ALSO TAUGHT YOU:
WHEN ONE PEOPLE UNJUSTLY HOLD SOMETHING FROM ANOTHER...
THERE CAN BE NO PEACE!

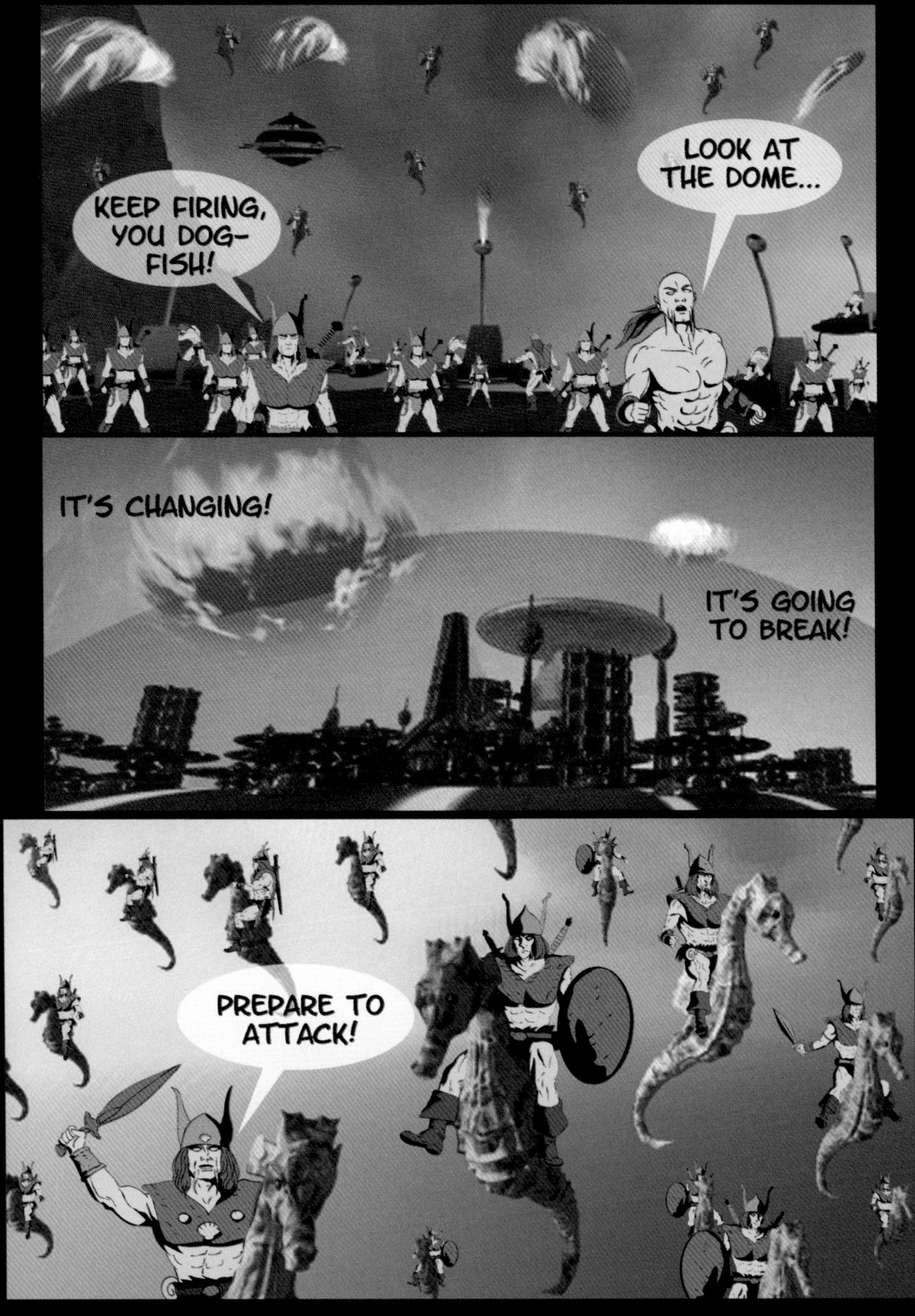
KEEP FIRING, YOU DOG-FISH!
LOOK AT THE DOME...
IT'S CHANGING!
IT'S GOING TO BREAK!
PREPARE TO ATTACK!

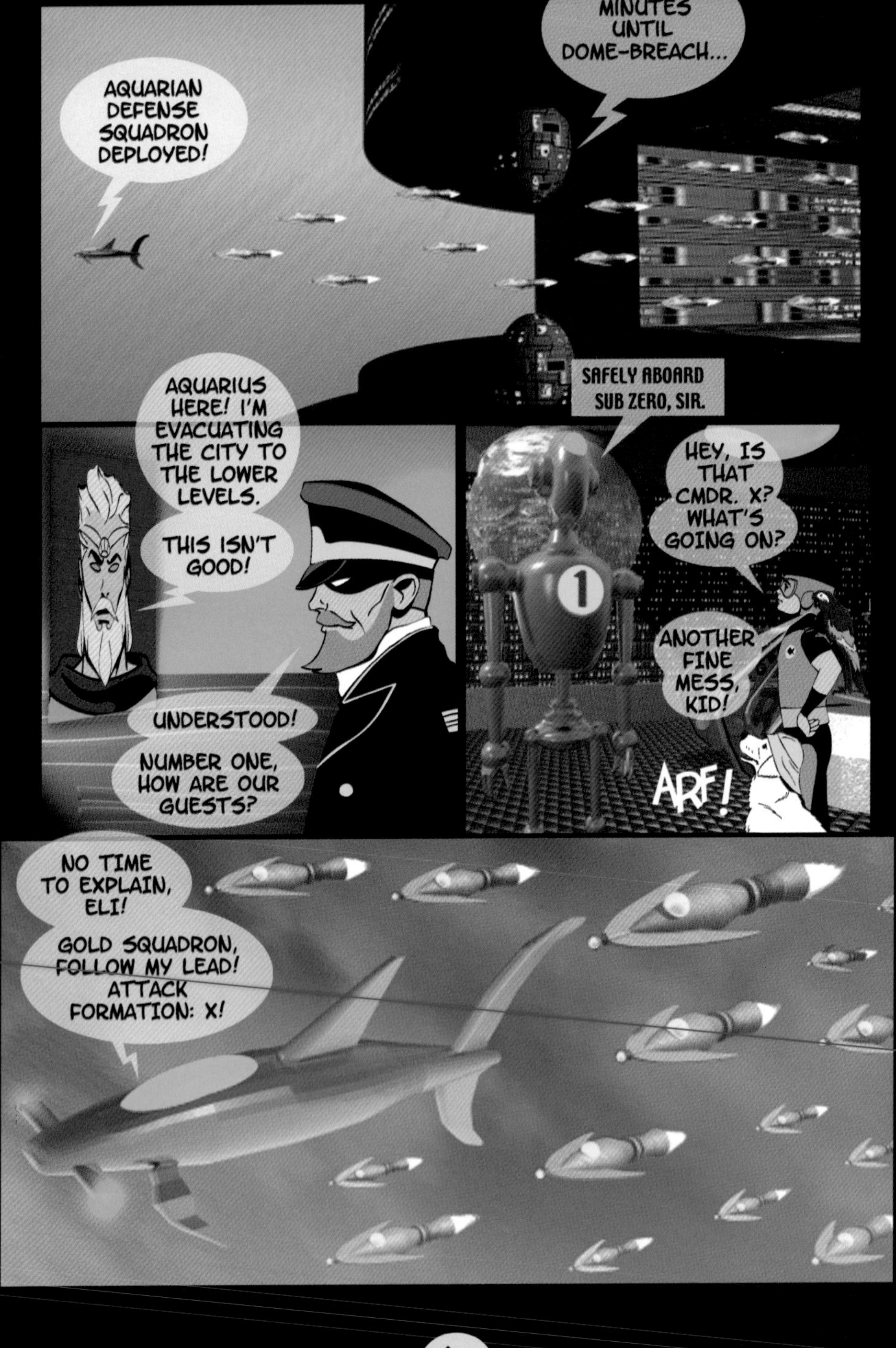
AQUARIAN DEFENSE SQUADRON DEPLOYED!
FIVE MINUTES UNTIL DOME-BREACH...
AQUARIUS HERE! I'M EVACUATING THE CITY TO THE LOWER LEVELS.
THIS ISN'T GOOD!
UNDERSTOOD!
NUMBER ONE, HOW ARE OUR GUESTS?
SAFELY ABOARD SUB ZERO, SIR.
1
HEY, IS THAT CMDR. X? WHAT'S GOING ON?
ANOTHER FINE MESS, KID!
ARF!
NO TIME TO EXPLAIN, ELI!
GOLD SQUADRON, FOLLOW MY LEAD! ATTACK FORMATION: X!

ACT 5 - THE BATTLE FOR AQUARIA

THE THRONE ROOM OF AQUARIA.

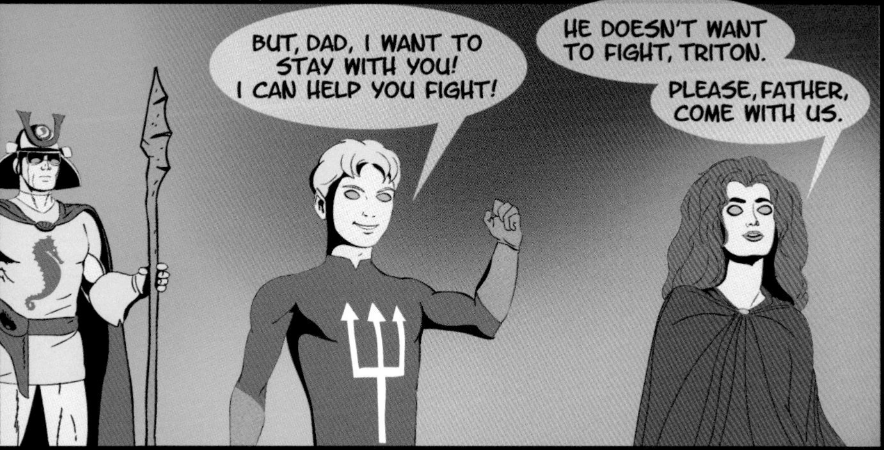
BUT, DAD, I WANT TO STAY WITH YOU! I CAN HELP YOU FIGHT!
HE DOESN'T WANT TO FIGHT, TRITON.
PLEASE, FATHER, COME WITH US.

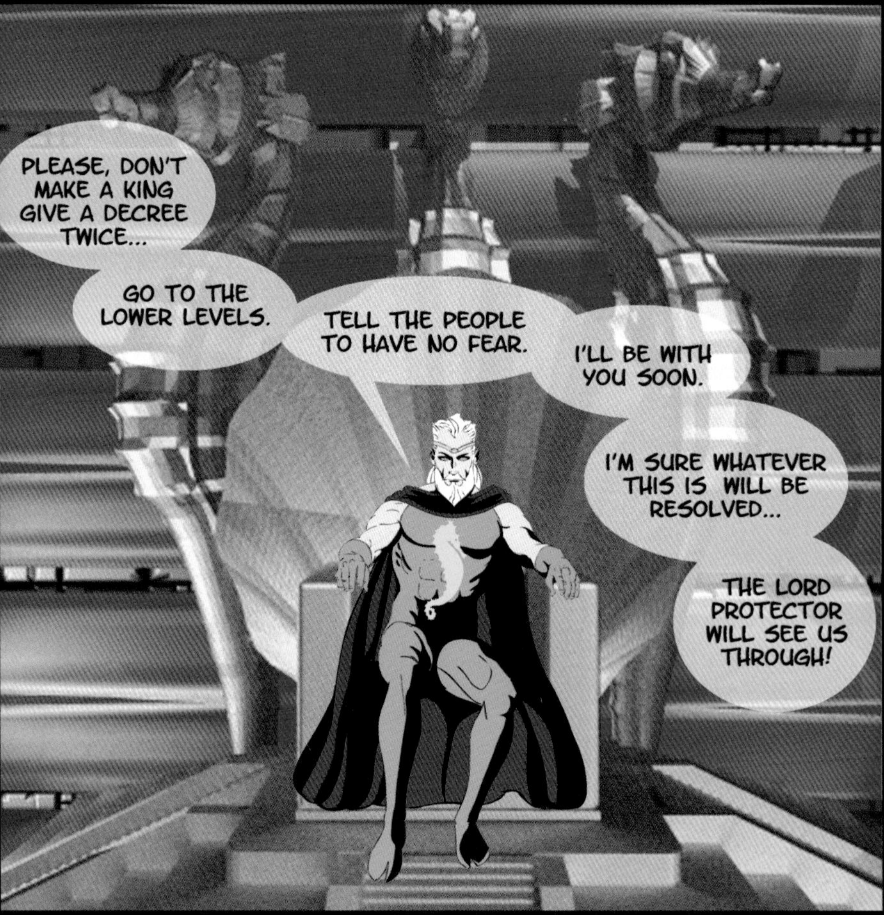
PLEASE, DON'T MAKE A KING GIVE A DECREE TWICE...
GO TO THE LOWER LEVELS.
TELL THE PEOPLE TO HAVE NO FEAR.
I'LL BE WITH YOU SOON.
I'M SURE WHATEVER THIS IS WILL BE RESOLVED...
THE LORD PROTECTOR WILL SEE US THROUGH!

THE BATTLE FOR AQUARIA CONTINUES.

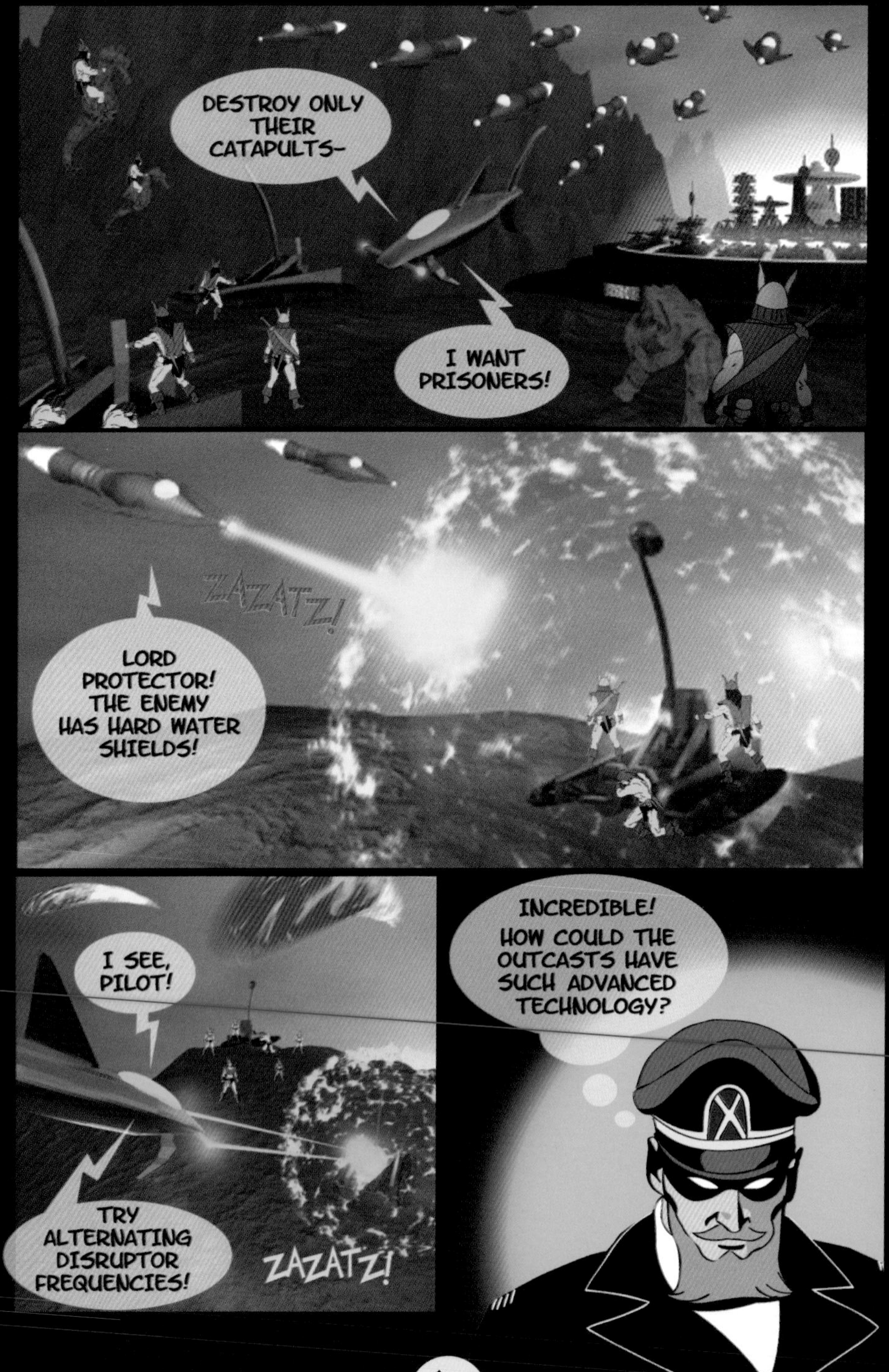
DESTROY ONLY THEIR CATAPULTS-
I WANT PRISONERS!
ZAZATZ!
LORD PROTECTOR! THE ENEMY HAS HARD WATER SHIELDS!
I SEE, PILOT!
TRY ALTERNATING DISRUPTOR FREQUENCIES!
ZAZATZ!
INCREDIBLE! HOW COULD THE OUTCASTS HAVE SUCH ADVANCED TECHNOLOGY?

Act 5 - The Battle for Aquaria

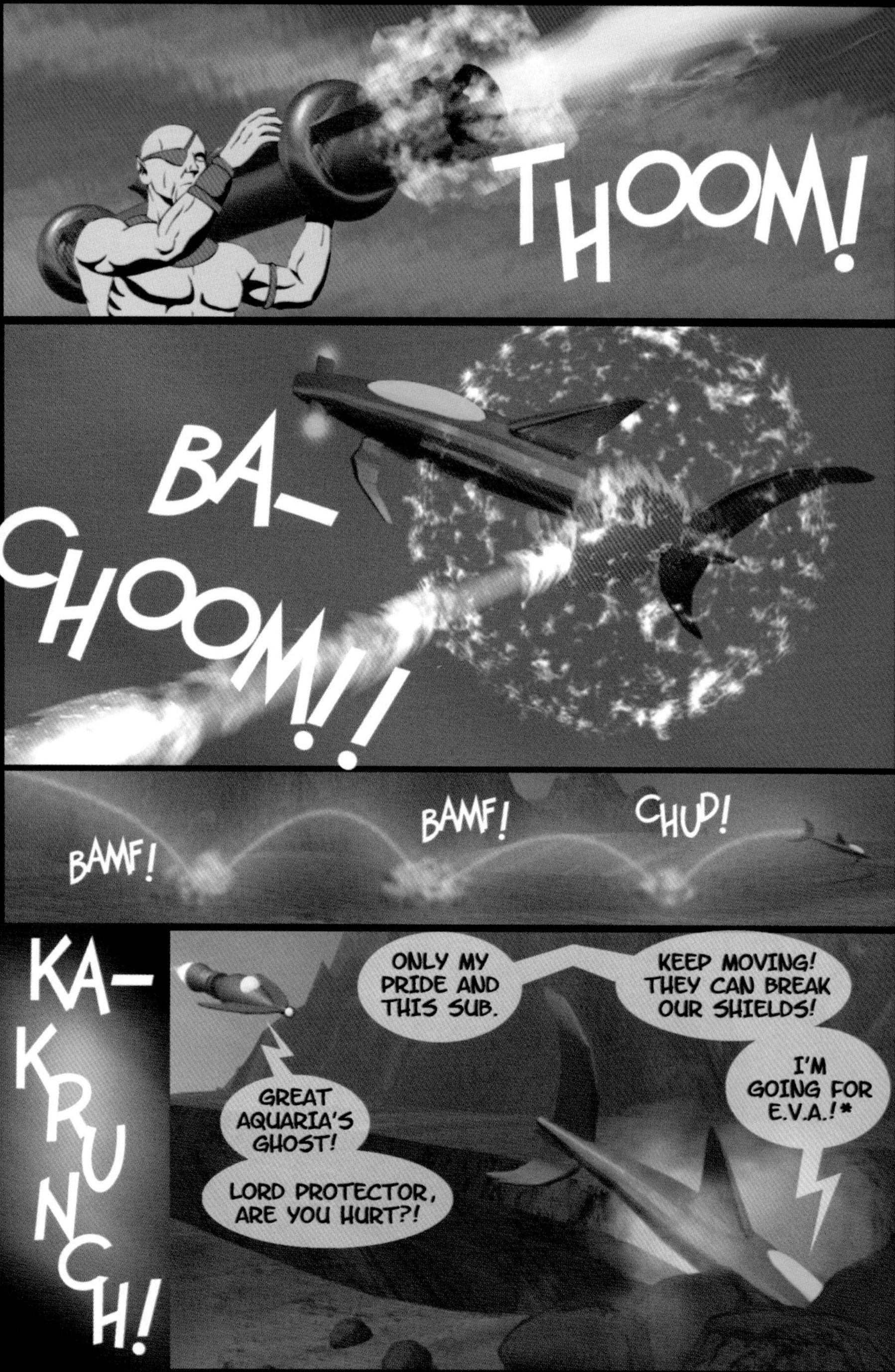
THOOM!
BA-CHOOM!!
BAMF!
BAMF!
CHUD!
KA-KRUNCH!
GREAT AQUARIA'S GHOST!
LORD PROTECTOR, ARE YOU HURT?!
ONLY MY PRIDE AND THIS SUB.
KEEP MOVING! THEY CAN BREAK OUR SHIELDS!
I'M GOING FOR E.V.A.!*

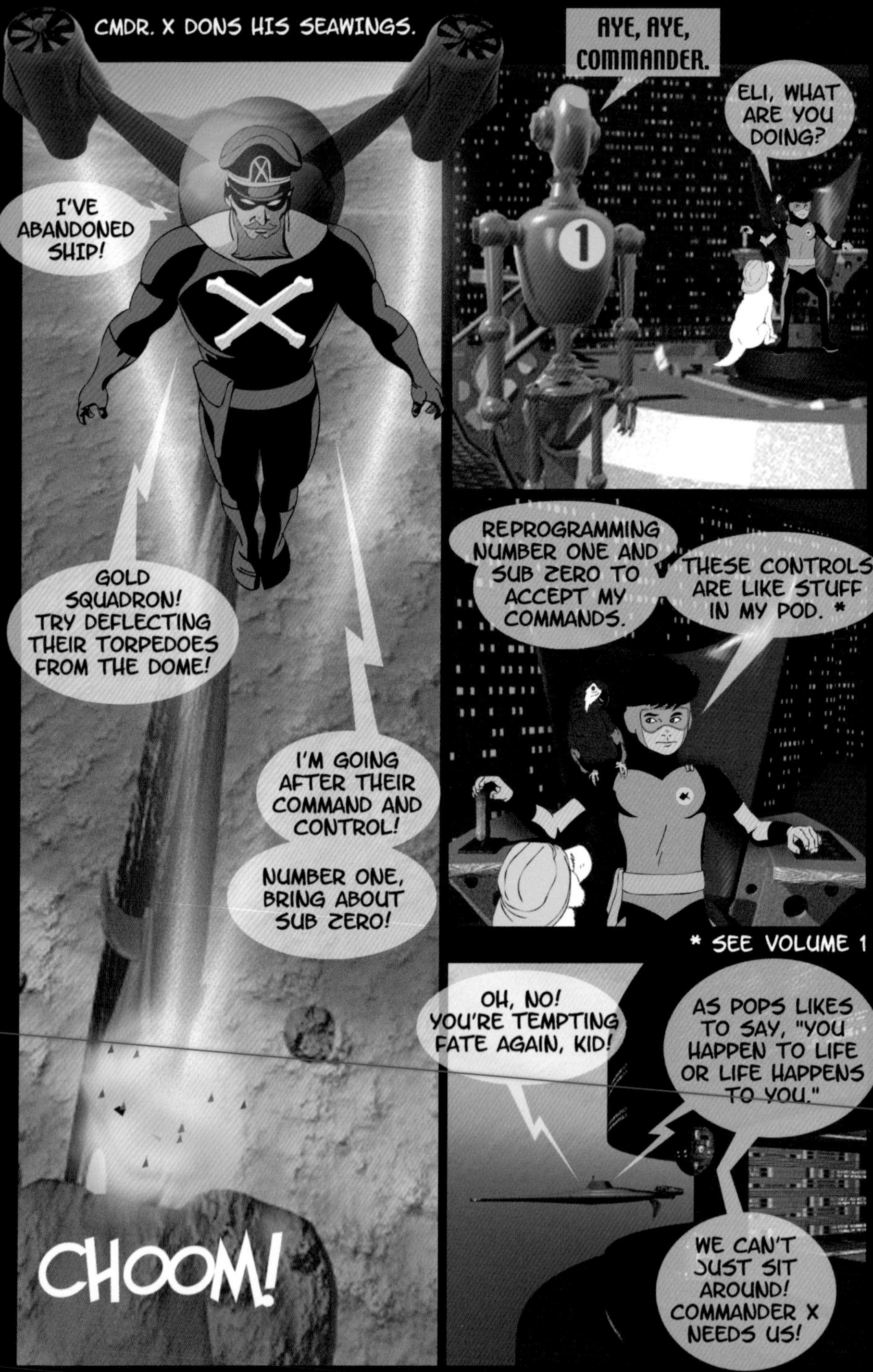
CMDR. X DONS HIS SEAWINGS.
I'VE ABANDONED SHIP!
GOLD SQUADRON! TRY DEFLECTING THEIR TORPEDOES FROM THE DOME!
I'M GOING AFTER THEIR COMMAND AND CONTROL!
NUMBER ONE, BRING ABOUT SUB ZERO!
CHOOM!
AYE, AYE, COMMANDER.
1
ELI, WHAT ARE YOU DOING?
REPROGRAMMING NUMBER ONE AND SUB ZERO TO ACCEPT MY COMMANDS.
THESE CONTROLS ARE LIKE STUFF IN MY POD. *
* SEE VOLUME 1
OH, NO! YOU'RE TEMPTING FATE AGAIN, KID!
AS POPS LIKES TO SAY, "YOU HAPPEN TO LIFE OR LIFE HAPPENS TO YOU."
WE CAN'T JUST SIT AROUND! COMMANDER X NEEDS US!

Act 5 - The Battle for Aquaria

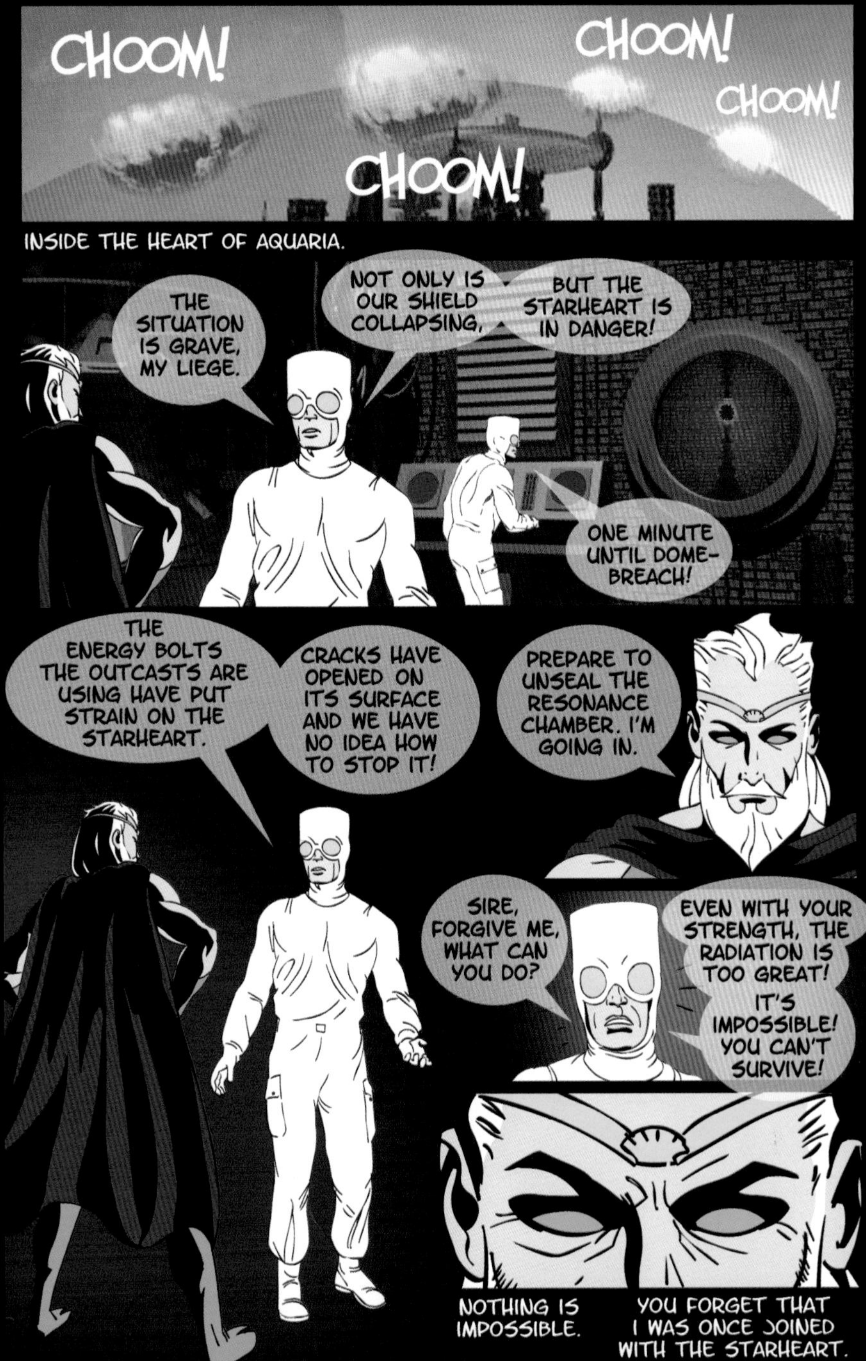
CHOOM!
CHOOM!
CHOOM!
CHOOM!
INSIDE THE HEART OF AQUARIA.
THE SITUATION IS GRAVE, MY LIEGE.
NOT ONLY IS OUR SHIELD COLLAPSING,
BUT THE STARHEART IS IN DANGER!
ONE MINUTE UNTIL DOME-BREACH!
THE ENERGY BOLTS THE OUTCASTS ARE USING HAVE PUT STRAIN ON THE STARHEART.
CRACKS HAVE OPENED ON ITS SURFACE AND WE HAVE NO IDEA HOW TO STOP IT!
PREPARE TO UNSEAL THE RESONANCE CHAMBER. I'M GOING IN.
SIRE, FORGIVE ME, WHAT CAN YOU DO?
EVEN WITH YOUR STRENGTH, THE RADIATION IS TOO GREAT!
IT'S IMPOSSIBLE! YOU CAN'T SURVIVE!
NOTHING IS IMPOSSIBLE.
YOU FORGET THAT I WAS ONCE JOINED WITH THE STARHEART.

KING AQUARIUS ENTERS THE RESONANCE CHAMBER.

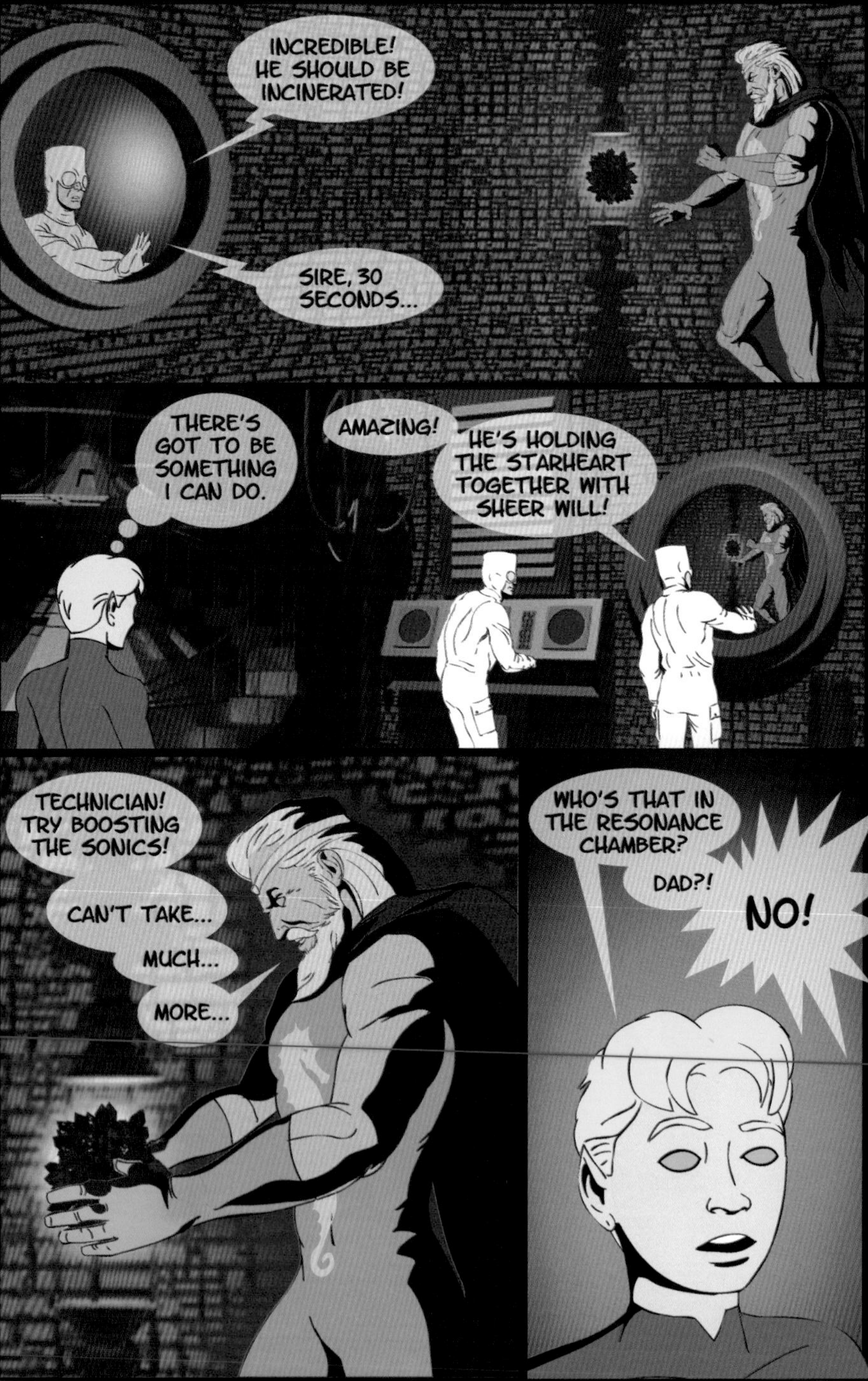
INCREDIBLE! HE SHOULD BE INCINERATED!
SIRE, 30 SECONDS...
THERE'S GOT TO BE SOMETHING I CAN DO.
AMAZING!
HE'S HOLDING THE STARHEART TOGETHER WITH SHEER WILL!
TECHNICIAN! TRY BOOSTING THE SONICS!
CAN'T TAKE...
MUCH...
MORE...
WHO'S THAT IN THE RESONANCE CHAMBER?
DAD?!
NO!

Act 5 - The Battle for Aquaria

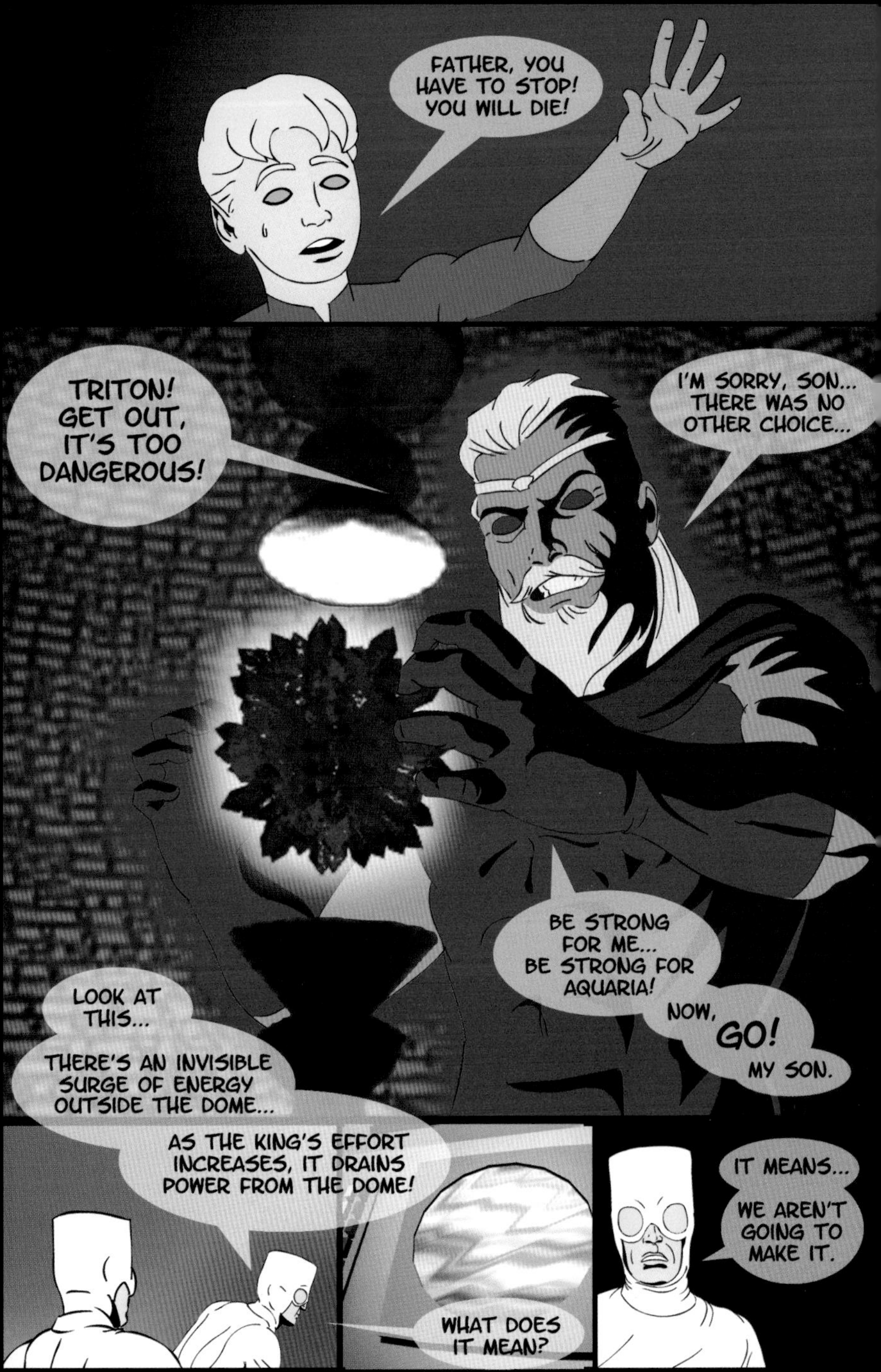
FATHER, YOU HAVE TO STOP! YOU WILL DIE!
TRITON! GET OUT, IT'S TOO DANGEROUS!
I'M SORRY, SON... THERE WAS NO OTHER CHOICE...
BE STRONG FOR ME... BE STRONG FOR AQUARIA!
NOW, GO! MY SON.
LOOK AT THIS...
THERE'S AN INVISIBLE SURGE OF ENERGY OUTSIDE THE DOME...
AS THE KING'S EFFORT INCREASES, IT DRAINS POWER FROM THE DOME!
WHAT DOES IT MEAN?
IT MEANS...
WE AREN'T GOING TO MAKE IT.

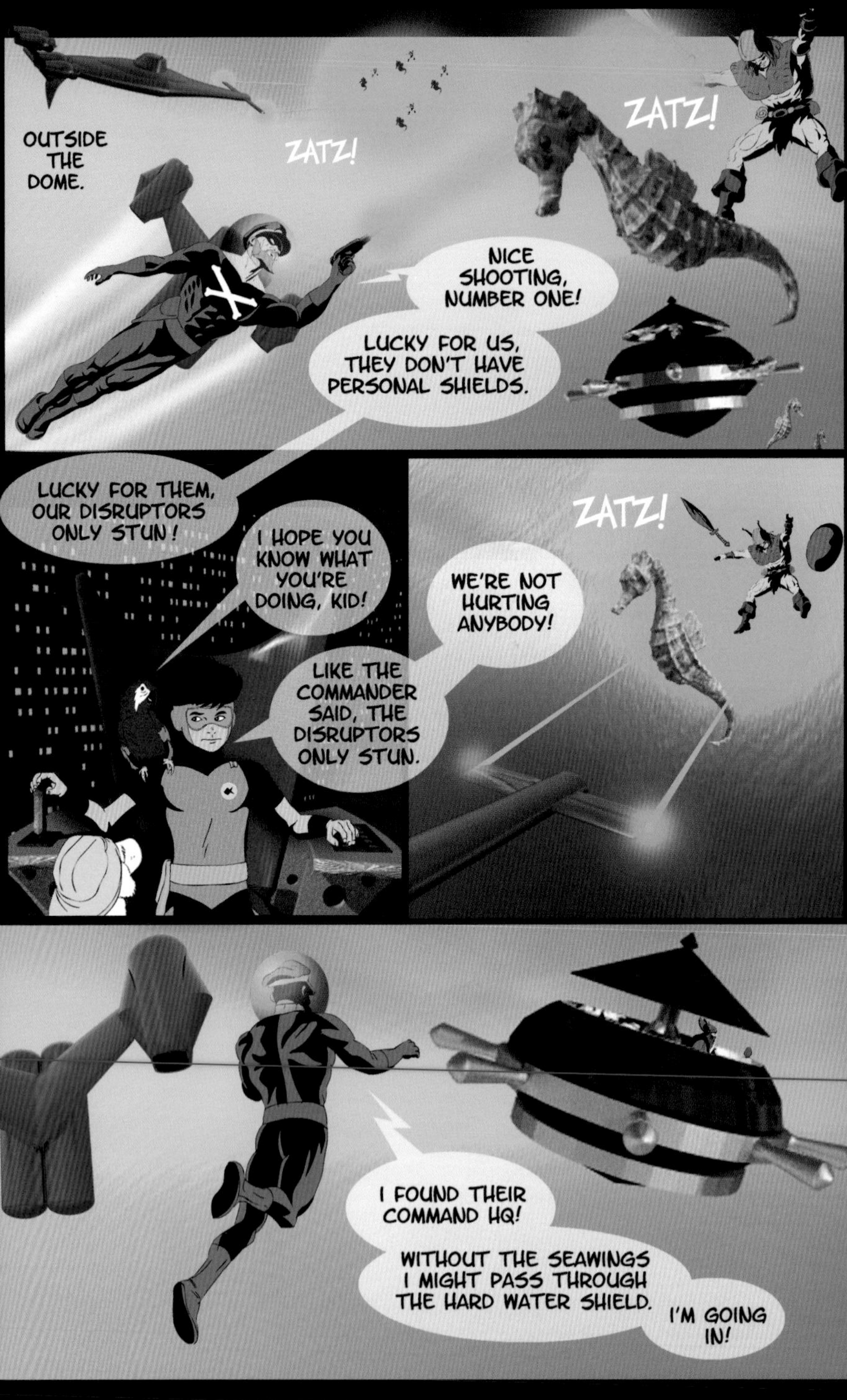
OUTSIDE THE DOME.
ZATZ!
ZATZ!
NICE SHOOTING, NUMBER ONE!
LUCKY FOR US, THEY DON'T HAVE PERSONAL SHIELDS.
LUCKY FOR THEM, OUR DISRUPTORS ONLY STUN!
I HOPE YOU KNOW WHAT YOU'RE DOING, KID!
WE'RE NOT HURTING ANYBODY!
LIKE THE COMMANDER SAID, THE DISRUPTORS ONLY STUN.
ZATZ!
I FOUND THEIR COMMAND HQ!
WITHOUT THE SEAWINGS I MIGHT PASS THROUGH THE HARD WATER SHIELD.
I'M GOING IN!

ACT 5 - THE BATTLE FOR AQUARIA

INSIDE THE OUTCAST HQ.

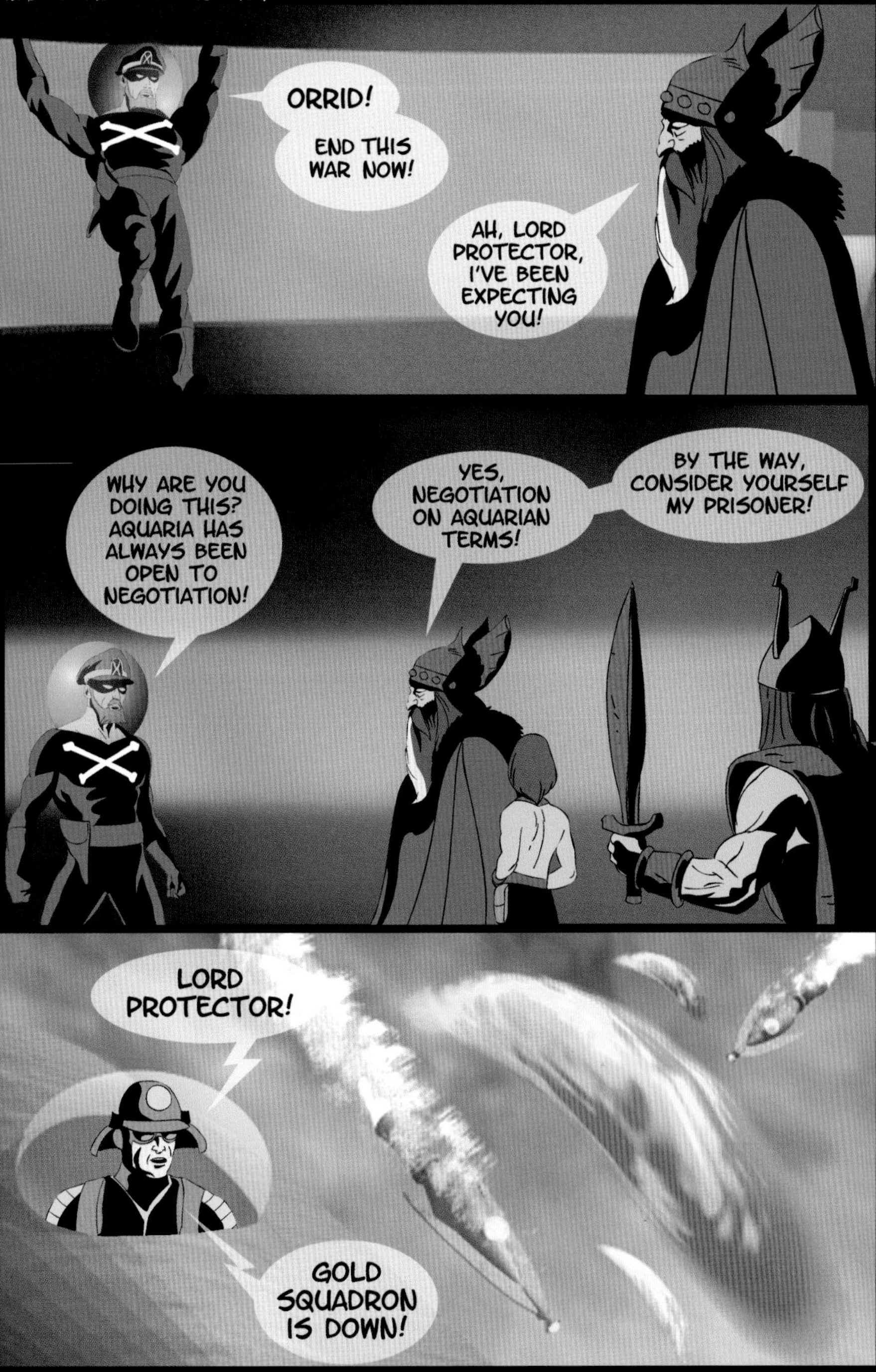

ORRID!
END THIS WAR NOW!
AH, LORD PROTECTOR, I'VE BEEN EXPECTING YOU!
WHY ARE YOU DOING THIS? AQUARIA HAS ALWAYS BEEN OPEN TO NEGOTIATION!
YES, NEGOTIATION ON AQUARIAN TERMS!
BY THE WAY, CONSIDER YOURSELF MY PRISONER!
LORD PROTECTOR!
GOLD SQUADRON IS DOWN!

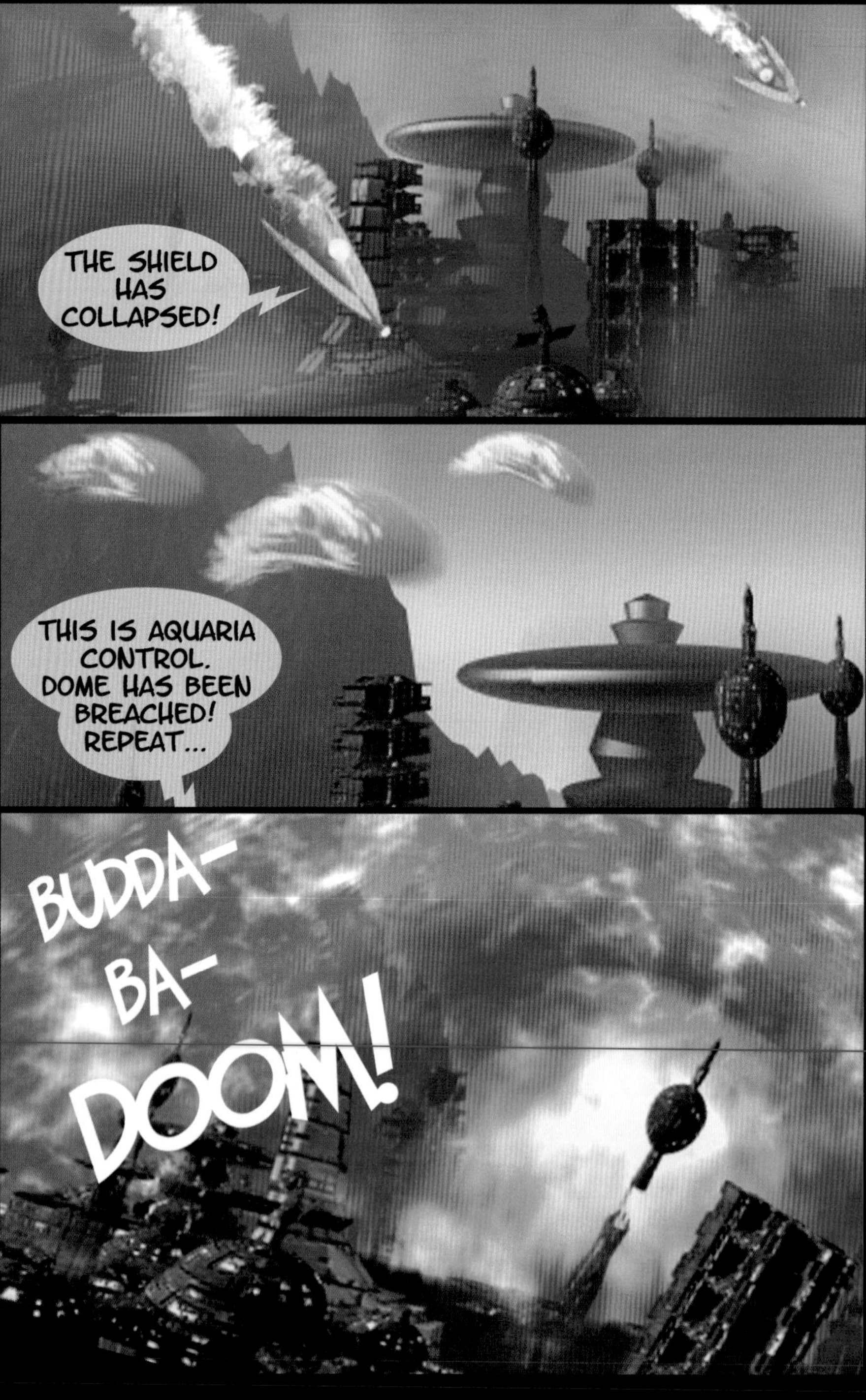
THE SHIELD HAS COLLAPSED!
THIS IS AQUARIA CONTROL. DOME HAS BEEN BREACHED! REPEAT...
BUDDA-BA-DOOM!

Act 5 - The Battle for Aquaria

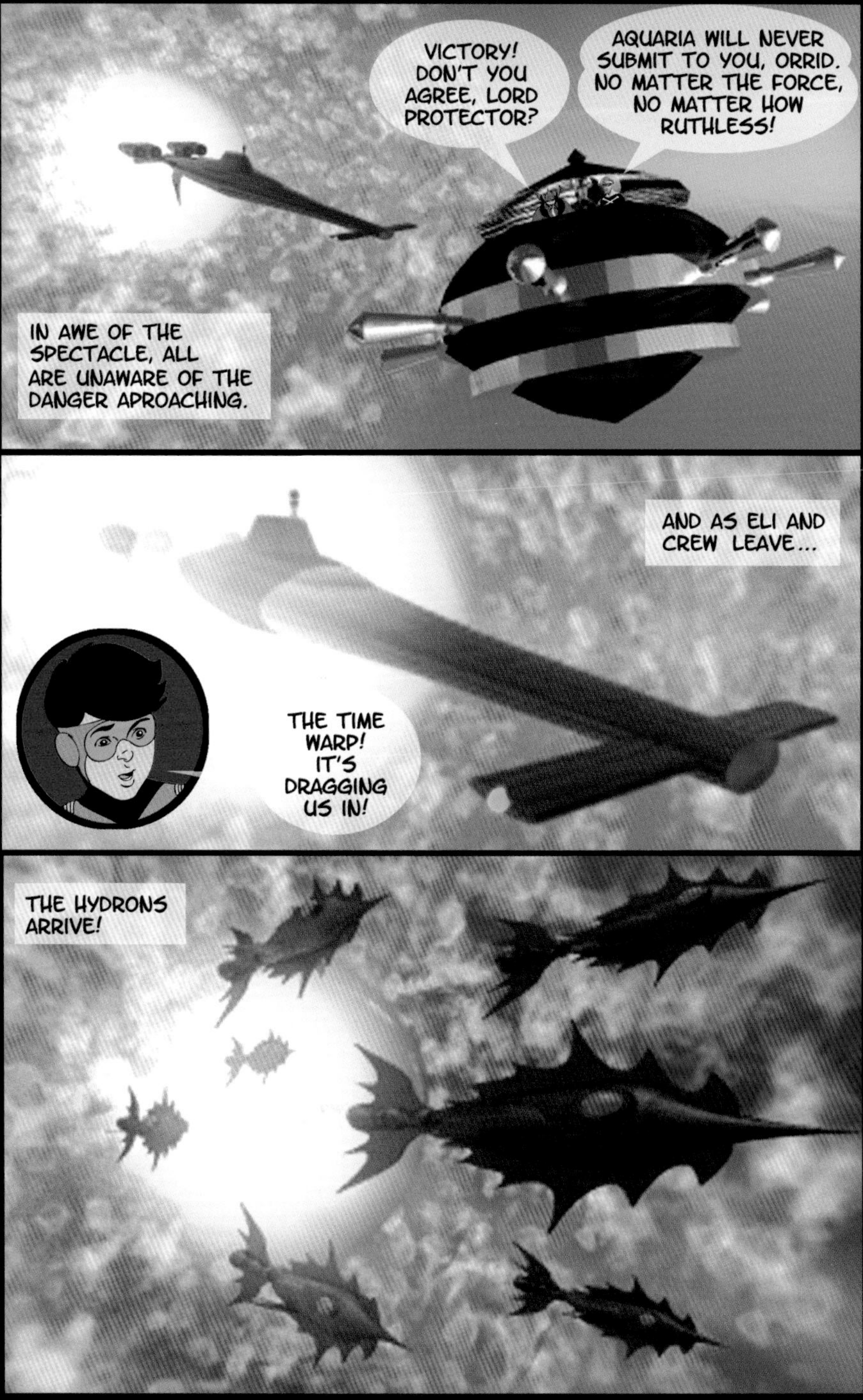
VICTORY! DON'T YOU AGREE, LORD PROTECTOR?
AQUARIA WILL NEVER SUBMIT TO YOU, ORRID. NO MATTER THE FORCE, NO MATTER HOW RUTHLESS!
IN AWE OF THE SPECTACLE, ALL ARE UNAWARE OF THE DANGER APROACHING.
AND AS ELI AND CREW LEAVE...
THE TIME WARP! IT'S DRAGGING US IN!
THE HYDRONS ARRIVE!

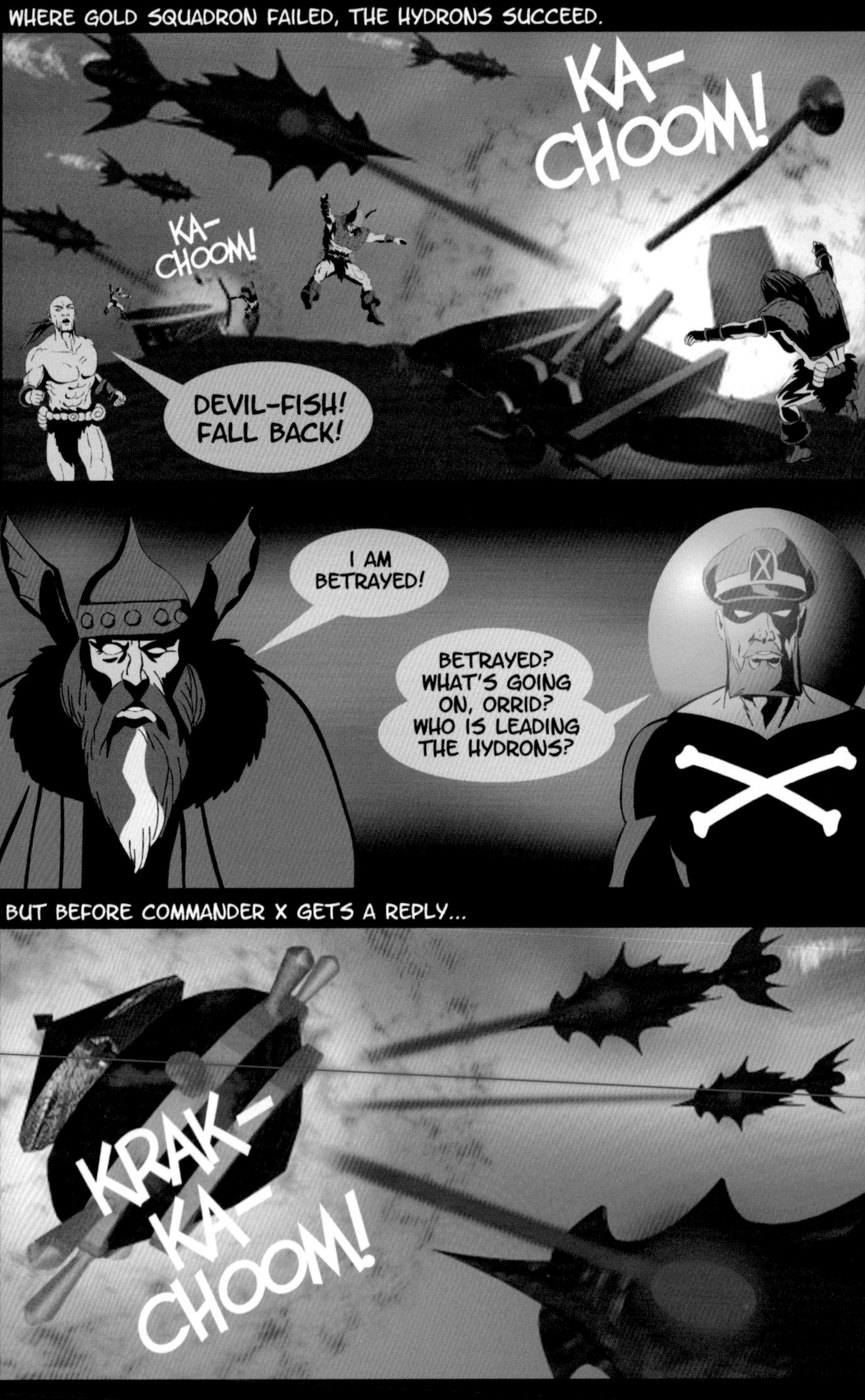
WHERE GOLD SQUADRON FAILED, THE HYDRONS SUCCEED.
KA-CHOOM!
KA-CHOOM!
DEVIL-FISH! FALL BACK!
I AM BETRAYED!
BETRAYED? WHAT'S GOING ON, ORRID? WHO IS LEADING THE HYDRONS?
BUT BEFORE COMMANDER X GETS A REPLY...
KRAK-KA-CHOOM!

ACT 5 - THE BATTLE FOR AQUARIA

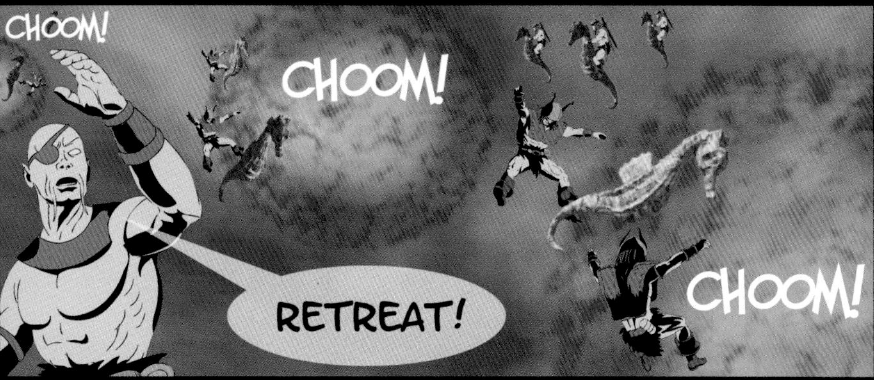
CHOOM!
CHOOM!
RETREAT!
CHOOM!

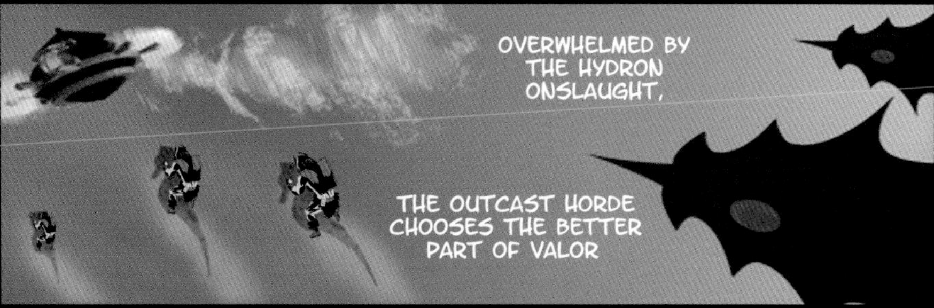
OVERWHELMED BY THE HYDRON ONSLAUGHT,
THE OUTCAST HORDE CHOOSES THE BETTER PART OF VALOR

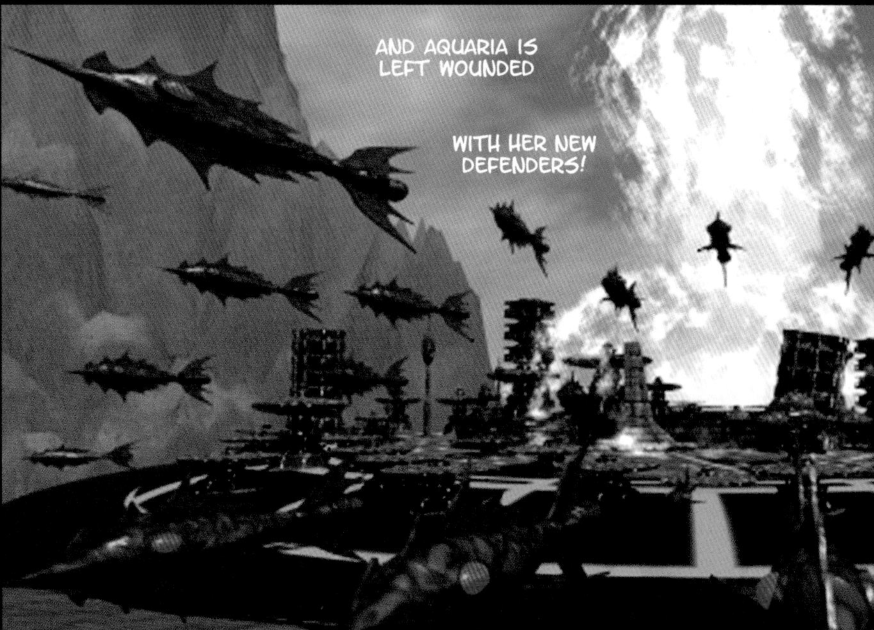
AND AQUARIA IS LEFT WOUNDED
WITH HER NEW DEFENDERS!

ELI TRAVELS THROUGH THE TIME WARP AGAIN.

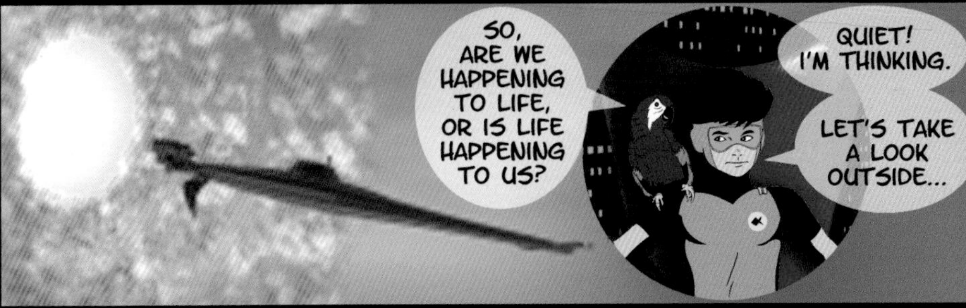
SO, ARE WE HAPPENING TO LIFE, OR IS LIFE HAPPENING TO US?
QUIET! I'M THINKING.
LET'S TAKE A LOOK OUTSIDE...

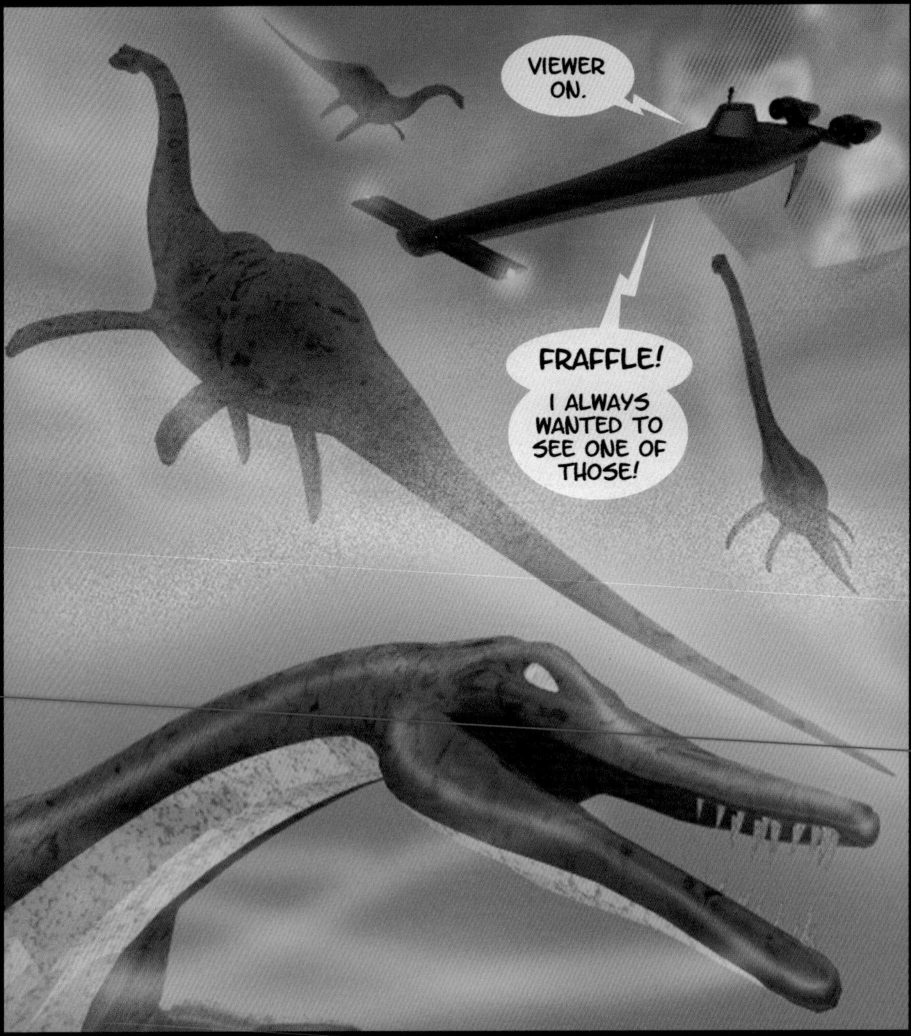
VIEWER ON.
FRAFFLE!
I ALWAYS WANTED TO SEE ONE OF THOSE!

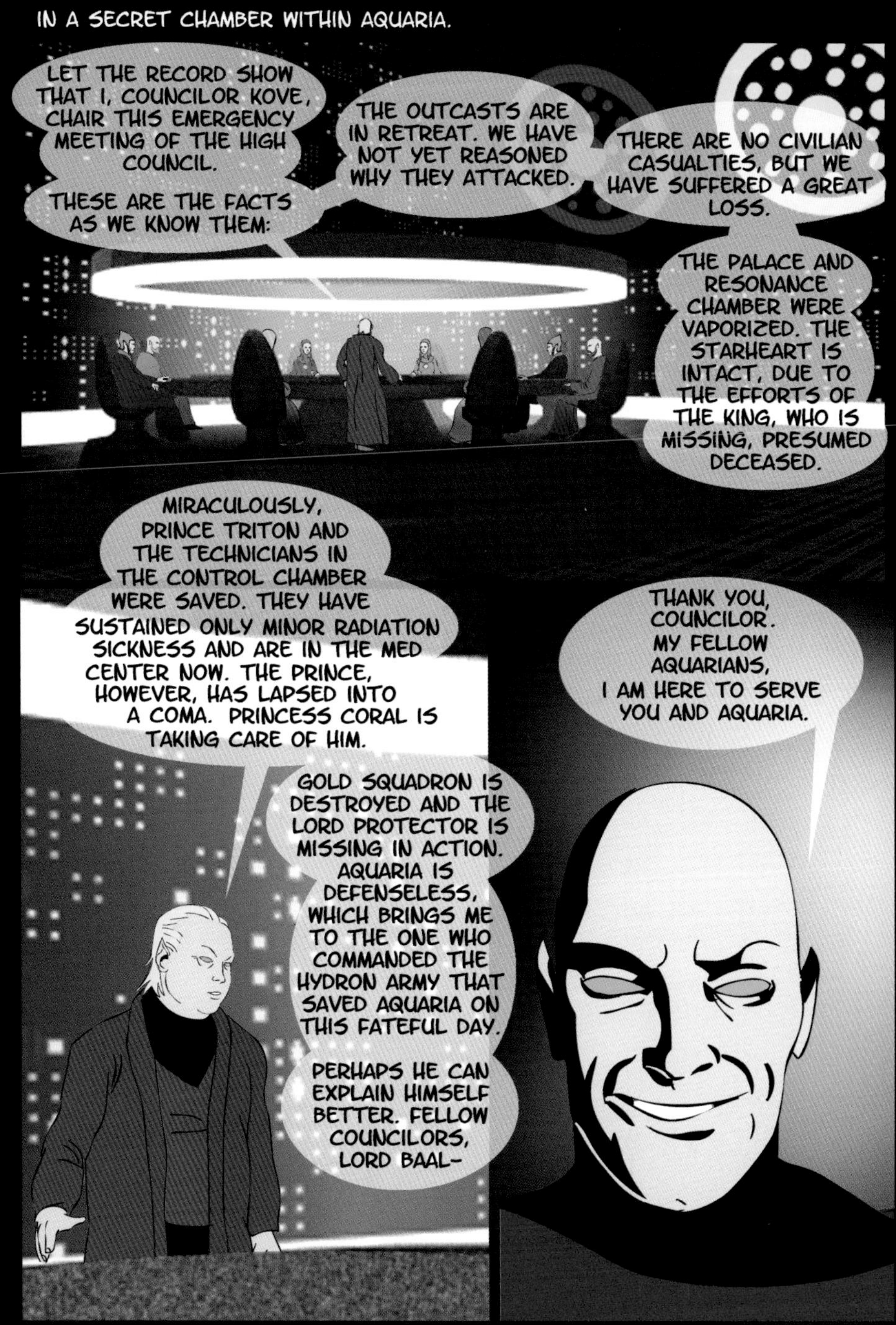
IN A SECRET CHAMBER WITHIN AQUARIA.
LET THE RECORD SHOW THAT I, COUNCILOR KOVE, CHAIR THIS EMERGENCY MEETING OF THE HIGH COUNCIL.
THESE ARE THE FACTS AS WE KNOW THEM:
THE OUTCASTS ARE IN RETREAT. WE HAVE NOT YET REASONED WHY THEY ATTACKED.
THERE ARE NO CIVILIAN CASUALTIES, BUT WE HAVE SUFFERED A GREAT LOSS.
THE PALACE AND RESONANCE CHAMBER WERE VAPORIZED. THE STARHEART IS INTACT, DUE TO THE EFFORTS OF THE KING, WHO IS MISSING, PRESUMED DECEASED.
MIRACULOUSLY, PRINCE TRITON AND THE TECHNICIANS IN THE CONTROL CHAMBER WERE SAVED. THEY HAVE SUSTAINED ONLY MINOR RADIATION SICKNESS AND ARE IN THE MED CENTER NOW. THE PRINCE, HOWEVER, HAS LAPSED INTO A COMA. PRINCESS CORAL IS TAKING CARE OF HIM.
GOLD SQUADRON IS DESTROYED AND THE LORD PROTECTOR IS MISSING IN ACTION. AQUARIA IS DEFENSELESS, WHICH BRINGS ME TO THE ONE WHO COMMANDED THE HYDRON ARMY THAT SAVED AQUARIA ON THIS FATEFUL DAY.
PERHAPS HE CAN EXPLAIN HIMSELF BETTER. FELLOW COUNCILORS, LORD BAAL-
THANK YOU, COUNCILOR. MY FELLOW AQUARIANS, I AM HERE TO SERVE YOU AND AQUARIA.

THE SEASEARCHERS SET OUT TO FIND ELI.

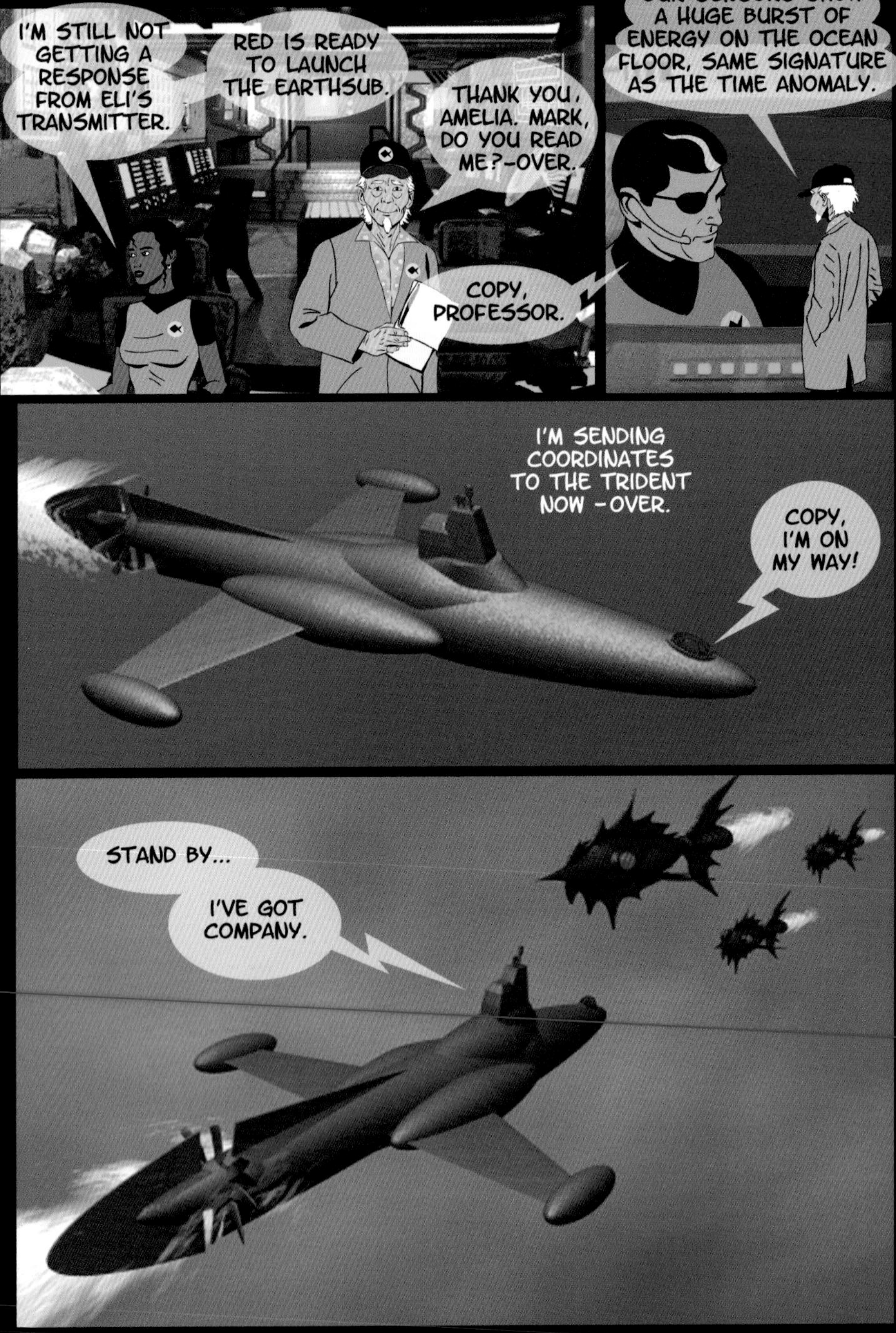
I'M STILL NOT GETTING A RESPONSE FROM ELI'S TRANSMITTER.
RED IS READY TO LAUNCH THE EARTHSUB.
THANK YOU, AMELIA. MARK, DO YOU READ ME?-OVER.
COPY, PROFESSOR.
OUR SENSORS SHOW A HUGE BURST OF ENERGY ON THE OCEAN FLOOR, SAME SIGNATURE AS THE TIME ANOMALY.
I'M SENDING COORDINATES TO THE TRIDENT NOW -OVER.
COPY, I'M ON MY WAY!
STAND BY...
I'VE GOT COMPANY.

END OF ACT 5

ZAZATZ!

THIS SHIP IS AMAZING! AUTOMATIC DEFENSE SYSTEM, HOLOGRAMS, JUST INCREDIBLE!

YEAH, BUT CAN IT GET US BACK TO WHERE WE BELONG?

COMMANDER X USED SUB ZERO TO TRAVEL THROUGH TIME BEFORE—

LET'S GIVE IT A TRY NOW—

NUMBER ONE, PLEASE RETURN US TO THE PRESENT!

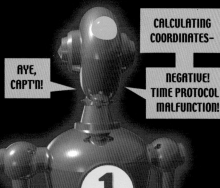

AYE, CAPT'N!

CALCULATING COORDINATES—

NEGATIVE! TIME PROTOCOL MALFUNCTION!

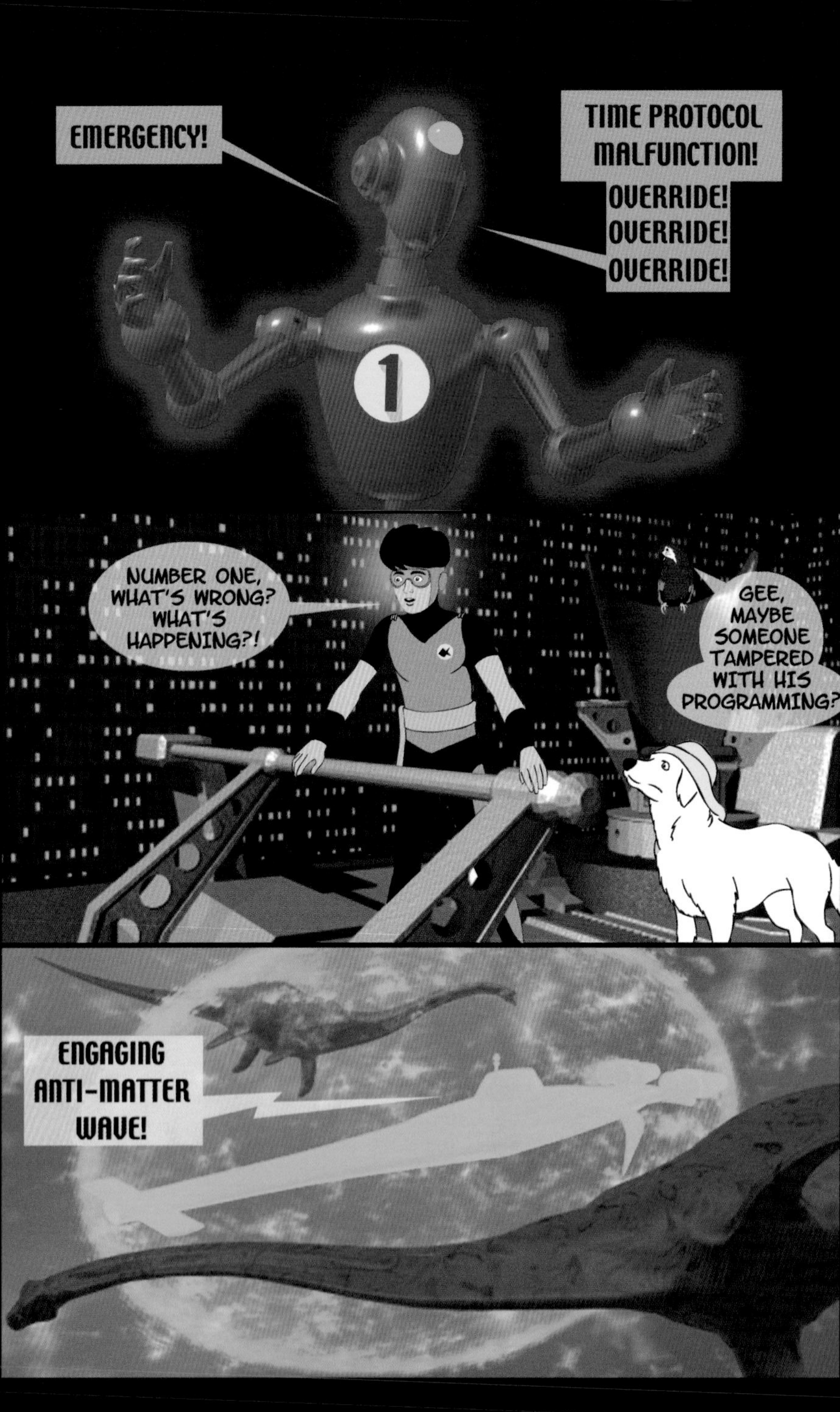
EMERGENCY!
TIME PROTOCOL MALFUNCTION!
OVERRIDE! OVERRIDE! OVERRIDE!
NUMBER ONE, WHAT'S WRONG? WHAT'S HAPPENING?!
GEE, MAYBE SOMEONE TAMPERED WITH HIS PROGRAMMING?
ENGAGING ANTI-MATTER WAVE!

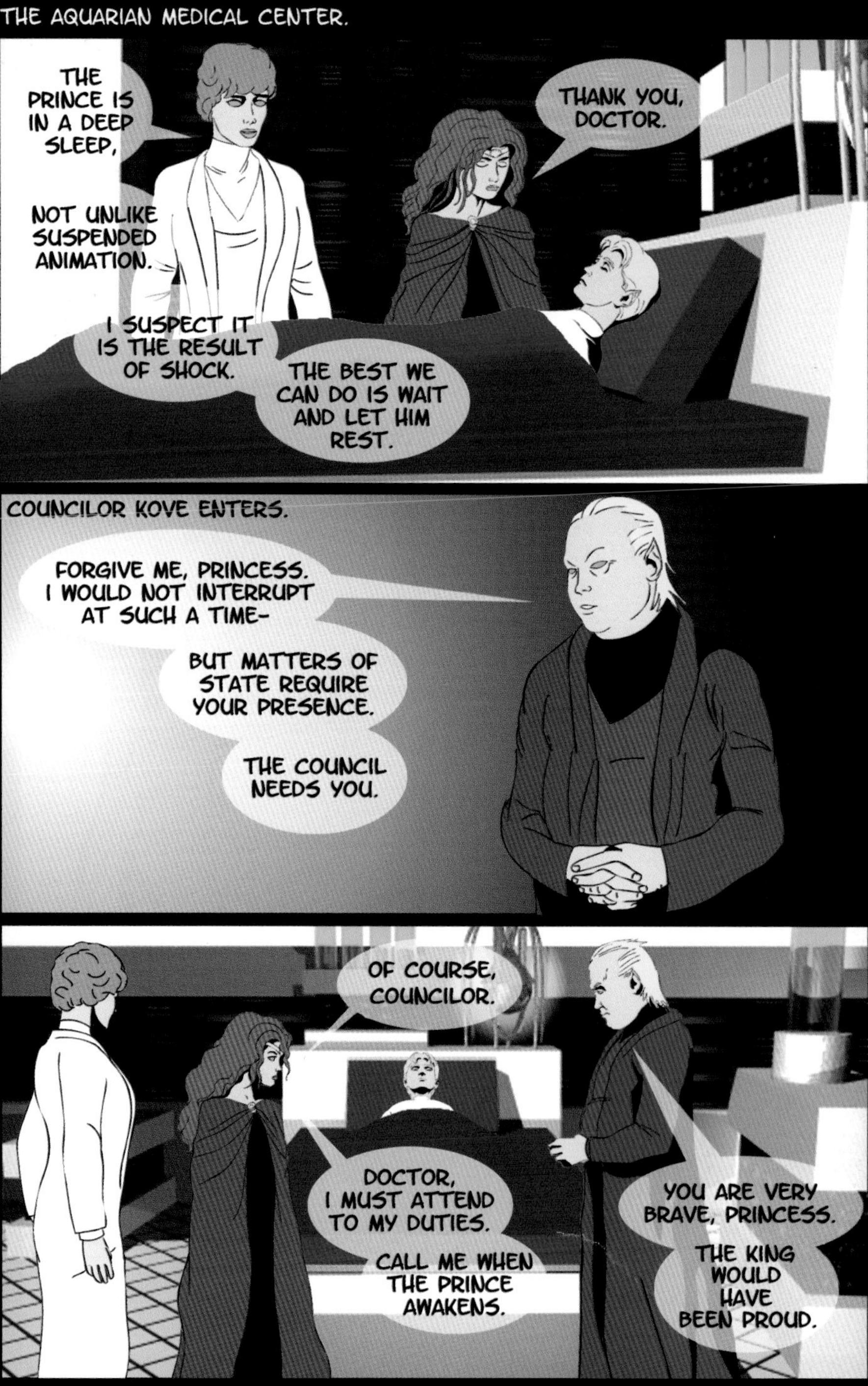
THE AQUARIAN MEDICAL CENTER.
THE PRINCE IS IN A DEEP SLEEP,
NOT UNLIKE SUSPENDED ANIMATION.
THANK YOU, DOCTOR.
I SUSPECT IT IS THE RESULT OF SHOCK.
THE BEST WE CAN DO IS WAIT AND LET HIM REST.
COUNCILOR KOVE ENTERS.
FORGIVE ME, PRINCESS. I WOULD NOT INTERRUPT AT SUCH A TIME-
BUT MATTERS OF STATE REQUIRE YOUR PRESENCE.
THE COUNCIL NEEDS YOU.
OF COURSE, COUNCILOR.
DOCTOR, I MUST ATTEND TO MY DUTIES.
CALL ME WHEN THE PRINCE AWAKENS.
YOU ARE VERY BRAVE, PRINCESS.
THE KING WOULD HAVE BEEN PROUD.

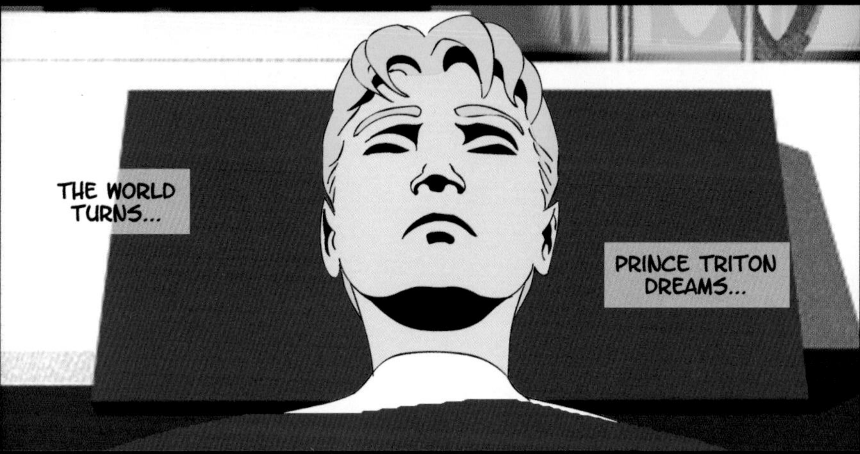
THE WORLD TURNS...
PRINCE TRITON DREAMS...

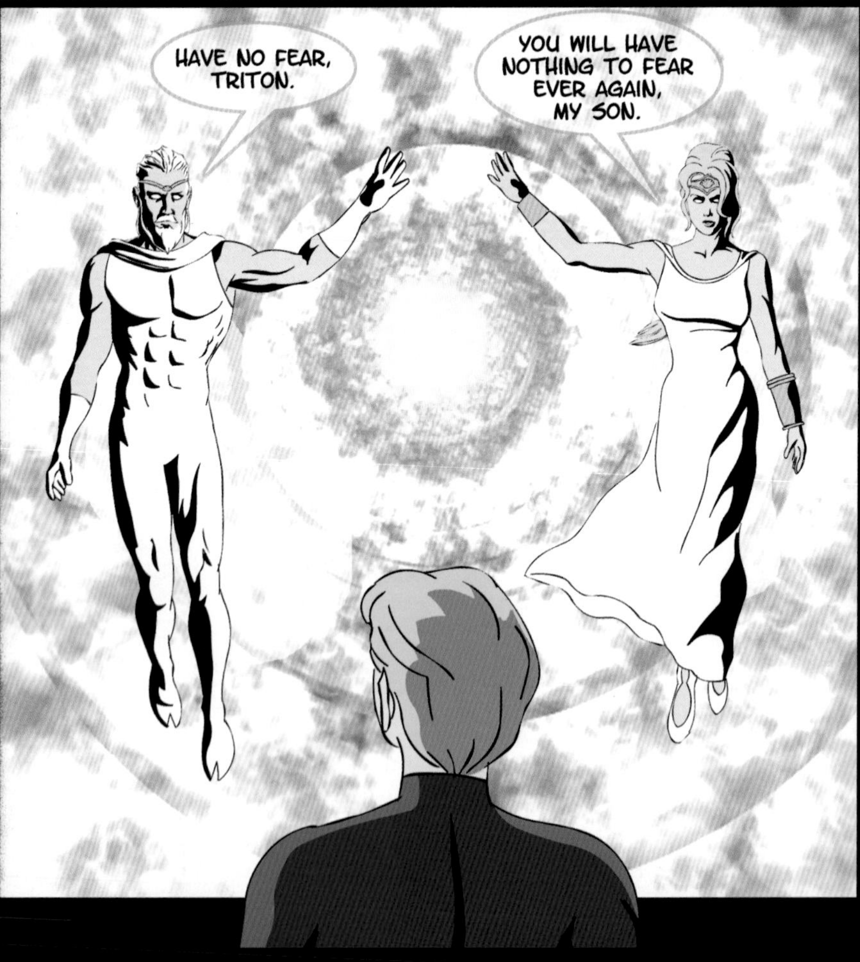
HAVE NO FEAR, TRITON.
YOU WILL HAVE NOTHING TO FEAR EVER AGAIN, MY SON.

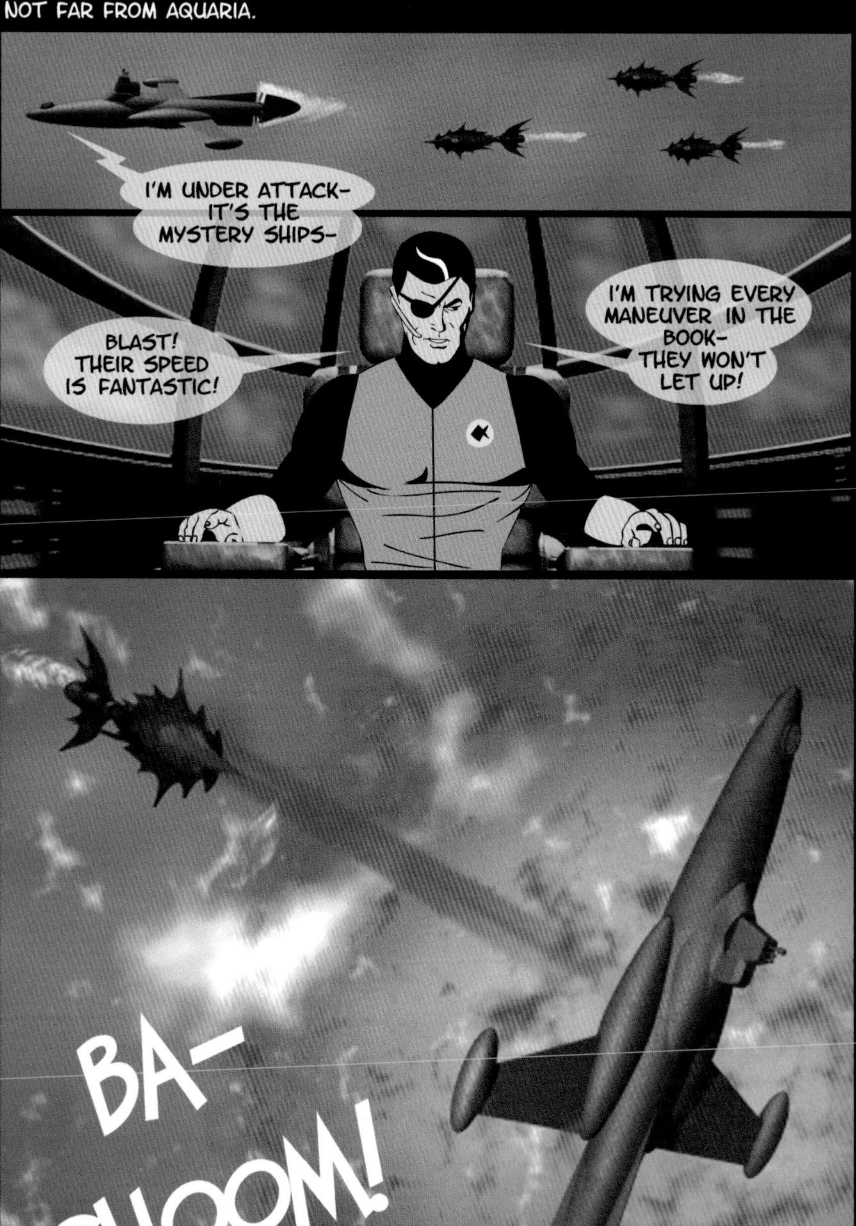
NOT FAR FROM AQUARIA.
I'M UNDER ATTACK- IT'S THE MYSTERY SHIPS-
BLAST! THEIR SPEED IS FANTASTIC!
I'M TRYING EVERY MANEUVER IN THE BOOK- THEY WON'T LET UP!
BA-CHOOM!

THE TRIDENT IS STOPPED.

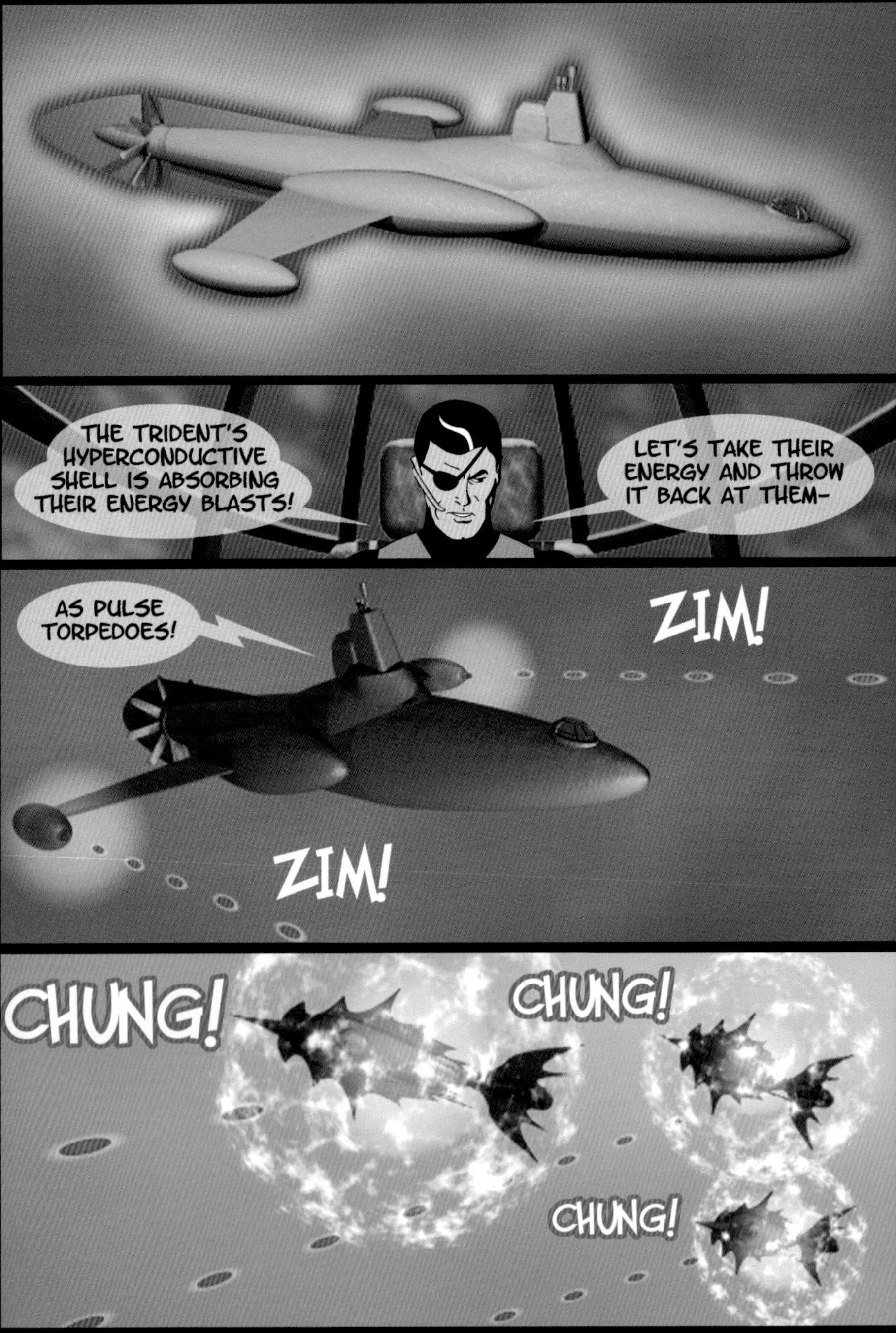
THE TRIDENT'S HYPERCONDUCTIVE SHELL IS ABSORBING THEIR ENERGY BLASTS!
LET'S TAKE THEIR ENERGY AND THROW IT BACK AT THEM-
AS PULSE TORPEDOES!
ZIM!
ZIM!
CHUNG!
CHUNG!
CHUNG!

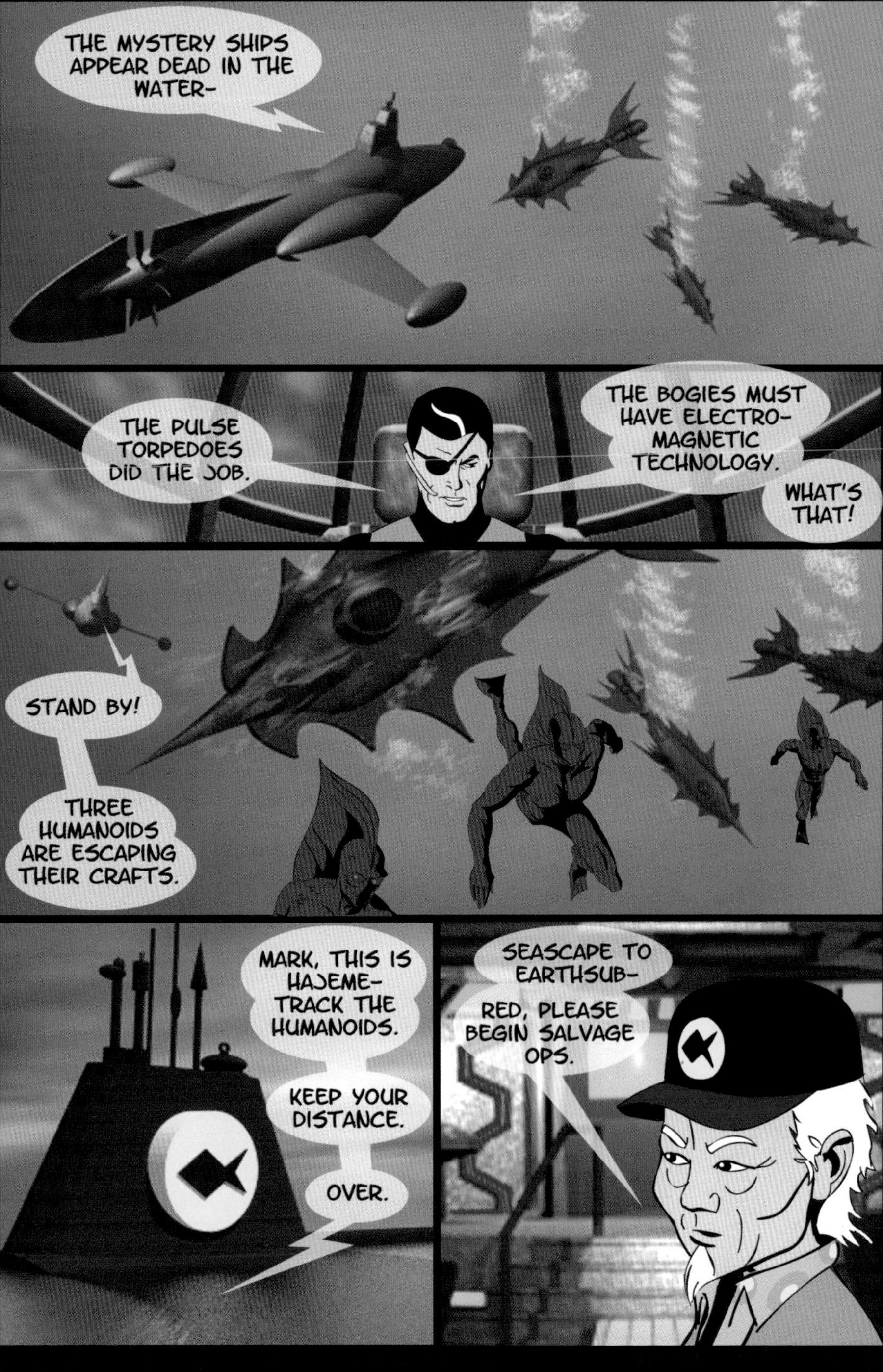
THE MYSTERY SHIPS APPEAR DEAD IN THE WATER-
THE PULSE TORPEDOES DID THE JOB.
THE BOGIES MUST HAVE ELECTRO-MAGNETIC TECHNOLOGY.
WHAT'S THAT!
STAND BY!
THREE HUMANOIDS ARE ESCAPING THEIR CRAFTS.
MARK, THIS IS HAJEME-TRACK THE HUMANOIDS.
KEEP YOUR DISTANCE.
OVER.
SEASCAPE TO EARTHSUB-
RED, PLEASE BEGIN SALVAGE OPS.

THE EARTHSUB GOES TO WORK.

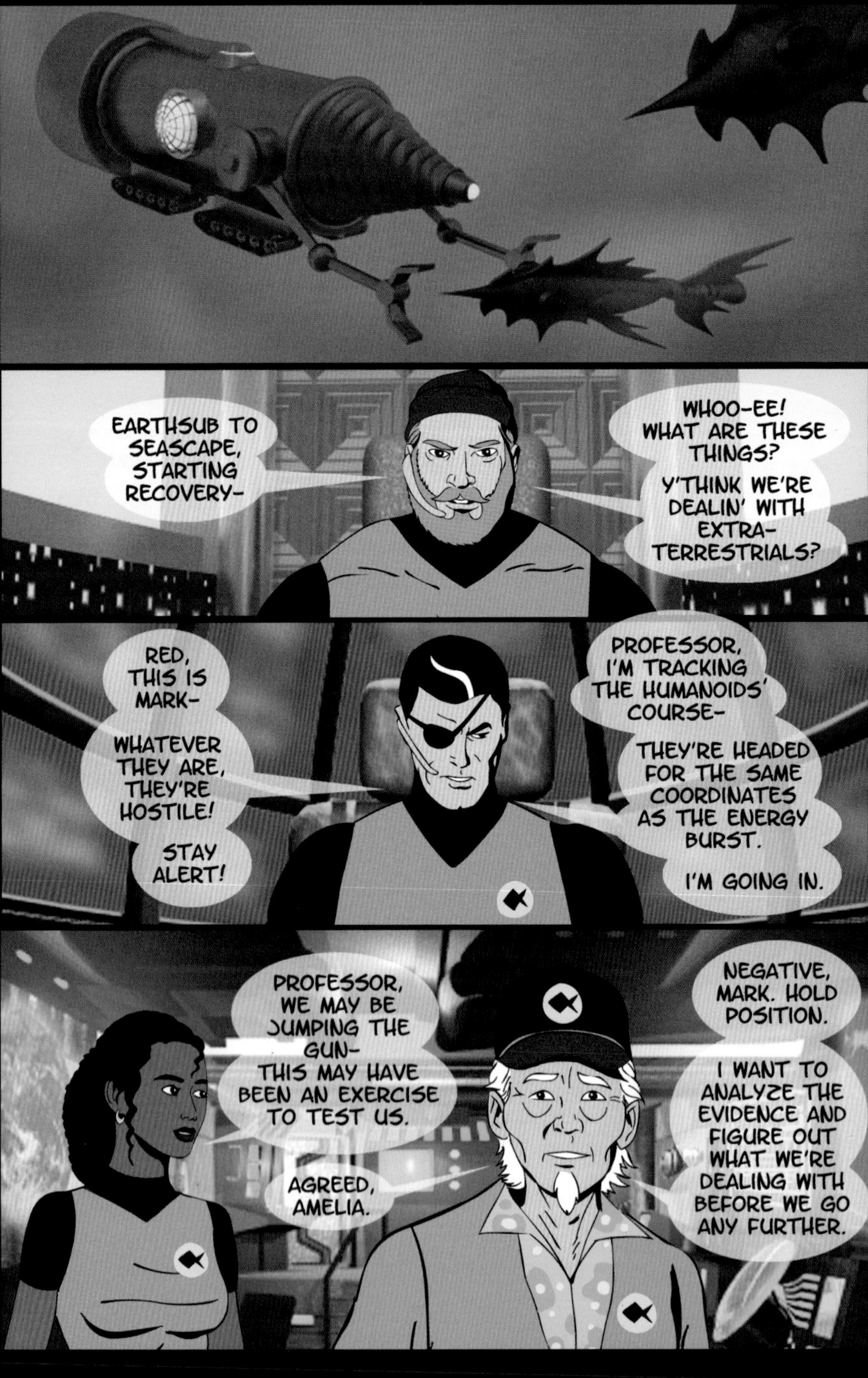
EARTHSUB TO SEASCAPE, STARTING RECOVERY-
WHOO-EE! WHAT ARE THESE THINGS?
Y'THINK WE'RE DEALIN' WITH EXTRA-TERRESTRIALS?
RED, THIS IS MARK-
WHATEVER THEY ARE, THEY'RE HOSTILE!
STAY ALERT!
PROFESSOR, I'M TRACKING THE HUMANOIDS' COURSE-
THEY'RE HEADED FOR THE SAME COORDINATES AS THE ENERGY BURST.
I'M GOING IN.
PROFESSOR, WE MAY BE JUMPING THE GUN-
THIS MAY HAVE BEEN AN EXERCISE TO TEST US.
AGREED, AMELIA.
NEGATIVE, MARK. HOLD POSITION.
I WANT TO ANALYZE THE EVIDENCE AND FIGURE OUT WHAT WE'RE DEALING WITH BEFORE WE GO ANY FURTHER.

SUB ZERO REMATERIALIZES.

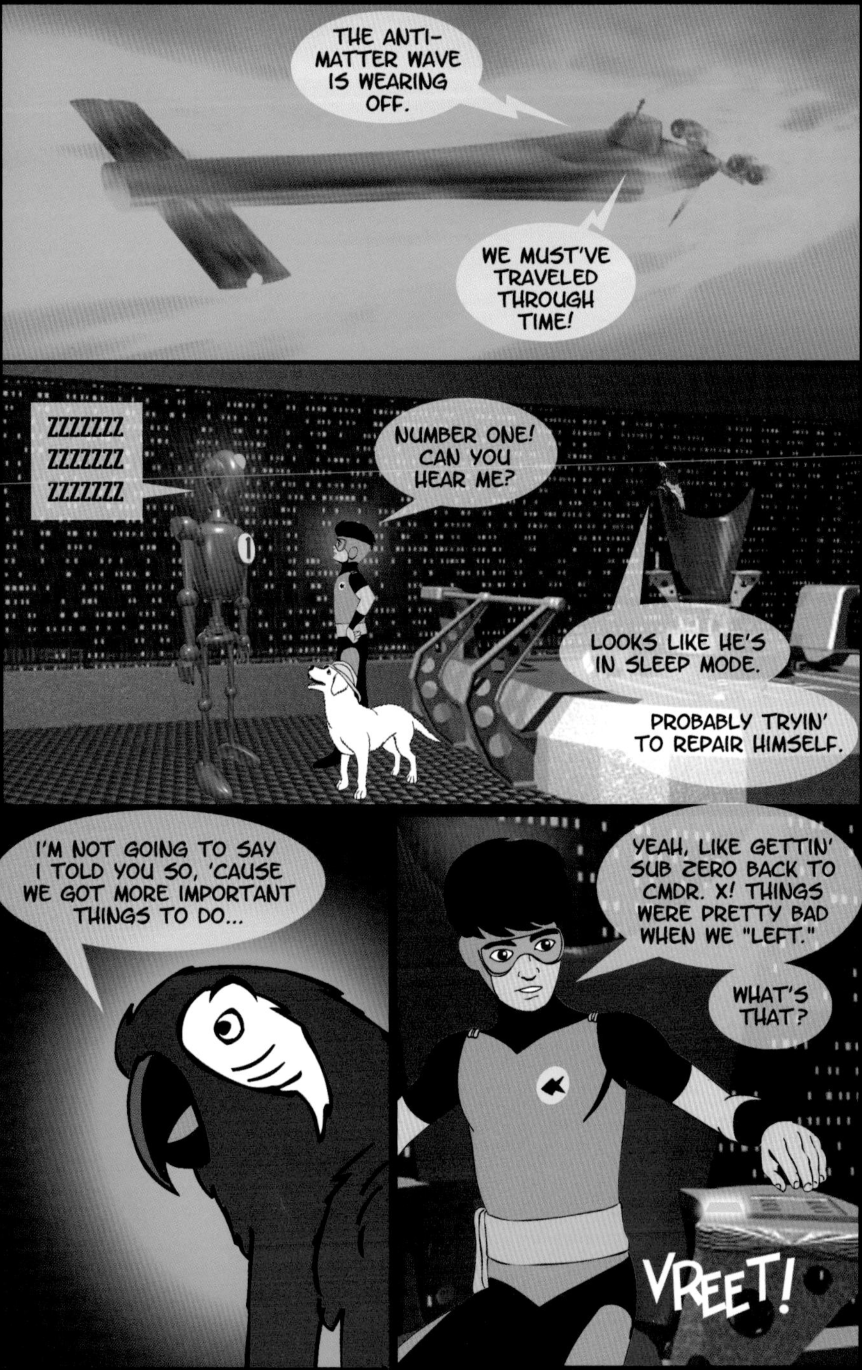
THE ANTI-MATTER WAVE IS WEARING OFF.
WE MUST'VE TRAVELED THROUGH TIME!
ZZZZZZZ ZZZZZZZ ZZZZZZZ
NUMBER ONE! CAN YOU HEAR ME?
LOOKS LIKE HE'S IN SLEEP MODE.
PROBABLY TRYIN' TO REPAIR HIMSELF.
I'M NOT GOING TO SAY I TOLD YOU SO, 'CAUSE WE GOT MORE IMPORTANT THINGS TO DO...
YEAH, LIKE GETTIN' SUB ZERO BACK TO CMDR. X! THINGS WERE PRETTY BAD WHEN WE "LEFT."
WHAT'S THAT?
VREET!

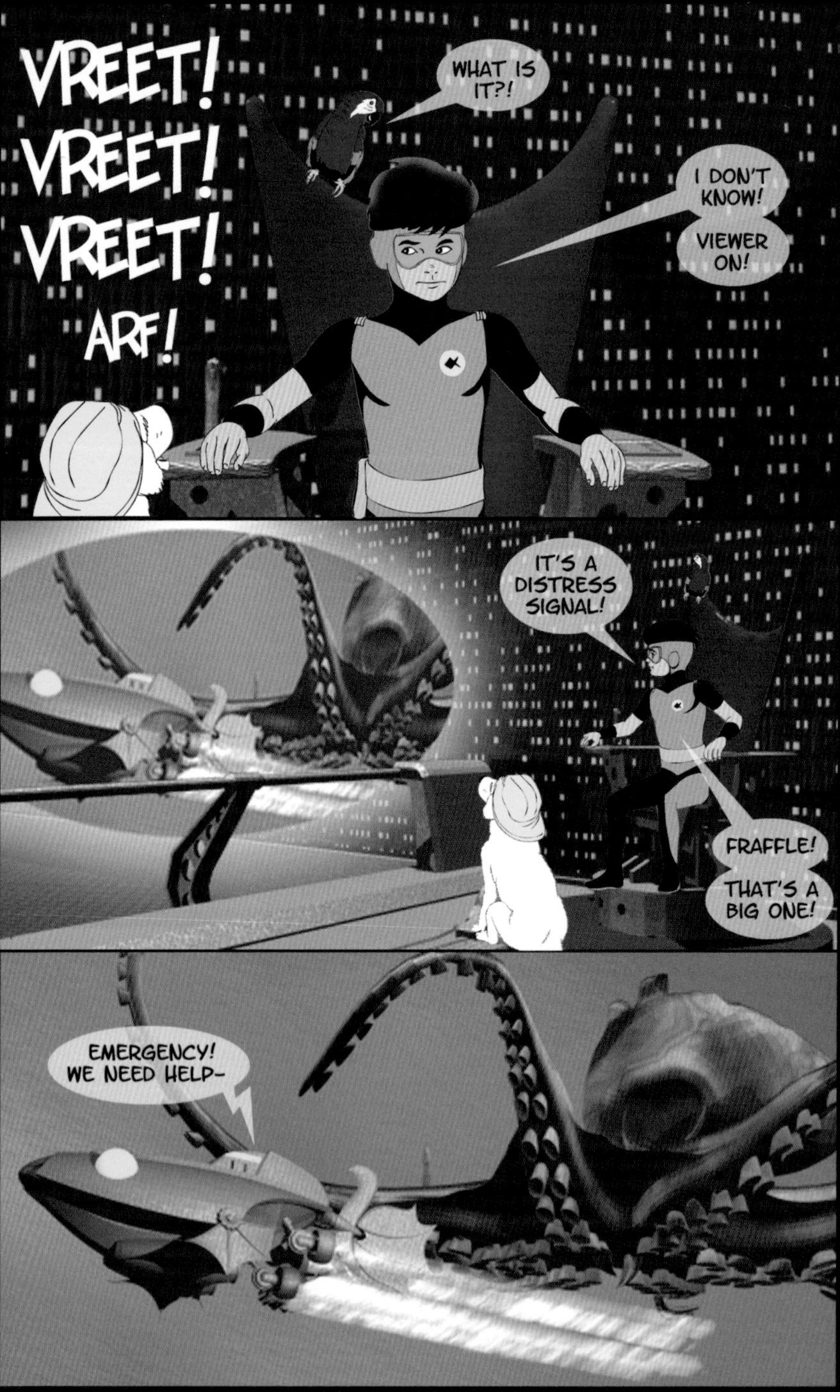
VREET! VREET! VREET!
ARF!
WHAT IS IT?!
I DON'T KNOW!
VIEWER ON!
IT'S A DISTRESS SIGNAL!
FRAFFLE!
THAT'S A BIG ONE!
EMERGENCY! WE NEED HELP-

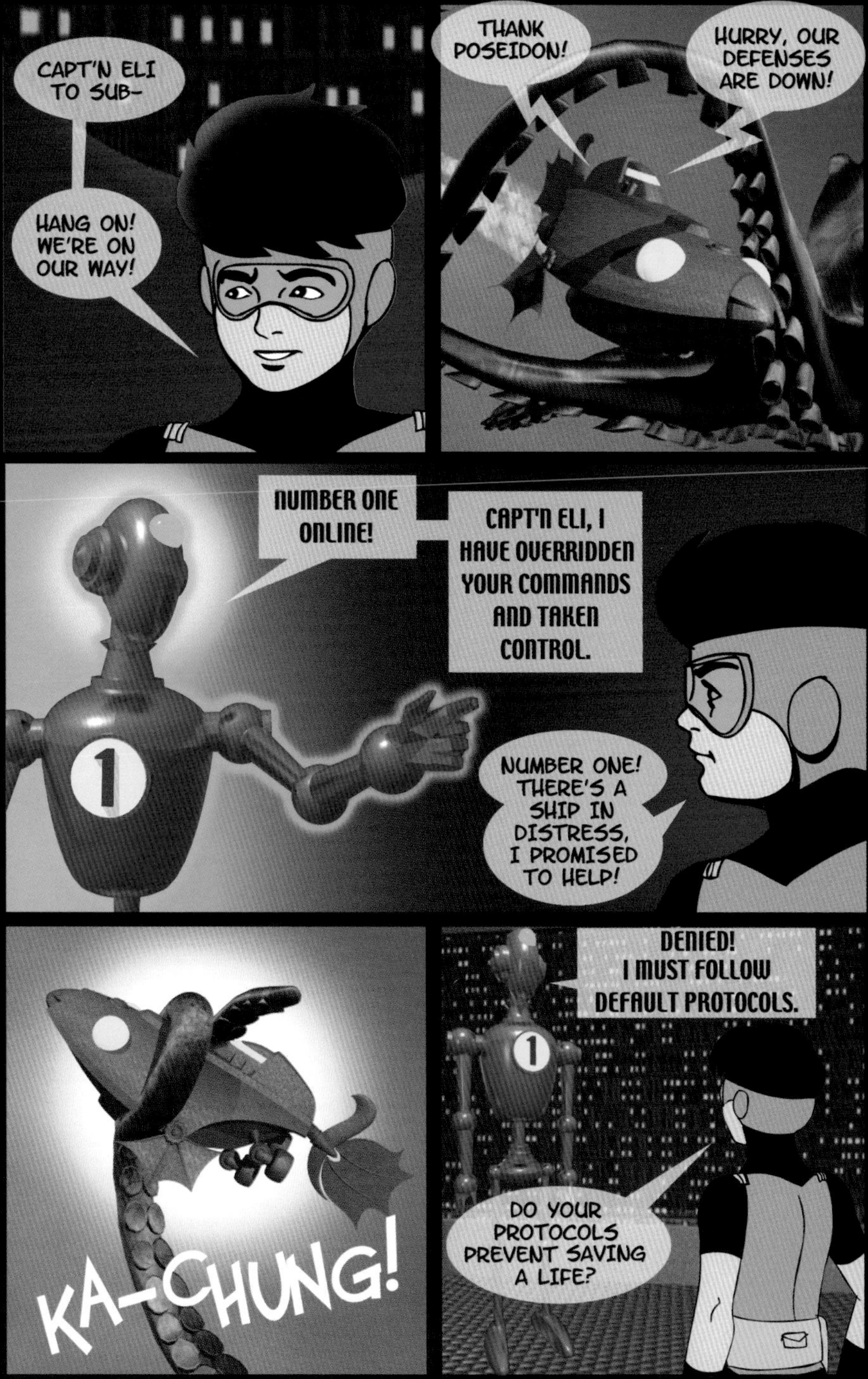
CAPT'N ELI TO SUB-
HANG ON! WE'RE ON OUR WAY!
THANK POSEIDON!
HURRY, OUR DEFENSES ARE DOWN!
NUMBER ONE ONLINE!
CAPT'N ELI, I HAVE OVERRIDDEN YOUR COMMANDS AND TAKEN CONTROL.
NUMBER ONE! THERE'S A SHIP IN DISTRESS, I PROMISED TO HELP!
KA-CHUNG!
DENIED! I MUST FOLLOW DEFAULT PROTOCOLS.
DO YOUR PROTOCOLS PREVENT SAVING A LIFE?

NUMBER ONE RESPONDS WITH STUN DISRUPTORS.

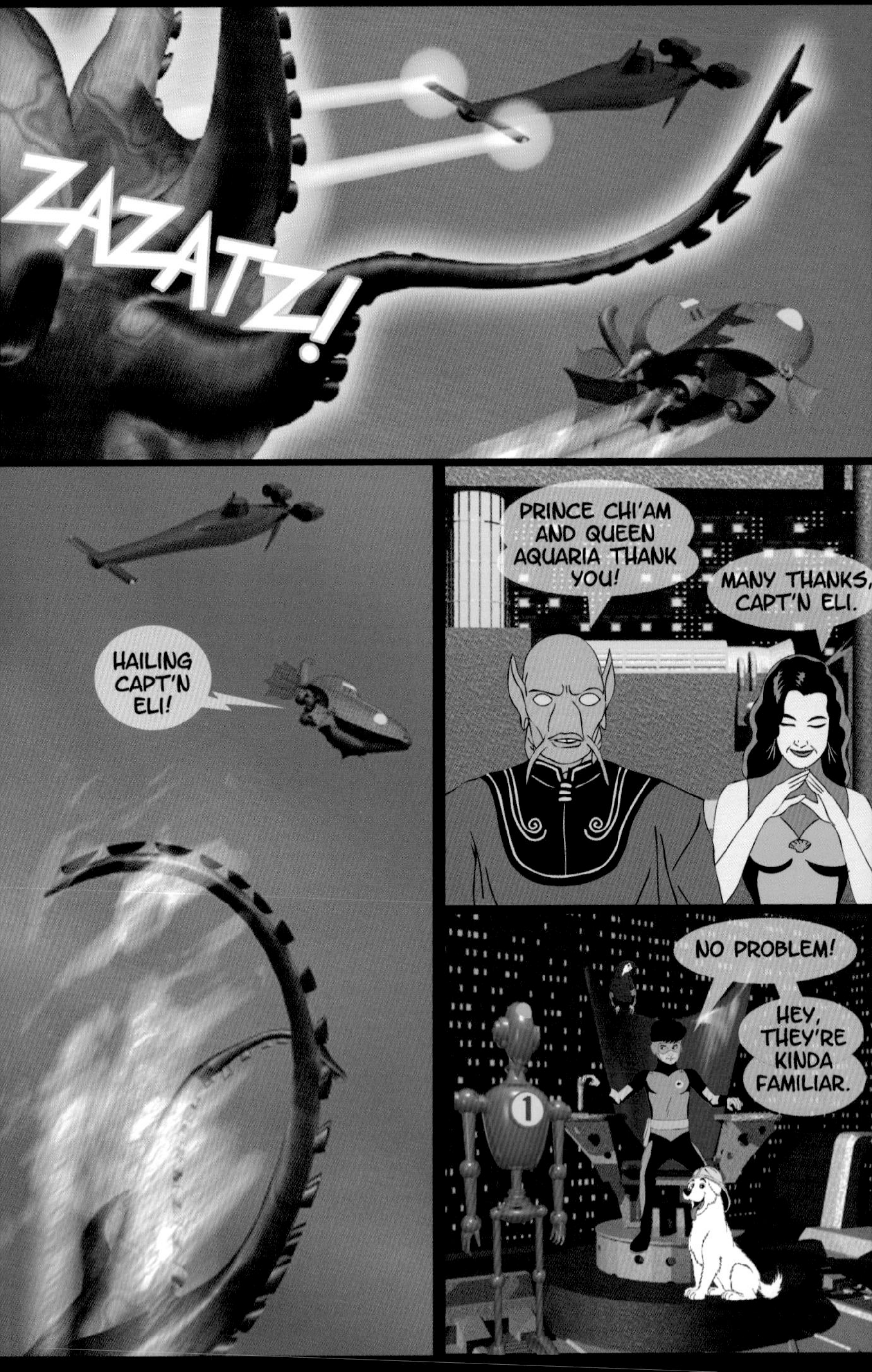
ZAZATZ!
HAILING CAPT'N ELI!
PRINCE CHI'AM AND QUEEN AQUARIA THANK YOU!
MANY THANKS, CAPT'N ELI.
NO PROBLEM!
HEY, THEY'RE KINDA FAMILIAR.

Act 6 - Past Imperfect

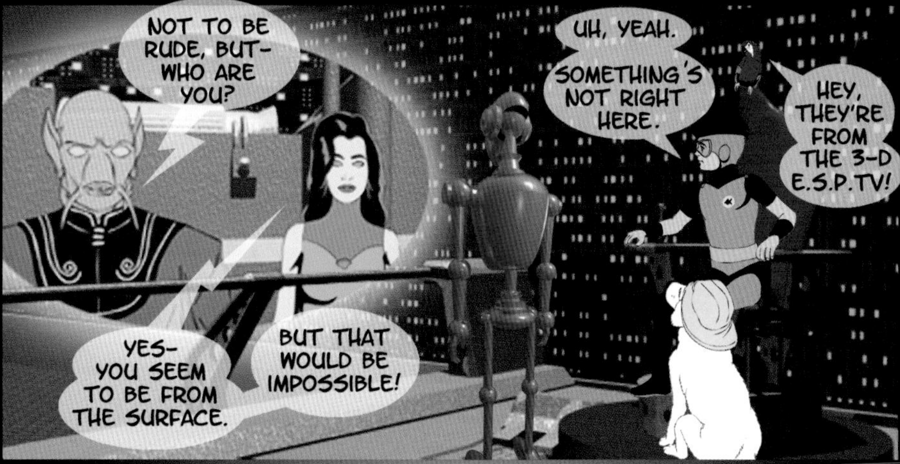
NOT TO BE RUDE, BUT- WHO ARE YOU?
YES- YOU SEEM TO BE FROM THE SURFACE.
BUT THAT WOULD BE IMPOSSIBLE!
UH, YEAH.
SOMETHING'S NOT RIGHT HERE.
HEY, THEY'RE FROM THE 3-D E.S.P.TV!

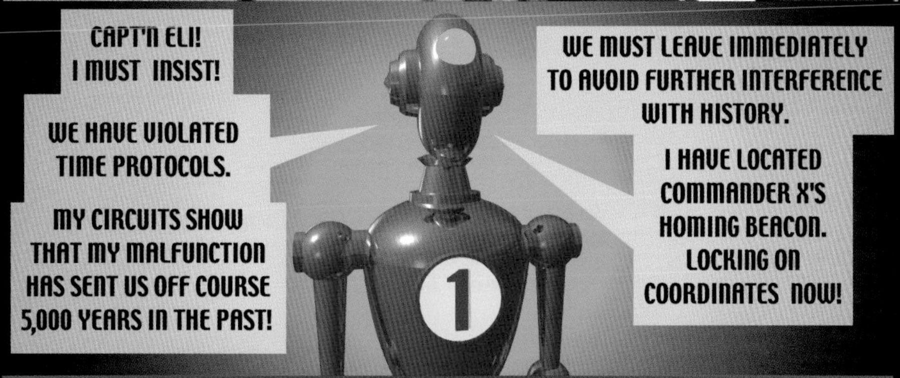
CAPT'N ELI! I MUST INSIST!
WE HAVE VIOLATED TIME PROTOCOLS.
MY CIRCUITS SHOW THAT MY MALFUNCTION HAS SENT US OFF COURSE 5,000 YEARS IN THE PAST!
WE MUST LEAVE IMMEDIATELY TO AVOID FURTHER INTERFERENCE WITH HISTORY.
I HAVE LOCATED COMMANDER X'S HOMING BEACON. LOCKING ON COORDINATES NOW!
1

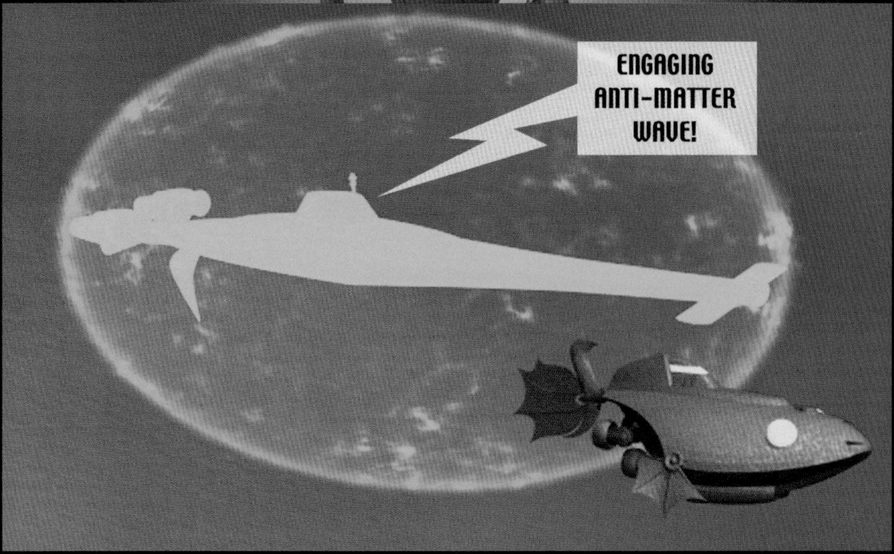
ENGAGING ANTI-MATTER WAVE!

THE AQUARIAN SENATE.

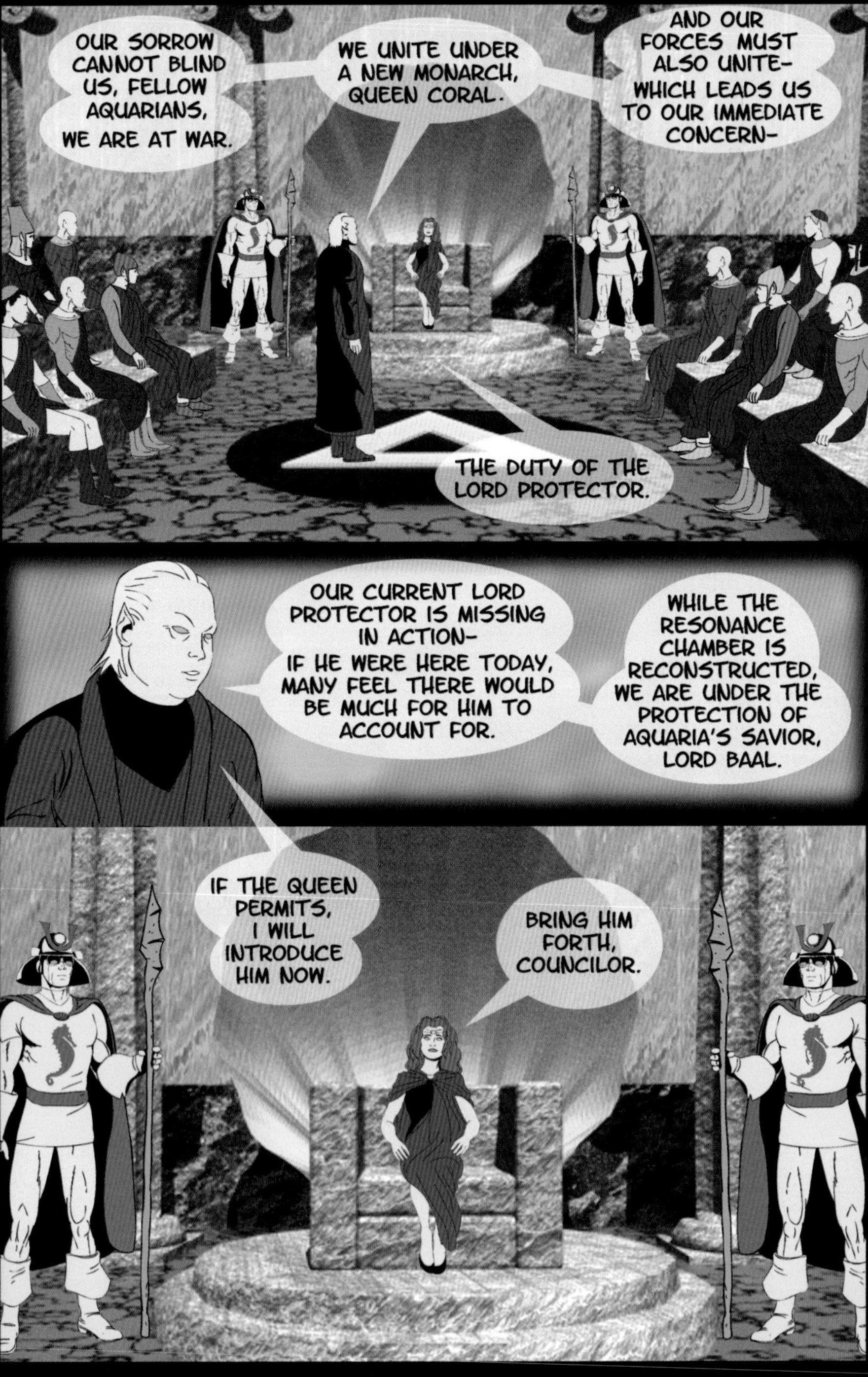
OUR SORROW CANNOT BLIND US, FELLOW AQUARIANS, WE ARE AT WAR.
WE UNITE UNDER A NEW MONARCH, QUEEN CORAL.
AND OUR FORCES MUST ALSO UNITE- WHICH LEADS US TO OUR IMMEDIATE CONCERN-
THE DUTY OF THE LORD PROTECTOR.
OUR CURRENT LORD PROTECTOR IS MISSING IN ACTION- IF HE WERE HERE TODAY, MANY FEEL THERE WOULD BE MUCH FOR HIM TO ACCOUNT FOR.
WHILE THE RESONANCE CHAMBER IS RECONSTRUCTED, WE ARE UNDER THE PROTECTION OF AQUARIA'S SAVIOR, LORD BAAL.
IF THE QUEEN PERMITS, I WILL INTRODUCE HIM NOW.
BRING HIM FORTH, COUNCILOR.

ACT 6 - PAST IMPERFECT

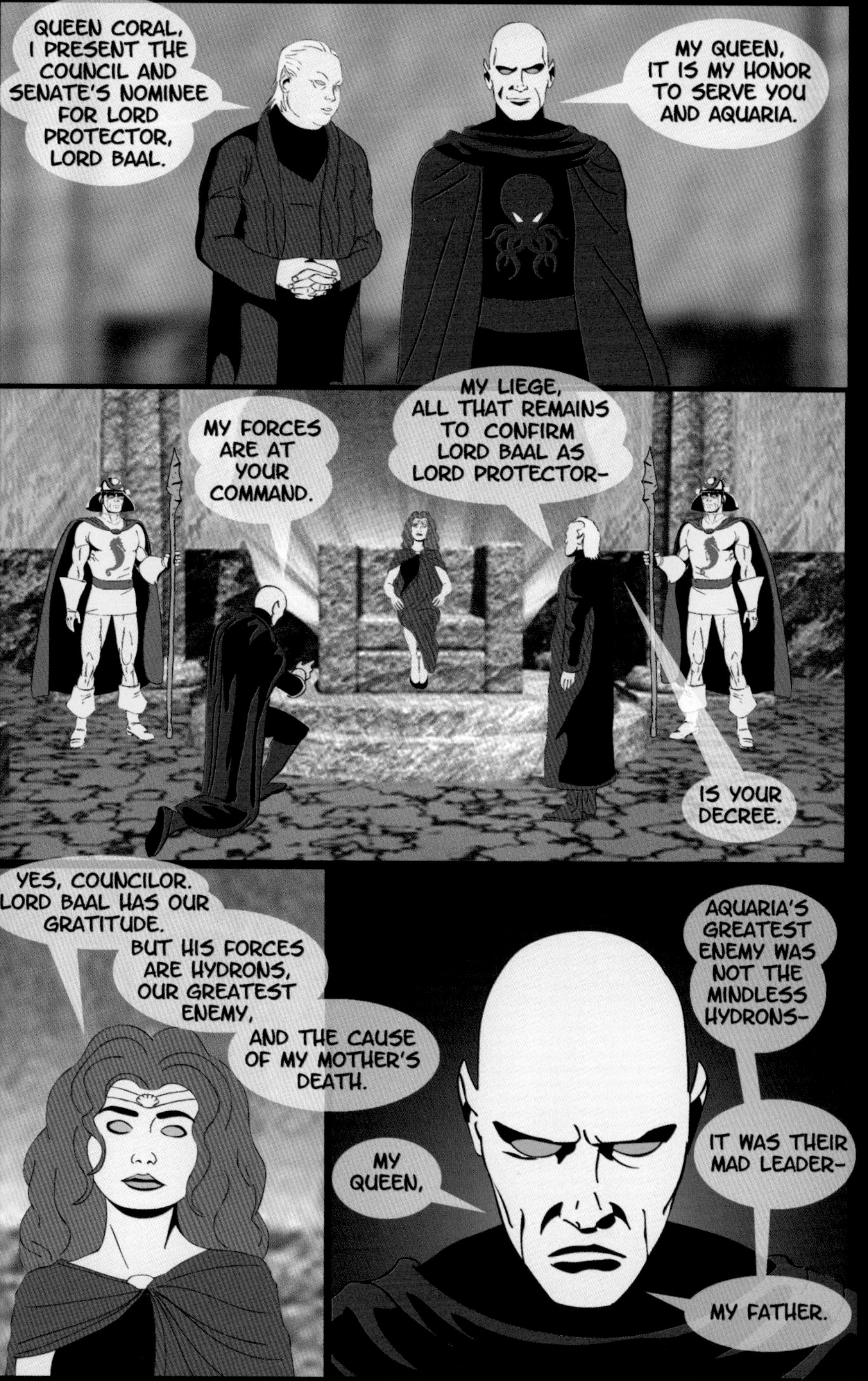
QUEEN CORAL, I PRESENT THE COUNCIL AND SENATE'S NOMINEE FOR LORD PROTECTOR, LORD BAAL.
MY QUEEN, IT IS MY HONOR TO SERVE YOU AND AQUARIA.
MY FORCES ARE AT YOUR COMMAND.
MY LIEGE, ALL THAT REMAINS TO CONFIRM LORD BAAL AS LORD PROTECTOR-
IS YOUR DECREE.
YES, COUNCILOR. LORD BAAL HAS OUR GRATITUDE.
BUT HIS FORCES ARE HYDRONS, OUR GREATEST ENEMY,
AND THE CAUSE OF MY MOTHER'S DEATH.
MY QUEEN,
AQUARIA'S GREATEST ENEMY WAS NOT THE MINDLESS HYDRONS-
IT WAS THEIR MAD LEADER-
MY FATHER.

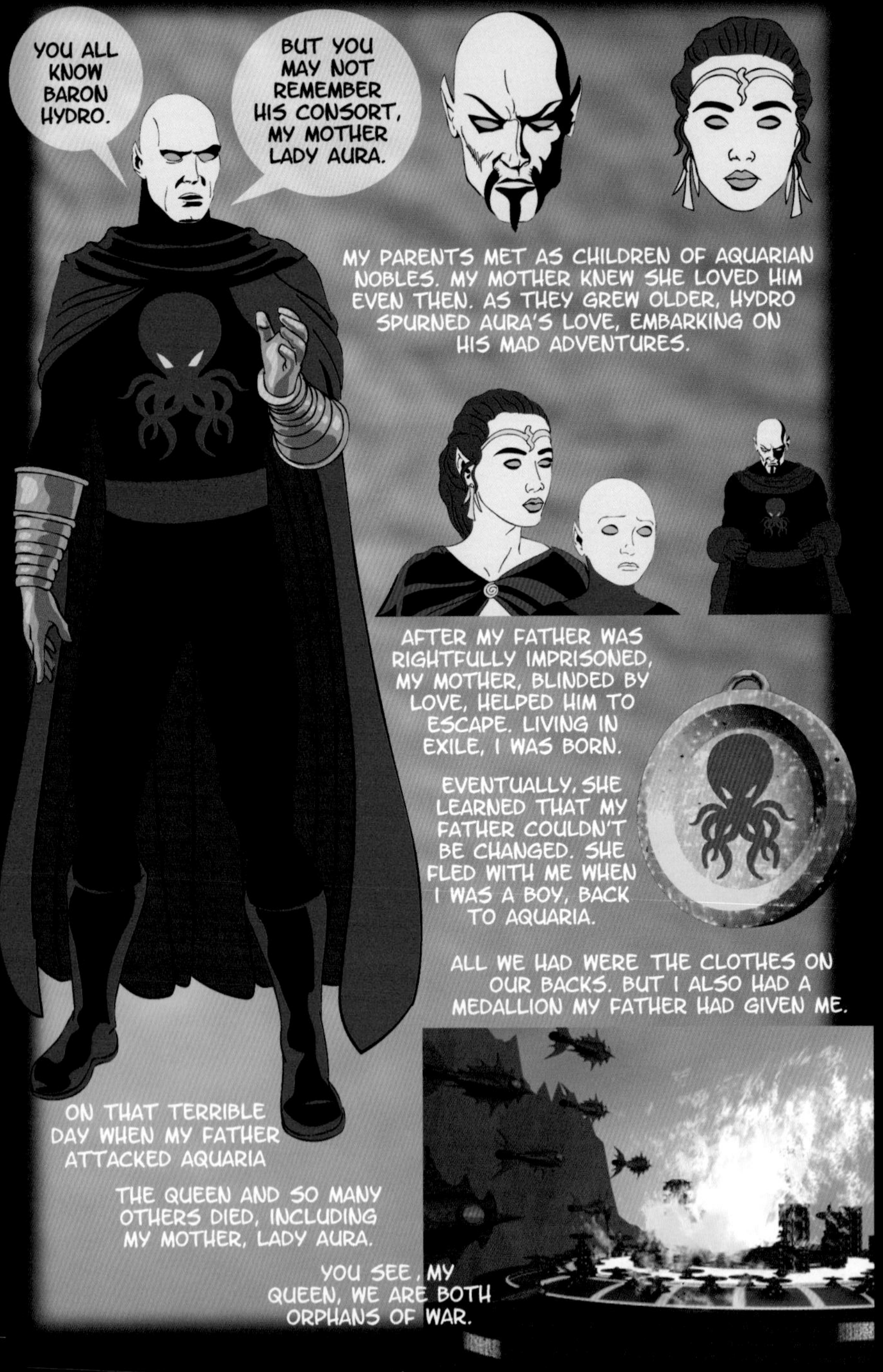
YOU ALL KNOW BARON HYDRO.
BUT YOU MAY NOT REMEMBER HIS CONSORT, MY MOTHER LADY AURA.
MY PARENTS MET AS CHILDREN OF AQUARIAN NOBLES. MY MOTHER KNEW SHE LOVED HIM EVEN THEN. AS THEY GREW OLDER, HYDRO SPURNED AURA'S LOVE, EMBARKING ON HIS MAD ADVENTURES.
AFTER MY FATHER WAS RIGHTFULLY IMPRISONED, MY MOTHER, BLINDED BY LOVE, HELPED HIM TO ESCAPE. LIVING IN EXILE, I WAS BORN.
EVENTUALLY, SHE LEARNED THAT MY FATHER COULDN'T BE CHANGED. SHE FLED WITH ME WHEN I WAS A BOY, BACK TO AQUARIA.
ALL WE HAD WERE THE CLOTHES ON OUR BACKS. BUT I ALSO HAD A MEDALLION MY FATHER HAD GIVEN ME.
ON THAT TERRIBLE DAY WHEN MY FATHER ATTACKED AQUARIA
THE QUEEN AND SO MANY OTHERS DIED, INCLUDING MY MOTHER, LADY AURA.
YOU SEE, MY QUEEN, WE ARE BOTH ORPHANS OF WAR.

Act 6 - Past Imperfect

BARON HYDRO MET HIS FATE AND I GREW UP AS AN ORPHAN IN AQUARIA. I WAS ACCEPTED BY SOME, BUT FOR OTHERS I WAS RESPONSIBLE FOR MY FATHER'S DEEDS.

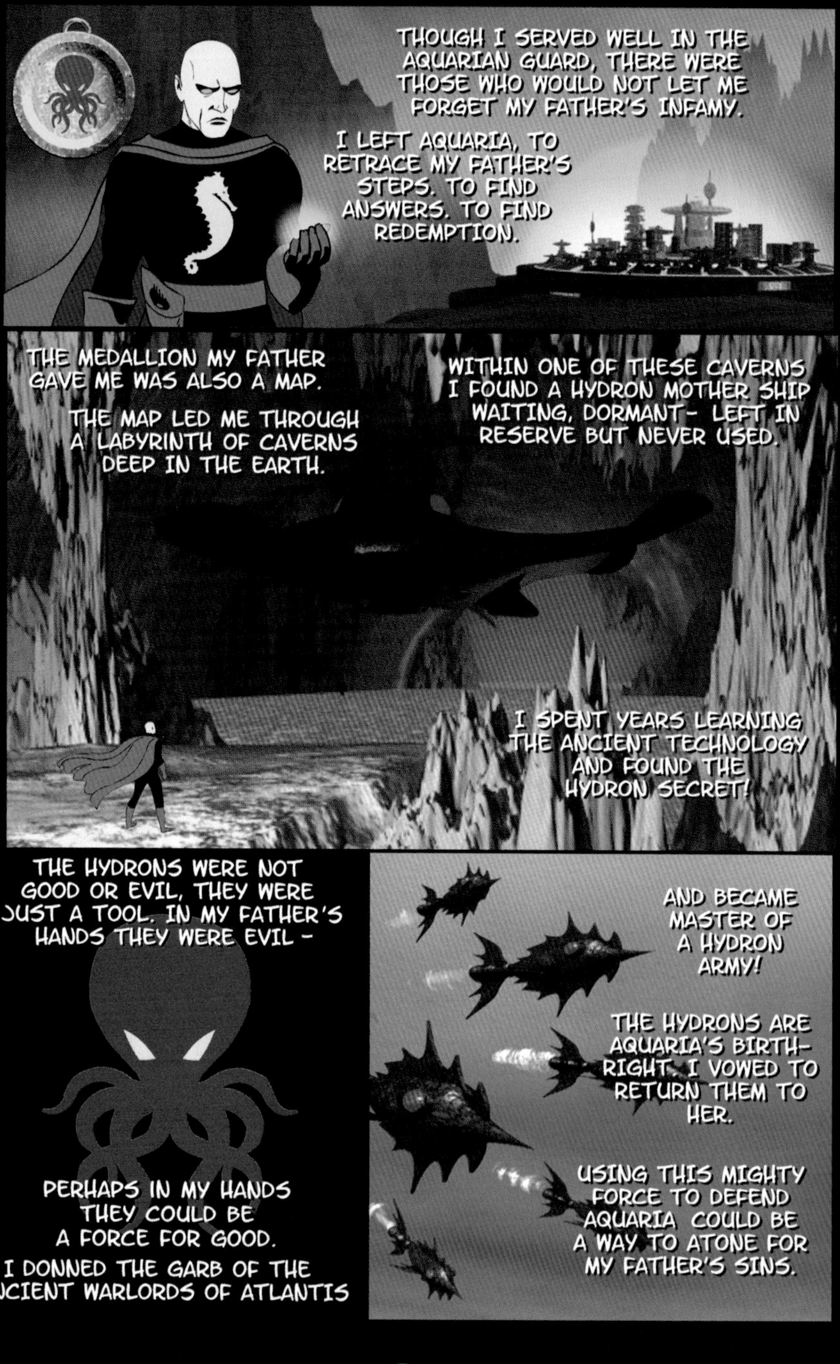

THOUGH I SERVED WELL IN THE AQUARIAN GUARD, THERE WERE THOSE WHO WOULD NOT LET ME FORGET MY FATHER'S INFAMY.
I LEFT AQUARIA, TO RETRACE MY FATHER'S STEPS. TO FIND ANSWERS. TO FIND REDEMPTION.
THE MEDALLION MY FATHER GAVE ME WAS ALSO A MAP.
THE MAP LED ME THROUGH A LABYRINTH OF CAVERNS DEEP IN THE EARTH.
WITHIN ONE OF THESE CAVERNS I FOUND A HYDRON MOTHER SHIP WAITING, DORMANT- LEFT IN RESERVE BUT NEVER USED.
I SPENT YEARS LEARNING THE ANCIENT TECHNOLOGY AND FOUND THE HYDRON SECRET!
THE HYDRONS WERE NOT GOOD OR EVIL, THEY WERE JUST A TOOL. IN MY FATHER'S HANDS THEY WERE EVIL -
PERHAPS IN MY HANDS THEY COULD BE A FORCE FOR GOOD.
I DONNED THE GARB OF THE ANCIENT WARLORDS OF ATLANTIS
AND BECAME MASTER OF A HYDRON ARMY!
THE HYDRONS ARE AQUARIA'S BIRTH-RIGHT. I VOWED TO RETURN THEM TO HER.
USING THIS MIGHTY FORCE TO DEFEND AQUARIA COULD BE A WAY TO ATONE FOR MY FATHER'S SINS.

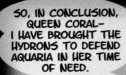

SO, IN CONCLUSION, QUEEN CORAL— I HAVE BROUGHT THE HYDRONS TO DEFEND AQUARIA IN HER TIME OF NEED.

AS FOR ME, I ASK— SHOULD A MAN BE JUDGED BY HIS OWN DEEDS AND NOT HIS FATHER'S?

AS FOR THE HYDRONS, I HUMBLY ASK— IS A SWORD EVIL? OR THE ONE WHO HOLDS IT?

I AM YOUR SERVANT!

THANK YOU, LORD BAAL.

YOUR WORDS ARE AS STRONG AS YOUR DEEDS— I WILL PROCLAIM YOU LORD PROTECTOR.

I AM HONORED BEYOND WORDS, MY QUEEN! I TAKE THE CEREMONIAL NAME OF HYDRO TO CLEAN MY PAST AND PAVE OUR FUTURE.

SO BE IT! ALL HAIL LORD HYDRO, LORD PROTECTOR OF AQUARIA!

HAIL, LORD HYDRO!!

ACT 6 - PAST IMPERFECT

BACK ABOARD THE SEASCAPE.

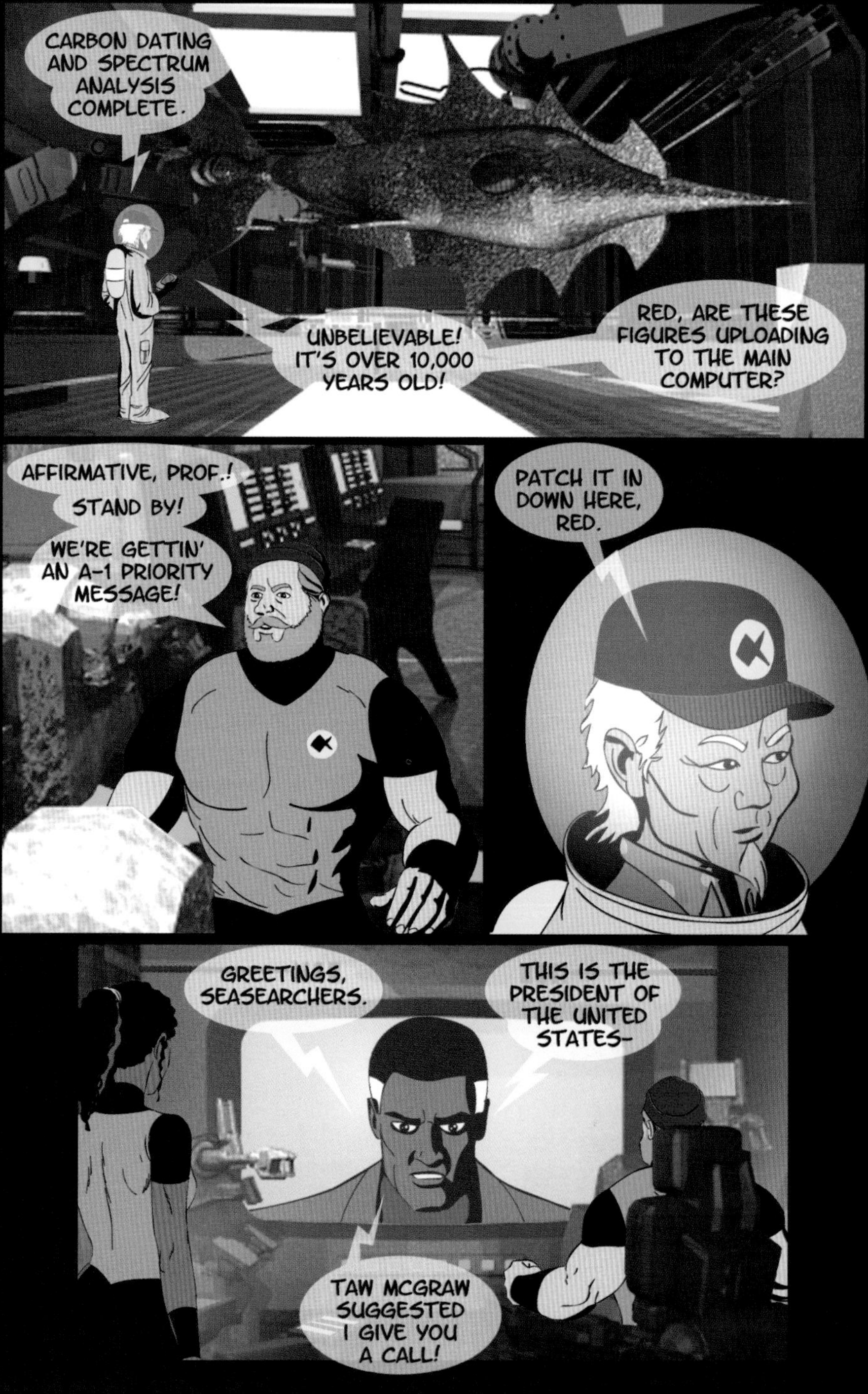
CARBON DATING AND SPECTRUM ANALYSIS COMPLETE.
UNBELIEVABLE! IT'S OVER 10,000 YEARS OLD!
RED, ARE THESE FIGURES UPLOADING TO THE MAIN COMPUTER?
AFFIRMATIVE, PROF.!
STAND BY!
WE'RE GETTIN' AN A-1 PRIORITY MESSAGE!
PATCH IT IN DOWN HERE, RED.
GREETINGS, SEASEARCHERS.
THIS IS THE PRESIDENT OF THE UNITED STATES-
TAW MCGRAW SUGGESTED I GIVE YOU A CALL!

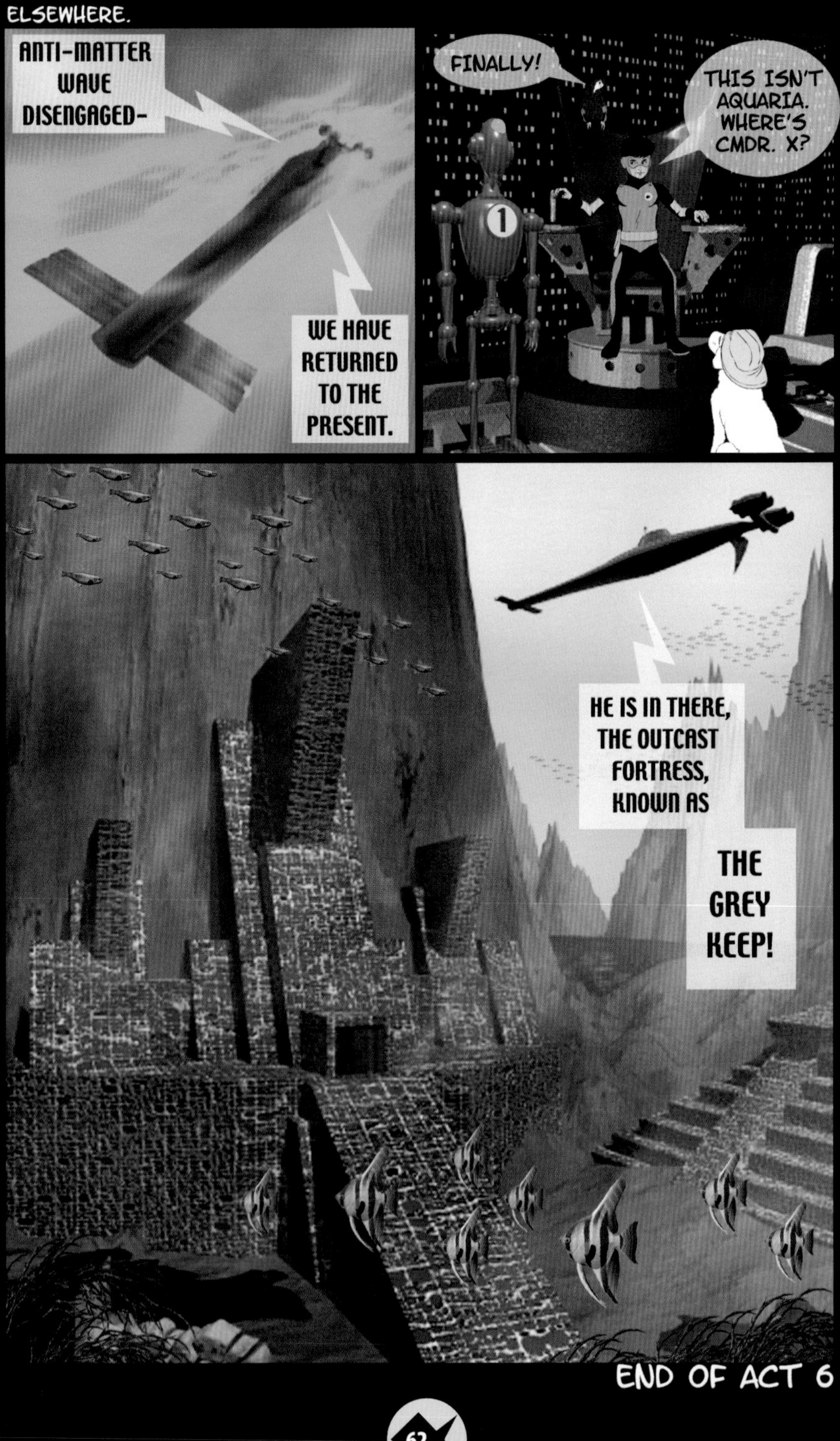
ELSEWHERE.
ANTI-MATTER WAVE DISENGAGED-
WE HAVE RETURNED TO THE PRESENT.
FINALLY!
THIS ISN'T AQUARIA. WHERE'S CMDR. X?
HE IS IN THERE, THE OUTCAST FORTRESS, KNOWN AS
THE GREY KEEP!
END OF ACT 6

ACT 7 - RENDEZVOUS WITH DESTINY

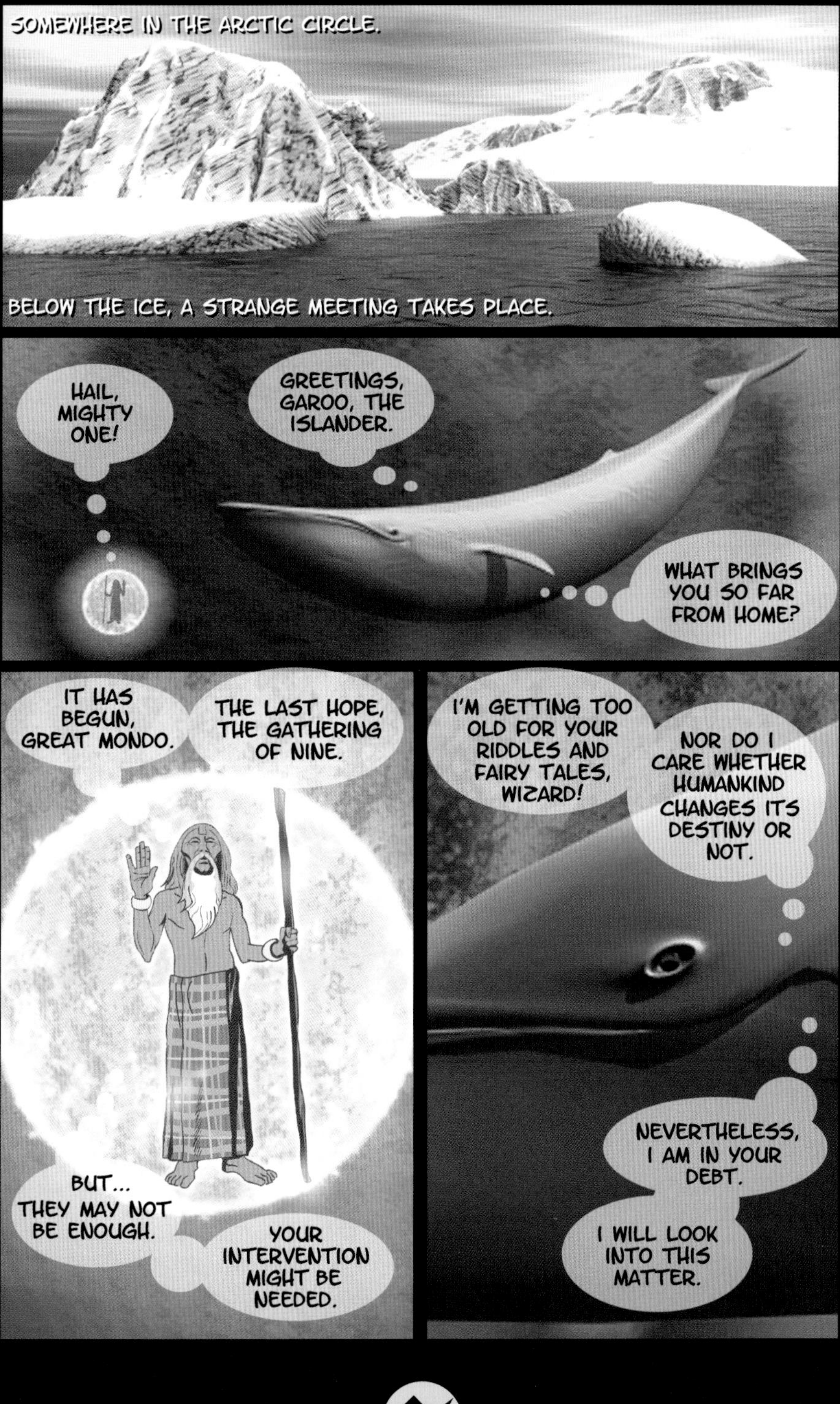
SOMEWHERE IN THE ARCTIC CIRCLE.
BELOW THE ICE, A STRANGE MEETING TAKES PLACE.
HAIL, MIGHTY ONE!
GREETINGS, GAROO, THE ISLANDER.
WHAT BRINGS YOU SO FAR FROM HOME?
IT HAS BEGUN, GREAT MONDO.
THE LAST HOPE, THE GATHERING OF NINE.
BUT... THEY MAY NOT BE ENOUGH.
YOUR INTERVENTION MIGHT BE NEEDED.
I'M GETTING TOO OLD FOR YOUR RIDDLES AND FAIRY TALES, WIZARD!
NOR DO I CARE WHETHER HUMANKIND CHANGES ITS DESTINY OR NOT.
NEVERTHELESS, I AM IN YOUR DEBT.
I WILL LOOK INTO THIS MATTER.

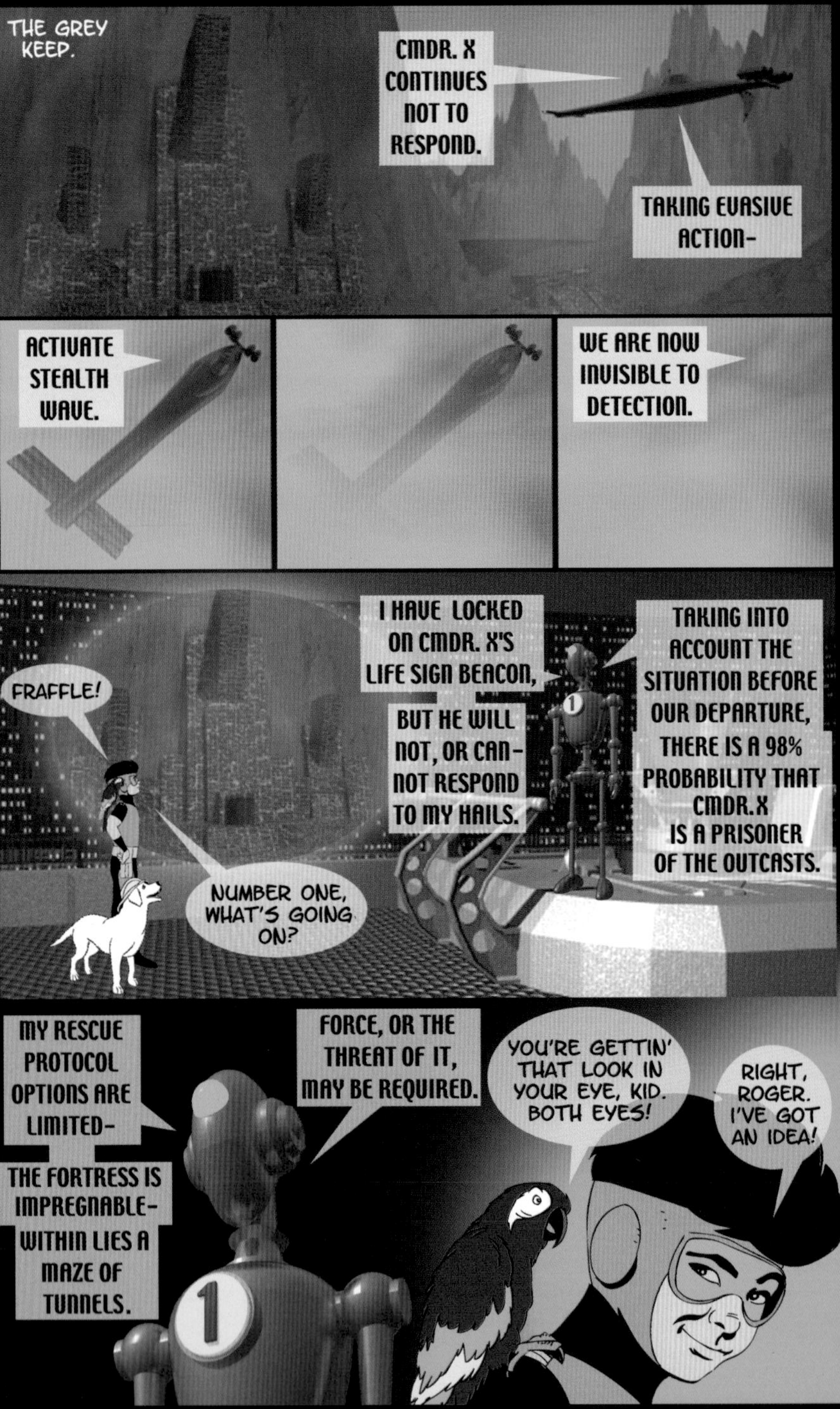
THE GREY KEEP.
CMDR. X CONTINUES NOT TO RESPOND.
TAKING EVASIVE ACTION-
ACTIVATE STEALTH WAVE.
WE ARE NOW INVISIBLE TO DETECTION.
FRAFFLE!
NUMBER ONE, WHAT'S GOING ON?
I HAVE LOCKED ON CMDR. X'S LIFE SIGN BEACON,
BUT HE WILL NOT, OR CAN-NOT RESPOND TO MY HAILS.
TAKING INTO ACCOUNT THE SITUATION BEFORE OUR DEPARTURE, THERE IS A 98% PROBABILITY THAT CMDR. X IS A PRISONER OF THE OUTCASTS.
MY RESCUE PROTOCOL OPTIONS ARE LIMITED-
THE FORTRESS IS IMPREGNABLE-
WITHIN LIES A MAZE OF TUNNELS.
FORCE, OR THE THREAT OF IT, MAY BE REQUIRED.
YOU'RE GETTIN' THAT LOOK IN YOUR EYE, KID. BOTH EYES!
RIGHT, ROGER. I'VE GOT AN IDEA!

ACT 7 - RENDEZVOUS WITH DESTINY

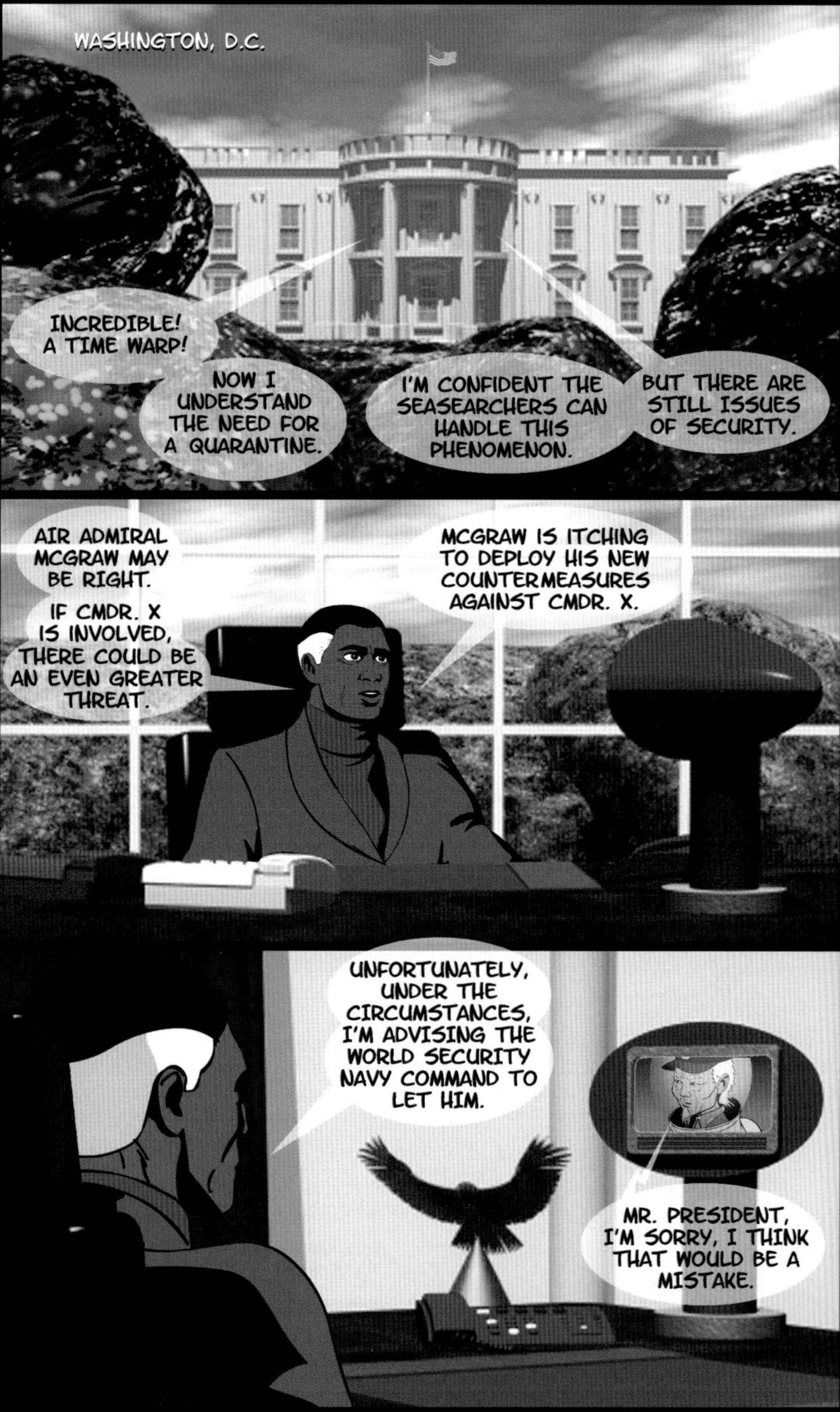
WASHINGTON, D.C.
INCREDIBLE! A TIME WARP!
NOW I UNDERSTAND THE NEED FOR A QUARANTINE.
I'M CONFIDENT THE SEASEARCHERS CAN HANDLE THIS PHENOMENON.
BUT THERE ARE STILL ISSUES OF SECURITY.
AIR ADMIRAL MCGRAW MAY BE RIGHT.
IF CMDR. X IS INVOLVED, THERE COULD BE AN EVEN GREATER THREAT.
MCGRAW IS ITCHING TO DEPLOY HIS NEW COUNTERMEASURES AGAINST CMDR. X.
UNFORTUNATELY, UNDER THE CIRCUMSTANCES, I'M ADVISING THE WORLD SECURITY NAVY COMMAND TO LET HIM.
MR. PRESIDENT, I'M SORRY, I THINK THAT WOULD BE A MISTAKE.

THE UNDERSEA ADVENTURES OF CAPT'N ELI

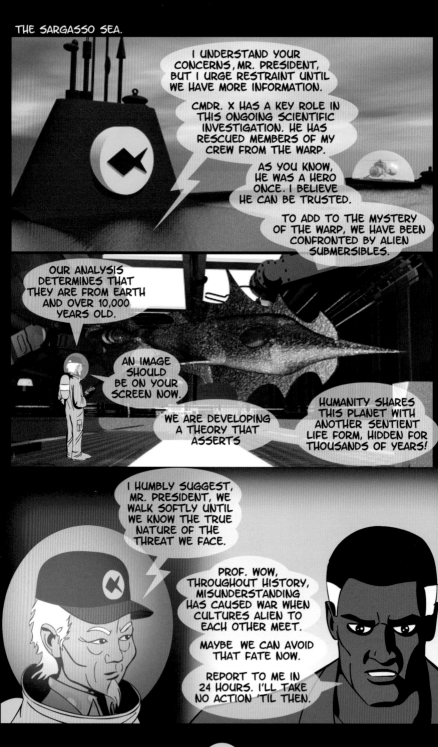

THE SARGASSO SEA.

I UNDERSTAND YOUR CONCERNS, MR. PRESIDENT, BUT I URGE RESTRAINT UNTIL WE HAVE MORE INFORMATION.

CMDR. X HAS A KEY ROLE IN THIS ONGOING SCIENTIFIC INVESTIGATION. HE HAS RESCUED MEMBERS OF MY CREW FROM THE WARP.

AS YOU KNOW, HE WAS A HERO ONCE. I BELIEVE HE CAN BE TRUSTED.

TO ADD TO THE MYSTERY OF THE WARP, WE HAVE BEEN CONFRONTED BY ALIEN SUBMERSIBLES.

OUR ANALYSIS DETERMINES THAT THEY ARE FROM EARTH AND OVER 10,000 YEARS OLD.

AN IMAGE SHOULD BE ON YOUR SCREEN NOW.

WE ARE DEVELOPING A THEORY THAT ASSERTS

HUMANITY SHARES THIS PLANET WITH ANOTHER SENTIENT LIFE FORM, HIDDEN FOR THOUSANDS OF YEARS!

I HUMBLY SUGGEST, MR. PRESIDENT, WE WALK SOFTLY UNTIL WE KNOW THE TRUE NATURE OF THE THREAT WE FACE.

PROF. WOW, THROUGHOUT HISTORY, MISUNDERSTANDING HAS CAUSED WAR WHEN CULTURES ALIEN TO EACH OTHER MEET.

MAYBE WE CAN AVOID THAT FATE NOW.

REPORT TO ME IN 24 HOURS. I'LL TAKE NO ACTION 'TIL THEN.

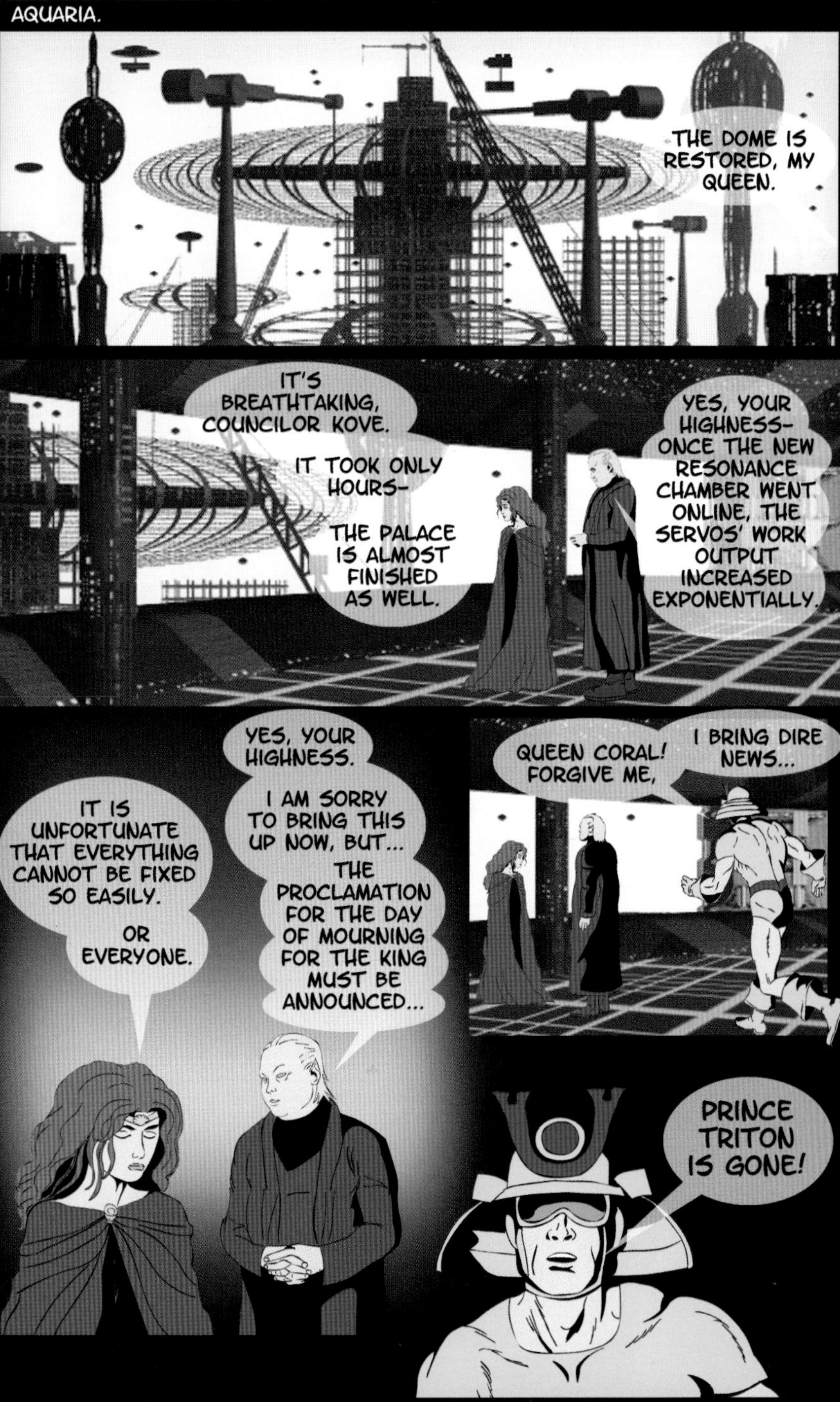
AQUARIA.
THE DOME IS RESTORED, MY QUEEN.
IT'S BREATHTAKING, COUNCILOR KOVE.
IT TOOK ONLY HOURS-
THE PALACE IS ALMOST FINISHED AS WELL.
YES, YOUR HIGHNESS- ONCE THE NEW RESONANCE CHAMBER WENT ONLINE, THE SERVOS' WORK OUTPUT INCREASED EXPONENTIALLY.
IT IS UNFORTUNATE THAT EVERYTHING CANNOT BE FIXED SO EASILY.
OR EVERYONE.
YES, YOUR HIGHNESS.
I AM SORRY TO BRING THIS UP NOW, BUT...
THE PROCLAMATION FOR THE DAY OF MOURNING FOR THE KING MUST BE ANNOUNCED...
QUEEN CORAL! FORGIVE ME,
I BRING DIRE NEWS...
PRINCE TRITON IS GONE!

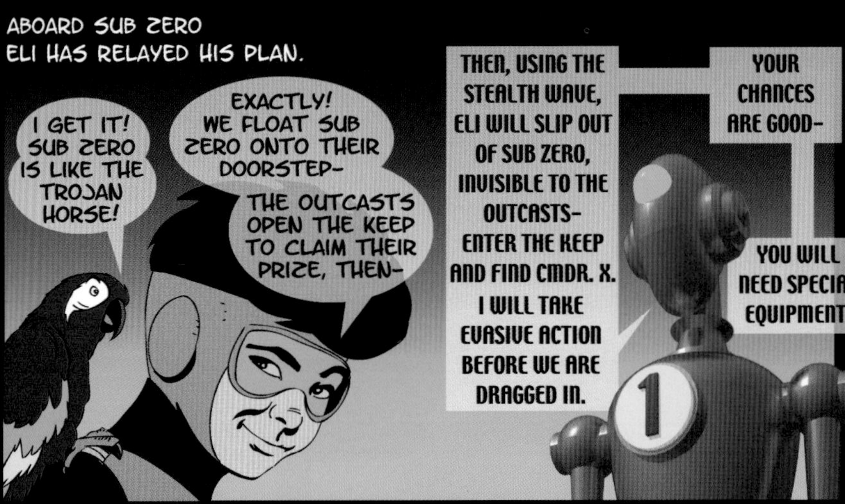
ABOARD SUB ZERO
ELI HAS RELAYED HIS PLAN.
I GET IT! SUB ZERO IS LIKE THE TROJAN HORSE!
EXACTLY! WE FLOAT SUB ZERO ONTO THEIR DOORSTEP-
THE OUTCASTS OPEN THE KEEP TO CLAIM THEIR PRIZE, THEN-
THEN, USING THE STEALTH WAVE, ELI WILL SLIP OUT OF SUB ZERO, INVISIBLE TO THE OUTCASTS- ENTER THE KEEP AND FIND CMDR. X.
I WILL TAKE EVASIVE ACTION BEFORE WE ARE DRAGGED IN.
YOUR CHANCES ARE GOOD-
YOU WILL NEED SPECIA EQUIPMENT
1

SOON, IN THE MINI-SUB BAY.

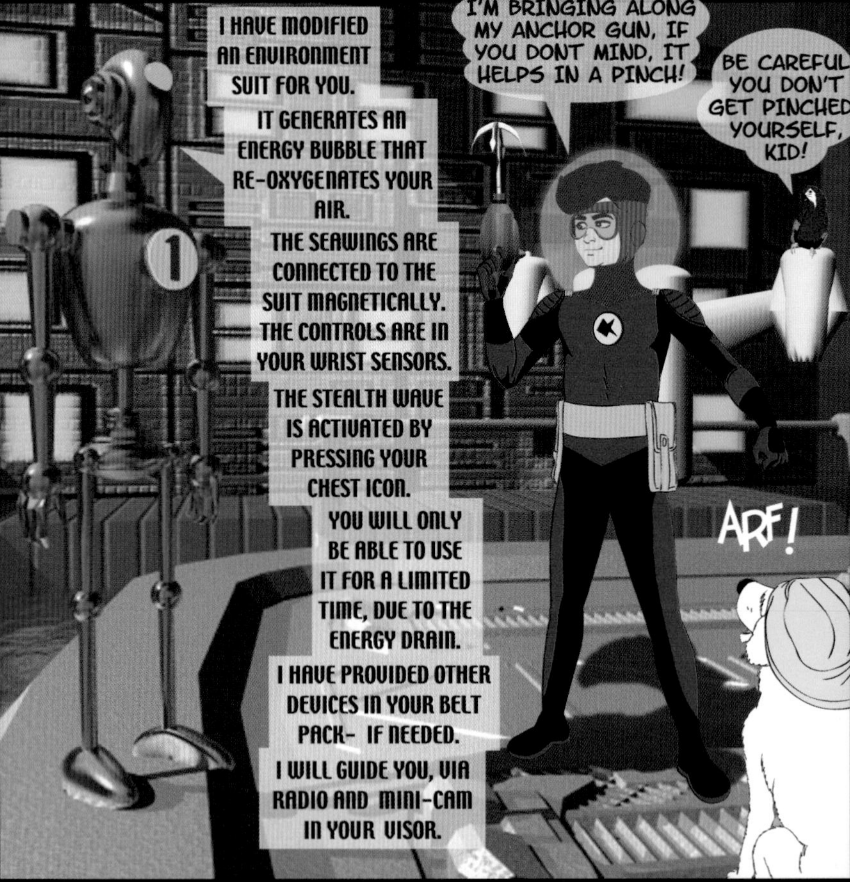
I HAVE MODIFIED AN ENVIRONMENT SUIT FOR YOU.
IT GENERATES AN ENERGY BUBBLE THAT RE-OXYGENATES YOUR AIR.
THE SEAWINGS ARE CONNECTED TO THE SUIT MAGNETICALLY.
THE CONTROLS ARE IN YOUR WRIST SENSORS.
THE STEALTH WAVE IS ACTIVATED BY PRESSING YOUR CHEST ICON.
YOU WILL ONLY BE ABLE TO USE IT FOR A LIMITED TIME, DUE TO THE ENERGY DRAIN.
I HAVE PROVIDED OTHER DEVICES IN YOUR BELT PACK- IF NEEDED.
I WILL GUIDE YOU, VIA RADIO AND MINI-CAM IN YOUR VISOR.
I'M BRINGING ALONG MY ANCHOR GUN, IF YOU DONT MIND, IT HELPS IN A PINCH!
BE CAREFUL YOU DON'T GET PINCHED YOURSELF, KID!
ARF!
1

ACT 7 - RENDEZVOUS WITH DESTINY

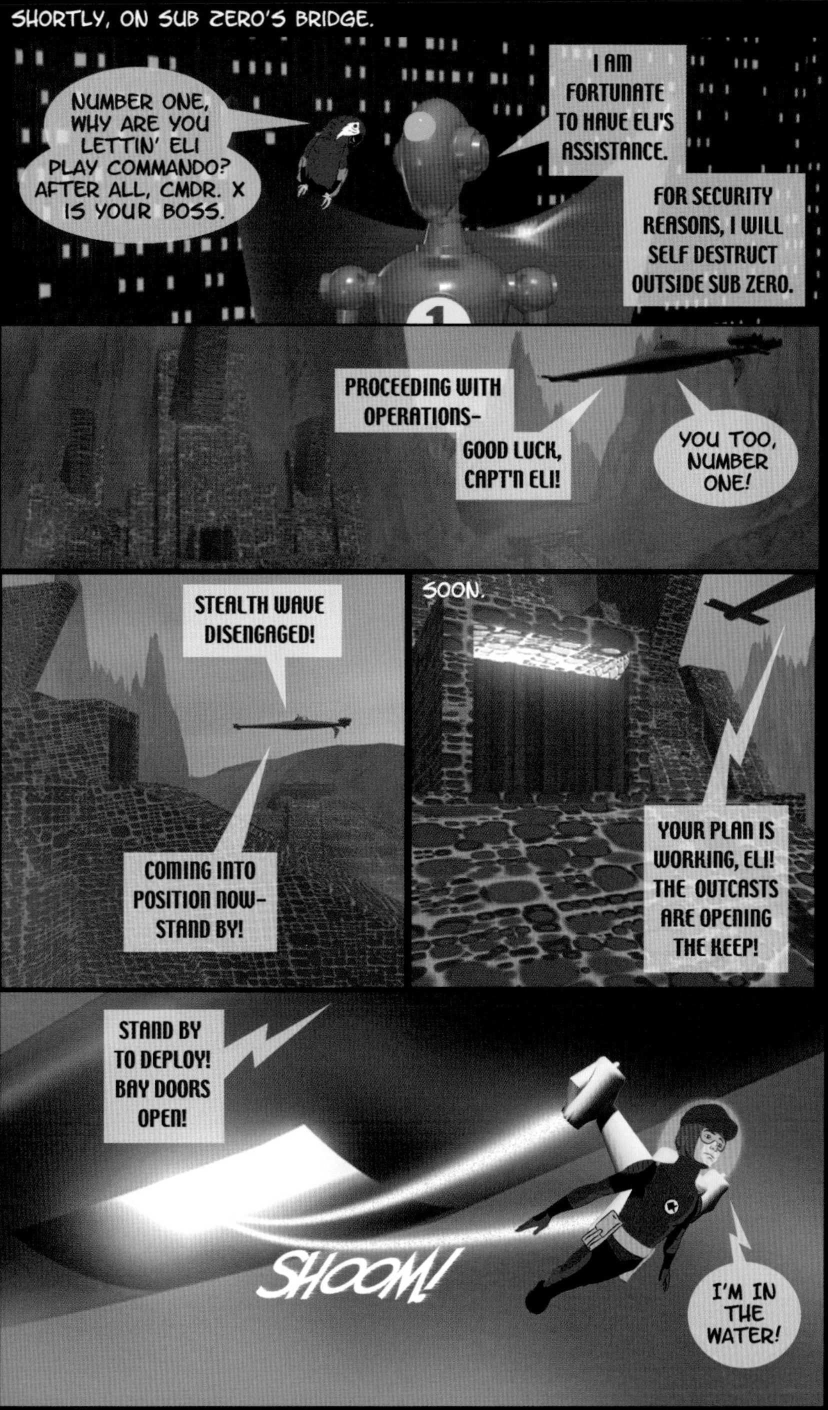
SHORTLY, ON SUB ZERO'S BRIDGE.
NUMBER ONE, WHY ARE YOU LETTIN' ELI PLAY COMMANDO? AFTER ALL, CMDR. X IS YOUR BOSS.
I AM FORTUNATE TO HAVE ELI'S ASSISTANCE.
FOR SECURITY REASONS, I WILL SELF DESTRUCT OUTSIDE SUB ZERO.
PROCEEDING WITH OPERATIONS–
GOOD LUCK, CAPT'N ELI!
YOU TOO, NUMBER ONE!
STEALTH WAVE DISENGAGED!
COMING INTO POSITION NOW– STAND BY!
SOON.
YOUR PLAN IS WORKING, ELI! THE OUTCASTS ARE OPENING THE KEEP!
STAND BY TO DEPLOY! BAY DOORS OPEN!
SHOOM!
I'M IN THE WATER!

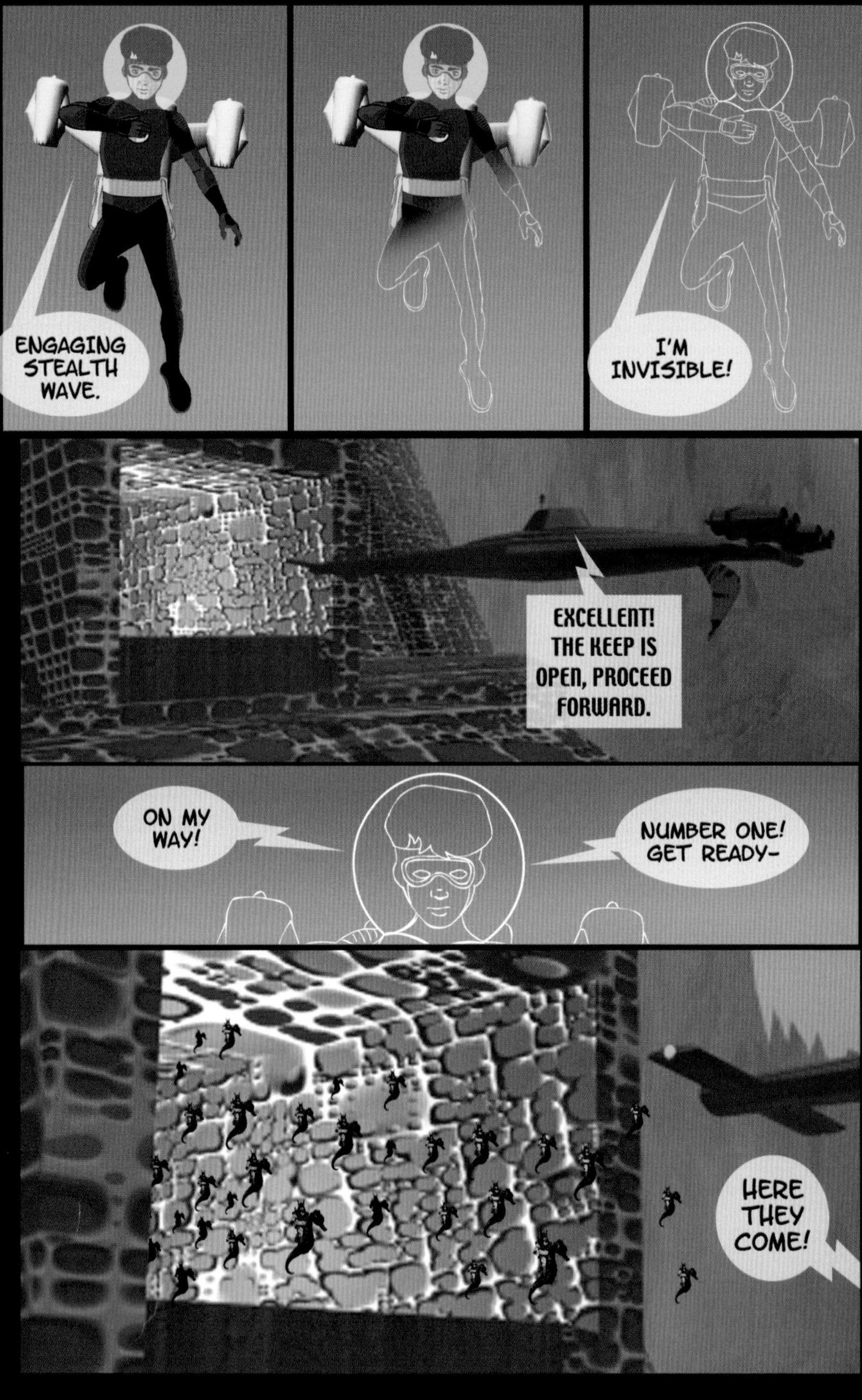
ENGAGING STEALTH WAVE.
I'M INVISIBLE!
EXCELLENT! THE KEEP IS OPEN, PROCEED FORWARD.
ON MY WAY!
NUMBER ONE! GET READY-
HERE THEY COME!

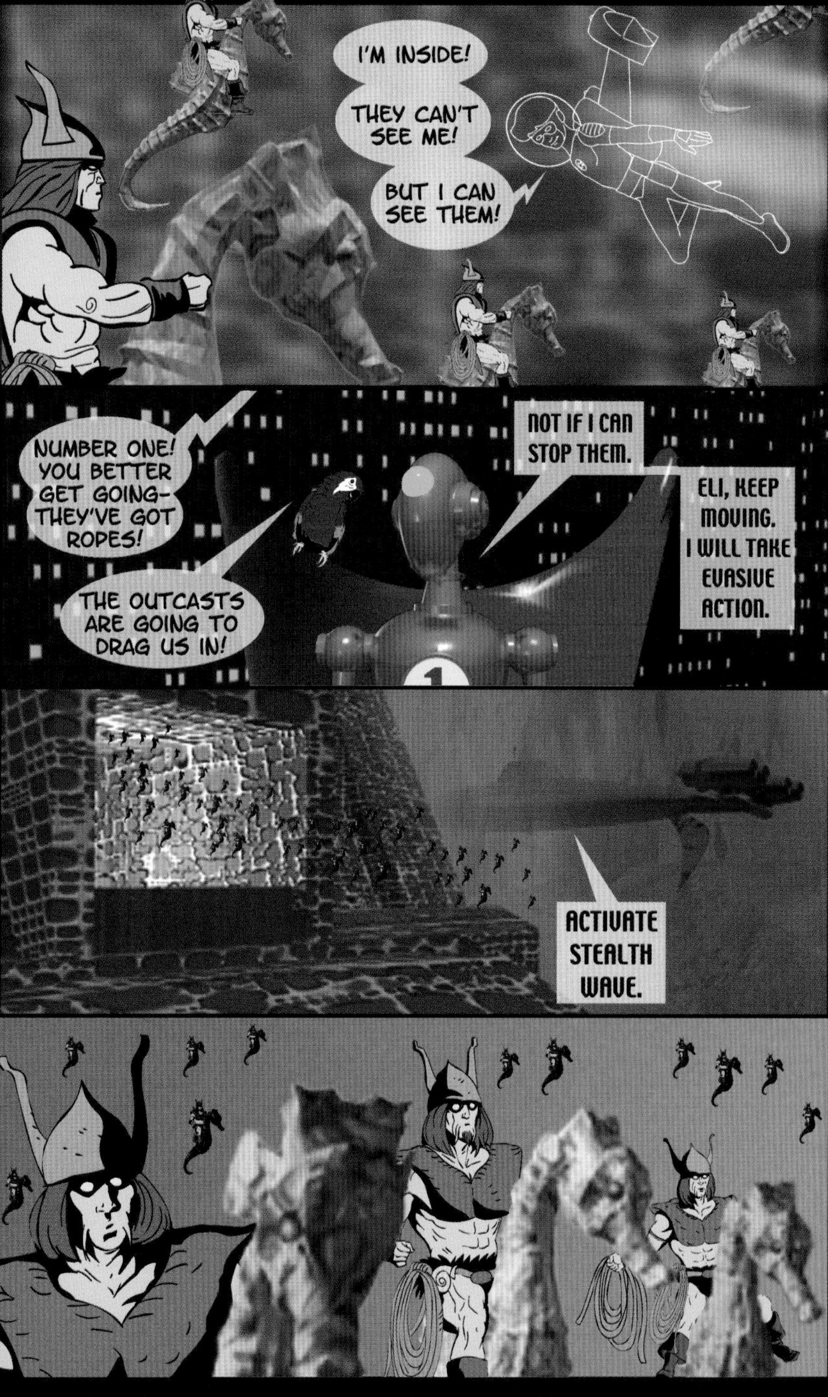
I'M INSIDE!
THEY CAN'T SEE ME!
BUT I CAN SEE THEM!
NUMBER ONE! YOU BETTER GET GOING- THEY'VE GOT ROPES!
THE OUTCASTS ARE GOING TO DRAG US IN!
NOT IF I CAN STOP THEM.
ELI, KEEP MOVING. I WILL TAKE EVASIVE ACTION.
ACTIVATE STEALTH WAVE.

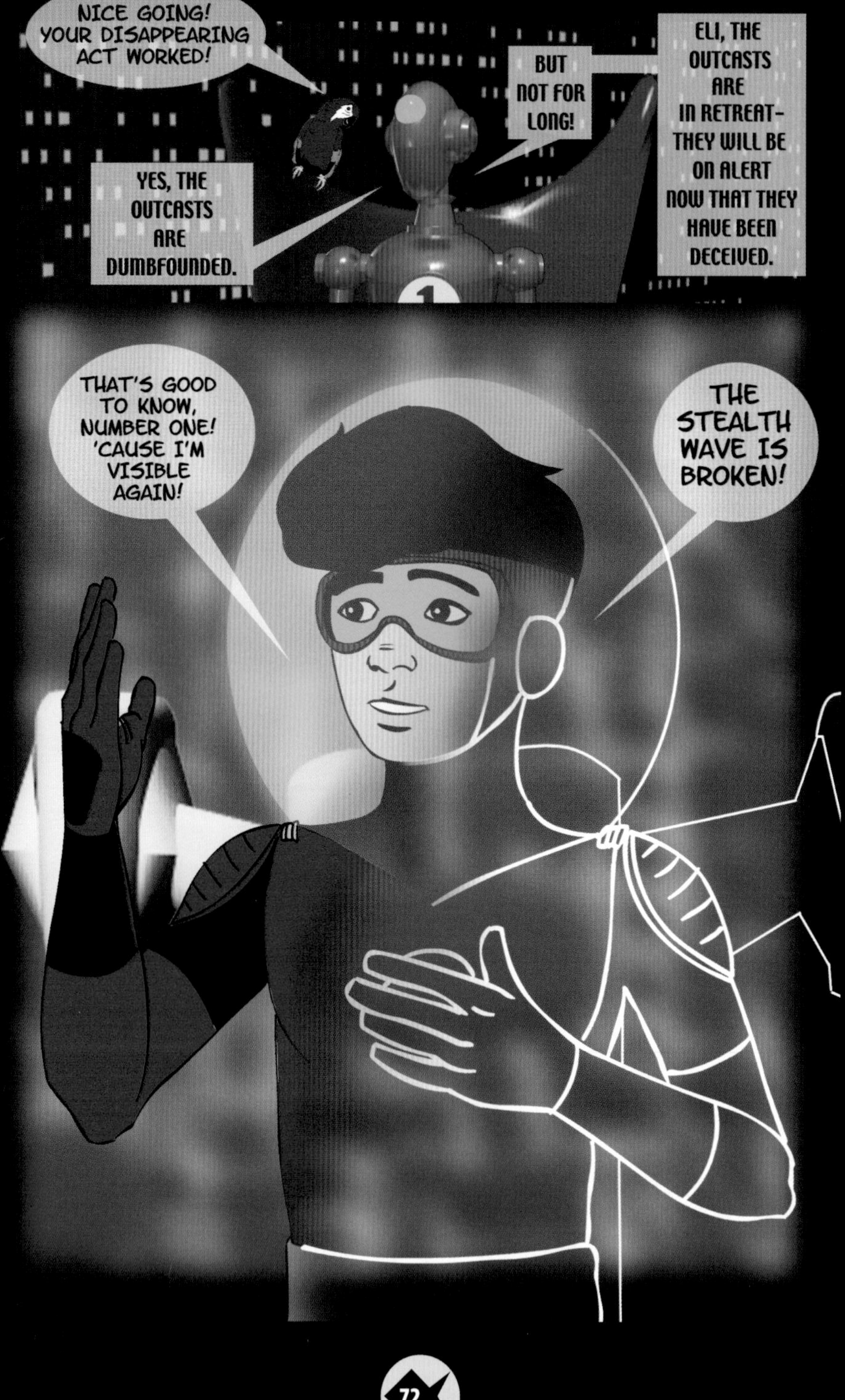
NICE GOING! YOUR DISAPPEARING ACT WORKED!
YES, THE OUTCASTS ARE DUMBFOUNDED.
BUT NOT FOR LONG!
ELI, THE OUTCASTS ARE IN RETREAT- THEY WILL BE ON ALERT NOW THAT THEY HAVE BEEN DECEIVED.
THAT'S GOOD TO KNOW, NUMBER ONE! 'CAUSE I'M VISIBLE AGAIN!
THE STEALTH WAVE IS BROKEN!

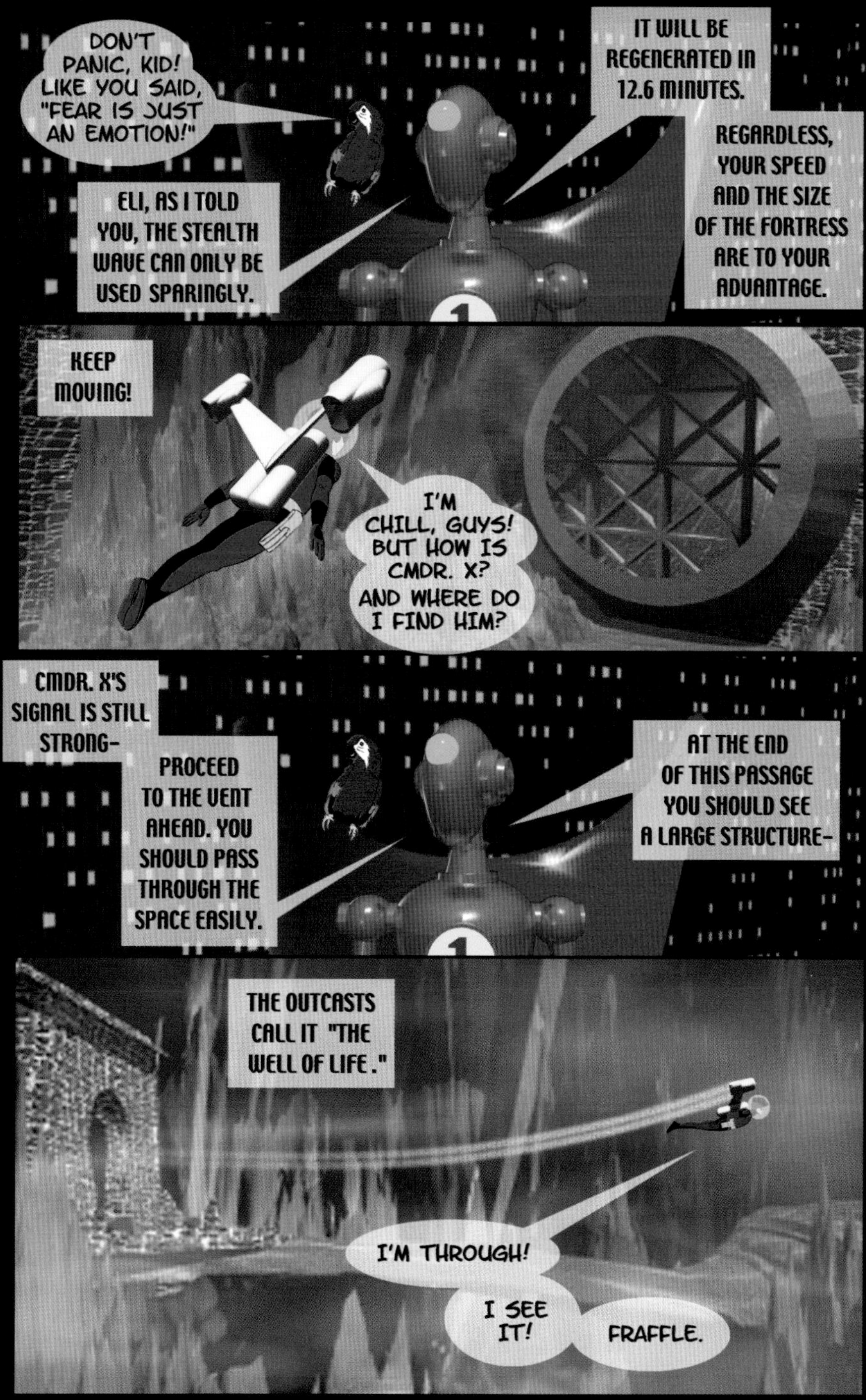
DON'T PANIC, KID! LIKE YOU SAID, "FEAR IS JUST AN EMOTION!"
IT WILL BE REGENERATED IN 12.6 MINUTES.
ELI, AS I TOLD YOU, THE STEALTH WAVE CAN ONLY BE USED SPARINGLY.
REGARDLESS, YOUR SPEED AND THE SIZE OF THE FORTRESS ARE TO YOUR ADVANTAGE.
KEEP MOVING!
I'M CHILL, GUYS! BUT HOW IS CMDR. X? AND WHERE DO I FIND HIM?
CMDR. X'S SIGNAL IS STILL STRONG-
PROCEED TO THE VENT AHEAD. YOU SHOULD PASS THROUGH THE SPACE EASILY.
AT THE END OF THIS PASSAGE YOU SHOULD SEE A LARGE STRUCTURE-
THE OUTCASTS CALL IT "THE WELL OF LIFE."
I'M THROUGH!
I SEE IT!
FRAFFLE.

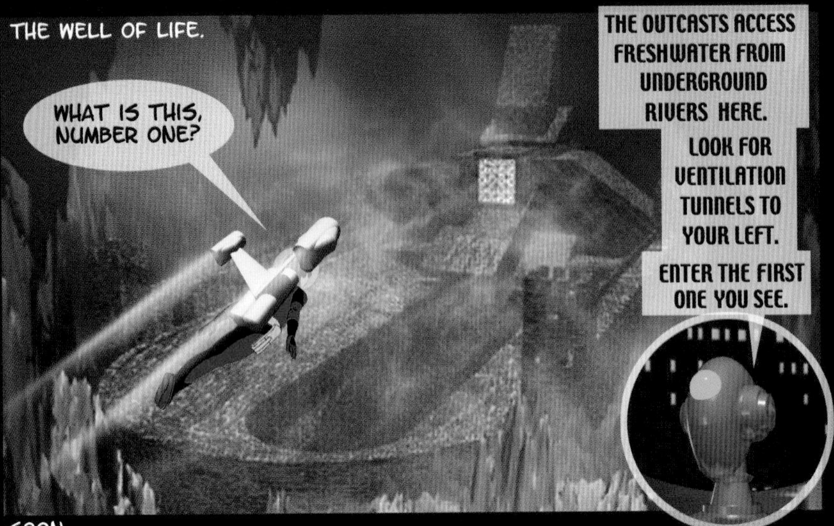
THE WELL OF LIFE.
THE OUTCASTS ACCESS FRESHWATER FROM UNDERGROUND RIVERS HERE.
WHAT IS THIS, NUMBER ONE?
LOOK FOR VENTILATION TUNNELS TO YOUR LEFT.
ENTER THE FIRST ONE YOU SEE.

SOON.

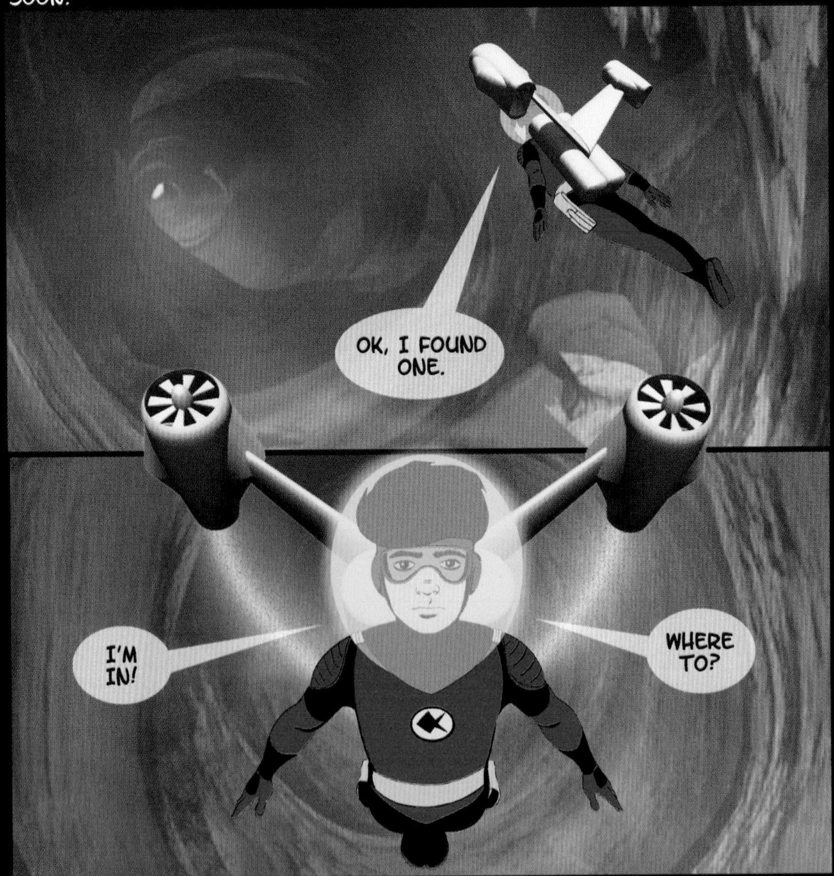
OK, I FOUND ONE.
I'M IN!
WHERE TO?

ACT 7 - RENDEZVOUS WITH DESTINY

SECONDS PASS AS NUMBER ONE GUIDES ELI TO CMDR. X.

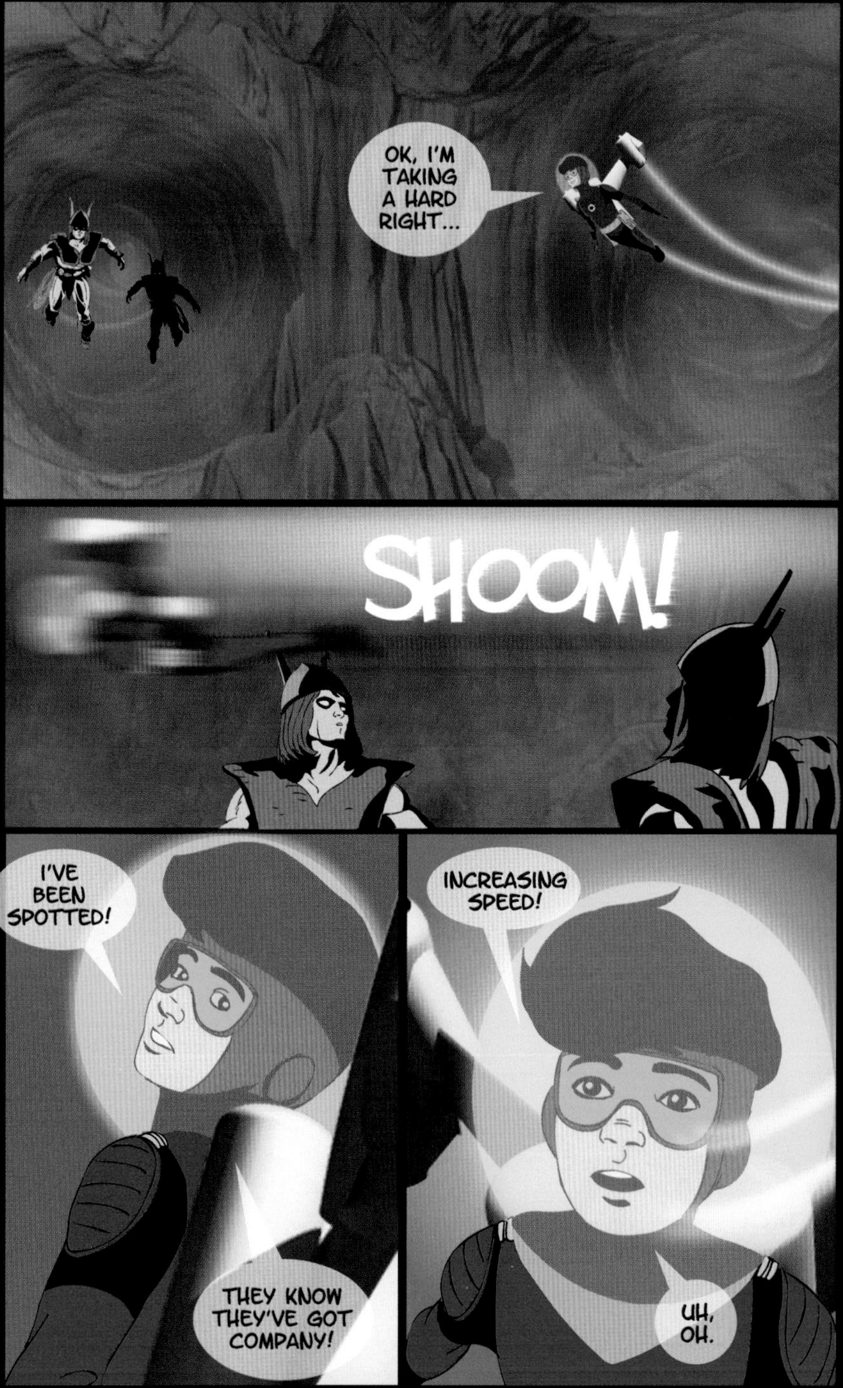
OK, I'M TAKING A HARD RIGHT...
SHOOM!
I'VE BEEN SPOTTED!
THEY KNOW THEY'VE GOT COMPANY!
INCREASING SPEED!
UH, OH.

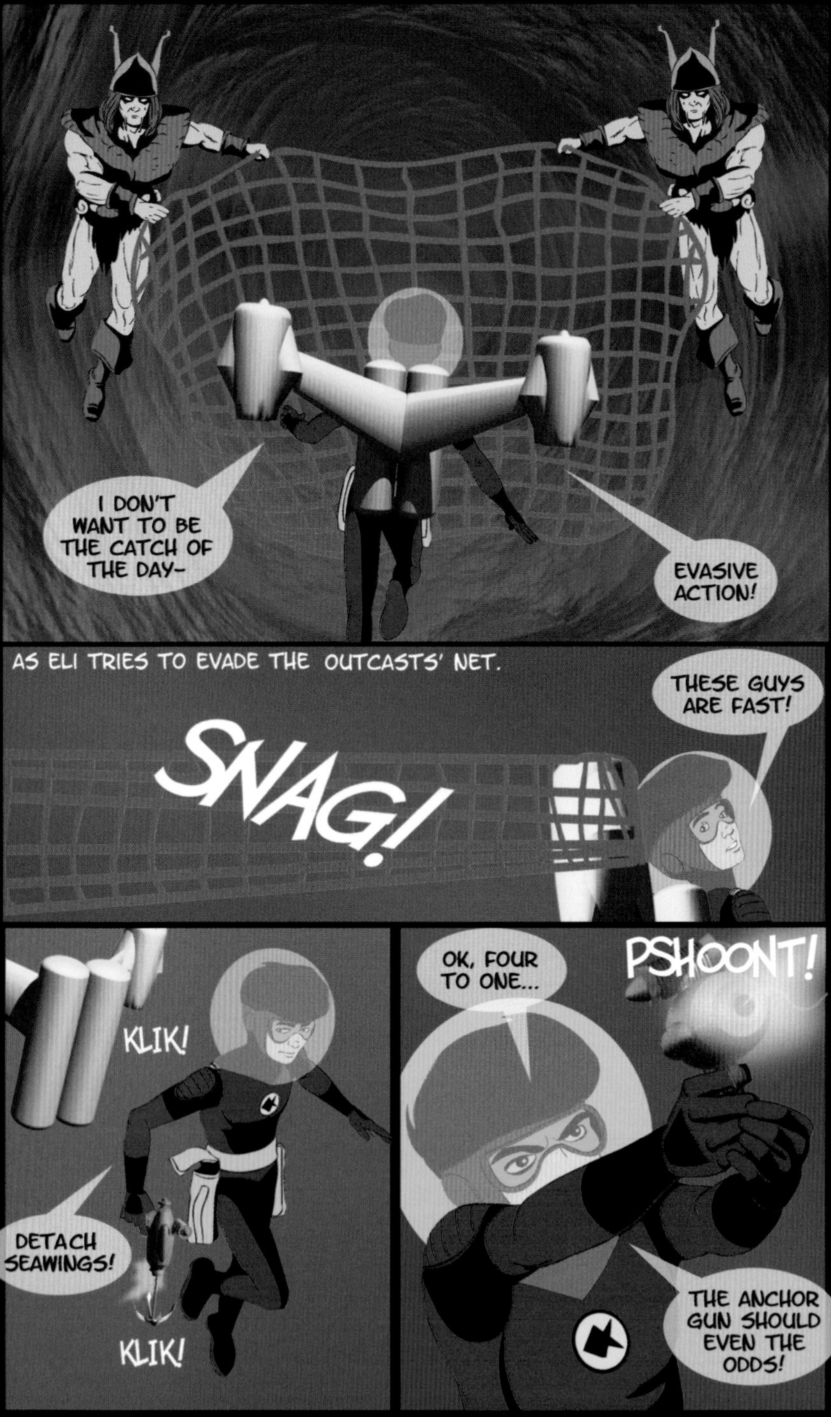
I DON'T WANT TO BE THE CATCH OF THE DAY-
EVASIVE ACTION!
AS ELI TRIES TO EVADE THE OUTCASTS' NET.
THESE GUYS ARE FAST!
SNAG!
KLIK!
DETACH SEAWINGS!
KLIK!
OK, FOUR TO ONE...
PSHOONT!
THE ANCHOR GUN SHOULD EVEN THE ODDS!

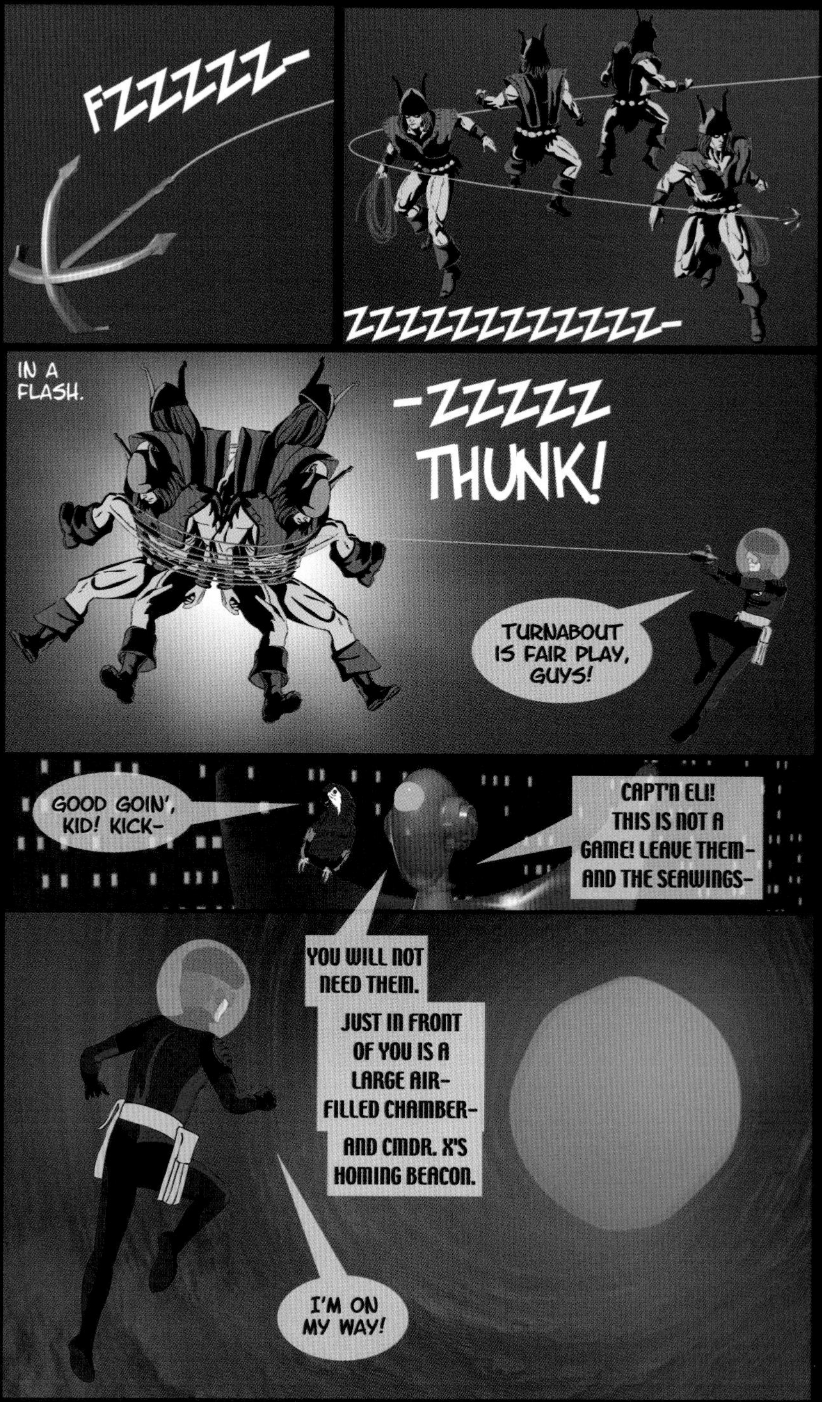
FZZZZZ-
ZZZZZZZZZZZZZZ-
IN A FLASH.
-ZZZZZ
THUNK!
TURNABOUT IS FAIR PLAY, GUYS!
GOOD GOIN', KID! KICK-
CAPT'N ELI! THIS IS NOT A GAME! LEAVE THEM- AND THE SEAWINGS-
YOU WILL NOT NEED THEM.
JUST IN FRONT OF YOU IS A LARGE AIR-FILLED CHAMBER-
AND CMDR. X'S HOMING BEACON.
I'M ON MY WAY!

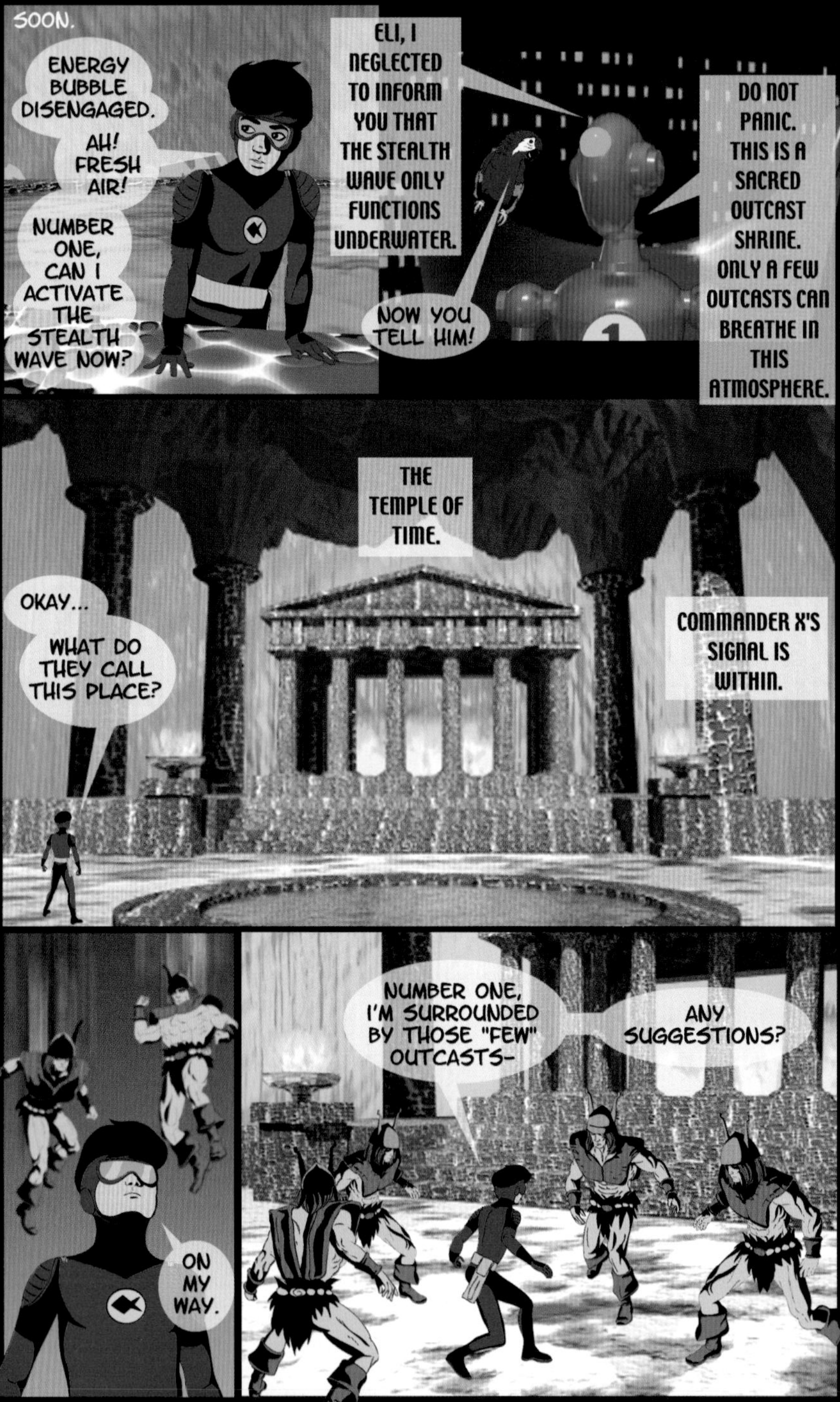
SOON.
ENERGY BUBBLE DISENGAGED.
AH! FRESH AIR!
NUMBER ONE, CAN I ACTIVATE THE STEALTH WAVE NOW?
ELI, I NEGLECTED TO INFORM YOU THAT THE STEALTH WAVE ONLY FUNCTIONS UNDERWATER.
NOW YOU TELL HIM!
DO NOT PANIC. THIS IS A SACRED OUTCAST SHRINE. ONLY A FEW OUTCASTS CAN BREATHE IN THIS ATMOSPHERE.
OKAY...
WHAT DO THEY CALL THIS PLACE?
THE TEMPLE OF TIME.
COMMANDER X'S SIGNAL IS WITHIN.
ON MY WAY.
NUMBER ONE, I'M SURROUNDED BY THOSE "FEW" OUTCASTS-
ANY SUGGESTIONS?

ACT 7 - RENDEZVOUS WITH DESTINY

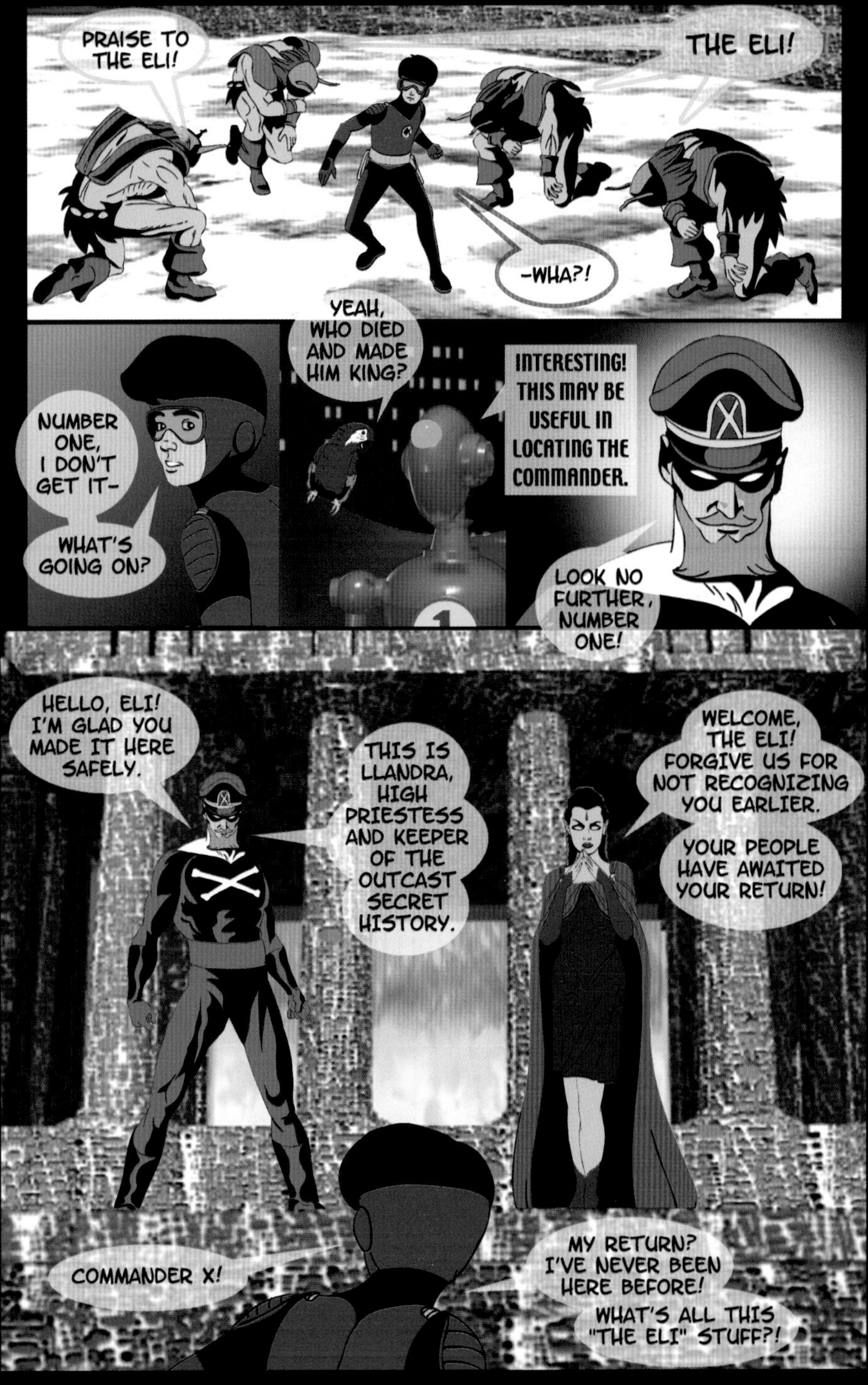
PRAISE TO THE ELI!
THE ELI!
-WHA?!
NUMBER ONE, I DON'T GET IT-
WHAT'S GOING ON?
YEAH, WHO DIED AND MADE HIM KING?
INTERESTING! THIS MAY BE USEFUL IN LOCATING THE COMMANDER.
LOOK NO FURTHER, NUMBER ONE!
HELLO, ELI! I'M GLAD YOU MADE IT HERE SAFELY.
THIS IS LLANDRA, HIGH PRIESTESS AND KEEPER OF THE OUTCAST SECRET HISTORY.
WELCOME, THE ELI! FORGIVE US FOR NOT RECOGNIZING YOU EARLIER.
YOUR PEOPLE HAVE AWAITED YOUR RETURN!
COMMANDER X!
MY RETURN? I'VE NEVER BEEN HERE BEFORE!
WHAT'S ALL THIS "THE ELI" STUFF?!

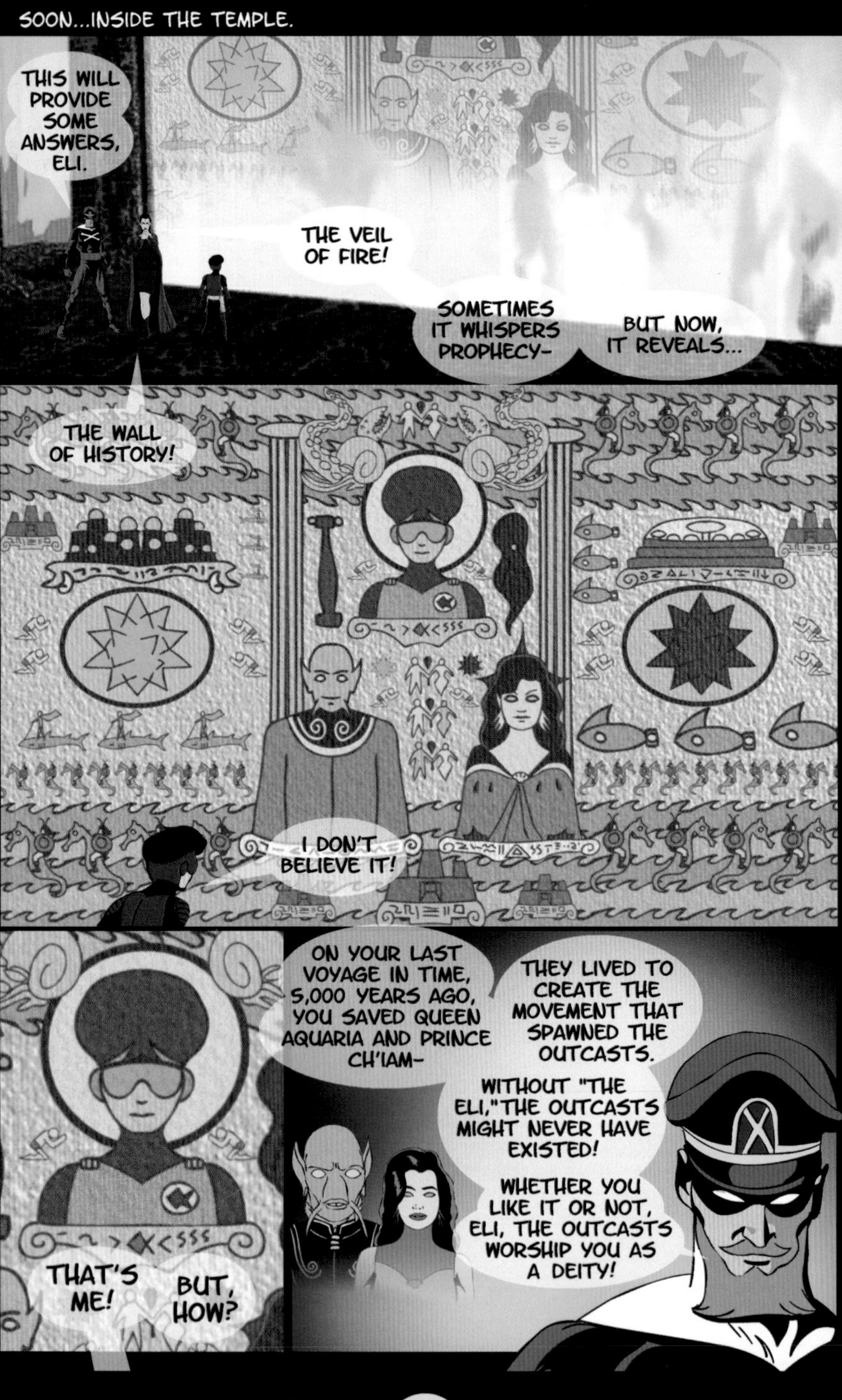
SOON...INSIDE THE TEMPLE.
THIS WILL PROVIDE SOME ANSWERS, ELI.
THE VEIL OF FIRE!
SOMETIMES IT WHISPERS PROPHECY-
BUT NOW, IT REVEALS...
THE WALL OF HISTORY!
I DON'T BELIEVE IT!
THAT'S ME!
BUT, HOW?
ON YOUR LAST VOYAGE IN TIME, 5,000 YEARS AGO, YOU SAVED QUEEN AQUARIA AND PRINCE CH'IAM-
THEY LIVED TO CREATE THE MOVEMENT THAT SPAWNED THE OUTCASTS.
WITHOUT "THE ELI," THE OUTCASTS MIGHT NEVER HAVE EXISTED!
WHETHER YOU LIKE IT OR NOT, ELI, THE OUTCASTS WORSHIP YOU AS A DEITY!

ACT 7 - RENDEZVOUS WITH DESTINY

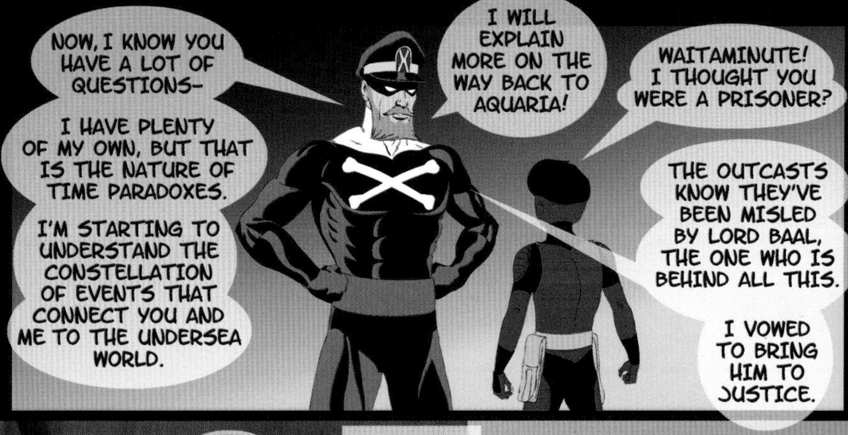
NOW, I KNOW YOU HAVE A LOT OF QUESTIONS–
I HAVE PLENTY OF MY OWN, BUT THAT IS THE NATURE OF TIME PARADOXES.
I'M STARTING TO UNDERSTAND THE CONSTELLATION OF EVENTS THAT CONNECT YOU AND ME TO THE UNDERSEA WORLD.
I WILL EXPLAIN MORE ON THE WAY BACK TO AQUARIA!
WAITAMINUTE! I THOUGHT YOU WERE A PRISONER?
THE OUTCASTS KNOW THEY'VE BEEN MISLED BY LORD BAAL, THE ONE WHO IS BEHIND ALL THIS.
I VOWED TO BRING HIM TO JUSTICE.

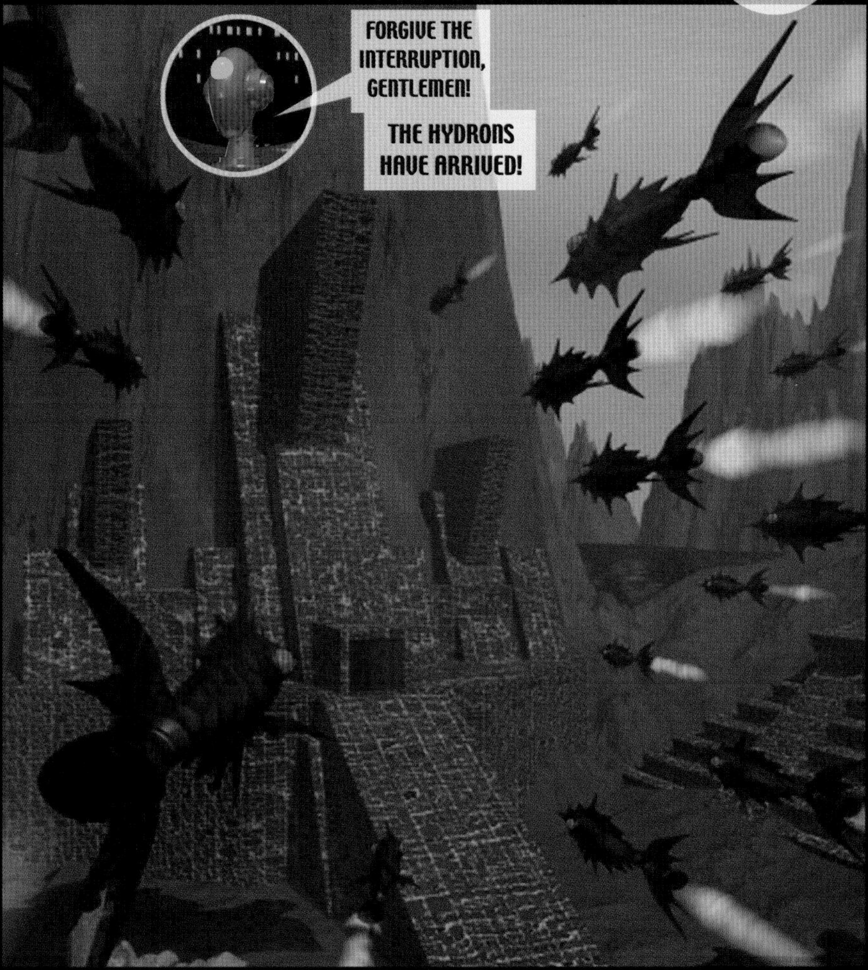
FORGIVE THE INTERRUPTION, GENTLEMEN!
THE HYDRONS HAVE ARRIVED!

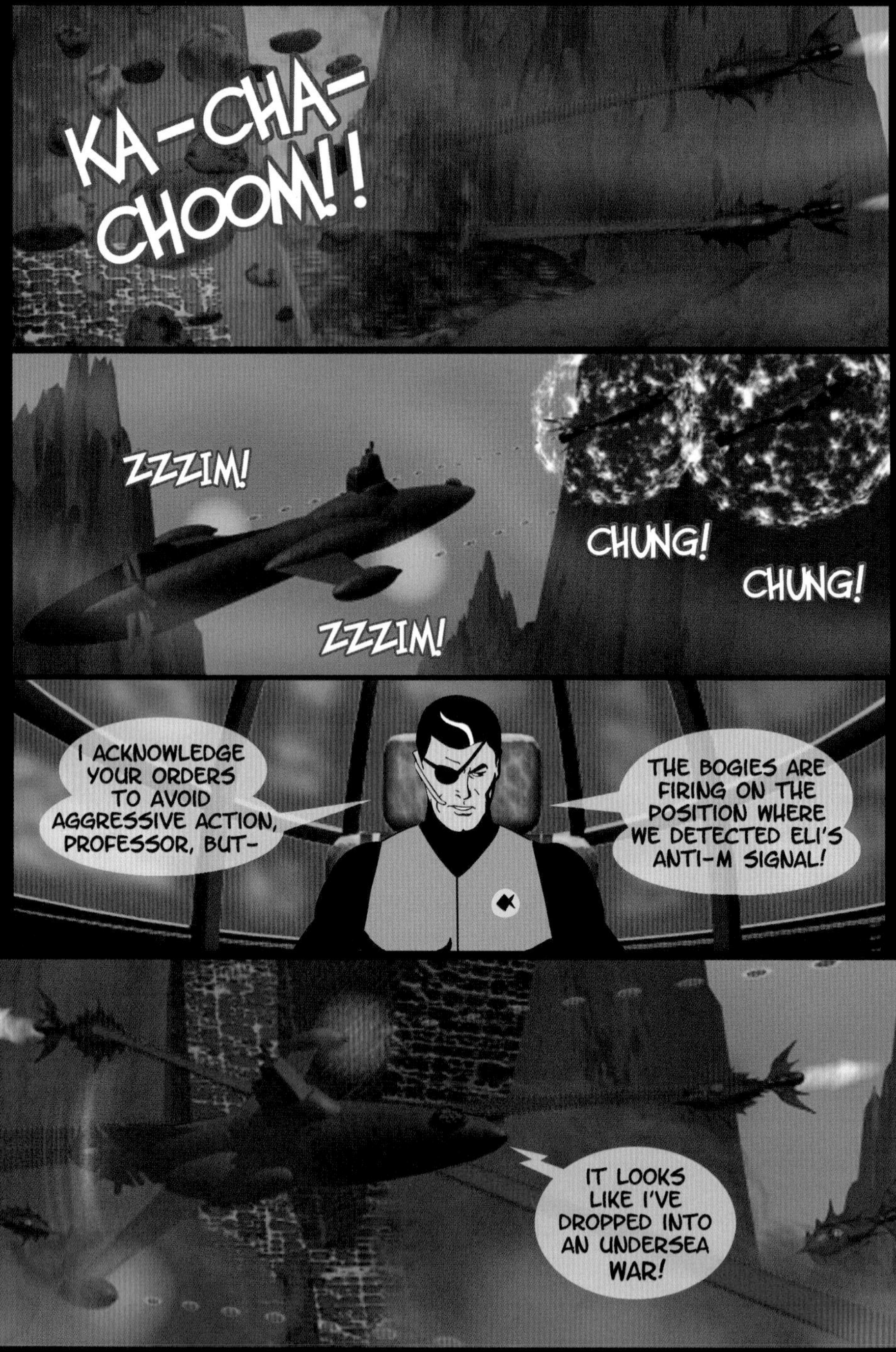
KA-CHA-CHOOM!!
ZZZIM!
CHUNG!
CHUNG!
ZZZIM!
I ACKNOWLEDGE YOUR ORDERS TO AVOID AGGRESSIVE ACTION, PROFESSOR, BUT-
THE BOGIES ARE FIRING ON THE POSITION WHERE WE DETECTED ELI'S ANTI-M SIGNAL!
IT LOOKS LIKE I'VE DROPPED INTO AN UNDERSEA WAR!

END OF ACT 7

ACT 8 - THE GATHERING STORM

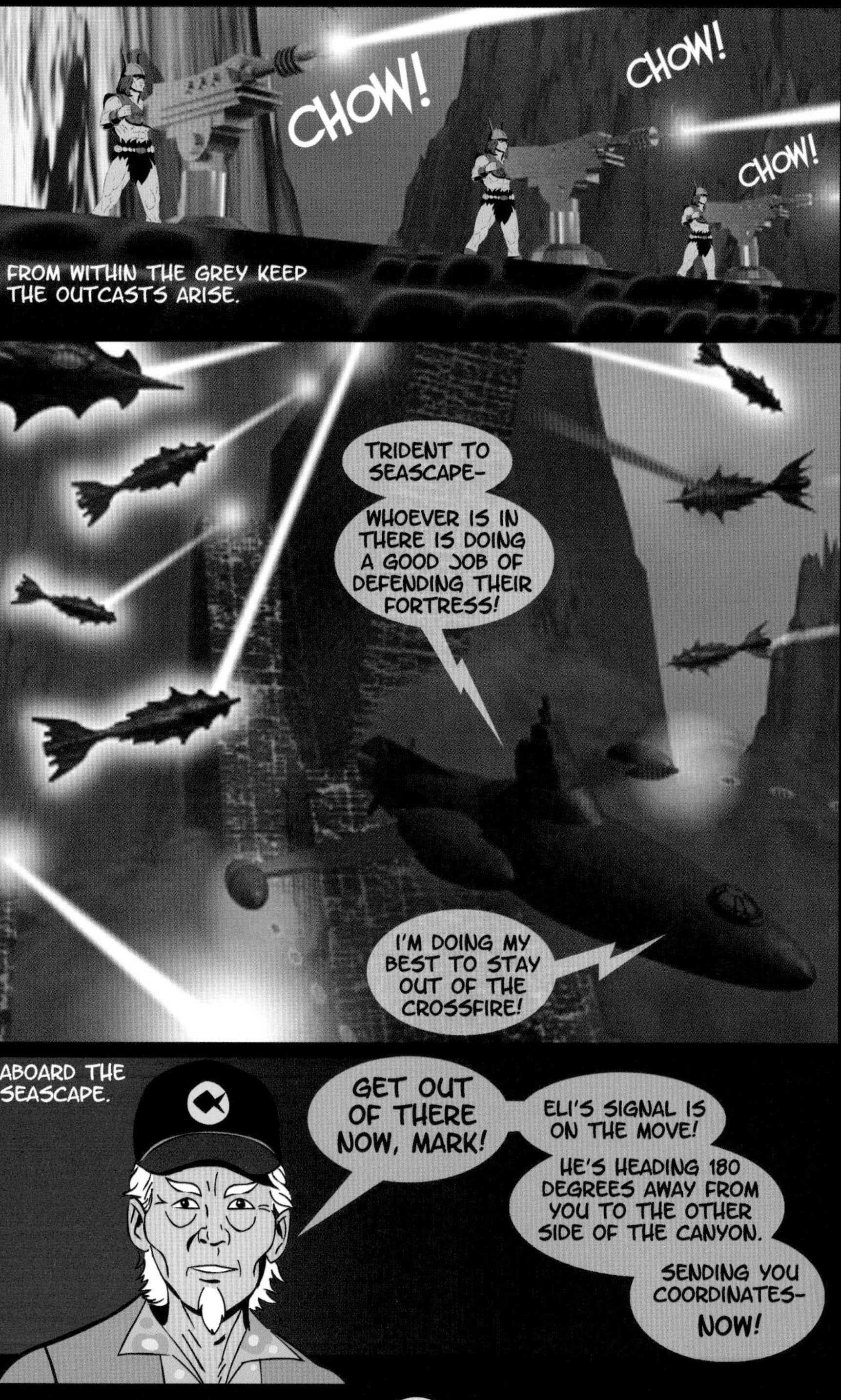
CHOW!
CHOW!
CHOW!
FROM WITHIN THE GREY KEEP THE OUTCASTS ARISE.
TRIDENT TO SEASCAPE-
WHOEVER IS IN THERE IS DOING A GOOD JOB OF DEFENDING THEIR FORTRESS!
I'M DOING MY BEST TO STAY OUT OF THE CROSSFIRE!
ABOARD THE SEASCAPE.
GET OUT OF THERE NOW, MARK!
ELI'S SIGNAL IS ON THE MOVE!
HE'S HEADING 180 DEGREES AWAY FROM YOU TO THE OTHER SIDE OF THE CANYON.
SENDING YOU COORDINATES- NOW!

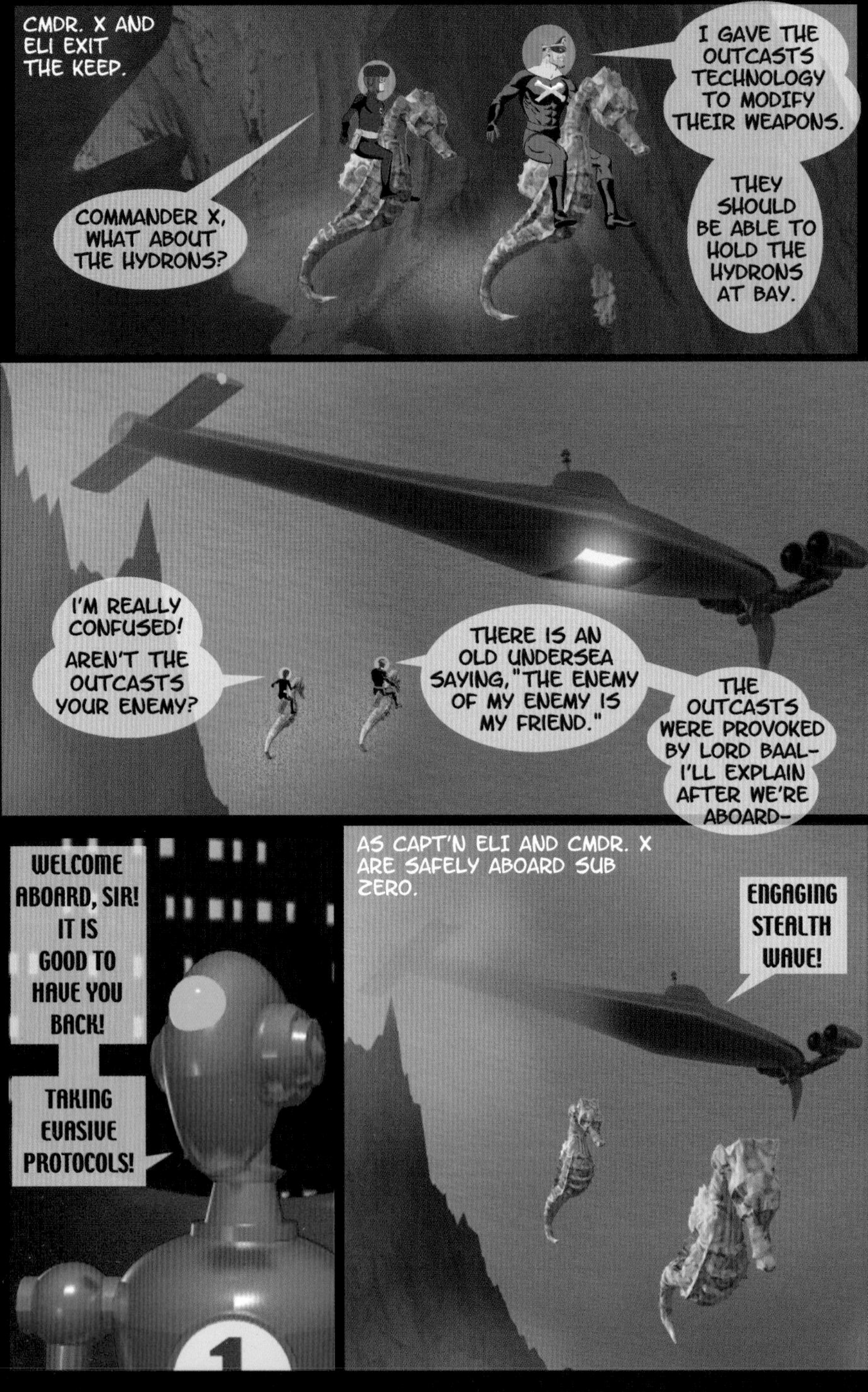
CMDR. X AND ELI EXIT THE KEEP.
COMMANDER X, WHAT ABOUT THE HYDRONS?
I GAVE THE OUTCASTS TECHNOLOGY TO MODIFY THEIR WEAPONS.
THEY SHOULD BE ABLE TO HOLD THE HYDRONS AT BAY.
I'M REALLY CONFUSED! AREN'T THE OUTCASTS YOUR ENEMY?
THERE IS AN OLD UNDERSEA SAYING, "THE ENEMY OF MY ENEMY IS MY FRIEND."
THE OUTCASTS WERE PROVOKED BY LORD BAAL- I'LL EXPLAIN AFTER WE'RE ABOARD-
WELCOME ABOARD, SIR! IT IS GOOD TO HAVE YOU BACK!
TAKING EVASIVE PROTOCOLS!
AS CAPT'N ELI AND CMDR. X ARE SAFELY ABOARD SUB ZERO.
ENGAGING STEALTH WAVE!

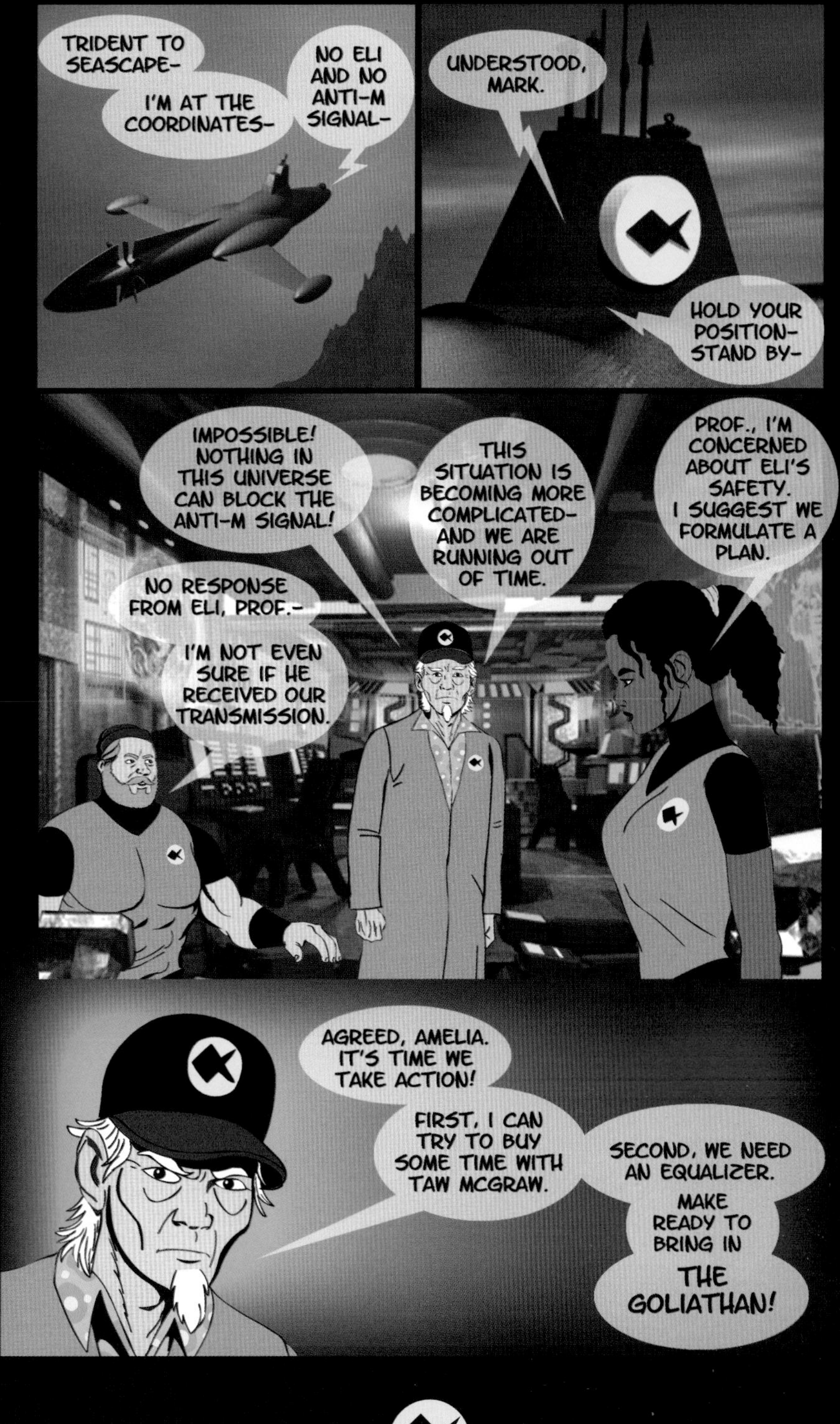
TRIDENT TO SEASCAPE-
I'M AT THE COORDINATES-
NO ELI AND NO ANTI-M SIGNAL-
UNDERSTOOD, MARK.
HOLD YOUR POSITION- STAND BY-
IMPOSSIBLE! NOTHING IN THIS UNIVERSE CAN BLOCK THE ANTI-M SIGNAL!
THIS SITUATION IS BECOMING MORE COMPLICATED- AND WE ARE RUNNING OUT OF TIME.
PROF., I'M CONCERNED ABOUT ELI'S SAFETY. I SUGGEST WE FORMULATE A PLAN.
NO RESPONSE FROM ELI, PROF.-
I'M NOT EVEN SURE IF HE RECEIVED OUR TRANSMISSION.
AGREED, AMELIA. IT'S TIME WE TAKE ACTION!
FIRST, I CAN TRY TO BUY SOME TIME WITH TAW MCGRAW.
SECOND, WE NEED AN EQUALIZER.
MAKE READY TO BRING IN
THE GOLIATHAN!

SOON, ELI IS REUNITED WITH ROGER AND BARNEY.

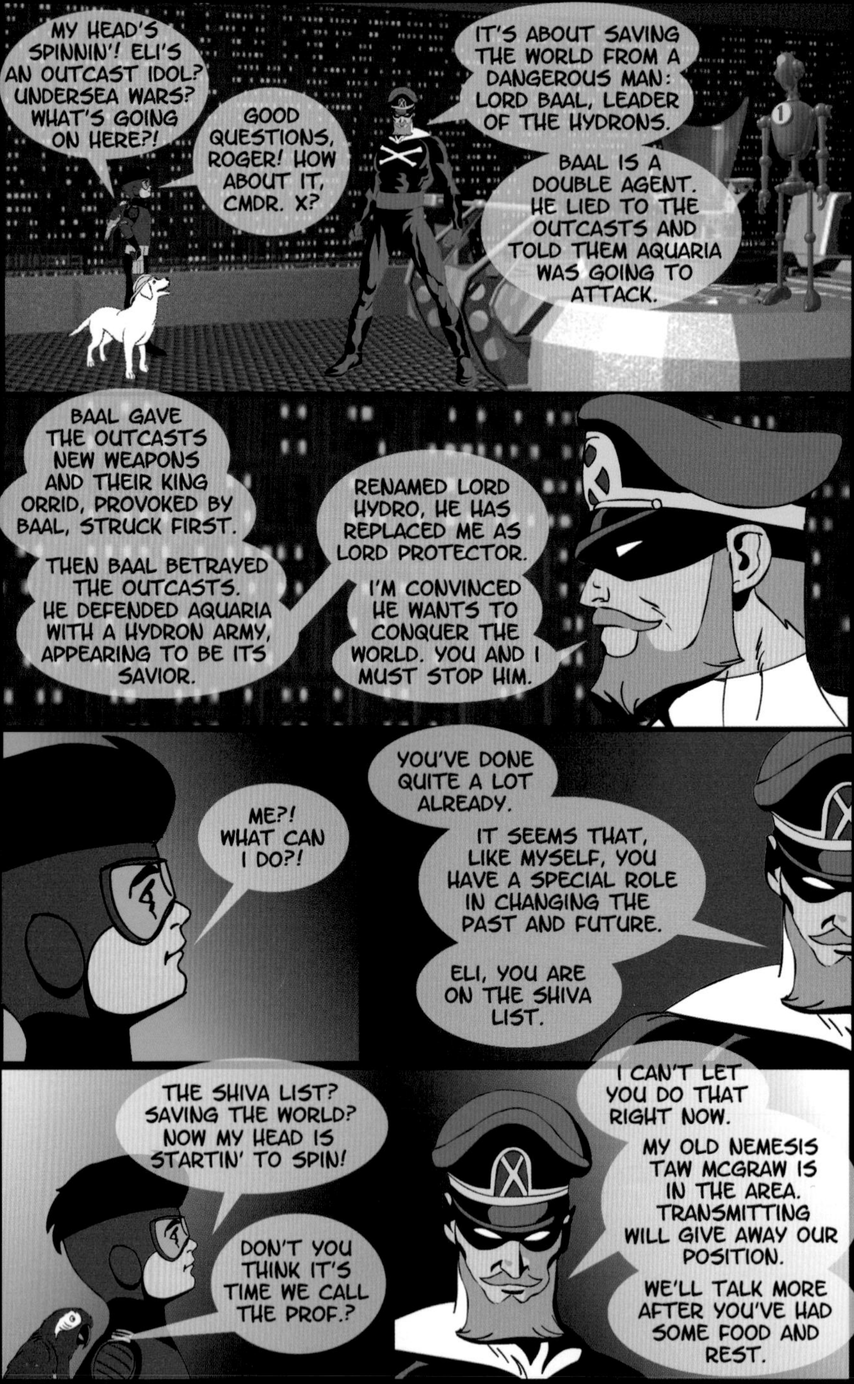
MY HEAD'S SPINNIN'! ELI'S AN OUTCAST IDOL? UNDERSEA WARS? WHAT'S GOING ON HERE?!
GOOD QUESTIONS, ROGER! HOW ABOUT IT, CMDR. X?
IT'S ABOUT SAVING THE WORLD FROM A DANGEROUS MAN: LORD BAAL, LEADER OF THE HYDRONS.
BAAL IS A DOUBLE AGENT. HE LIED TO THE OUTCASTS AND TOLD THEM AQUARIA WAS GOING TO ATTACK.
BAAL GAVE THE OUTCASTS NEW WEAPONS AND THEIR KING ORRID, PROVOKED BY BAAL, STRUCK FIRST.
THEN BAAL BETRAYED THE OUTCASTS. HE DEFENDED AQUARIA WITH A HYDRON ARMY, APPEARING TO BE ITS SAVIOR.
RENAMED LORD HYDRO, HE HAS REPLACED ME AS LORD PROTECTOR.
I'M CONVINCED HE WANTS TO CONQUER THE WORLD. YOU AND I MUST STOP HIM.
ME?! WHAT CAN I DO?!
YOU'VE DONE QUITE A LOT ALREADY.
IT SEEMS THAT, LIKE MYSELF, YOU HAVE A SPECIAL ROLE IN CHANGING THE PAST AND FUTURE.
ELI, YOU ARE ON THE SHIVA LIST.
THE SHIVA LIST? SAVING THE WORLD? NOW MY HEAD IS STARTIN' TO SPIN!
DON'T YOU THINK IT'S TIME WE CALL THE PROF.?
I CAN'T LET YOU DO THAT RIGHT NOW.
MY OLD NEMESIS TAW MCGRAW IS IN THE AREA. TRANSMITTING WILL GIVE AWAY OUR POSITION.
WE'LL TALK MORE AFTER YOU'VE HAD SOME FOOD AND REST.

ACT 8 - THE GATHERING STORM

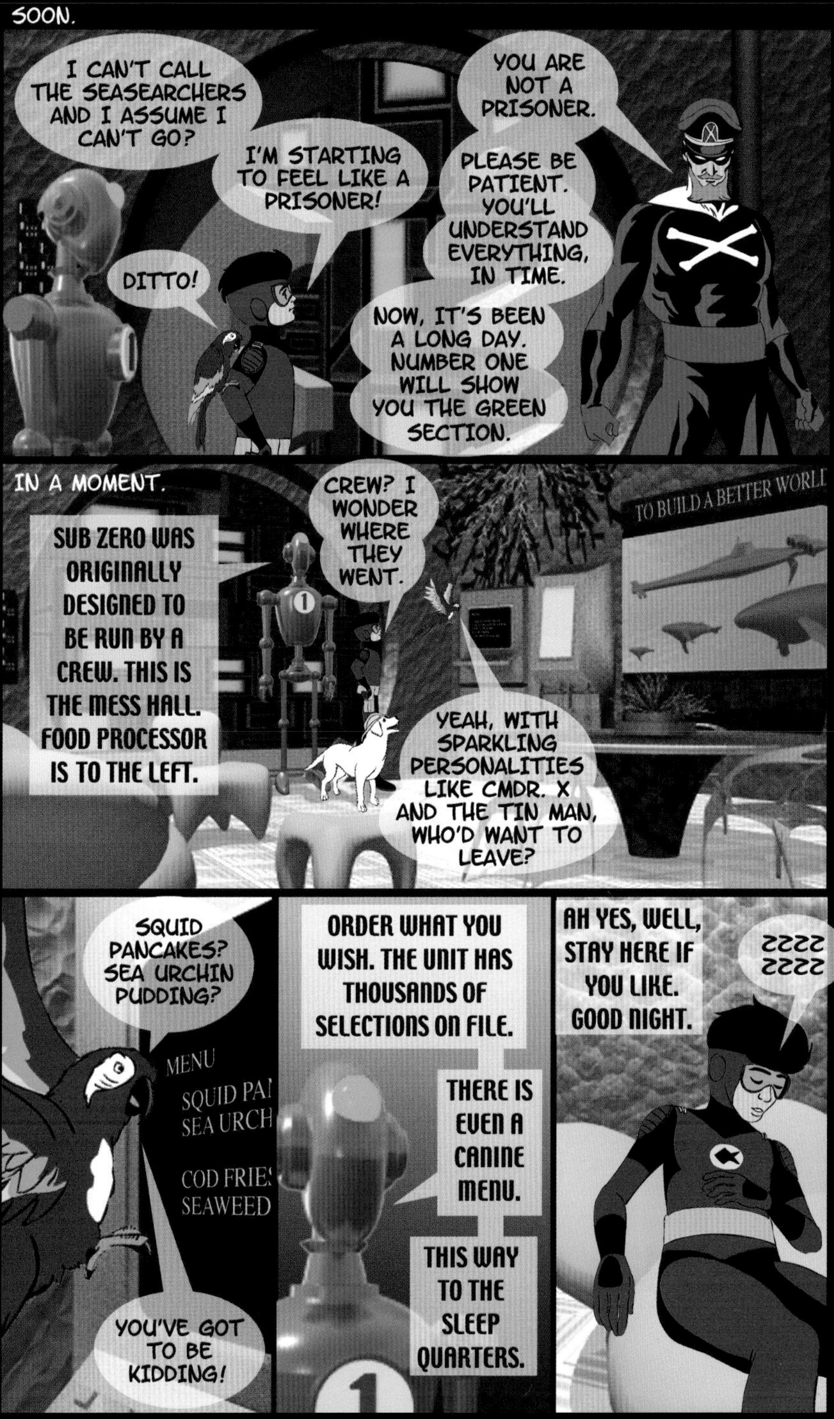
SOON.
I CAN'T CALL THE SEASEARCHERS AND I ASSUME I CAN'T GO?
I'M STARTING TO FEEL LIKE A PRISONER!
DITTO!
YOU ARE NOT A PRISONER.
PLEASE BE PATIENT. YOU'LL UNDERSTAND EVERYTHING, IN TIME.
NOW, IT'S BEEN A LONG DAY. NUMBER ONE WILL SHOW YOU THE GREEN SECTION.
IN A MOMENT.
SUB ZERO WAS ORIGINALLY DESIGNED TO BE RUN BY A CREW. THIS IS THE MESS HALL. FOOD PROCESSOR IS TO THE LEFT.
CREW? I WONDER WHERE THEY WENT.
YEAH, WITH SPARKLING PERSONALITIES LIKE CMDR. X AND THE TIN MAN, WHO'D WANT TO LEAVE?
TO BUILD A BETTER WORL
SQUID PANCAKES? SEA URCHIN PUDDING?
MENU
SQUID PA
SEA URCH
COD FRIE
SEAWEED
YOU'VE GOT TO BE KIDDING!
ORDER WHAT YOU WISH. THE UNIT HAS THOUSANDS OF SELECTIONS ON FILE.
THERE IS EVEN A CANINE MENU.
THIS WAY TO THE SLEEP QUARTERS.
AH YES, WELL, STAY HERE IF YOU LIKE. GOOD NIGHT.
ZZZZ ZZZZ

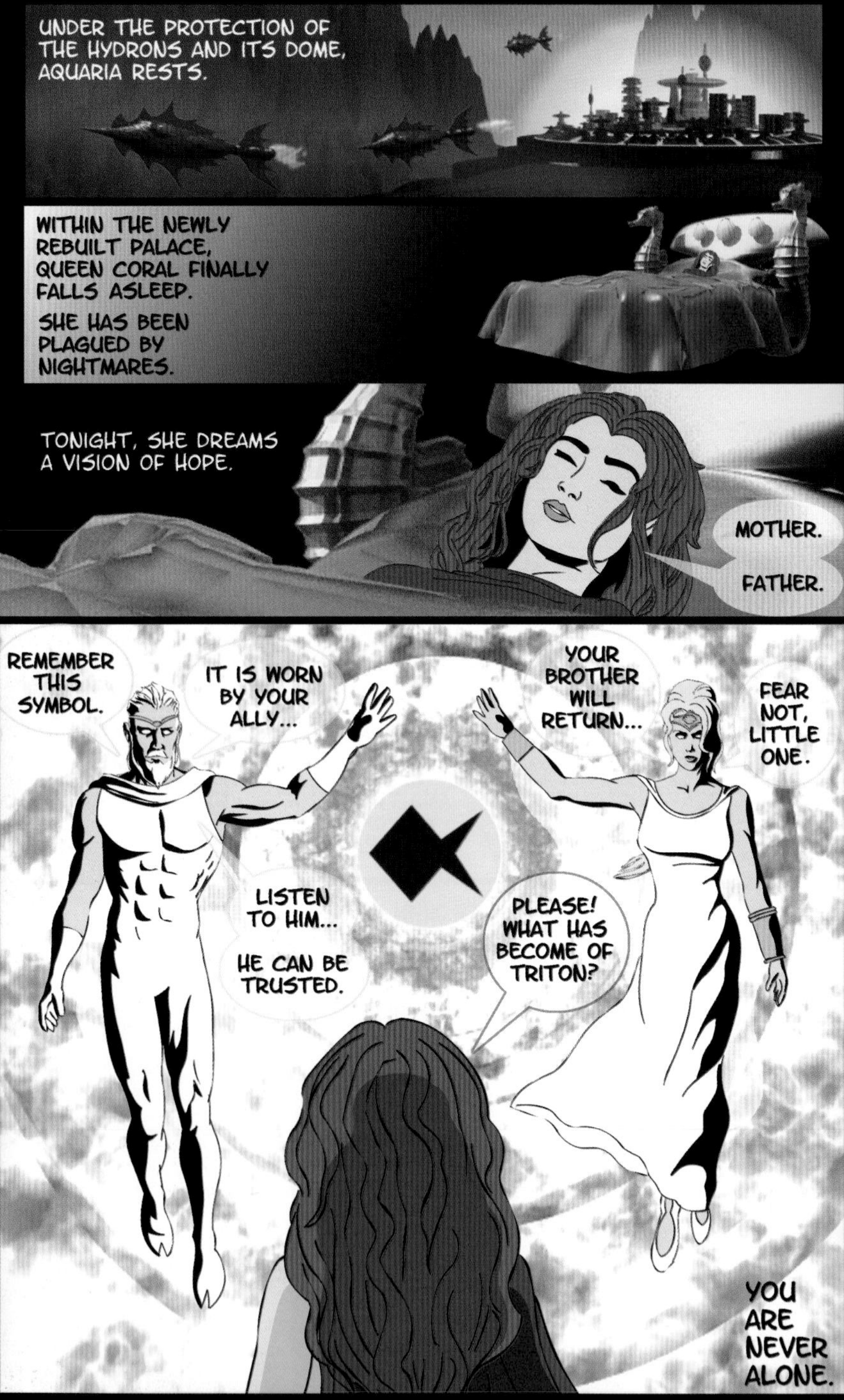
UNDER THE PROTECTION OF THE HYDRONS AND ITS DOME, AQUARIA RESTS.
WITHIN THE NEWLY REBUILT PALACE, QUEEN CORAL FINALLY FALLS ASLEEP.
SHE HAS BEEN PLAGUED BY NIGHTMARES.
TONIGHT, SHE DREAMS A VISION OF HOPE.
MOTHER.
FATHER.
REMEMBER THIS SYMBOL.
IT IS WORN BY YOUR ALLY...
YOUR BROTHER WILL RETURN...
FEAR NOT, LITTLE ONE.
LISTEN TO HIM...
HE CAN BE TRUSTED.
PLEASE! WHAT HAS BECOME OF TRITON?
YOU ARE NEVER ALONE.

ACT 8 - THE GATHERING STORM

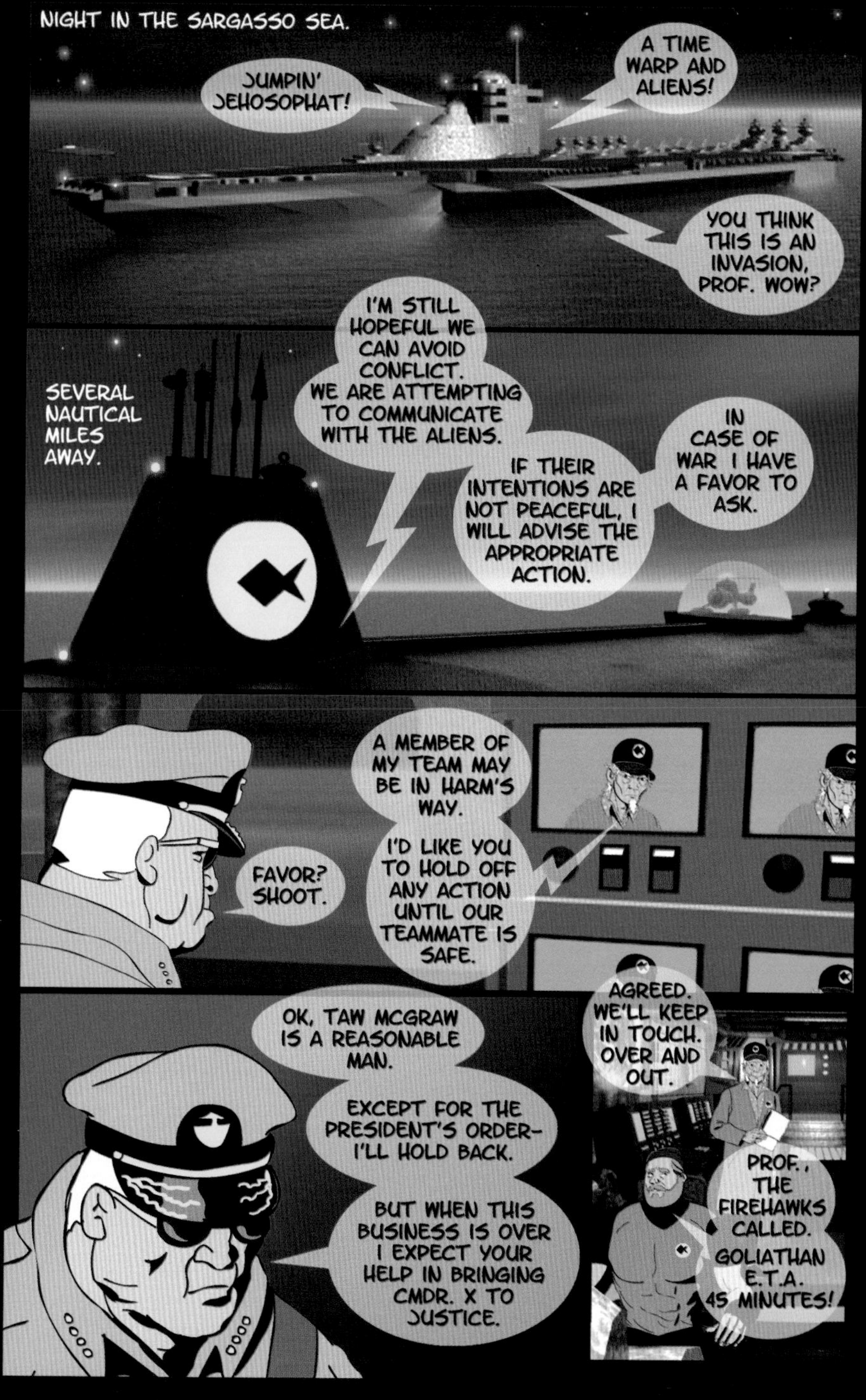
NIGHT IN THE SARGASSO SEA.
JUMPIN' JEHOSOPHAT!
A TIME WARP AND ALIENS!
YOU THINK THIS IS AN INVASION, PROF. WOW?
SEVERAL NAUTICAL MILES AWAY.
I'M STILL HOPEFUL WE CAN AVOID CONFLICT. WE ARE ATTEMPTING TO COMMUNICATE WITH THE ALIENS.
IF THEIR INTENTIONS ARE NOT PEACEFUL, I WILL ADVISE THE APPROPRIATE ACTION.
IN CASE OF WAR I HAVE A FAVOR TO ASK.
FAVOR? SHOOT.
A MEMBER OF MY TEAM MAY BE IN HARM'S WAY.
I'D LIKE YOU TO HOLD OFF ANY ACTION UNTIL OUR TEAMMATE IS SAFE.
OK, TAW MCGRAW IS A REASONABLE MAN.
EXCEPT FOR THE PRESIDENT'S ORDER– I'LL HOLD BACK.
BUT WHEN THIS BUSINESS IS OVER I EXPECT YOUR HELP IN BRINGING CMDR. X TO JUSTICE.
AGREED. WE'LL KEEP IN TOUCH. OVER AND OUT.
PROF., THE FIREHAWKS CALLED.
GOLIATHAN E.T.A. 45 MINUTES!

AIR ADMIRAL MCGRAW PREPARES FOR WAR.

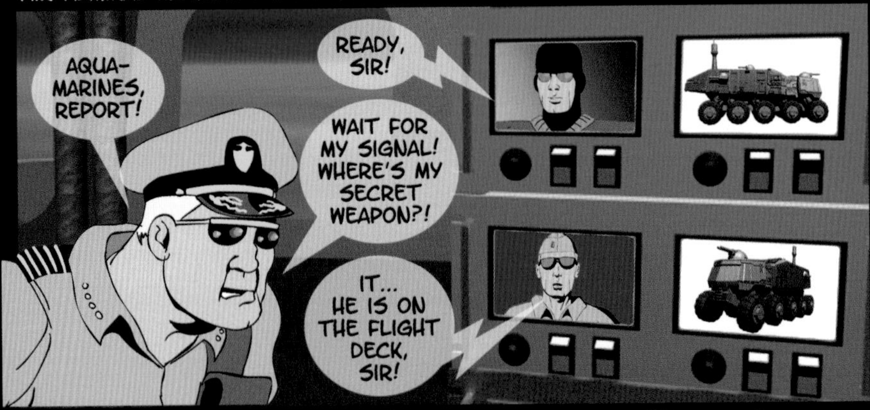
AQUA-MARINES, REPORT!
READY, SIR!
WAIT FOR MY SIGNAL! WHERE'S MY SECRET WEAPON?!
IT... HE IS ON THE FLIGHT DECK, SIR!

THE FLIGHT DECK.

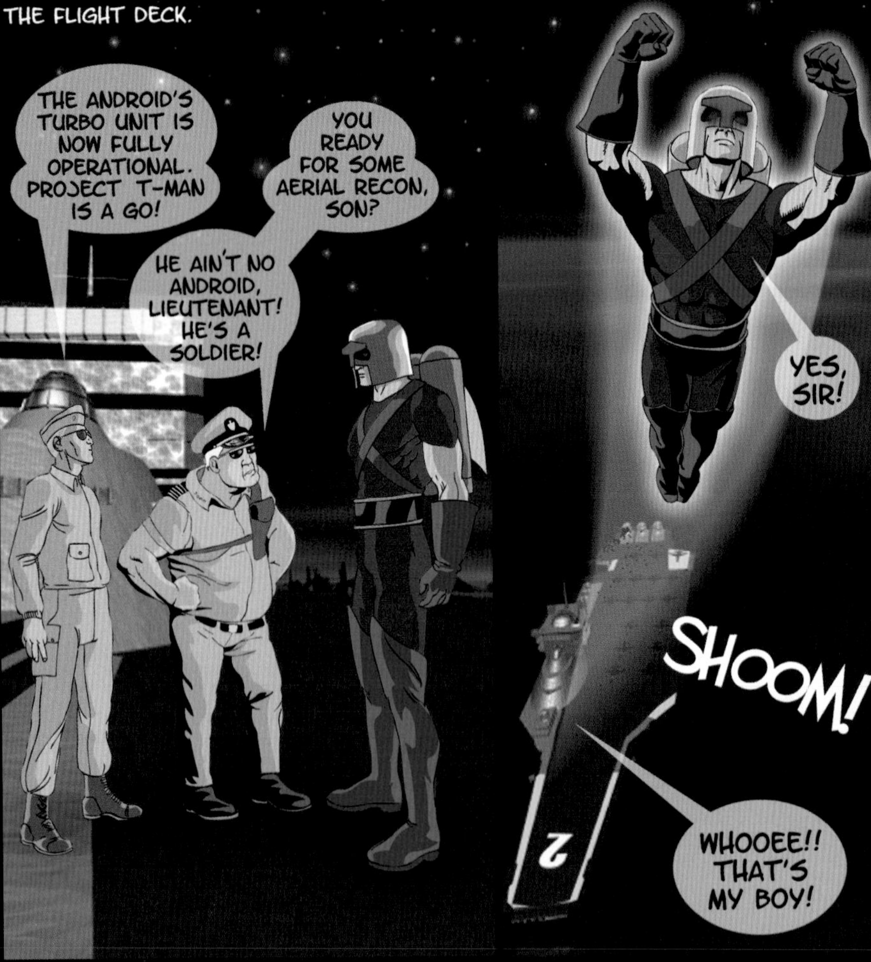
THE ANDROID'S TURBO UNIT IS NOW FULLY OPERATIONAL. PROJECT T-MAN IS A GO!
YOU READY FOR SOME AERIAL RECON, SON?
HE AIN'T NO ANDROID, LIEUTENANT! HE'S A SOLDIER!
YES, SIR!
SHOOM!
WHOOEE!! THAT'S MY BOY!

ACT 8 - THE GATHERING STORM

SOMEWHERE IN THE SARGASSO SEA.

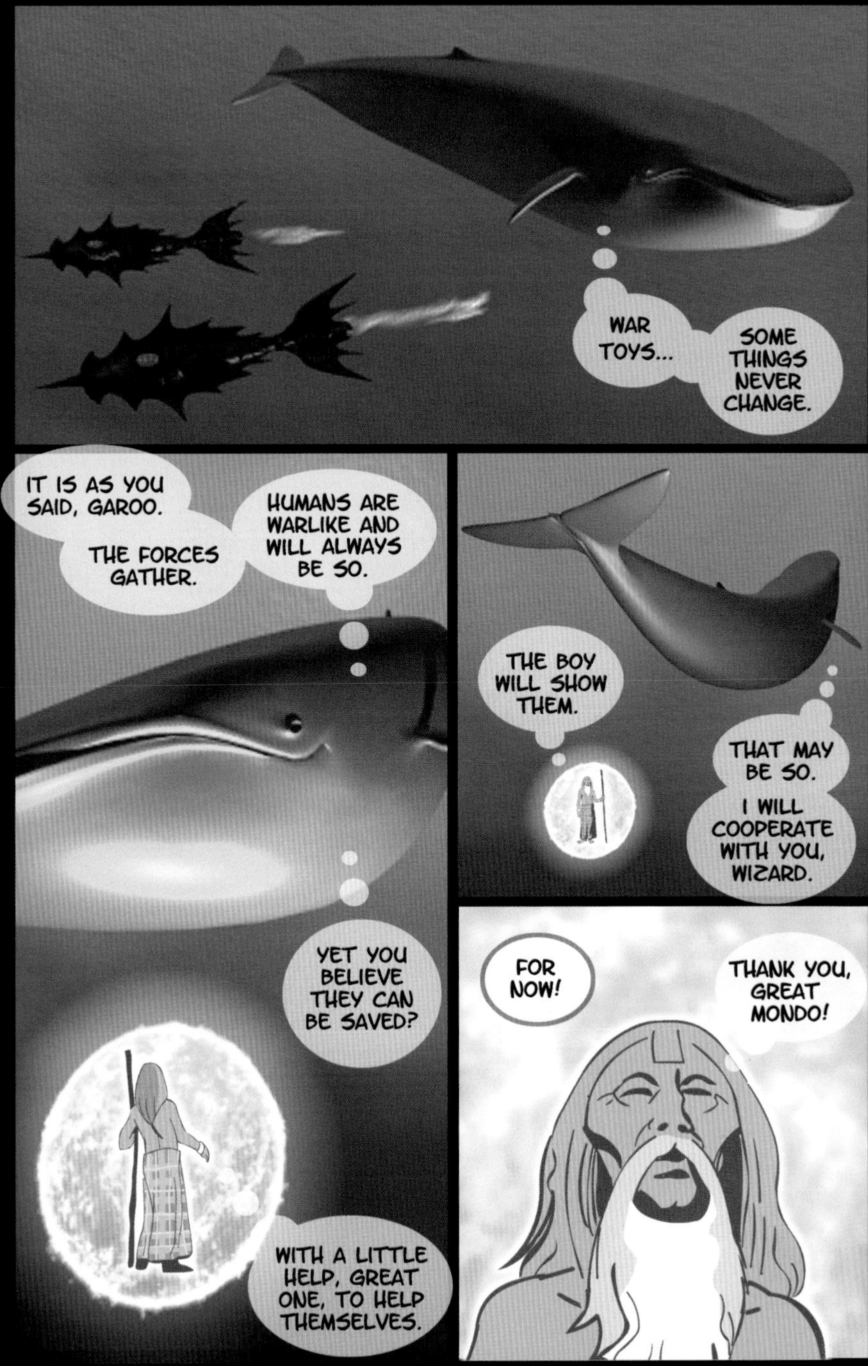

WAR TOYS...
SOME THINGS NEVER CHANGE.
IT IS AS YOU SAID, GAROO.
THE FORCES GATHER.
HUMANS ARE WARLIKE AND WILL ALWAYS BE SO.
YET YOU BELIEVE THEY CAN BE SAVED?
WITH A LITTLE HELP, GREAT ONE, TO HELP THEMSELVES.
THE BOY WILL SHOW THEM.
THAT MAY BE SO.
I WILL COOPERATE WITH YOU, WIZARD.
FOR NOW!
THANK YOU, GREAT MONDO!

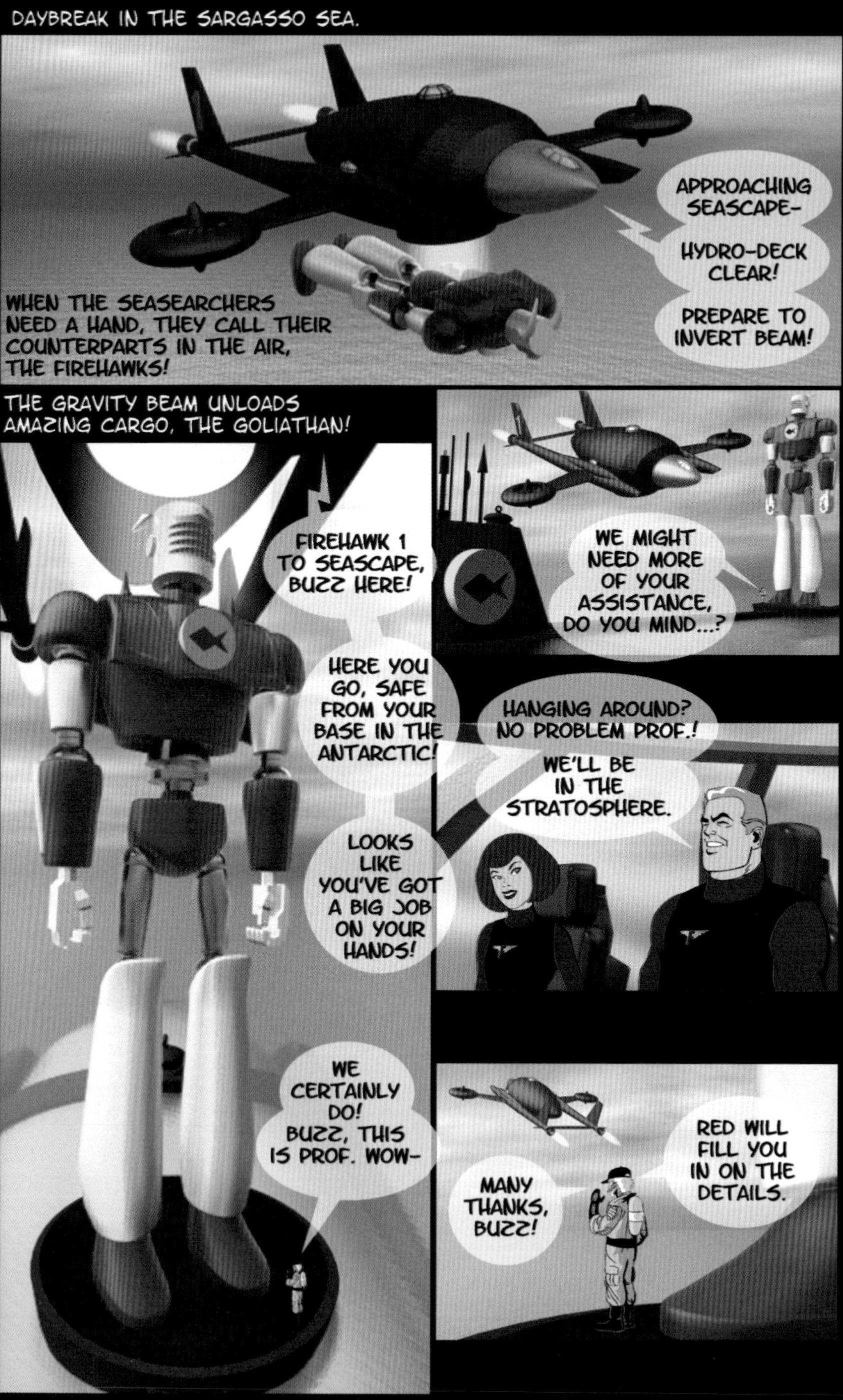
DAYBREAK IN THE SARGASSO SEA.
APPROACHING SEASCAPE-
HYDRO-DECK CLEAR!
PREPARE TO INVERT BEAM!
WHEN THE SEASEARCHERS NEED A HAND, THEY CALL THEIR COUNTERPARTS IN THE AIR, THE FIREHAWKS!
THE GRAVITY BEAM UNLOADS AMAZING CARGO, THE GOLIATHAN!
FIREHAWK 1 TO SEASCAPE, BUZZ HERE!
HERE YOU GO, SAFE FROM YOUR BASE IN THE ANTARCTIC!
LOOKS LIKE YOU'VE GOT A BIG JOB ON YOUR HANDS!
WE CERTAINLY DO! BUZZ, THIS IS PROF. WOW-
WE MIGHT NEED MORE OF YOUR ASSISTANCE, DO YOU MIND...?
HANGING AROUND? NO PROBLEM PROF.!
WE'LL BE IN THE STRATOSPHERE.
RED WILL FILL YOU IN ON THE DETAILS.
MANY THANKS, BUZZ!

ACT 8 - THE GATHERING STORM

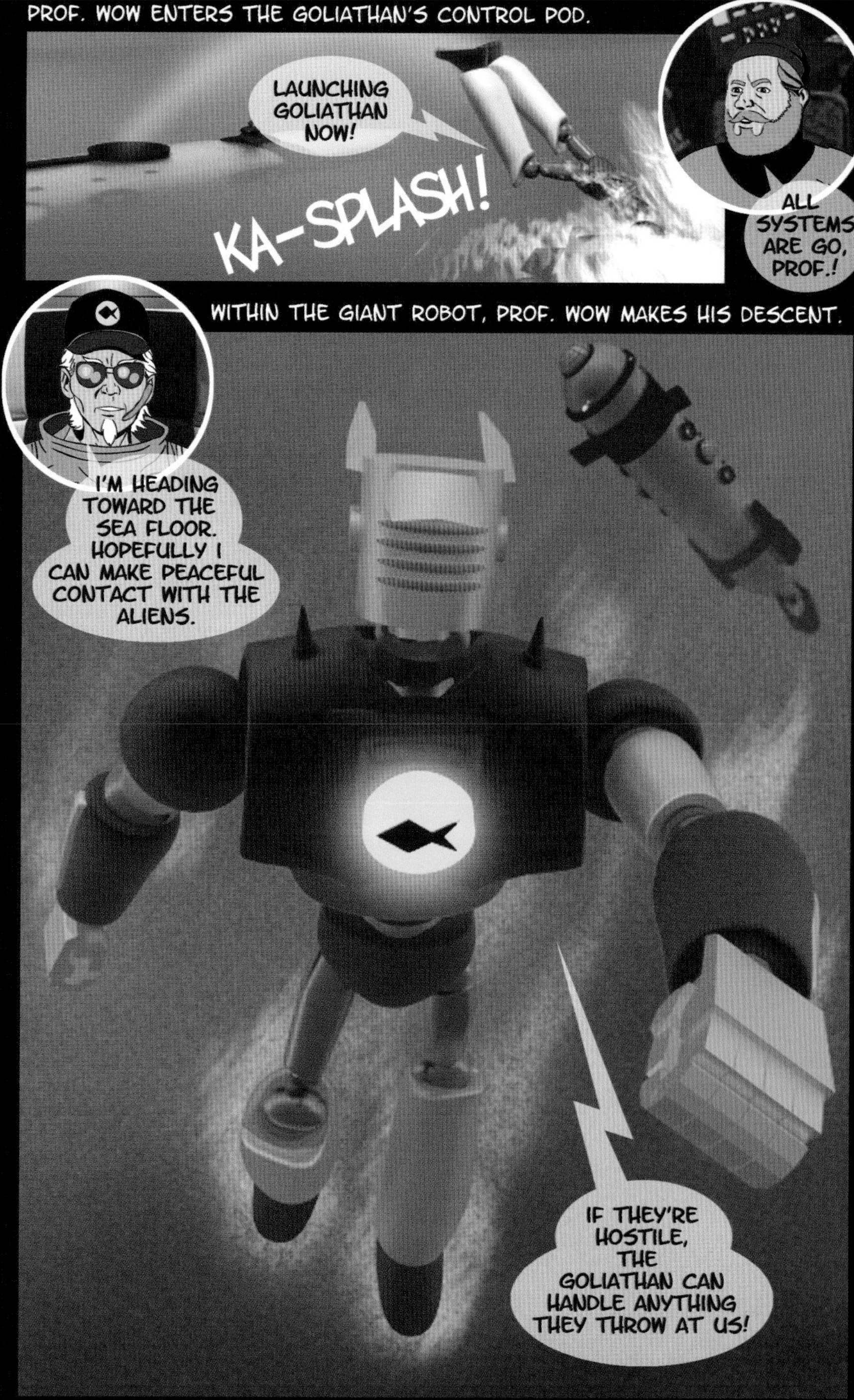
PROF. WOW ENTERS THE GOLIATHAN'S CONTROL POD.
LAUNCHING GOLIATHAN NOW!
KA-SPLASH!
ALL SYSTEMS ARE GO, PROF.!
WITHIN THE GIANT ROBOT, PROF. WOW MAKES HIS DESCENT.
I'M HEADING TOWARD THE SEA FLOOR. HOPEFULLY I CAN MAKE PEACEFUL CONTACT WITH THE ALIENS.
IF THEY'RE HOSTILE, THE GOLIATHAN CAN HANDLE ANYTHING THEY THROW AT US!

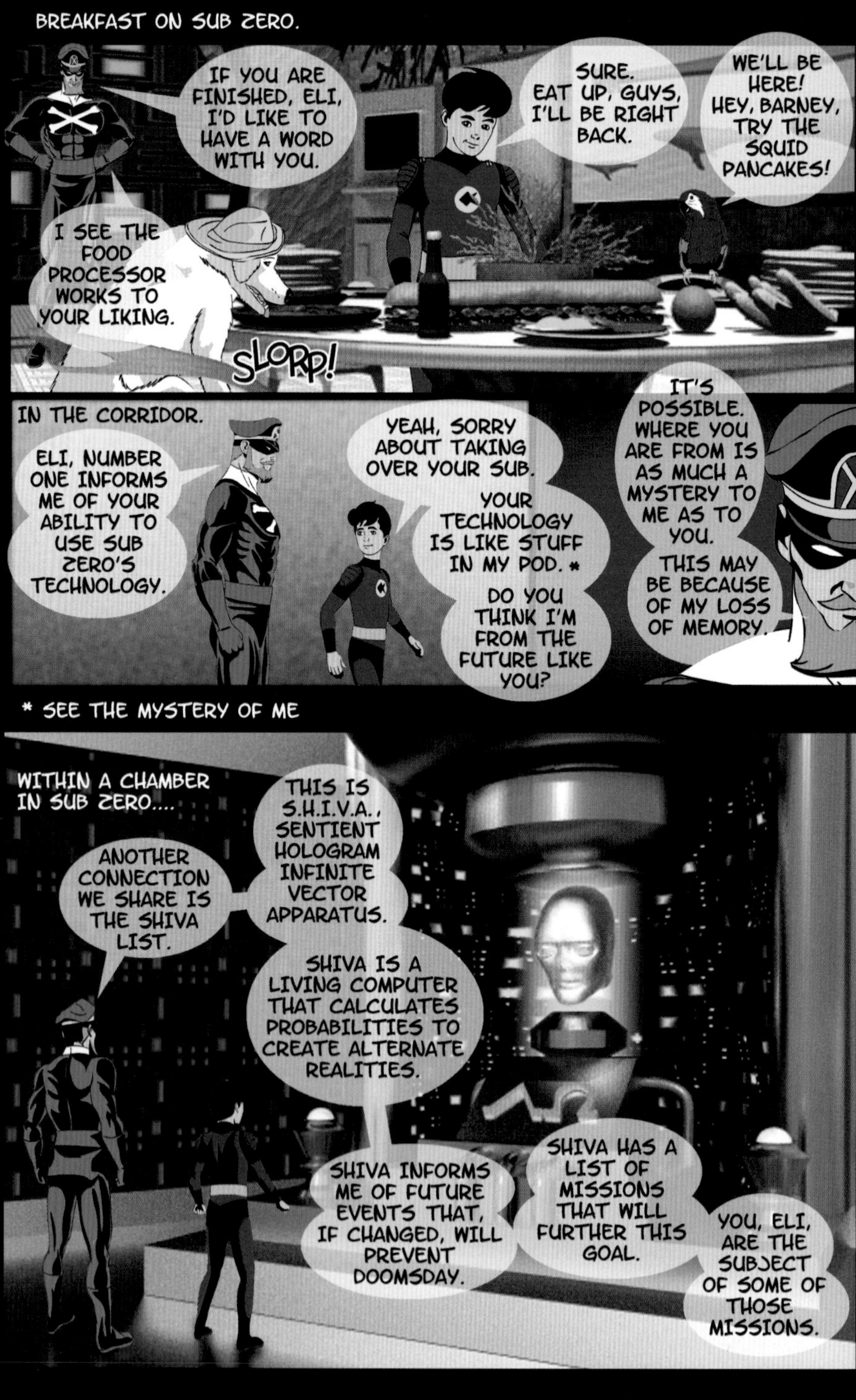
BREAKFAST ON SUB ZERO.
IF YOU ARE FINISHED, ELI, I'D LIKE TO HAVE A WORD WITH YOU.
I SEE THE FOOD PROCESSOR WORKS TO YOUR LIKING.
SURE. EAT UP, GUYS, I'LL BE RIGHT BACK.
WE'LL BE HERE! HEY, BARNEY, TRY THE SQUID PANCAKES!
SLORP!
IN THE CORRIDOR.
ELI, NUMBER ONE INFORMS ME OF YOUR ABILITY TO USE SUB ZERO'S TECHNOLOGY.
YEAH, SORRY ABOUT TAKING OVER YOUR SUB.
YOUR TECHNOLOGY IS LIKE STUFF IN MY POD. *
DO YOU THINK I'M FROM THE FUTURE LIKE YOU?
IT'S POSSIBLE. WHERE YOU ARE FROM IS AS MUCH A MYSTERY TO ME AS TO YOU.
THIS MAY BE BECAUSE OF MY LOSS OF MEMORY.
* SEE THE MYSTERY OF ME
WITHIN A CHAMBER IN SUB ZERO....
ANOTHER CONNECTION WE SHARE IS THE SHIVA LIST.
THIS IS S.H.I.V.A., SENTIENT HOLOGRAM INFINITE VECTOR APPARATUS.
SHIVA IS A LIVING COMPUTER THAT CALCULATES PROBABILITIES TO CREATE ALTERNATE REALITIES.
SHIVA INFORMS ME OF FUTURE EVENTS THAT, IF CHANGED, WILL PREVENT DOOMSDAY.
SHIVA HAS A LIST OF MISSIONS THAT WILL FURTHER THIS GOAL.
YOU, ELI, ARE THE SUBJECT OF SOME OF THOSE MISSIONS.

ACT 8 - THE GATHERING STORM

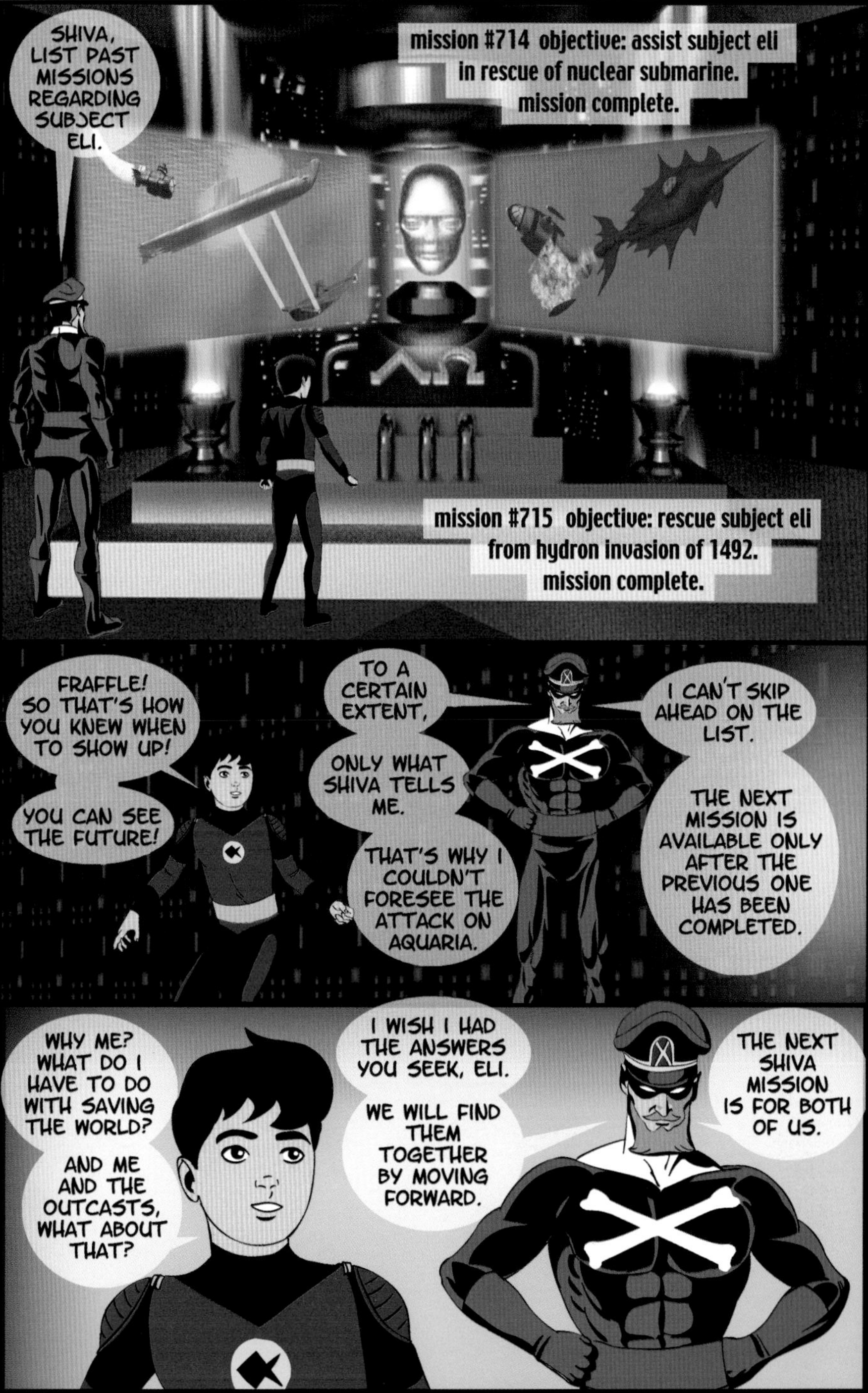

SHIVA, LIST PAST MISSIONS REGARDING SUBJECT ELI.
mission #714 objective: assist subject eli in rescue of nuclear submarine. mission complete.
mission #715 objective: rescue subject eli from hydron invasion of 1492. mission complete.
FRAFFLE! SO THAT'S HOW YOU KNEW WHEN TO SHOW UP!
YOU CAN SEE THE FUTURE!
TO A CERTAIN EXTENT,
ONLY WHAT SHIVA TELLS ME.
THAT'S WHY I COULDN'T FORESEE THE ATTACK ON AQUARIA.
I CAN'T SKIP AHEAD ON THE LIST.
THE NEXT MISSION IS AVAILABLE ONLY AFTER THE PREVIOUS ONE HAS BEEN COMPLETED.
WHY ME? WHAT DO I HAVE TO DO WITH SAVING THE WORLD?
AND ME AND THE OUTCASTS, WHAT ABOUT THAT?
I WISH I HAD THE ANSWERS YOU SEEK, ELI.
WE WILL FIND THEM TOGETHER BY MOVING FORWARD.
THE NEXT SHIVA MISSION IS FOR BOTH OF US.

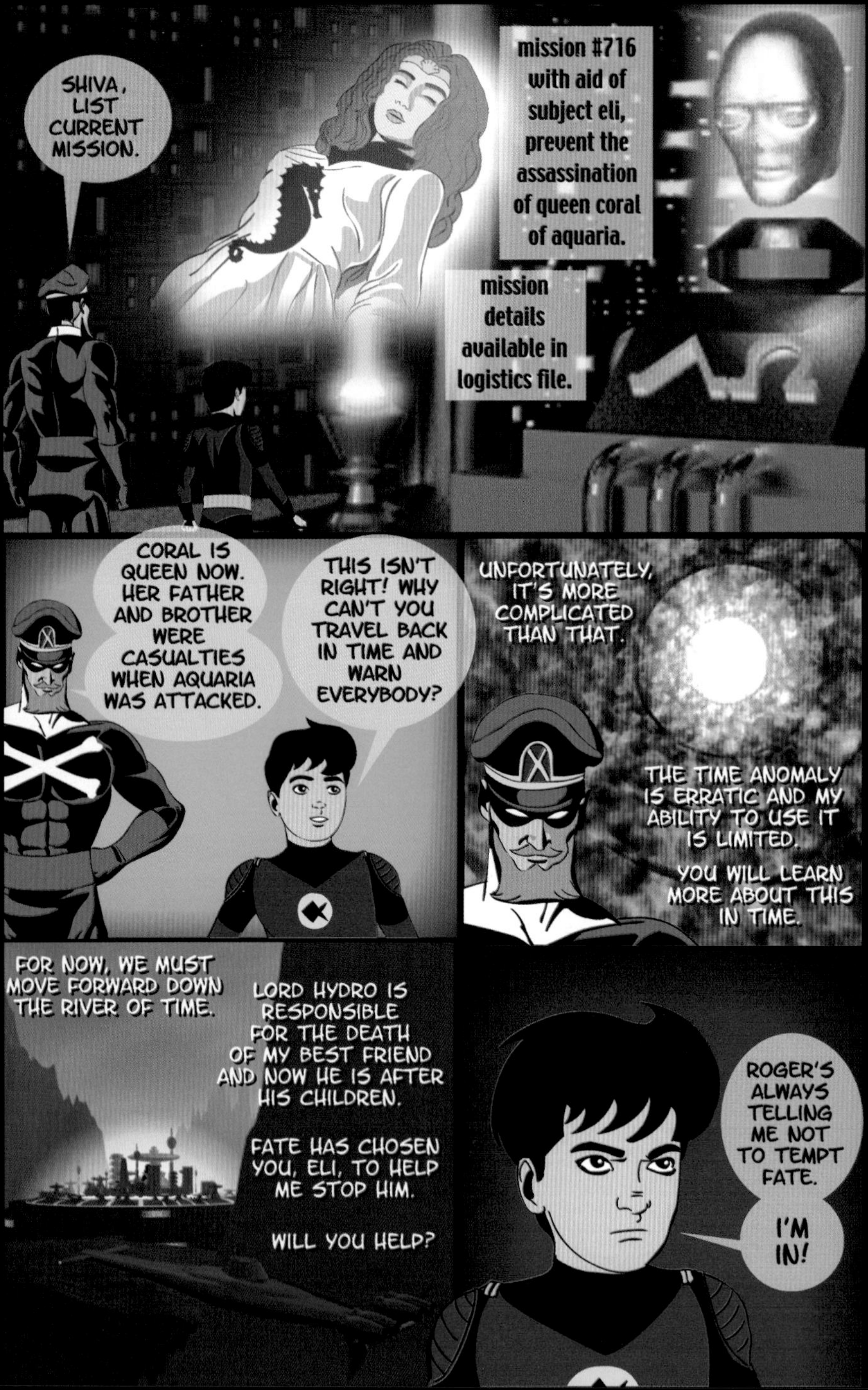
SHIVA, LIST CURRENT MISSION.
mission #716 with aid of subject eli, prevent the assassination of queen coral of aquaria.
mission details available in logistics file.
CORAL IS QUEEN NOW. HER FATHER AND BROTHER WERE CASUALTIES WHEN AQUARIA WAS ATTACKED.
THIS ISN'T RIGHT! WHY CAN'T YOU TRAVEL BACK IN TIME AND WARN EVERYBODY?
UNFORTUNATELY, IT'S MORE COMPLICATED THAN THAT.
THE TIME ANOMALY IS ERRATIC AND MY ABILITY TO USE IT IS LIMITED.
YOU WILL LEARN MORE ABOUT THIS IN TIME.
FOR NOW, WE MUST MOVE FORWARD DOWN THE RIVER OF TIME.
LORD HYDRO IS RESPONSIBLE FOR THE DEATH OF MY BEST FRIEND AND NOW HE IS AFTER HIS CHILDREN.
FATE HAS CHOSEN YOU, ELI, TO HELP ME STOP HIM.
WILL YOU HELP?
ROGER'S ALWAYS TELLING ME NOT TO TEMPT FATE.
I'M IN!

ACT 8 - THE GATHERING STORM

SOMEWHERE AMONG THE RUINS OF SUNKEN ATLANTIS.

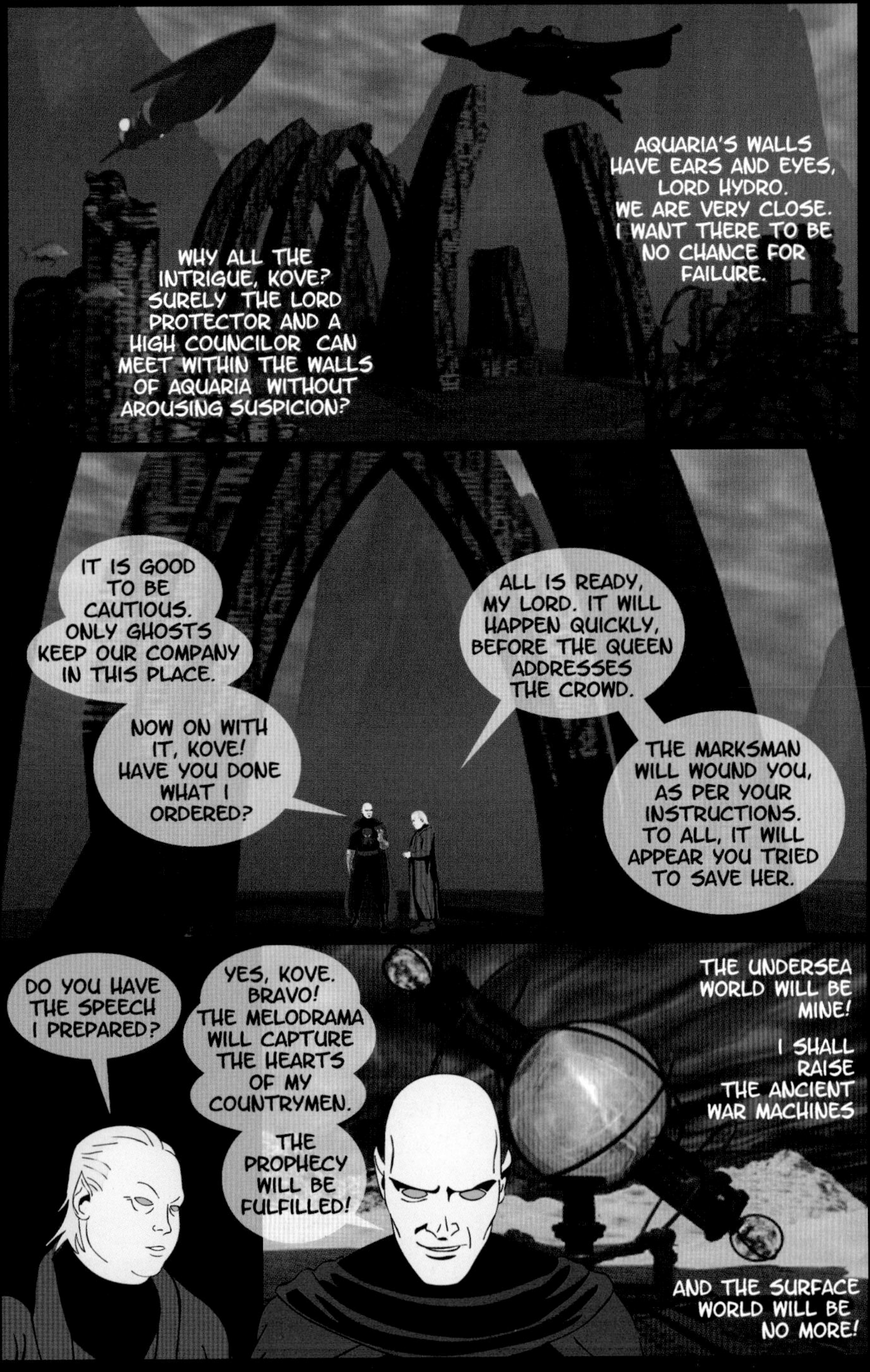
WHY ALL THE INTRIGUE, KOVE? SURELY THE LORD PROTECTOR AND A HIGH COUNCILOR CAN MEET WITHIN THE WALLS OF AQUARIA WITHOUT AROUSING SUSPICION?
AQUARIA'S WALLS HAVE EARS AND EYES, LORD HYDRO. WE ARE VERY CLOSE. I WANT THERE TO BE NO CHANCE FOR FAILURE.
IT IS GOOD TO BE CAUTIOUS. ONLY GHOSTS KEEP OUR COMPANY IN THIS PLACE.
NOW ON WITH IT, KOVE! HAVE YOU DONE WHAT I ORDERED?
ALL IS READY, MY LORD. IT WILL HAPPEN QUICKLY, BEFORE THE QUEEN ADDRESSES THE CROWD.
THE MARKSMAN WILL WOUND YOU, AS PER YOUR INSTRUCTIONS. TO ALL, IT WILL APPEAR YOU TRIED TO SAVE HER.
DO YOU HAVE THE SPEECH I PREPARED?
YES, KOVE. BRAVO! THE MELODRAMA WILL CAPTURE THE HEARTS OF MY COUNTRYMEN.
THE PROPHECY WILL BE FULFILLED!
THE UNDERSEA WORLD WILL BE MINE!
I SHALL RAISE THE ANCIENT WAR MACHINES
AND THE SURFACE WORLD WILL BE NO MORE!

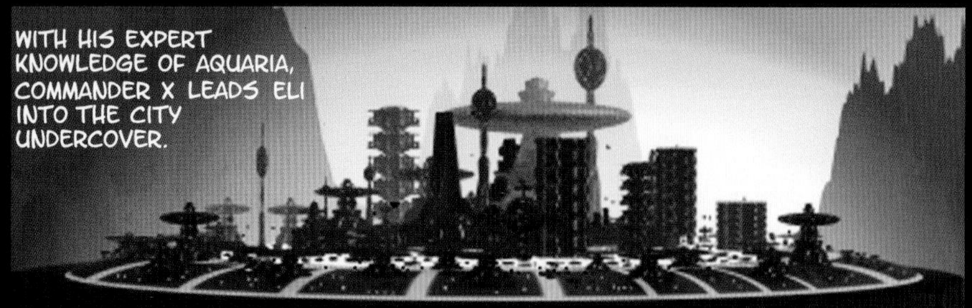
WITH HIS EXPERT KNOWLEDGE OF AQUARIA, COMMANDER X LEADS ELI INTO THE CITY UNDERCOVER.

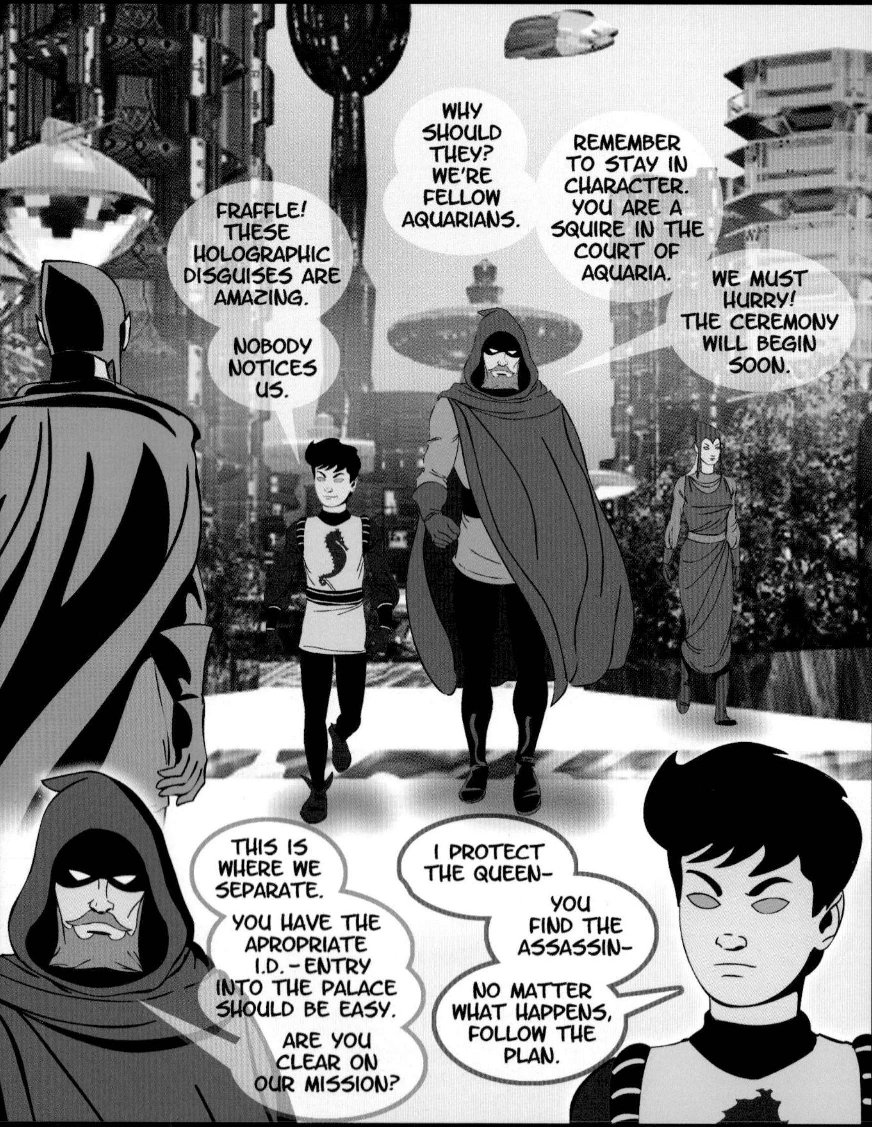
FRAFFLE! THESE HOLOGRAPHIC DISGUISES ARE AMAZING.
NOBODY NOTICES US.
WHY SHOULD THEY? WE'RE FELLOW AQUARIANS.
REMEMBER TO STAY IN CHARACTER. YOU ARE A SQUIRE IN THE COURT OF AQUARIA.
WE MUST HURRY! THE CEREMONY WILL BEGIN SOON.
THIS IS WHERE WE SEPARATE.
YOU HAVE THE APROPRIATE I.D. - ENTRY INTO THE PALACE SHOULD BE EASY.
ARE YOU CLEAR ON OUR MISSION?
I PROTECT THE QUEEN-
YOU FIND THE ASSASSIN-
NO MATTER WHAT HAPPENS, FOLLOW THE PLAN.

ACT 8 - THE GATHERING STORM

ALL EYES ARE ON THE PALACE.
TODAY, AQUARIANS SAY GOODBYE TO THEIR KING
AND GREET THEIR NEW QUEEN.

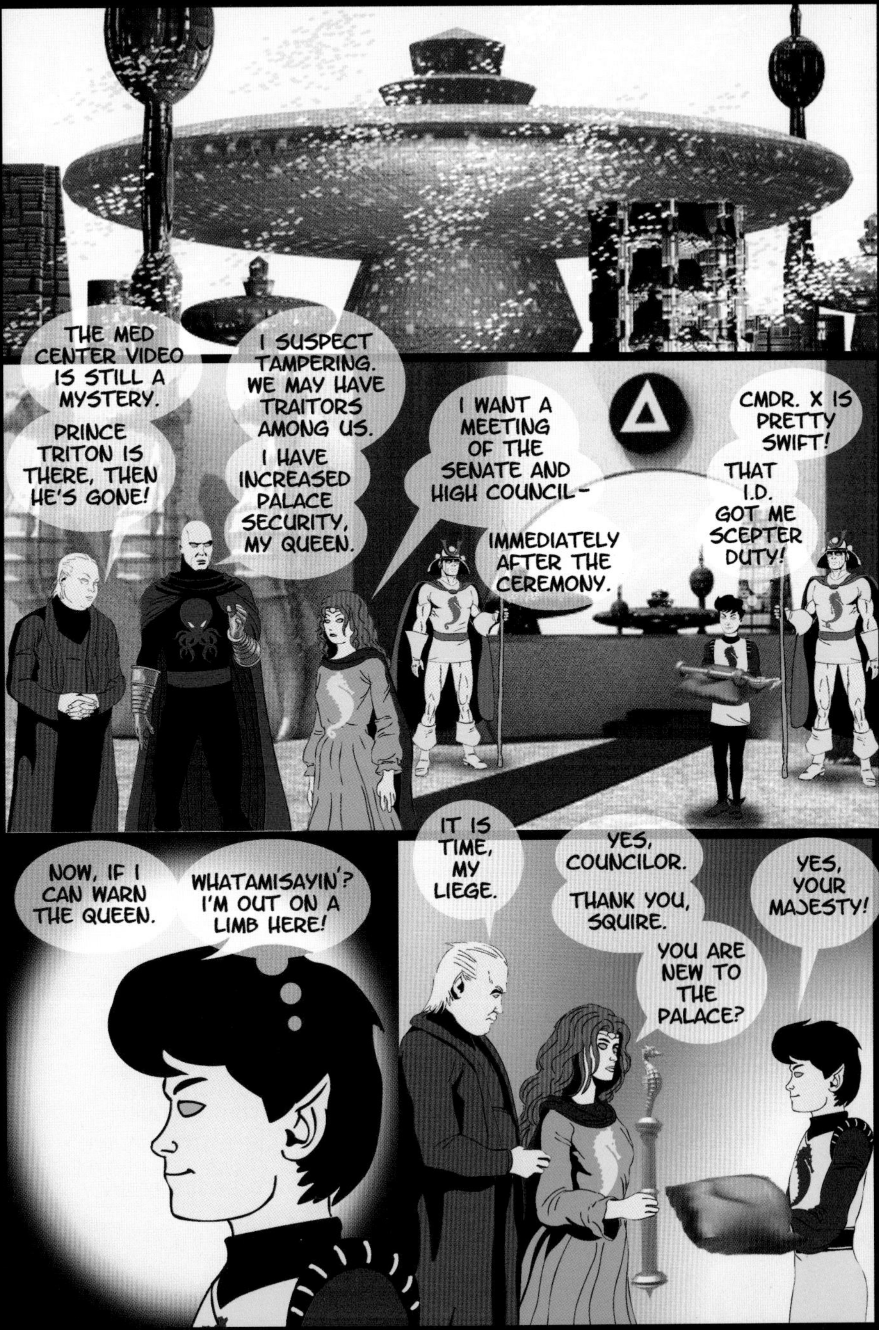
THE MED CENTER VIDEO IS STILL A MYSTERY.
PRINCE TRITON IS THERE, THEN HE'S GONE!
I SUSPECT TAMPERING. WE MAY HAVE TRAITORS AMONG US.
I HAVE INCREASED PALACE SECURITY, MY QUEEN.
I WANT A MEETING OF THE SENATE AND HIGH COUNCIL-
IMMEDIATELY AFTER THE CEREMONY.
CMDR. X IS PRETTY SWIFT!
THAT I.D. GOT ME SCEPTER DUTY!
NOW, IF I CAN WARN THE QUEEN.
WHATAMISAYIN'? I'M OUT ON A LIMB HERE!
IT IS TIME, MY LIEGE.
YES, COUNCILOR.
THANK YOU, SQUIRE.
YOU ARE NEW TO THE PALACE?
YES, YOUR MAJESTY!

THE CEREMONY BEGINS.

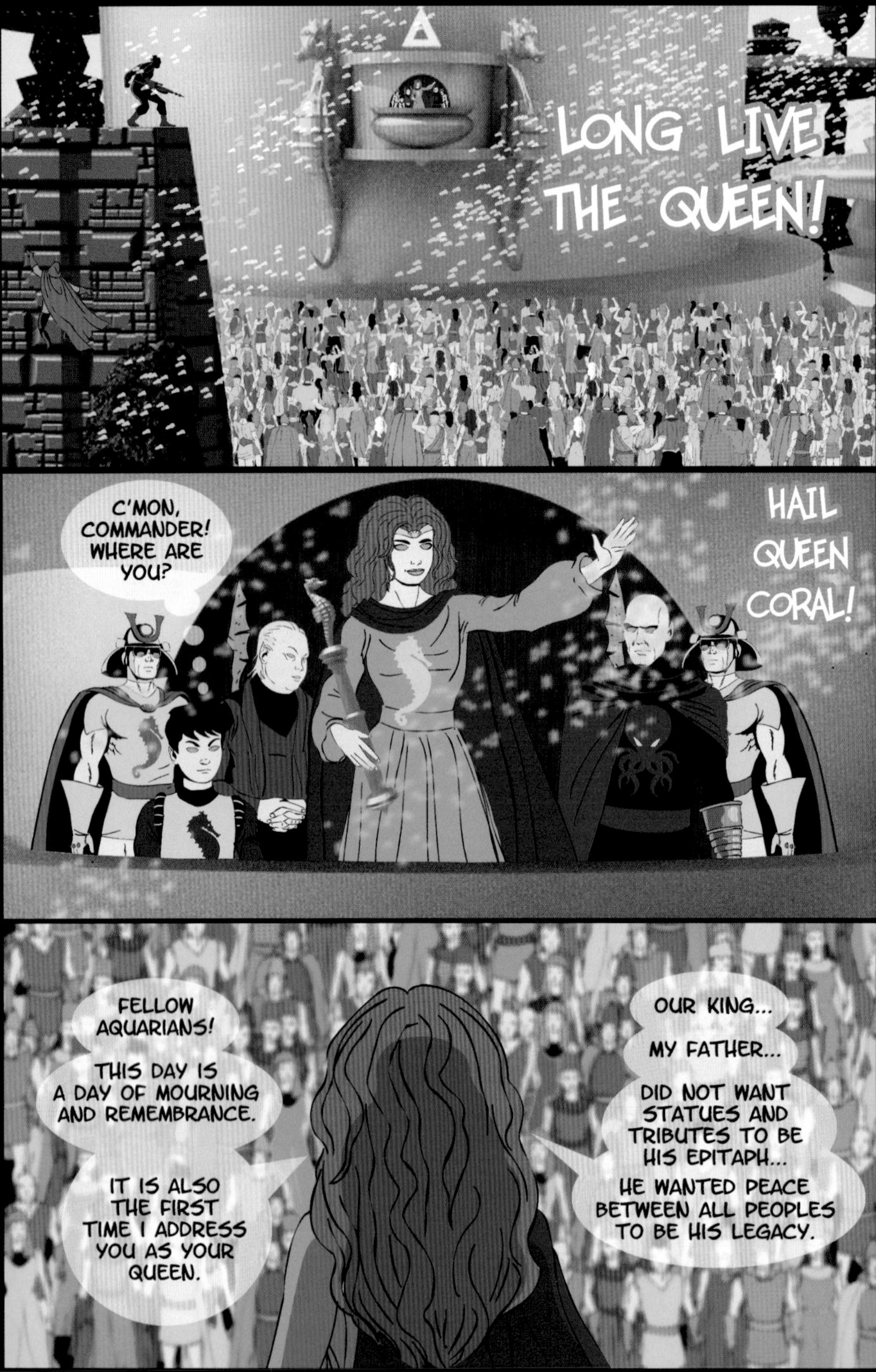
LONG LIVE THE QUEEN!
C'MON, COMMANDER! WHERE ARE YOU?
HAIL QUEEN CORAL!
FELLOW AQUARIANS!
THIS DAY IS A DAY OF MOURNING AND REMEMBRANCE.
IT IS ALSO THE FIRST TIME I ADDRESS YOU AS YOUR QUEEN.
OUR KING...
MY FATHER...
DID NOT WANT STATUES AND TRIBUTES TO BE HIS EPITAPH...
HE WANTED PEACE BETWEEN ALL PEOPLES TO BE HIS LEGACY.

ACT 8 - THE GATHERING STORM

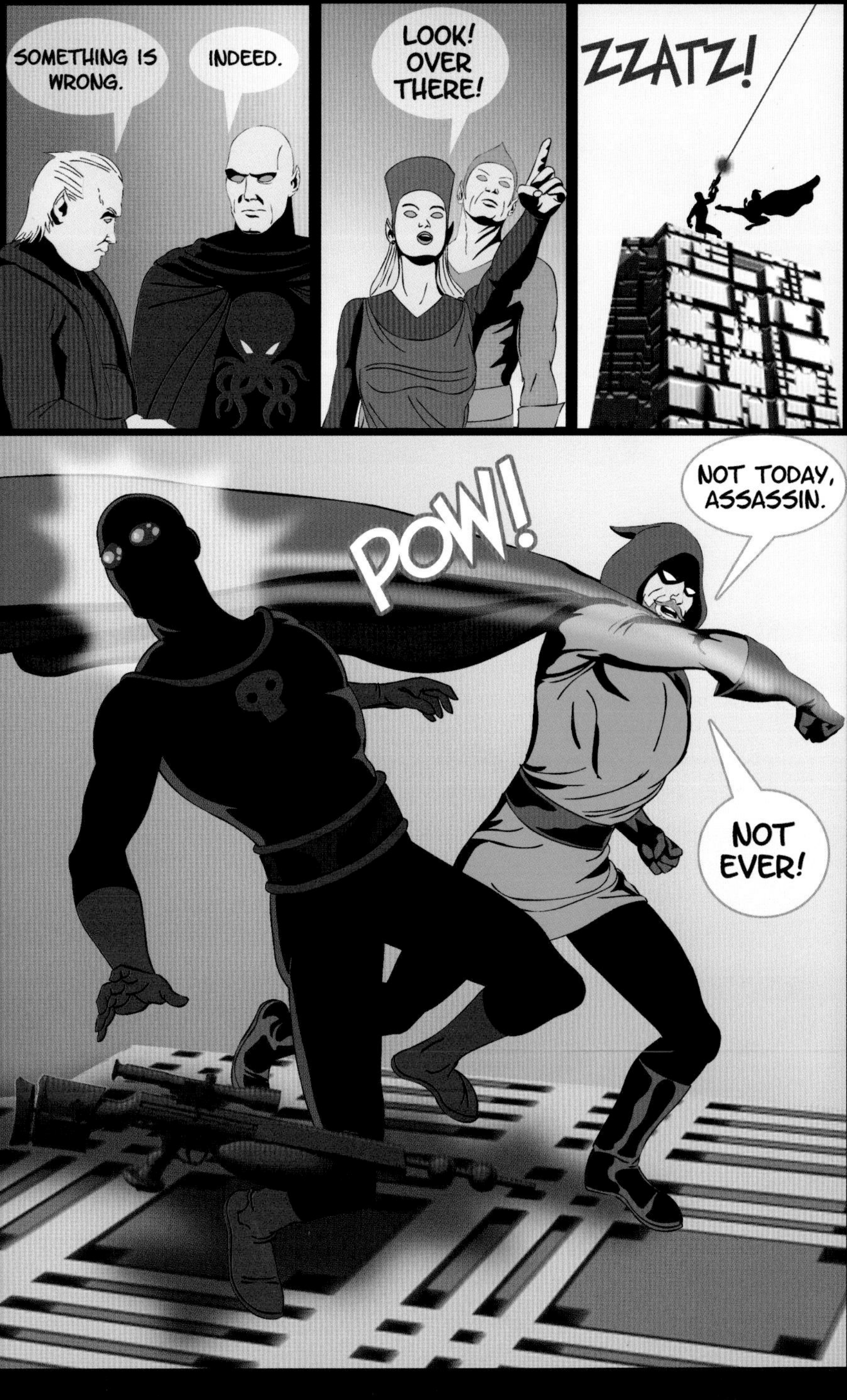
SOMETHING IS WRONG.
INDEED.
LOOK! OVER THERE!
ZZATZ!
POW!
NOT TODAY, ASSASSIN.
NOT EVER!

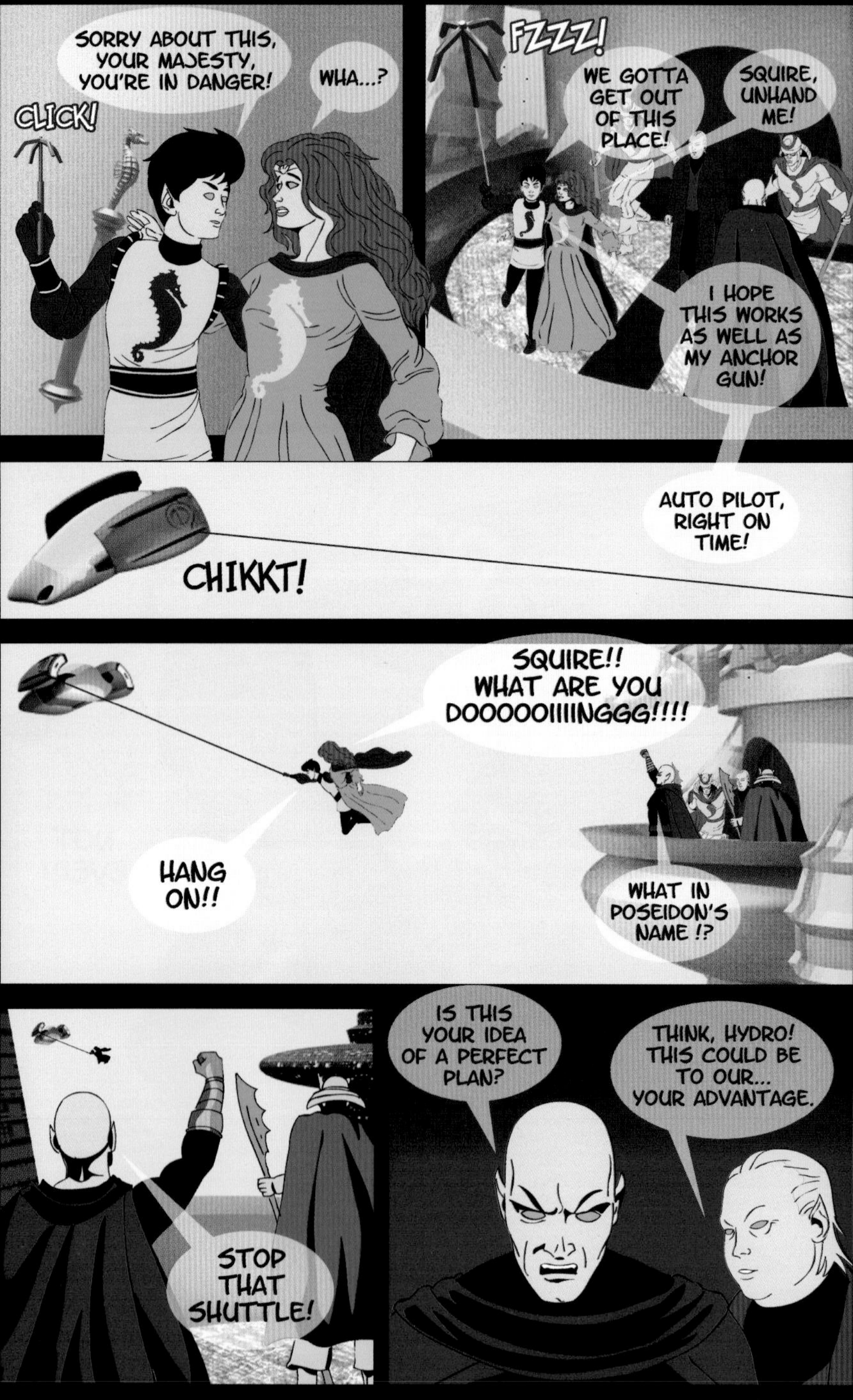
SORRY ABOUT THIS, YOUR MAJESTY, YOU'RE IN DANGER!
WHA...?
CLICK!
FZZZ!
WE GOTTA GET OUT OF THIS PLACE!
SQUIRE, UNHAND ME!
I HOPE THIS WORKS AS WELL AS MY ANCHOR GUN!
AUTO PILOT, RIGHT ON TIME!
CHIKKT!
SQUIRE!! WHAT ARE YOU DOOOOOIIIINGGG!!!!
HANG ON!!
WHAT IN POSEIDON'S NAME !?
STOP THAT SHUTTLE!
IS THIS YOUR IDEA OF A PERFECT PLAN?
THINK, HYDRO! THIS COULD BE TO OUR... YOUR ADVANTAGE.

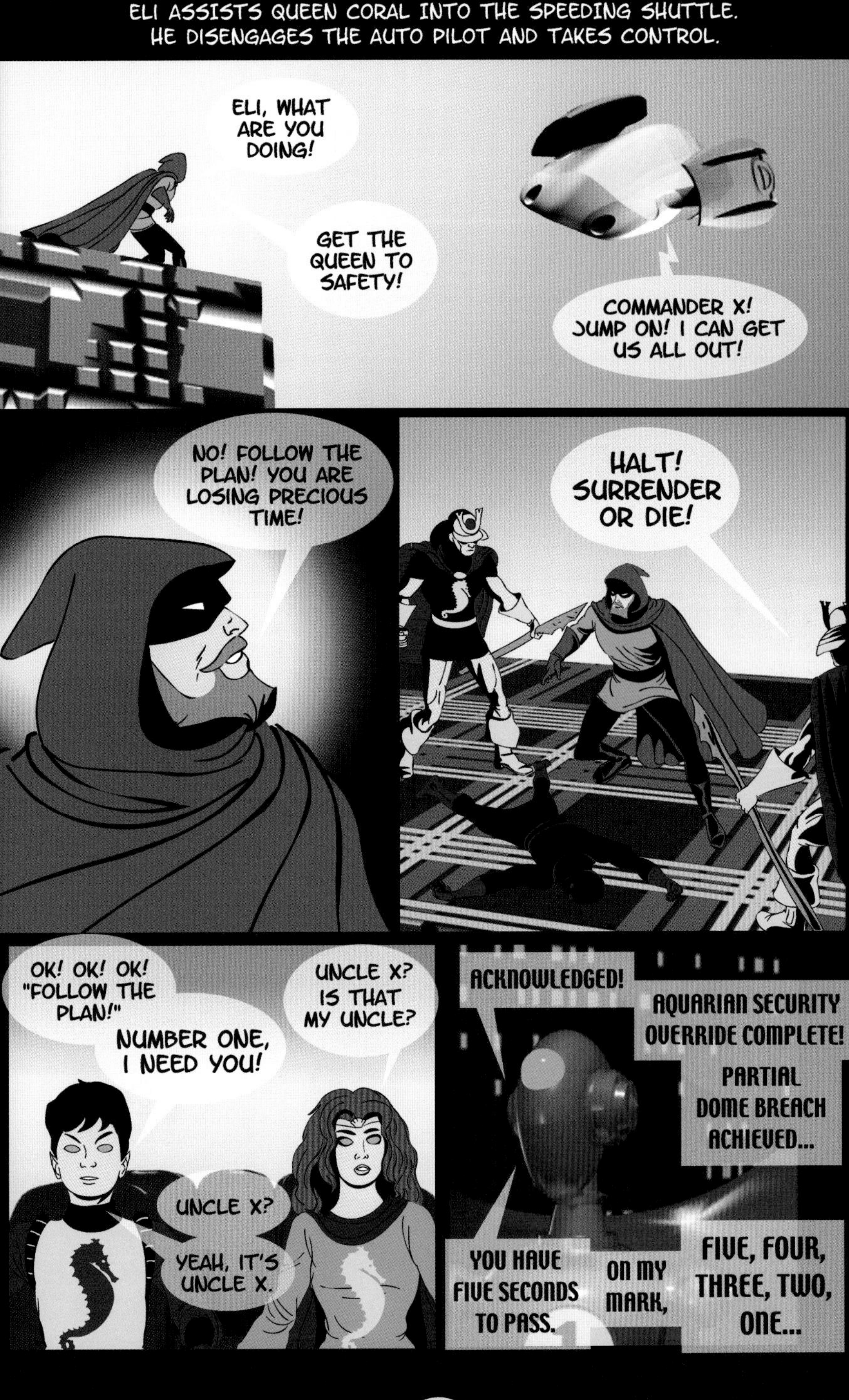
ELI ASSISTS QUEEN CORAL INTO THE SPEEDING SHUTTLE. HE DISENGAGES THE AUTO PILOT AND TAKES CONTROL.
ELI, WHAT ARE YOU DOING!
GET THE QUEEN TO SAFETY!
COMMANDER X! JUMP ON! I CAN GET US ALL OUT!
NO! FOLLOW THE PLAN! YOU ARE LOSING PRECIOUS TIME!
HALT! SURRENDER OR DIE!
OK! OK! OK! "FOLLOW THE PLAN!"
NUMBER ONE, I NEED YOU!
UNCLE X? IS THAT MY UNCLE?
UNCLE X?
YEAH, IT'S UNCLE X.
ACKNOWLEDGED!
AQUARIAN SECURITY OVERRIDE COMPLETE!
PARTIAL DOME BREACH ACHIEVED...
YOU HAVE FIVE SECONDS TO PASS.
ON MY MARK,
FIVE, FOUR, THREE, TWO, ONE...

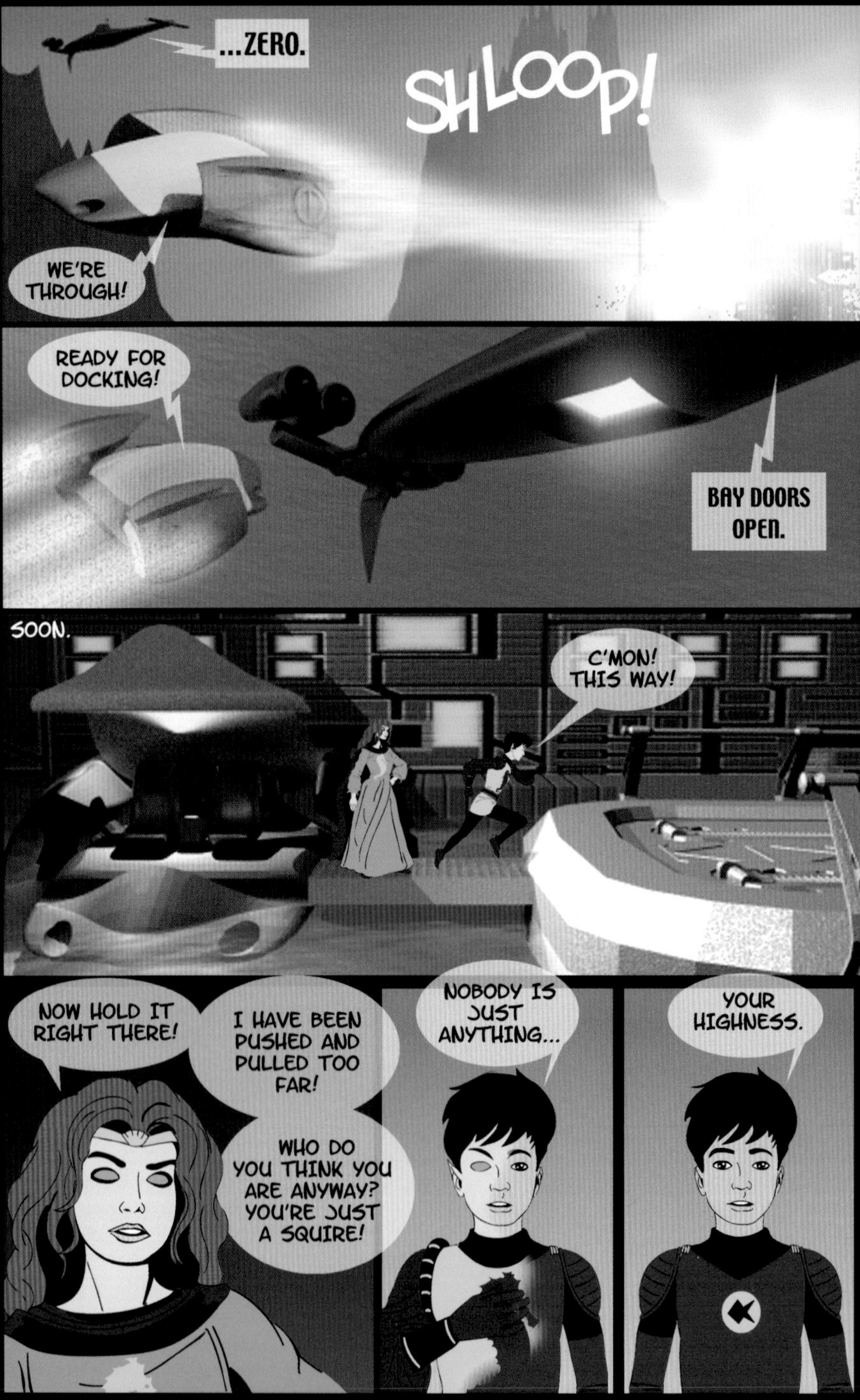
...ZERO.
SHLOOP!
WE'RE THROUGH!
READY FOR DOCKING!
BAY DOORS OPEN.
SOON.
C'MON! THIS WAY!
NOW HOLD IT RIGHT THERE!
I HAVE BEEN PUSHED AND PULLED TOO FAR!
WHO DO YOU THINK YOU ARE ANYWAY? YOU'RE JUST A SQUIRE!
NOBODY IS JUST ANYTHING...
YOUR HIGHNESS.

ACT 8 - THE GATHERING STORM

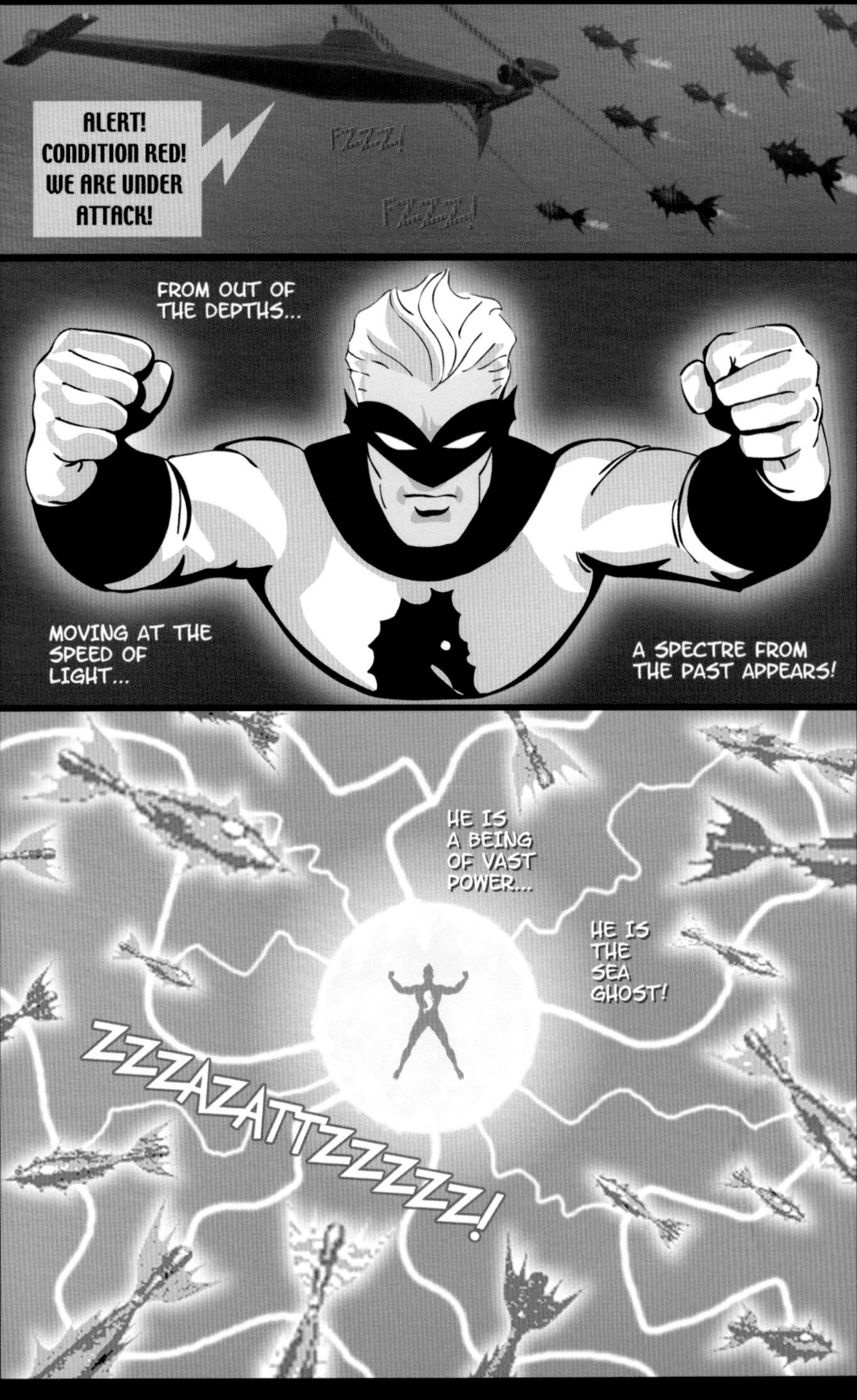
ALERT! CONDITION RED! WE ARE UNDER ATTACK!
FROM OUT OF THE DEPTHS...
MOVING AT THE SPEED OF LIGHT...
A SPECTRE FROM THE PAST APPEARS!
HE IS A BEING OF VAST POWER...
HE IS THE SEA GHOST!
ZZZAZATTZZZZZ!

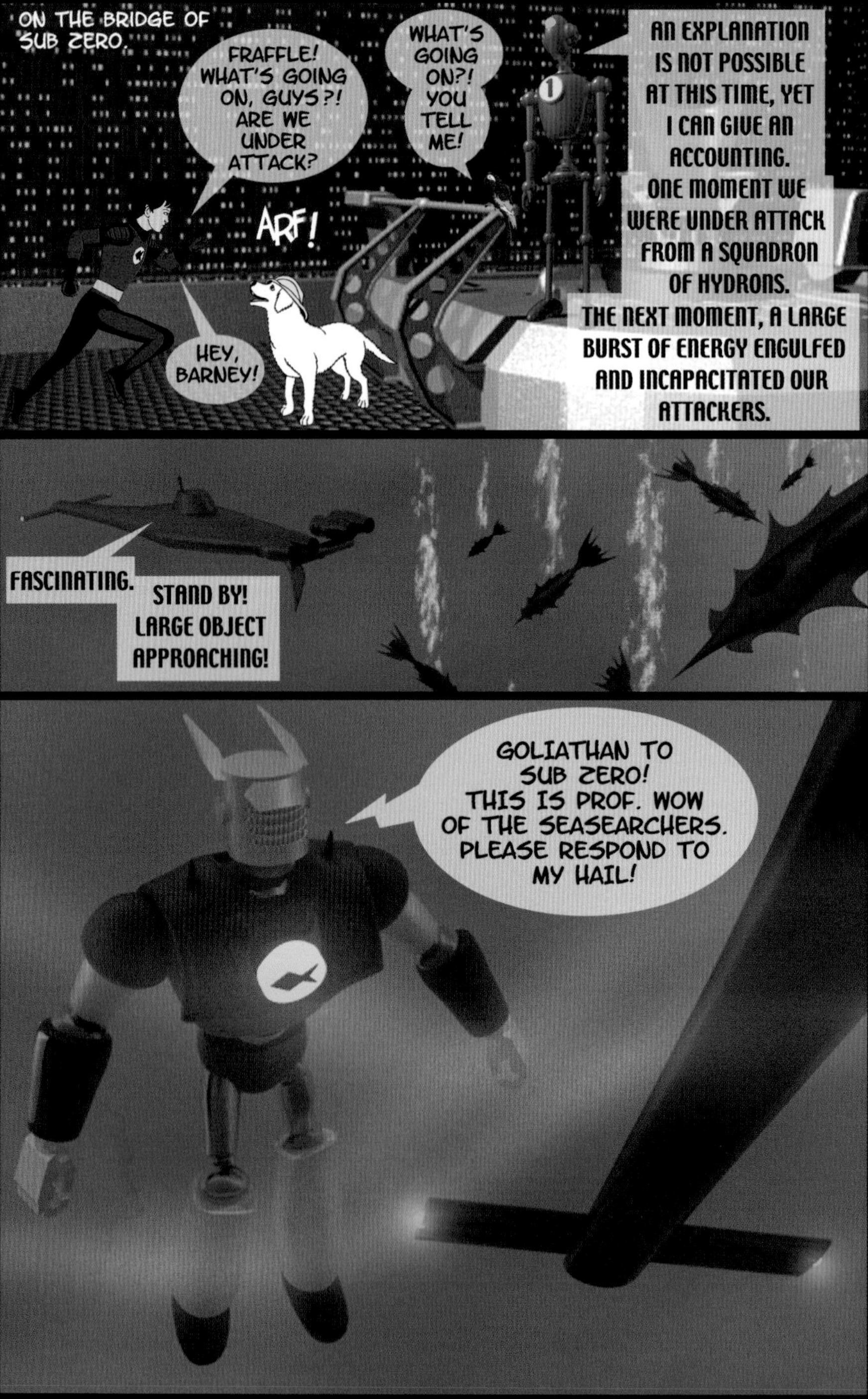
ON THE BRIDGE OF SUB ZERO.
FRAFFLE! WHAT'S GOING ON, GUYS?! ARE WE UNDER ATTACK?
HEY, BARNEY!
ARF!
WHAT'S GOING ON?! YOU TELL ME!
AN EXPLANATION IS NOT POSSIBLE AT THIS TIME, YET I CAN GIVE AN ACCOUNTING.
ONE MOMENT WE WERE UNDER ATTACK FROM A SQUADRON OF HYDRONS.
THE NEXT MOMENT, A LARGE BURST OF ENERGY ENGULFED AND INCAPACITATED OUR ATTACKERS.
FASCINATING.
STAND BY! LARGE OBJECT APPROACHING!
GOLIATHAN TO SUB ZERO! THIS IS PROF. WOW OF THE SEASEARCHERS. PLEASE RESPOND TO MY HAIL!

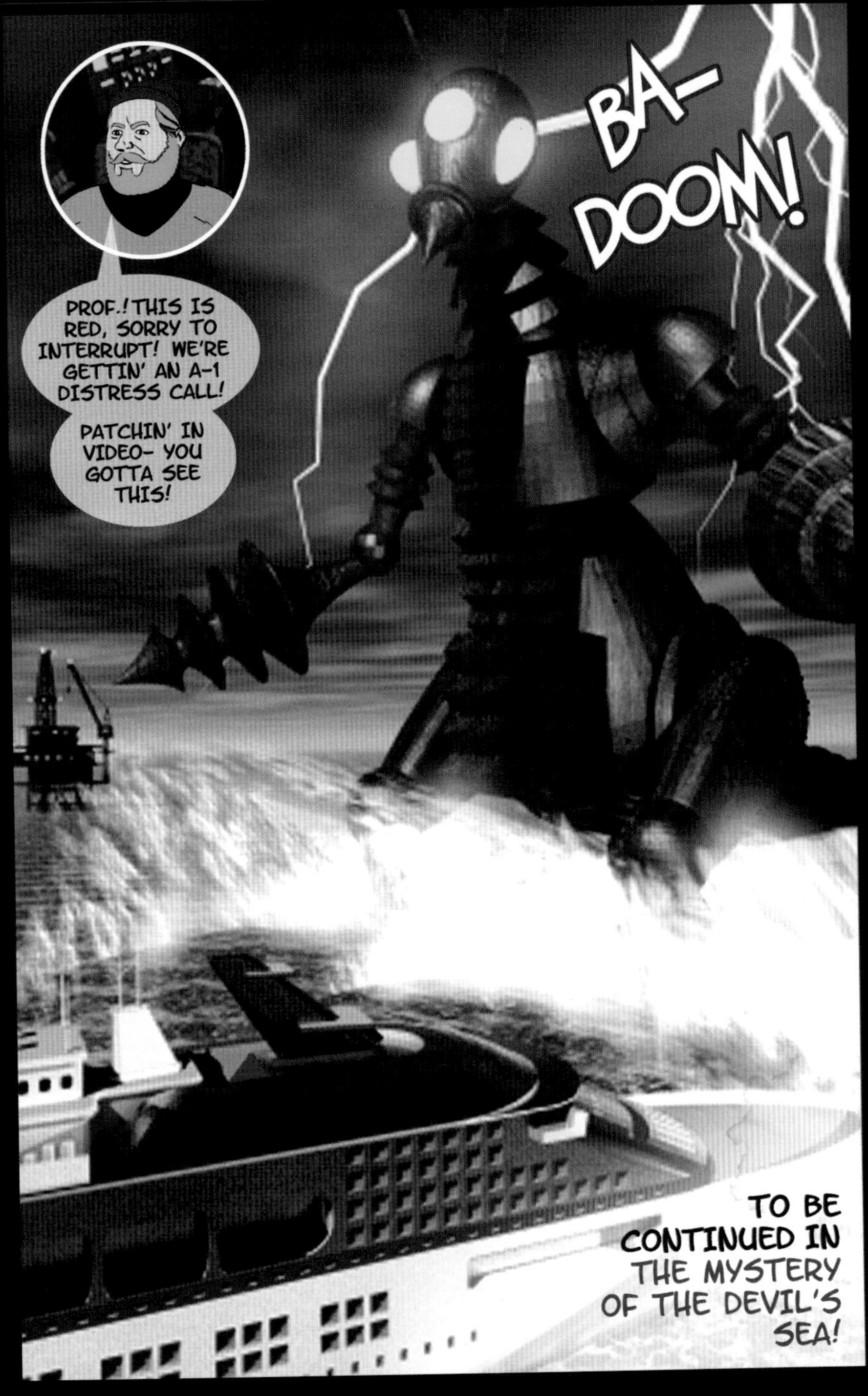
PROF.! THIS IS RED, SORRY TO INTERRUPT! WE'RE GETTIN' AN A-1 DISTRESS CALL!
PATCHIN' IN VIDEO- YOU GOTTA SEE THIS!
BA-DOOM!
TO BE CONTINUED IN THE MYSTERY OF THE DEVIL'S SEA!

GUEST ARTIST GALLERY

I am honored to have contributions from these fantastic artists! In the last book, the focus was on the Golden Age. In this volume, the Silver Age is in the spotlight. The unique style of each of these artists helps illustrate why the Silver Age was such a wonderful era in the history of comics.

HERB TRIMPE'S amazing work spans decades. In the Silver Age, he drew the Hulk for an unbroken run of seven years. As a Marvel mainstay, he's drawn all of Marvel's major characters and in 2008 returned to draw the Hulk in a King-Size special. I think one of the reasons Herb's work is so cherished by fans and pros alike is because he never forgets what comics should be – FUN! www.herbtrimpe.com

JOE ZIERMAN'S illustrations show a love and appreciation for the great comic art of the Silver Age. I first saw Joe's incredible work for Big Bang Comics' *Venus*. After seeing *Teen Rex*, I was blown away and hoped one day Joe could contribute to *Capt'n Eli*. I love the amazing cover he did for this book as well as his T-Man pin-up. Look for more from Joe in the next volume where he brings his style to a pin-up of the Sea Ghost. www.comicspace.com/mightyjoe

LAUREN MONARDO is an extraordinary artist. She is a character designer, illustrator, comics artist, and animator. She has storyboarded for the Silver Age-inspired *The Venture Bros.* on Cartoon Network. She has a flair for action and humor, as you can see in her spectacular pin-up of Capt'n Eli. Lauren is a prolific creator and works on a variety of projects for print and film. www.lmonardo.blogspot.com

Special thanks to ROY THOMAS. Roy is the writer and editor who succeeded Stan Lee as Marvel editor-in-chief in the early 1970's. Check out his legendary fanzine *Alter Ego* where he champions the work and creators of the Golden and Silver Ages - www.twomorrows.com. In a recent conversation, Roy compared *Capt'n Eli* to Herge's *Tintin*. Thanks for that, Roy, and extra special thanks for teaching me how to pronounce Tintin properly!

JAY

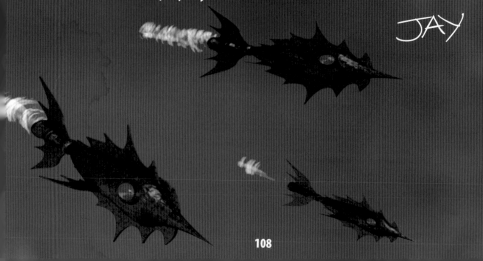

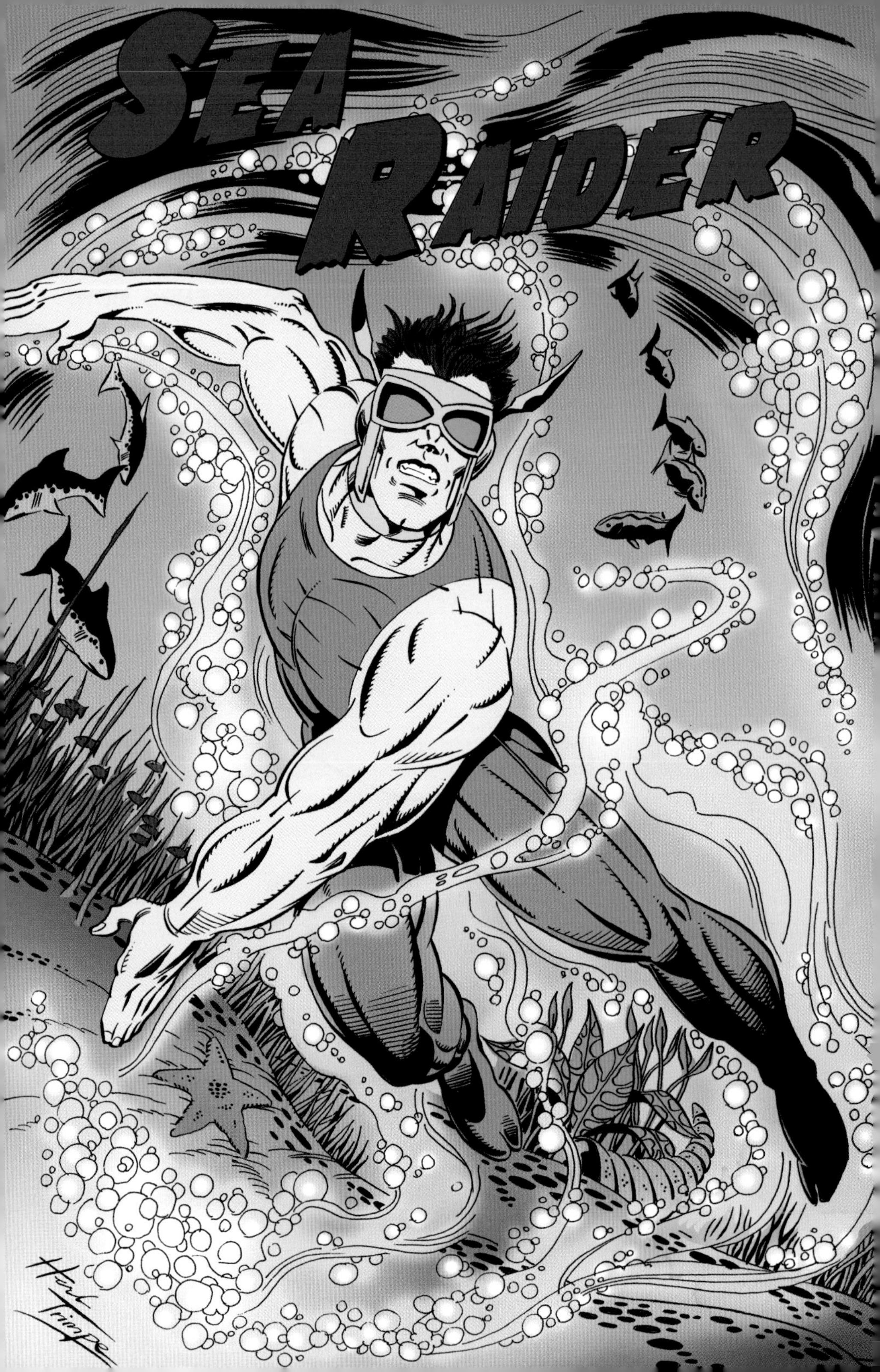
SEA RAIDER
Kurt Trimpe

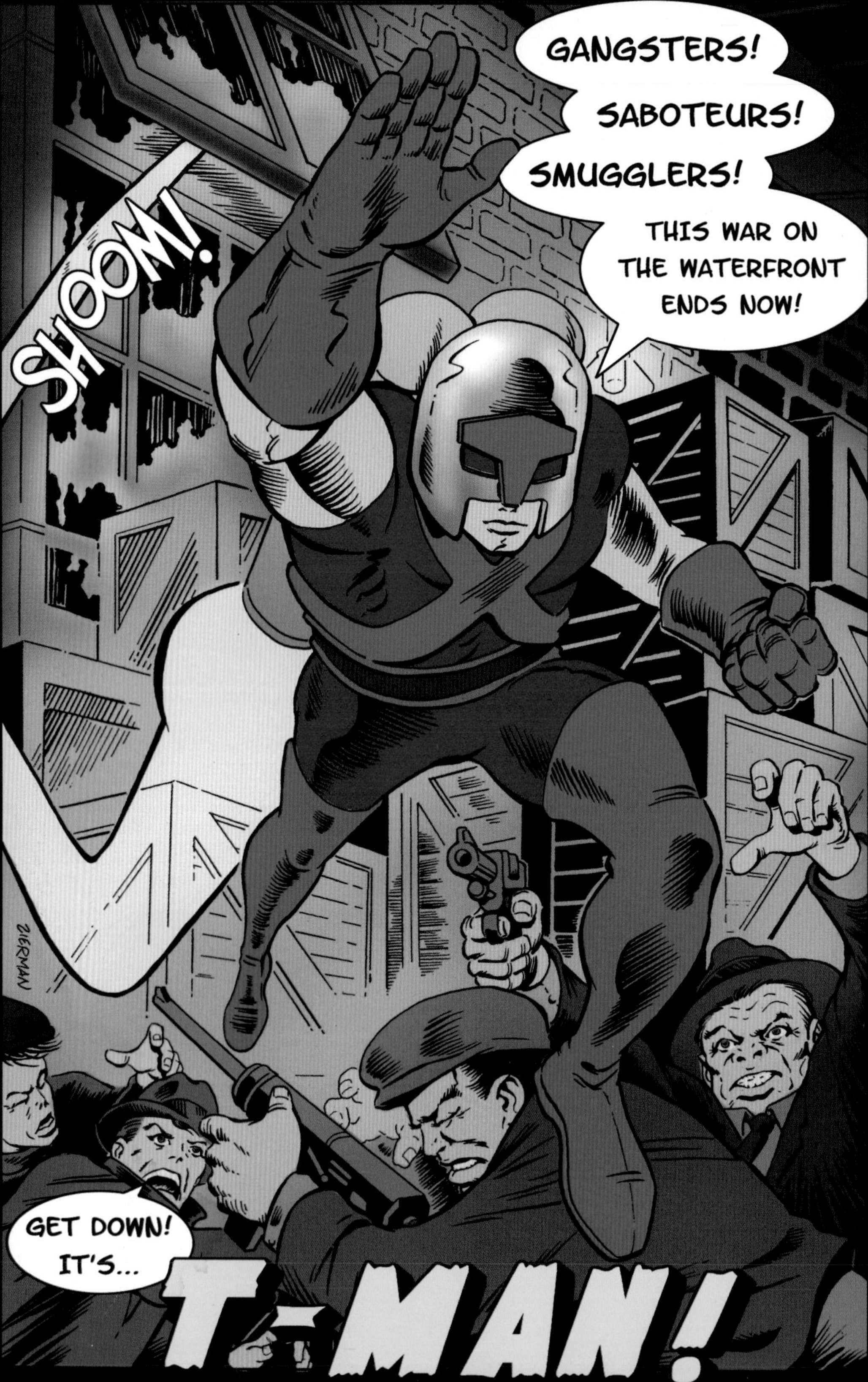
GANGSTERS!
SABOTEURS!
SMUGGLERS!
THIS WAR ON THE WATERFRONT ENDS NOW!
SHOOM!
GET DOWN! IT'S...
T-MAN!
ZIERMAN

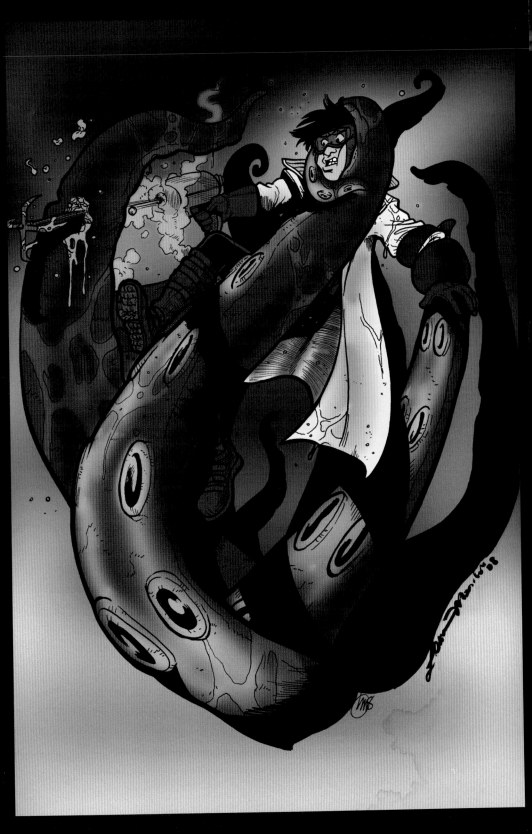

THE STORY BEHIND THE STORY

Everybody has a first comic book, mine was Adam Strange.

When I was about five, we moved to a town called Yarmouth, Maine. This was around 1970. Five is a tender age and moving to a new town can be scary.

One day, my father walked me up the street to the barber shop for a haircut. I had some fear about this as well. But, waiting for my haircut, I discovered my first comic book! It was Adam Strange and it was an amazing story! He was teleported by a beam of energy to a planet called Rann where he met his true love, Alanna. Together, they fought monsters and other galactic threats. At the end of each story, Adam would disappear and we'd have to wait until the next time he was teleported for another adventure.

As you can see, Adam Strange made a lasting impression on me. Making a lasting impression and taking responsibility for who that impression is made on is the idea behind being an all-ages story. And that's what *The Undersea Adventures of Capt'n Eli* is all about.

Adam Strange was created during a period of time called the Silver Age, which began in the 1960's. The people who created comics back then geared their stories to eight- to thirteen-year-olds but were aware adults also read comics. Wallace Wood, Jack Kirby, and Alex Toth were three masters of the comic art form who came to prominence at this time. If you want to know anything there is to know about comics, these guys wrote and drew the books!

At the same time I discovered comics I was also reading adventure and science fiction stories. I loved *20,000 Leagues Under the Sea* and *The Mysterious Island* by Jules Verne as well as H.G. Wells' *The War of the Worlds* and *The Time Machine*. I was introduced to Tom Swift, boy inventor. He created a sub called the Supermarine. Yup, there's a lot of Tom Swift in *Capt'n Eli*!

I also enjoyed learning about world mythology and, over time, began to recognize how the ancient adventure stories are retold again and again through television, movies and comics.

The lasting impression Adam Strange made on me makes me aware that, today, *The Undersea Adventures of Capt'n Eli* might be your first comic! Whether you're five or fifty, my hope is that this book leaves the same positive and lasting impression on you as the stories I grew up with did on me.

Thanks for reading and drop me a note anytime at jaypiscopo@captneli.com.

Until then, *STAND BY FOR ADVENTURE!*